Houses
of
Stone

Also published in Large Print
from G.K. Hall by Barbara Michaels:

Vanish with the Rose
Into the Darkness
Smoke and Mirrors
Search the Shadows
Shattered Silk
The Grey Beginning
Sons of the Wolf
The Master of Blacktower

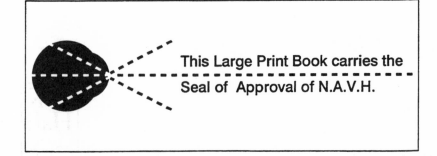

Houses
of
Stone

Barbara Mertz

Barbara
Michaels, [pseud.]

G.K. Hall & Co.
Thorndike, Maine

Published in 1994 by arrangement with Simon & Schuster, Inc.

G.K. Hall Large Print Core Collection.

The text of this Large Print edtion is unabridged.
Other aspects of the book may vary from the original edition.

Set in 16 pt. News Plantin by Ginny Beaulieu.

Printed in the United States on acid-free, high opacity paper. ∞

Library of Congress Cataloging in Publication Data

Mertz, Barbara

Michaels, Barbara, 1927–
    Houses of stone / Barbara Michaels.
      p.   cm.
    ISBN 0-8161-5936-X (alk. paper : lg. print)
    ISBN 0-8161-5937-8 (alk. paper : lg. print : pbk.)
    1. Man-woman relationships — United States — Fiction. 2. Women college teachers — United States — Fiction. 3. Large type books.
I. Title.
[PS3563.E747H68 1994]
813'.54—dc20

522 p. (large print) ; 24 cm.

93-40498

This one, especially, is for Kristen.

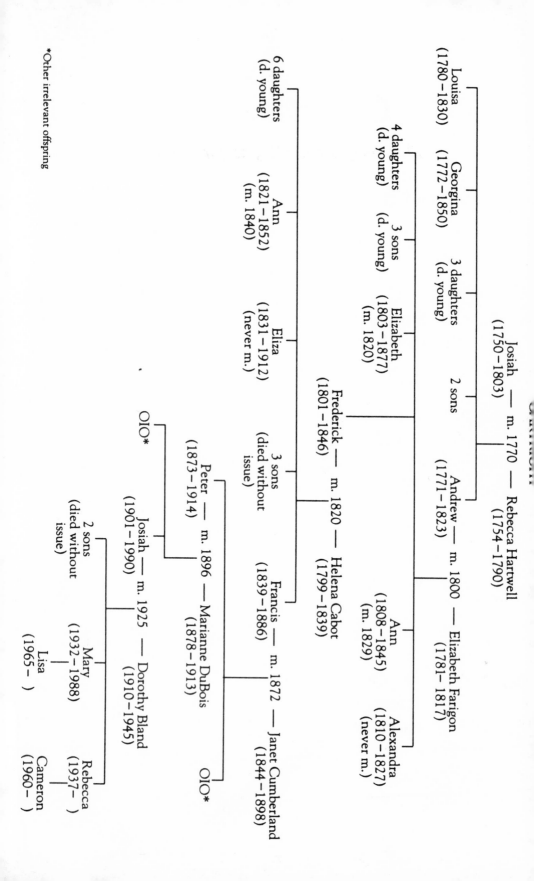

Josiah — m. 1770 — Rebecca Harwell
(1750–1803)   (1754–1790)

Louisa
(1780–1830)

Georgina
(1772–1850)

2 sons

Andrew — m. 1800 — Elizabeth Farigon
(1771–1823)   (1781–1817)

4 daughters
(d. young)

3 daughters
(d. young)

3 sons
(d. young)

Elizabeth
(1803–1877)
(m. 1820)

Frederick — m. 1820 — Helena Cabot
(1801–1846)   (1799–1839)

Ann
(1808–1845)
(m. 1829)

Alexandra
(1810–1827)
(never m.)

6 daughters
(d. young)

Ann
(1821–1852)
(m. 1840)

Eliza
(1831–1912)
(never m.)

3 sons
(died without
issue)

Francis — m. 1872 — Janet Cumberland
(1839–1886)   (1844–1898)

OIO*

Peter — m. 1896 — Marianne DuBois
(1873–1914)   (1878–1913)

OIO*

Josiah — m. 1925 — Dorothy Bland
(1901–1990)   (1910–1945)

2 sons
(died without
issue)

Mary
(1932–1988)

Rebecca
(1937–)

Lisa
(1965–)

Cameron
(1960–)

*Other irrelevant offspring

Chapter One

Literature is not the business of a woman's life, and it cannot be.

Letter from SOUTHEY
to CHARLOTTE BRONTË, *1837*

If only Simon weren't such a practical joker!

The other booksellers with whom she dealt were not given to joking about their profession — as one of them gloomily put it, peddling the printed word to a nation of semiliterates was no laughing matter — and Simon, of all people, ought to have been free of that weakness. He specialized in rare antiquarian books and resembled a romantic novelist's conception of a dignified elderly European count. But the last time he had summoned her to Baltimore with breathless hints of a fantastic discovery, the treasure had turned out to be the complete oeuvre of Barbara Cartland.

"But," said Simon innocently, as Karen sputtered with outrage, "that's your field, isn't it? Women novelists?"

Their friendship was strong enough to survive such episodes; in fact, the ongoing debate between them, marked by withering sarcasm on Simon's part and heated argument on hers, lent an element of charm to a relationship that was inherently improbable. In every way, Simon was Karen's exact opposite. He was in his late sixties or early seventies; she was almost forty years younger. He was tall and lean, she was five-five and — to put it nicely — well-rounded. Simon was a self-proclaimed male chauvinist, her academic specialty was women's literature. She had her doctorate and an assistant professorship at a women's college; Simon had never mentioned attending a college or university. Yet he was one of the best-educated people she had ever met. He had at least a nodding acquaintance with hundreds of subjects, from baseball to Bartók, politics to Plato, dogs to dendrochronology. He and Karen did not agree on any of the above — except, possibly, dendrochronology. It was hard to start an argument about tree-ring dating.

What was it that had drawn them together and preserved an affection that grew ever stronger, despite infrequent contact and violent differences of opinion? Karen pondered the question as she drove along Route 70 toward the Baltimore Beltway. Traffic was light, and she had been over the route so many times she could have driven it in total darkness.

It was dark enough, though the morning was only half advanced. Clouds blustered across the sky, their swollen surfaces pewter-gray. Karen had already switched on the headlights. It wouldn't dare snow, she thought. Not in April. Not even in Maryland. At least she hoped it wouldn't dare. The distance from Baltimore to her home was almost a hundred miles, some of it over winding mountain roads, and she had a full schedule of classes and conferences the following day. But she could no more have resisted Simon's tempting hints than she could have refused food after a month of fasting. He had been typically, tantalizingly vague. "No, I can't possibly describe it. You'll have to see it for yourself. But if I'm right — and I always am — this is the find of a lifetime for you."

What the devil could it be? A few tentative snowflakes melted against the windshield, and Karen switched on the radio, hoping for a weather forecast — a futile gesture, for there was nothing she could do about the weather anyhow, and she had no intention of turning back. If Simon was pulling another stunt like "the Cartland Collection," she would murder him.

Her finger paused in the process of punching buttons as the strains of "Eine Kleine Nachtmusik" reached her ears. That was one answer to the question she had asked herself about her friendship with Simon. Music. Before she met him, she had never cared for the classical composers, but if you spent time with Simon, you hadn't much choice. He always had music playing in the background — or, at times, loudly in the foreground, when he raised the volume to hear a favorite passage. Simon considered Mozart the greatest composer who had ever lived, with John Lennon a close second.

What else? Simon's sense of humor, of course.

9

Even at his most outrageous he was funny. His sardonic view of the world as a planet-sized insane asylum helped steady her whenever some fresh example of stupidity or cruelty sent her adrenaline soaring.

There was another element. She had acknowledged it early in their acquaintance, with some surprise; it had never occurred to her until she met Simon that the attraction between male and female could be an abstract quality, unrelated to age or any other practical factor. He had never done or said anything to make her feel self-conscious or defensive. She knew he never would. It was only a game, a game he played with enormous skill, and one whose archaic rules she had learned to enjoy, though she would never be as good at it as he was.

And, of course, there was their shared passion for books.

Who knows whence such passions derive? Karen sometimes felt she had been born with hers. She had never been more than temporarily distracted by television; she read while she walked to school, while she brushed her teeth, while she dusted and vacuumed. She favored baths over showers, because it was impossible to read under a waterfall. She read the back of the cereal box at breakfast, when her mother refused to let her bring a book to the table. She loved the smell of books, the feel of books, the look of them on a shelf.

Simon felt the same. Unlike some booksellers, he was as interested in the contents of his wares as in the volumes themselves. The Cartland Collection had been an aberration, a joke he could not resist; on several other occasions he had supplied her with books of genuine interest.

What could it be this time? Karen hit the brake as a tractor trailer lunged into her lane. She was nearing the beltway, with its heavier traffic; she had better concentrate on her driving and stop dreaming about fantastic discoveries — the missing, probably apocryphal, chapters of Charlotte Brontë's last novel, or an unknown poem by Emily Dickinson. Such things did turn up, but not often, and she had already had one big find.

Hers hadn't been anything so impressive as a lost manuscript by a recognized author, but it had been her own, stemming from the bookcollecting mania that had driven her long-suffering family to threats of violence. They didn't mind (her father explained patiently) having to buy a new bookcase every month. They weren't annoyed (her mother insisted, through clenched teeth) at having to move a pile of books when they wanted to sit in a chair or use a telephone or set the table. What they objected to were books on the stairs and under her bed and on the piano. The attic was full of books, the basement was full of books, the guest room . . .

By the time she began working on her doctorate, she had little time for outside reading or for browsing, but she celebrated the completion of her dissertation by going on an orgy of book buying — not in expensive antiquarian stores like Simon's,

11

but dark musty cubbyholes where the cheapest book was a quarter. It was in one of these shops that she had found the slim volume of poems by the woman who called herself Ismene. It had been tossed into a carton with a number of other battered volumes. The hand-lettered sign read, "Two bits each, three for fifty cents."

Even Karen was not tempted by a forty-year-old chemistry textbook or a paperback reprint of *Lady Audley's Secret*. (She already had a copy of *Lady Audley's Secret*.) But only Karen would have looked twice at the thin volume whose front cover was missing and whose water-stained pages seemed to be glued into a solid mass. She inserted a fingernail at random. Only the edges were stuck together; the book opened.

Later she wondered what her reaction would have been if she had not happened to read that particular poem first. Faulty and faltering though it was, some of the lines had a haunting quality. "They have shut me in a house of stone . . . There is no victory in death — only the mute darkness . . ." Squatting on the dusty pavement, she pried other pages apart, and gradually the importance of what she had found began to dawn on her.

The title page, exposed by the removal of the front cover, was so stained and torn she could only make out two words: "Verses" and what must be the author's name or pseudonym: Ismene. There was no date visible, but she had seen other books like this one. It had probably been printed during the first half of the nineteenth century. That was her field — nineteenth-century women's literature. She had never heard of a writer who called herself Ismene.

She paid her two bits and went home with her discovery. It took her six weeks to search the literature to make certain no such writer was known. It took another six months to prepare her edition of the poems, annotated, footnoted and equipped with all the necessary scholarly apparatus.

Ismene was no Emily Dickinson; her verses were not so sure, and certainly not so enigmatic. In fact, Karen had never been able to determine who she really was. Ismene had to be a pseudonym, derived from the name of the sister of Antigone in the classic Greek drama. Women who aspired to authorship in those early days seldom dared use their own names. If they didn't hide behind the anonymous "By a Lady," they chose masculine or ambiguous names — Currer, Ellis and Acton instead of Charlotte, Emily and Anne. The use of a pseudonym supported the other evidence as to the date of the book — the handmade paper, the printing technique — but it proved impossible to identify even the publisher. The book must have been privately printed, in a very limited edition; the product of a vanity press, paid for by the author herself.

Could Simon's discovery be something as significant? Crawling along the city streets, slowed by construction and thickening traffic, Karen tried to control her expectations. Yet, she argued with herself, they weren't completely unreasonable.

13

Women writers had been ignored, snubbed by the literary establishment, for centuries. There must be more of them out there in limbo, waiting to be found. Simon knew her interests. "Right up your alley," he had said. "You won't believe it. I can hardly believe it myself . . ." He surely couldn't be so cruel as to lure her all the way to Baltimore on a wild-goose chase. Simon was no pathetic old man, hungry for her companionship. He had dozens of friends, and he preferred his own company to that of most people.

The shop was on Charles Street, north of the railroad station, in a neighborhood that clung by its fingernails to the crumbling edge of respectability. She had to park several blocks away. Snow drifted down as she walked, fat, feathery flakes that stuck to her eyelashes. Opening the shop door, she cleared her throat and began to sing: "These are a few of my favorite things . . ."

The soft music from the back of the shop soared to ear-aching pitch. It was the coruscating aria of the Queen of the Night, from *Zauberflöte*, and the high notes seemed to drill into her head. Karen covered her ears with her hands. In the shadows at the back she saw Simon sitting behind his desk. A lamp cast Satanic shadows across his lean, sculptured face.

"Turn it down!" she yelled.

Simon blinked at her. "Can't hear you," he mouthed. But the volume dropped, and he came to her, taking both her hands in his.

"How dare you warble sentimental popular

14

drivel at me while the Master's work is playing?"

Karen laughed and let him help her off with her coat. Hanging it neatly on a hook, he remarked, "It is damp. Does it snow hard? Perhaps you had better spend the night."

She had done it once or twice before, but she hated putting him out, for he always insisted on giving up his own bed to her and curling his lean length on the living-room couch. She answered, "I can't, I've got too much to do tomorrow. The snow doesn't seem to be sticking. I should make it back all right, if I don't stay too long."

Simon got the hint. His thin lips quirked in a half-smile, but he said nothing as he escorted her toward the back of the shop. Soft, overstuffed chairs slipcovered in faded chintz, reading lamps, an electric teakettle emitting a cloud of steam, and a time-softened Persian rug furnished a cozy alcove walled with books — Simon's sanctum, to which only favored customers were admitted.

Karen let out a sigh as she sank into one of the chairs and allowed Simon to serve her coffee and a plate of flaky pastry. She hadn't realized how tense she was, not only with anticipation over Simon's mysterious find, but with the constant everyday aggravation and bustle. It all seemed to slip away here; muscles relaxed, unfinished tasks became unimportant, worries faded. The friendly, intimate ambience Simon had created was partially responsible, but the books themselves had an almost physical effect upon her. What they represented was little short of a miracle — contact, as

15

direct as any spiritualist medium could claim, with minds long dead.

"Fresh-baked an hour ago," said Simon, proffering the plate. "From that Polish bakery around the corner."

Karen waved the plate away. "I'm trying to lose weight. You're putting me off, Simon. I hate it when you do this! Where is it? What is it?"

"Please." Raising a hand for silence, Simon turned up the volume again. The great basso of Alexander Kipnis filled the room. It was one of Karen's favorite arias too, but she lacked the skill to listen with the intensity that held Simon's face rapt. It was a wonderful face, so thin it had the pure, bare beauty of bone. His hair clung to his skull like a cap of polished steel. He was still a handsome man; he must have been knockdown gorgeous when he was young.

The great music faded into silence, and Simon let out his breath. "The only music that might without blasphemy be put in the mouth of God himself," he quoted.

"Mmm." Karen knew the futility of pushing him, but she needed some outlet for her frustration. Wickedly she said, "The music is sublime, but you must admit the words are pretty corny. And chauvinist. 'Keep it up, my boy, and you'll be a man.' What about poor Pamina? She trudged through the seven hells with her boyfriend; how come she doesn't get to be a Mensch too?"

Simon bit into a pastry with a vehemence that sent flakes showering down his shirtfront. He brushed them away and said forcefully, "You don't understand the meaning of the word. The German for man, male person, is 'Mann.' Mensch means —"

"Superman."

"No! A more accurate translation might be 'superior person.' Superior in the sense of courageous, noble, honorable —"

"Never mind. We've discussed this before. You're just trying to prolong the suspense, Simon. How can you be so mean?"

"No."

"What do you mean, no?"

"If I show it to you now, you will snatch it and run away, and then we will not have our nice little visit."

"Simon!"

"And also, I would have to call the police to follow you and arrest you for stealing a valuable object."

"Valuable? In monetary terms or —"

"In all terms." He leaned back in his chair. The lamplight shaded his face, deepening the lines around his smiling mouth and hiding his eyes in pools of shadow. He looked like an elegant Art Nouveau Mephistopheles. "I have made for lunch my famous goulash. But you do not need to lose weight, you are young and should have a healthy appetite. Have a kalashke."

Resignedly Karen took one of the pastries.

"How is Norman?"

The fact that Karen's mouth was full gave her

an excuse to delay answering. She couldn't imagine why Simon was inquiring about her ex-husband. He had been painstakingly polite to Norman on the few occasions when they had met — an unmistakable indication, to anyone who knew Simon, that he didn't care much for the other man. When Simon liked people he teased them and argued with them. Norman hadn't taken to Simon either. Karen's affection for the older man had left him baffled and obscurely uneasy, and he had objected vehemently to her filling the bookcases with "those dirty old books." His were all lined up in neat rows, arranged by size instead of subject, with nice clean dust jackets on them.

She swallowed. "All right, I guess."

"When will the divorce become final?"

"It is final. I got the papers last week."

"You are very calm about it."

"My heart isn't broken, Simon. We were married for less than three years, and I never liked him very much."

"What a cynic you have become!" He appeared to be genuinely shocked.

"A realist," Karen corrected. "I fell in love. When I fell out of love, I discovered there was nothing left — not liking, nor mutual respect, nor even forbearance. Do you know what his pet endearment for me was? Baby."

She knew Simon would never understand why that seemingly frivolous habit of Norman's had enraged her so. His forehead furrowed as he struggled to grasp the idea; then he shrugged it away.

"It is none of my business. But a young woman like yourself should not be alone."

"Simon, darling, you are hopelessly old-fashioned." Karen gave him an affectionate smile. "What do you mean by alone — unmarried, or celibate?"

"That is a vulgar question," Simon said severely.

"It is not. I phrased it very genteelly. And you were the one who brought the subject up."

He returned her smile. "Touché. Well, then — I certainly would not want you to marry the first lout who asked you."

"I'm relieved to hear it. Good men are hard to find. As for being celibate — what makes you suppose I am?"

"You are not foolhardy. In these times, only a permanent relationship (how I despise that word!) is completely safe. I would know if you had established one. There are," said Simon delicately, "certain indications."

Karen gave up. She usually backed away when they got onto this subject. "You're trying to start another argument. I don't provoke, Simon. Stop trying to change the subject. If you don't tell me —"

"Ah, excuse me. I hear the bell ring."

He disappeared around the bookshelf. A customer had come into the shop; Karen heard a murmur of voices and then another tinkle from the bell over the door of the shop. Simon came back, wearing a look of disgust.

"Some fool in search of best-sellers. The latest

Stephen King, he wanted. As if I would carry such a book."

"Ah," said Karen. "So there is a type of literature you haven't read."

"There is no type I have not read."

"Stephen King?"

"Certainly. He does what he does very well. I don't care for what he does. It is a matter of personal taste. I prefer horror to be more delicate — a frisson, a suggestion, instead of a catalog of disgusting details. The whisper from an invisible throat, the shadow where there is no object to cast it, a sudden breath of cold air in a warm room. Don't you agree?"

"I don't read horror stories," Karen said.

" 'The Yellow Wallpaper'?"

"Oh, but that isn't . . . Well, yes, it is; but the horror is psychological; it is a brilliant study of a woman retreating into madness from —"

"Ah, bah. More of your feminist jargon. What does it matter if the victim is a woman being driven mad by the constraints of male-dominated society or an unbeliever tormented by a narrow concept of religion?"

"It isn't a question of better or worse," Karen protested. "You can't compare absolute evil; all you can do is fight it whenever it manifests itself."

"Precisely what I was saying. The agony is the same and the cause is the same: a rigid moral absolutism that inflicts pain under the pretext of kindness."

"What story are you referring to? Sounds like Poe."

"No; I doubt you have heard of the author. The story is called 'The Torture of Hope.' It is about a prisoner trying to escape from the cells of the Inquisition, only to find, just as he seems to reach freedom, that his captors have allowed him to hope as the ultimate torture. And the worst thing about both stories is that the tormentor is not a perverted sadist. Quite the contrary; the husband and the Grand Inquisitor have noble motives. They wish to save their victims from damnation, by society or by God."

"Simon, I promise I won't steal your precious surprise. Please let me see it."

"Not just yet. First you must listen to this. Where did I put that book . . ." Turning, he ran his finger along the shelf behind him.

Karen bit her lip. Simon wasn't being deliberately sadistic either. His attitude was typical of the world from which he had come — Europe between the wars, sophisticated, intellectual, more than a little decadent. Though he had never told her his precise age, he must have been in his teens when his native Vienna had fallen to the forces of evil and his family and friends had vanished into the death camps. The values of that vanished age, remembered by an impressionable boy, were all the more to be cherished because of the horror that had swept them away. Whatever their failings, the aristocrats and intellectuals of old Europe had realized that the deliberate, delicate prolongation

21

of pleasure was an art to be cultivated in all aspects of life, from the enjoyment of sculpture to the appreciation of music, from dining to making love.

"You are flushed," Simon said, turning back to her with the book in his hand. "Is it too warm? Old people have cold bones; I will lower the heat."

Karen wiped the smile off her face. Maybe Simon was right; she had been "alone" too long. "I'm not too warm," she assured him. "I was thinking about . . . something else."

"If it makes you blush I don't want to hear it," Simon said reprovingly. "Now listen."

He had only read a few sentences when the shop door opened again and he went out to attend to the customer, leaving the book open on his chair. This time he was gone for some time. Karen picked up the book. When Simon returned she started and let out a strangled shriek.

Chuckling, Simon took the book from her hands. "Where had you got to? Ah, yes. 'He pressed forward faster on his knees, his hands, at full length, dragging himself painfully along, and soon entered the dark portion of this terrible corridor.' "

"You startled me," Karen mumbled. "Creeping in like that."

Simon raised an elegant eyebrow at her and went on reading. " 'Oh Heaven, if the door should open outward. Every nerve in the miserable fugitive's body thrilled with hope.' "

He started to close the book. "You see what I mean. The physical tortures inflicted on the rabbi are never described in detail, only hinted at. It is his mental suffering —"

"Okay," Karen said. "Finish it. Please."

"I wouldn't want to bore you with third-rate fiction."

"You did that on purpose. I know he doesn't make it, but I'll never sleep tonight if I don't find out what happens."

Simon did as she asked. He had a sonorous, flexible voice and he knew he read well. He gave the dreadful story everything he had. Scarcely had the poor rabbi reached the gardens and raised his eyes toward Heaven to praise God for his escape than he was clasped in a tender embrace and he realized that "all the phases of this fatal evening were only a prearranged torture, that of HOPE." "The Grand Inquisitor, with an accent of touching reproach and a look of consternation, murmured in his ear, his breath parched and burning from long fasting: 'What, my son! On the eve, perchance, of salvation — you wished to leave us?' "

Karen shuddered, then laughed — at herself. "I concede your point. But I'm afraid modern readers wouldn't be affected."

"They have become jaded — too many chain saws, too many decomposing corpses. And few comprehend that mental torture is the worst of all — the constriction of hope and of ambition."

"But that's what women's writing is all about," Karen said. "That's the theme of Ismene's poem. 'They have shut me in a house of stone.' She wasn't talking about a physical prison."

Much of Simon's business was conducted by mail; drop-in customers were rare, and the dismal weather did not encourage shoppers. They were not interrupted again. However, Simon waited until the stroke of twelve before locking the front door. Karen preceded him up the stairs at the back of the shop, moving slowly so that the necessary deliberation of his own ascent would not humiliate him.

The apartment over the shop was small and a little shabby, but it was impeccably neat — except for the books. They lined the walls, covered all the flat surfaces, stood stacked in uneven piles beside chairs and sofa. Simon turned on the lights and led the way to the kitchen.

The rich, spicy smell of the goulash filled the room. Simon held a chair for Karen and moved back and forth with wineglasses, a basket of bread, and the steaming tureen. She knew better than to offer assistance.

After they finished eating Simon took out one of his thin black cigars. "May I smoke?" he inquired.

Karen jumped up. Snatching his plate and hers, she carried them to the sink, and finished clearing the table. Then she sat down and stared fixedly at him. "Now, Simon."

With a sigh Simon rose and left the room. The set of his shoulders expressed the resignation of a long-suffering male yielding to feminine whims. When he came back he was carrying a parcel and a clean white cloth, which he spread carefully across the table. "Now may I smoke?" he inquired, handing her the parcel.

He took her silence for consent; she had realized early on that he would be unmoved by lectures on the dangers of smoking and would regard any comment on his habits as rude and impertinent. In fact, she scarcely heard the question. She was too intent on the parcel.

It was small but bulky. Carefully Karen removed an outer covering of padded cloth to disclose a layer of the inert plastic used by museum conservators. Unlike ordinary plastic, it would not react chemically with fragile substances such as paper and cloth.

Her mouth was dry and her hands shook as she unwrapped the plastic. The object felt like a book. Well, she had expected that, hadn't she? Something old, something rare . . .

It wasn't a printed book. It was a pile of loose papers — a manuscript. If there had been covers, they were missing. The pages were raveled along one side, like mouse-nibbled wool, and the corners were so worn that the shape was more elliptical than rectangular. The lower edge was black and crumbling. She could just make out traces of writing on the topmost sheet, though it was so darkened by time and by disfiguring spots of brown — a condition known in the trade as "foxing" — that only a few words were legible.

Karen tried to control her voice. "I can't . . . I don't . . ."

25

"Don't be afraid to touch it, it is not as fragile as it appears," Simon said. "Except along the edges. The paper is hand-made, lacking the destructive chemicals modern paper manufacturers employ. Well? What are you waiting for? All morning you nagged me to see it, and now you sit with folded hands staring at a blank page."

"Not . . . completely blank. I can read a few words." She turned to face him. "Simon. This isn't a joke, is it? You wouldn't . . ."

"No." A single sharp word; the accusation had hurt and angered him. She held out her hands in silent apology, and his stiff features relaxed as he took them in his. "Well, I can hardly blame you. I could not believe it myself at first. But the name is there. Ismene."

"Maybe it's not the same woman. Maybe some other writer used that name. Maybe this isn't . . . What is it? More poems? A diary?"

"Why don't you look for yourself?"

"I'm afraid to. I'm afraid I'm imagining this. I'm afraid it will crumble when I touch it."

"It is not a diary," Simon said patiently. "It appears to be a novel, or part of one. The first pages are missing, and so are the last."

"I don't believe it!"

"What don't you believe? As a literary form, the novel is two and a half centuries old. Richardson's *Pamela* was published in 1740. Also eighteenth-century in date were *The Mysteries of Udolpho* and *The Castle of Otranto*. This appears to be an example of the latter genre — the true

Gothic novel, as opposed to the so-called Gothics of this century, which bear little resemblance to —"

"Don't you dare lecture me on my own subject!"

Simon laughed aloud. "So, you are yourself again."

"Dammit, Simon, I've written two articles on the Gothic novel."

"And you are now wringing your hands," Simon said, grinning. "How appropriate!"

"I'm trying to keep them off that book," Karen said, returning his smile. He knew her well; he had chosen the most effective method of calming her. "I want to grab it and start reading."

"Go ahead. We have all afternoon. And if you care to spend the night, all evening."

"Not the original, it's too precious. I'll have a copy made . . . ." She broke off as she saw his face change, and a wave of genuine physical sickness swamped her. "Simon! You are going to let me have it? You wouldn't show it to me and then take it away? You haven't sold it to someone else? You couldn't!"

"Calm yourself," Simon exclaimed. "Let me get you a glass of wine, or —"

"Don't treat me like some Victorian lady with the vapors! Oh, all right. I'll have some coffee. Please," she added sulkily.

He filled two cups and joined her at the table. "My dear Karen, you are the first person other than myself to see this. How could I do less? But I can't let you have it — not now, at any rate.

27

No, don't speak! You would only say something you would regret. Let me explain."

She seized on the words that offered hope. "Not now? When?"

"After the proper procedures have been followed. Listen to me! Do you have any idea what this battered object is worth? I am talking of money, Karen — crude and vulgar of me, no doubt, but this is how I earn my living, by buying and selling books."

"Well, of course. I expected to pay for it, that's the only way I would . . ." She heard her voice start to rise, and fought to control it. This was business, not friendship. That was how she wanted it. One didn't take advantage of a friend. "How much are you asking for it?"

Undeceived by her pretense at coolness, Simon eyed her warily. "Are you familiar with the motto of antiquities dealers? 'An object is worth only what someone is willing to pay for it.' It is possible to estimate the value of a particular book by studying what comparable volumes have brought in the market. But that's the problem. With what can I compare this? I could make an educated guess as to what a Brontë or Dickens manuscript might bring; the original manuscripts of known works do appear on the market from time to time. But an unknown, unpublished manuscript by a little-known writer . . . who knows? The only way to find out is to offer it for sale."

"Where? At auction?"

He remained maddeningly calm. "I could do

that, but I won't. If it sold to a private collector, he or she might not make it available to scholars, which would be a pity. I intend instead to invite bids from major universities and libraries."

"I'll top your highest bid. Isn't there a procedure for that in your business? Preferred bidder, or something?"

"Karen —" His eyes moved from hers. Following his gaze, she saw that, without being conscious of movement, she had placed both hands on the manuscript, fingers flexed, palms pressing down.

"I understand your position, Simon," she said steadily. "Now hear mine. The first person to get hold of this manuscript, by hook or crook or legal purchase, will be the one to publish it. If it goes to a university or library, they'll pick one of their own people to handle it. I wouldn't have a chance."

"You believe you can persuade your college to —"

"Simon, you're not listening! Even if the college would put up the money, which is unlikely, there's at least one other person on the faculty who would lay claim to it. He'd probably succeed, too, because he sucks up to the board and the faculty senate and I don't. Bill Meyer at Yale, and Dorothea Angelo at Berkeley — to name only two — would kill for the chance to get this. And both institutions have a hell of a lot more money than my college."

"Yes, I understand that. But you —"

"Let me finish." He hated being interrupted, and now she had done it twice. She plunged on, desperately seeking words that would convince him. "Do you know what a less scrupulous person would do in my place? Accept your invitation to spend the night, slip you a sleeping pill and sneak out, with the manuscript, to one of those all-night copying places."

Simon's eyes widened. "That would be a despicable act."

"Of course. I'd never commit it, but I can think of several other people who wouldn't hesitate for a second. You of all people ought to know that the definition of legal ownership with regard to old manuscripts is hideously complex. The pages themselves, the physical manuscript, can be bought or sold, inherited, given away. I would be guilty of theft if I stole It. But what about the text — the words? They can't be copyrighted, they are old enough to be in the public domain. If I had a copy of the text, I doubt very much if you could prevent me from publishing it. I'd sure as hell be willing to take that chance — and so would Bill Meyer, or dear old Joe Cropsey, my favorite departmental chairman. That's why I have to own it, Simon, and guard it with my life — to keep other people from getting their hands on it. It wouldn't take more than two hours to have a copy made."

She was breathless when she finished, but she had made her point. Simon was looking very sober. "I hadn't thought of it that way. It is true that there are other interested parties. Your own fault, Karen; you were the one who made Ismene famous. How many copies of your edition of the poems were sold? How many articles on her have appeared since then?"

Karen didn't answer. It was particularly embittering to realize that if she hadn't made Ismene famous, in the scholarly world at least, she wouldn't have to fear competition. On the other hand, Simon would not have called her first if she had not been the acknowledged authority. The manuscript itself might have been overlooked, discarded, if she had not publicized that vital name. The very idea made her break into a cold sweat.

"Where did you get it?" she asked.

"From a trunk in a dusty attic, of course. Isn't that the traditional source for such finds? In fact, most discoveries of this nature do come from places like that. Remember the first half of the Huckleberry Finn manuscript that was found a few years ago? Mark Twain had sent it to a friend, who evidently mislaid it; it remained in a trunk in Gluck's attic for over a century."

Karen smiled sweetly. "If you think you are going to distract me, Simon, you are sadly mistaken."

Simon sighed. "The house from which this manuscript came belonged to an old gentleman who was a pack rat, like his ancestors before him. When he died, the new owner called in a local auctioneer and told him to clear the place out in preparation for a sale. The auctioneer is a man with whom I've dealt before; local dealers often consult me about books and manuscripts. He and the owner agreed to let me handle this particular

31

item, since it was — shall we say — somewhat esoteric."

"Who —" she began.

"You know I can't tell you that," Simon interrupted with a frown.

"Are you selling on consignment?"

"No. I bought it outright." He hesitated for a moment, and then named a figure. It was less than she had feared, but more than she had hoped. Simon was too damned honorable; he could have told the owner the manuscript was worthless, and offered him ten dollars as a gesture of goodwill.

"I'll top your highest bid," she repeated. "Whatever it is." Reaching into her purse, she took out her checkbook. "I've got seven thousand, six hundred in my savings account. I'll give you seven thousand as a deposit. And yes, thank you — I will spend the night."

Chapter Two

All women, as authors, are feeble and tiresome. I wish they were forbidden to write, on pain of having their faces deepley scarified with an oyster shell.

NATHANIEL HAWTHORNE,
letter to his publisher, 1852

Darkness solid as stone weighted her limbs, filled her open mouth and flaring nostrils as she struggled for breath. Darkness like moist black earth, heavy, airless, imprisoning the hands that struggled to free themselves, pressing down upon her staring eyes . . .

She fought out of sleep into waking, the scream she had not been able to utter still trapped in her throat. The streetlight outside her bedroom window cast a pale illumination into the room. It was some time before her gasps settled into normal breathing; longer before she dared sleep again.

Karen had reached the faculty parking lot before she realized the sound — repeated, peremptory, vaguely familiar — was that of her own name. She turned. The form bearing down on her was also familiar: Dr. Margaret Finneyfrock, professor of American history, known to her friends as

Peggy. She insisted on the diminutive, for reasons Karen had never understood; it certainly didn't suit her. Her crop of short gray curls looked as if it had been trimmed with garden shears, her weathered face was devoid of makeup, her stocky frame was clad in one of her legendary tweed suits. Her students claimed that when she bought a new one she weighted the pockets with stones and left it hanging in her closet until it had been suitably aged before putting it on. The skirts always bagged at the seat and the pockets always sagged and the fabric was always frayed by the claws of Peggy's cats.

Peggy was not wearing a coat, and Karen realized it was a mild, sunny day. She hadn't taken notice of the weather or the flowerbeds, which were bright with crocuses and daffodils.

"Are you going deaf, or just trying to avoid me?" Peggy demanded. "I've been bellowing at you for five minutes. Where the hell do you think you're going?"

"Home. Why the hell shouldn't I?"

"There is an extremely exasperated young woman outside your office door who could answer that. She claims she had an appointment with you at eleven."

"Oh, Lord." Karen bit her lip. "Debbie. This is the second . . . I suppose I'll have to see her."

"Don't bother. She went stamping off after she'd unloaded on me. I don't know why they all unload on ME. I certainly don't invite — Hey, wait a minute!" Karen turned. Peggy caught her by the arm.

"I didn't chase you all this way just to tell you you'd screwed up. Why do you think I went by your office in the first place? I haven't seen you for over a week. Let's go have lunch."

"Sorry. I really don't have time."

Peggy gripped Karen's other arm and swung her around so that they stood face-to-face. The expression was not entirely accurate; Peggy was five inches shorter than Karen, and she had to tip her head back in order to meet the latter's eyes. Apparently she did not approve of what she saw.

"You look terrible," she said bluntly. "What have you been doing? Not eating or sleeping, obviously. Is something wrong?"

Not sleeping, Karen thought. Dreaming. The flash of memory — palpable darkness, weighting her down — shivered through her body, and Peggy's grip tightened. "What is it?"

"Nothing. I'm fine. I've been working, that's all. A new project. I've got to get back to it, I don't have time for —"

"Then you'd damned well better make time. You'll fall ill if you go on like this, and then where will your precious project be? This isn't an invitation, it's an order."

"Did Joan put you up to this?" Karen demanded. "Or Sharon?"

"They're worried about you too. You didn't show up for lunch last week, or call to tell them you weren't coming. You aren't answering your phone and you're hardly ever in your office."

"So? I've been busy. Those lunches aren't formal meetings, we just get together when we can. They aren't my keepers, I don't owe them —"

"They are your friends," Peggy interrupted. "You owe them. It was Sharon who called me; you know these psychologists, they're always reading sinister meanings into sudden alterations of behavior. Joan's theory is that you have a new boyfriend."

Karen smiled in spite of herself. She didn't need Peggy's critical stare to know she did not look like a woman in love. Her panty hose had a run and her lipstick must be . . . Had she put on makeup that morning? She couldn't remember. "Oh, all right," she said ungraciously. "Where do you want to go?"

"Anyplace that has a liquor license and does not serve tofu in any form. Come on. I'll drive."

Once she had her prisoner safely in the car, Peggy relapsed into tactful silence, and Karen felt herself beginning to relax. Wilmington was a pretty town, nestled in the folds of the hills Marylanders euphemistically referred to as mountains; the spring sunshine freshened the facades of the old houses, and the new green of the lawns was freckled with bright-yellow dandelions. Quite a contrast to that gloomy day a week ago when she had driven back from Baltimore through a last-of-the-season snowstorm. Spring had come on unnoticed by her; she had scarcely left the house since, except when she happened to remember she had a class or a faculty meeting.

They passed through the old town and headed west toward one of the shopping centers that had sprung up, with their cluster of surrounding subdivisions. "I thought we'd try that new Mexican restaurant at the mall," Peggy explained. "They say the food is pretty good."

"You're just trying to get as far away from campus as possible," Karen said. "Don't worry, I won't leap out and try to escape. You were right; I do need a break. Thanks."

"For what? My motives were purely selfish, as they always are."

Karen studied her with an affectionate smile. Peggy's gruff voice, deepened to bass-baritone by years of chain smoking, and her disdain for feminine fripperies concealed a personality as soft as marshmallow. It wasn't surprising that Joan and Sharon, Karen's closest friends on the faculty, had appealed to Peggy; everybody unloaded on her, including students in other departments. Even the least perceptive of them realized within a week that there was a mother hen under the gruff facade. Peggy yelled at them and scolded them and was always there when they needed her.

As she was for me, Karen thought, dutifully stuffing herself with the taco salad Peggy had made her order. She hadn't realized how hungry she was until she had actually eaten most of the monstrous object — chili, guacamole, lettuce and tomatoes and shredded cheese and a mound of sour cream in a casing of puffed dough.

"You can have a margarita now if you want,"

said Peggy. She had had two.

"No, thanks."

"Coffee, then." Peggy summoned the waitress with a peremptory flourish of her arm. With a wry smile, Karen nodded agreement. The preliminaries having been concluded, Peggy was about to get down to the real business of the meeting.

"Has somebody been complaining about me?" Karen asked for openers. She was pretty sure she knew the answer.

"You've missed two classes and God knows how many student conferences," Peggy said. "But of course you know who's done the complaining — your favorite departmental chairman, Joe Cropsey. All under the guise of fatherly solicitude. Perhaps you've been ill? Perhaps you've had bad news from home? Perhaps — giggle, smirk, nudge, nudge — your personal life has gone sour?"

"He would think of that," Karen muttered, shoving a wilted scrap of taco around the plate.

"He wants to be part of your personal life," Peggy said. She added dispassionately, "Nasty little prick. You'd better tell me, or you'll have him oozing around offering to console you."

"A fate worse than death. I'd like to tell you, actually. I guess I've reached the stage where I need some dispassionate advice. I hadn't . . ." She brushed a lock of limp brown hair away from her face. It was long overdue for a shampoo. She went on, "I hadn't realized how madly preoccupied I've been. It may take a while; do you have the time?"

"I have all day," Peggy said.

38

She had finished her coffee by the time the tale was told. She accepted a refill and asked the waitress to replace Karen's untouched, tepid tea.

"So did you dope the old gent?"

"Of course not." With a wry smile, Karen added, "I wouldn't have gotten away with it; he watched me like a hawk. In the end he consented to take my check. He made me read some of the manuscript first, though, honorable soul that he is. Not that he had to force me. That's why I stayed the night and missed half my appointments next day. I'm too noble to steal and copy it, but I'm not noble enough to resist the chance to read as much as I could."

"So what is it?"

"It is a novel. A Gothic novel."

"Ruined castles, dastardly villains in hot pursuit of the helpless heroine's virginity?" Peggy grinned. "I used to read that sort of thing. I was still in my twenties, which is some excuse."

"You're thinking about the imitation Gothics, most of which were nothing of the sort, that were all over the bookstores thirty years ago." Unconsciously Karen assumed her lecturer's pose. "The original Gothic novel began with *The Castle of Otranto* in 1764, and reached its height in the novels of Mrs. Radcliffe thirty years later. They were certainly overburdened with dastardly villains and vapid heroines, ancient castles and Deadly Secrets; but the Gothic romance represents a significant development in the history of the modern novel. The images of imprisonment and danger represent the social, intellectual and economic frustration of women in a rigid paternalistic society —"

"Spare me. I'm not knocking literary criticism, but I just don't give a damn about analysis of that sort, be it Freudian or feminist. The only thing I care about is whether it's a good read."

"Do you consider *Jane Eyre* a good read? How about *Wuthering Heights?*"

"They aren't Gothic novels."

"They are in the Gothic tradition. Gloomy, isolated old houses, glowering Byronic heroes, threatened heroines —"

Peggy's eyes narrowed. "But those are great works of literature. Are you saying that this manuscript is of the same caliber?"

"I don't know what it is yet," Karen said in a low voice. "Simon gave me a copy of the first thirty pages. He's doing the same, damn him, for all the other potential buyers. I've spent the last week going over and over those pages and making a typewritten copy. The text is awfully hard to read. The ink has faded, the handwriting is minuscule — paper was expensive in those days, they crammed as much as they could onto a page — and there are a lot of interpolations and abbreviations and interlineations. I can only do a few pages at a time before my eyes start aching."

"I see." Peggy lit another cigarette. "At least I think I do. This is really important to you, isn't it?"

"It could be the most important thing that's ever happened to me. Or ever will happen. Grants, job offers from big universities, a step, maybe two steps, up the academic ladder, national recognition."

"Whew. That big, huh? For heaven's sake, relax," she added in some alarm. "You're bending that spoon into a circle. Your friend the bookseller promised it to you, didn't he?"

"He promised me I could top the highest bid. It's not like a regular auction, he's only giving the others a chance to make one offer. That's damned decent of him, really, he's doing me a big favor. He says this is the only way he can determine what it's worth."

Peggy's eyes narrowed. "What kind of money are we talking about here? And where are you proposing to get it?"

"I don't know; I don't know." Karen brushed at the fog of smoke hovering over the table. "I haven't even thought about it. I've been too absorbed —"

"Obsessed is more like it." Peggy blew out a rather wobbly smoke ring. "Don't bother defending yourself; I know how I'd feel if a comparable discovery came into my hands. There's no sense worrying about money yet. Maybe the other bidders won't be interested. Maybe they won't be able to come up with the cash."

"You don't understand."

"So tell me."

"Simon has contacted a number of people. Two of them have expressed interest and asked to see the merchandise. He won't tell me their names,

41

but I'm sure one of them is Bill Meyer. Once that bastard sees it . . ." Her voice rose.

"Calm down," Peggy said. "Who's Bill Meyer?"

"Yale. Associate professor. Specializes in Early American literature and in smart-ass, nasty reviews. His critique of my edition of Ismene's poems was a masterpiece of snottiness. He's also a die-hard male chauvinist and a defender of the canon." Seeing Peggy's look of exasperation, she explained, "The traditional literary canon of great works was defined by men, and consists mostly of male authors. One major book on nineteenth-century literature doesn't even admit Jane Austen or the Brontës or George Eliot into the sacred ranks. Meyer and his kind claim there aren't any great books by women on the list because women didn't *write* any great books."

"Huh," said Peggy. "Then why would he want —"

"This is a major discovery, Peggy, whatever its eventual literary status may be. There are a number of eighteenth-century novels by women — more than most people realize, because they have been neglected and rejected by critics. For example, I'll bet you've never heard of *Charlotte Temple*. Yet it was the first American best-seller; it went through over two hundred editions, official and pirated, after it was published in 1791, and it was still being read in 1912 by 'housemaids and shop-girls,' as some critic condescendingly put it. That was its problem, of course; any book popular with women was by definition —"

"You've made your point, and exposed my ignorance. Let's concentrate, for the moment, on this particular book. I take it that most of the neglected and rejected books were in print at one time. This is completely new — never published?"

"I've checked every reference I can think of. That's why it's so important, Peggy. Even Bill Meyer, male chauvinist though he is, would love to be the discoverer of an unknown American author."

"You think he can talk Yale into coming up with an offer? Money's tight these days."

"You're telling me. The other buyer has to be Dorothea Angelo, from Berkeley. She's a full professor and she's got a lot of clout. She was green with envy when I published the poems; she's been sniping at me ever since, in print and in person. She'd kill to get her hands on this."

"But Simon promised you —"

"I may not be able to raise the money." It was the first time Karen had admitted it, even to herself. Her voice was unsteady. "And even if I can, they will have seen it. Simon won't let it out of his hands, he'll insist that they examine it in his office; at least I hope that's what he'll do. But I wouldn't put it past either of them to steal the damned thing."

"Your friend Simon doesn't sound like a patsy."

"Well . . . maybe not. But there's another aspect to this business — the author's identity. The poems gave no clue to her real name, or even what part

43

of the country she came from. It would be an additional feather in my professional cap to identify her. In fact, without that background it will be impossible to do a proper study of her novel — show how she fits into the tradition, what other writers influenced her, and so on. There's no way I could prevent someone else from pursuing that search, even if I owned the manuscript. I couldn't stand it if —"

She broke off, biting her lip. The last thing she wanted to do was sound like one of the hysterical heroines of the novels they had discussed. Peggy seemed to find her reaction reasonable, though. "Yes, I see. The manuscript offers clues to her identity?"

"I think it may," Karen said cautiously. "Even more important is where it was found. Simon bought it from a person — he wouldn't even tell me whether it was a man or a woman — who had inherited an old house and its contents. He said something about 'local dealers,' so I'm assuming the house is somewhere in this area. He also said the manuscript had been found in a trunk in the attic of the house. You see what that means?"

"Who, me? I'm just an ignorant historian," Peggy said with ineffable sarcasm. But her eyes were bright and intent. " 'In this area' is pretty vague; it could cover the whole East Coast. However you would probably be safe in limiting yourself to the Mid-Atlantic region — from Pennsylvania to the Carolinas. There are a lot of old houses and old families in that part of the country . . ." She ended on a questioning note; then she said, "The former owner may have been an auction hound. He could have picked up the manuscript in a box lot at some country sale."

"Then the auctioneer's records would give me the name of the person who put it up for sale," Karen said. "You're right, it may have passed through many hands; tracking it down would be like those treasure-hunt games we used to play, with one clue leading to another."

"Or tracing the ownership of a plot of land." Peggy lit another cigarette from the stub of the last. Karen could tell she was hooked. She wondered why she hadn't thought of confiding in Peggy earlier. This part of the problem required historical rather than literary research and Peggy loved puzzles in all forms, from mystery stories to double-crostics.

"There's another possibility, of course," Peggy went on musingly. "From Mrs. Radcliffe to the Brontës; you're talking about a literary type that flourished around the turn of the eighteenth century, right? This part of the country was well settled by 1800. The author must have been a member of a wealthy, land-owning family; only the upper classes bothered to have their sons educated, much less their daughters. They were lordly aristocrats — slave owners — flaunting their wealth, importing books and furniture from England, building great mansions . . ." She had been talking to herself, letting her agile and informed imagination build up a theory. Now she looked directly at

Karen and said, "That's what you believe, isn't it? That the seller is one of Ismene's descendants. That the house where the manuscript was found is her home."

"I don't know why the weather is always foul when I go to Baltimore," Karen grumbled. "If I were superstitious I'd regard it as an omen, and turn back."

It was rain, not sleet or snow, that darkened the highway that morning. Patches of mist drifted across the road.

Peggy checked her seat belt for the tenth time. She had offered to drive, but Karen had overruled her, even though she knew Peggy hated being a passenger.

"You wouldn't turn back if the clouds opened up and God threw a thunderbolt at you." Peggy reached in her purse, which squatted on the floor at her feet like a malignant black gnome, and then made a face and withdrew her hand.

"Go ahead and smoke," Karen said resignedly.

"And deprive you of ten minutes of your busy, productive, happy, interminable life?"

"I don't want to see a premature end to *your* busy, productive, happy, interminable life. And I hate having the smell of it in the car. But I'd rather put up with that than have you twitching and snapping at me all the way to Baltimore."

Peggy grinned. "Oh, well. If you insist."

She lit her cigarette, cracked the window, and then leaned back, looking more relaxed. "I'm looking forward to meeting your friend Simon. Do you think he'll mind my coming along?"

"If he does, he won't show it. He's a perfect gent. Your presence will add a certain legitimacy to my claim on the manuscript; he'll think you represent the college."

"Just watch what you say," Peggy warned her. "I don't represent the college, and I don't particularly want to be sued for misrepresentation — by Simon or the board of trustees."

"Don't worry."

"Huh," said Peggy. "Are you still set on that crazy scheme of yours?"

"I have to know who the other bidders are, Peggy! Simon wouldn't tell me."

"You didn't expect him to, did you?"

"Well — no. I certainly wouldn't want him to give the others my name. Call it idle curiosity if you like —"

"Oh, I can see why you're interested."

"Will you please stop interrupting me?"

Peggy laughed aloud. After a moment Karen laughed too. "Am I being prickly?"

"Uh-huh. And overly defensive. Hell, you don't have to explain why you're curious about the competition. I am too. I wouldn't miss this for the world. Skulking in doorways with my hat pulled down over my eyes, snapping pictures with my hidden camera, trailing suspects through the byways of Baltimore . . ."

Karen groaned. "I knew I'd regret letting you come."

It was a lie; she could only thank heaven that chance had involved Peggy in her project. Not only was her historical expertise proving invaluable, but her practical, commonsense presence steadied Karen's imagination. She had been in danger of going off the deep end that first week; excitement had muddled her thinking processes and endangered not only her job but the acquisition of the precious manuscript. With Peggy nagging her, she had resumed her normal academic schedule and managed to refrain from hassling Simon. Her enforced patience had paid off when he called to tell her she wouldn't have to wait much longer, he had volunteered the information that he expected the other interested parties that weekend, and when she asked if she might have another look at the prize, he had agreed.

"You're sure Bill Meyer is coming today?" Peggy asked. "I don't mind playing spy, even in the rain, so long as it isn't a waste of time."

"I'm not sure who the client is," Karen said. "Simon's too damned discreet to mention a name. But someone will be there today or tomorrow."

"Goody, goody. I can play spy two days in a row."

"That's why I suggested you bring an overnight bag. Simon mentioned two prospects. If both show up today, we won't have to stay over, but just in case . . ."

"Fine with me. For God's sake," Peggy added irritably, "you're driving fifty miles an hour and every damned vehicle on the road is passing us.

Can't you go a little faster?"

"Have another cigarette," Karen said.

The rain slackened when they approached the city; only a dismal drizzle dampened their coats as they walked toward Simon's shop. Peggy had covered her head with a garish red-and-purple tie-dyed scarf. She explained she was saving her hat for surveillance purposes.

Simon was waiting at the door. His bushy eyebrows lifted when he saw Peggy, but he acknowledged the introduction with a slight bow and took the hand she extended.

They made one of the oddest couples Karen had ever seen. Simon's lean height dwarfed Peggy's stocky form, though he bent gallantly at the waist in order not to seem to loom over her. Peggy stood with her feet firmly planted; the pockets of her shabby raincoat sagged, and the hideous scarf drooped over her face. She pushed it back and grinned up at him. "I've heard a lot about you, Mr. Hallett."

"I am of course familiar with your work, Dr. Finneyfrock. But I mustn't keep you standing in your wet coat. Let me hang it up, here . . . And now, what about something hot to drink? Tea or coffee?"

He ushered her into the sitting area, leaving Karen to follow.

The manuscript, encased in its wrappings, lay on the table. Karen didn't wait for Simon's gesture of permission; she snatched it up like a mother embracing a missing child. This time she was not tempted to read on. A few more pages would not satisfy her urgent need.

It took the other two less than five minutes to get into a violent argument. Simon had never mentioned to Karen that he had read Peggy's book, but it was clear that he had, and it was only to be expected that he would take exception to her views on the role of women in pioneer America. Peggy was no more reluctant than he to express her opinions. Before long the dangerous word "herstory" had been mentioned and Peggy's voice had deepened to a growl. "Conventional history completely ignores half the human race. What do you think women were doing while their men were shooting Indians and slaughtering animals and cutting down the forests — embroidering doilies? The progress of civilization . . ."

Karen listened with amused enjoyment. She had thought Simon would like Peggy, but she hadn't dared hope they would hit it off so quickly and thoroughly. Simon never waxed sarcastic with people unless he approved of them.

He kept an unobtrusive eye on the clock, however, and finally he smiled and shrugged. "Greatly as I am enjoying this discussion, I fear I must excuse myself. We must talk again, Dr. Finneyfrock; I will not abandon hope of convincing such a rational woman of her small errors."

"I'll send you a copy of that article," Peggy said. "If it doesn't convince you, I will be forced to the conclusion that you are not as rational a man as you give occasional evidence of being."

Simon laughed aloud. "I will read it with pleasure. Your presence here makes me suspect that you are also interested in the manuscript. May I ask whether that interest is financial?"

Peggy returned his smile. "To whatever extent proves necessary."

Karen choked on the mouthful of coffee she had been about to swallow, and had to retire behind her napkin. It had never occurred to her to ask Peggy for financial help. There were some limits friends didn't cross, even when they were in the grip of an obsession like hers.

"I see." Simon stroked his chin and studied Peggy thoughtfully. "You are aware of the terms of the agreement? We have not committed it to writing; neither of us felt the need —"

"Nor do I," Peggy said. "Your word is good enough for me. I assure you I can and will match any offer you receive, but if you would like financial references —"

Simon's smile broadened. "I didn't require them of Karen. I can hardly do less for her . . . partner?"

"Whatever," said Peggy amiably. "Our arrangements need not concern you, Mr. Hallett."

Simon wasn't accustomed to being snubbed with such courteous finality. His brows drew together and he committed the outrageous rudeness of rising, to signal that the visit was at an end. "Very well. I'll be in touch with you as soon as I have the requisite information."

He helped them on with their coats and ushered them out the door.

Karen had so many questions and comments, she could not decide what to say first. As soon as the shop door had closed behind them, she burst out, "I didn't ask you for financial backing. When did you —"

"Save it." Peggy took her arm and started walking. "First things first. Let's get away from the shop. As soon as we're out of sight we'll put on our disguises and sneak back."

"What disguises? I didn't bring —"

"I've got one of those rainbonnets for you. Our coats are conveniently generic, in color and cut. I'll remove my glasses —"

"You're blind as a bat without them," Karen protested.

"Just till we're in position. You can lead me. The main thing is this scarf. Why do you think I wore such a garish article of attire? Once I take it off and put on my hat, I'll be unrecognizable."

She looked so pleased with herself, Karen hadn't the heart to point out the flaws in her plan. Peggy's most distinctive characteristic — her height, or lack thereof — couldn't easily be disguised. Karen decided not to mention it, for fear Peggy would rush off in search of a shoestore and a pair of four-inch heels.

They turned the corner and sought refuge from the thickening rain in a doorway. Peggy rummaged in her purse, fished out an amorphous wad of fabric and punched it into shape. It looked more like a decaying tan pyramid than a hat. Peggy replaced her scarf with this object and smirked complacently. "See? Now where did I put the . . . ah, here it is."

The plastic strip unfolded into a headcovering of sorts. It was printed with bright-red balloons. Resignedly Karen allowed her friend to arrange it over her damp hair.

"What position did you have in mind?" she asked. "This isn't the sort of neighborhood where it's safe to stand on a street corner."

"There's a bar practically across the street from the shop." Before Karen could object, Peggy went on, "And we'd better hurry. He was getting fidgety; his client must be due soon."

She was right, and Karen gave her credit for spotting Simon's impatience. She wouldn't have noticed it herself if she hadn't known him so well.

If she had been alone, Karen would have preferred the perils of a street corner to the ambiguous ambience Peggy had selected. Peggy did not share her qualms. "A nice, typical neighborhood bar," she proclaimed happily. "I hope they serve sandwiches. I'm starved."

The menu reminded Karen of a classic "Saturday Night Live" routine: hamburgers, cheeseburgers, and — as a concession to health-conscious customers — cheese sandwiches. It took Peggy less than five minutes to get them established at a table next to the window, where they could peer out between the dusty café curtains covering the lower half of that aperture. It took Karen a little longer to regain her composure.

"My God, Peggy! Did you have to tell him that

pack of lies?" she whispered.

"Certainly I did. It accomplished two things. First, my story eliminated any suspicion that we're lesbians. People who practice alternate life-styles aren't popular in places like —"

"Why would he think that?" Karen exclaimed.

"Two women enjoying one another's company are automatically suspect," Peggy said cynically. "Especially in blue-collar bars; especially when one of them is a tough-looking old broad and the other is young and pretty. Second, I had to think of an excuse for requesting a table next to the window and sitting here half the afternoon. There's nothing like a cheating husband to arouse chivalrous sympathy. Try to remember to call me Mom."

"I don't think I can do it," Karen gasped. "Peggy, this isn't going to work! I'm not even wearing a wedding ring!"

"Hell," said Peggy. "I forgot. Here." She slipped a ring from her finger and passed it to Karen under the table. It was a tight fit, but Karen managed to force it on. She turned it so that the glittering stones were hidden and only the plain gold shank showed. The central stone was very green and rather large. An emerald? If so, it suggested more affluence than she had suspected Peggy possessed. Which reminded her . . .

"I appreciate your offer of financial assistance, Peggy, but I can't accept it."

"We'll discuss that after Simon has settled on a price." Peggy took a long swallow of beer. "He's divine, Karen. I absolutely adore him. Fortunately he's too old for you."

"Peggy, you . . . " Karen shook her head. "I never knew you were like this."

"Neither did I. What a vast wasteland my life has been! I've had more fun in the last two hours than in the past ten years. Hey, look! Someone's going in the shop."

Karen pulled back the curtain and looked out. "It's nobody I know. Probably a regular customer."

Visibly disappointed, Peggy settled back. "You might not recognize all the potential buyers."

"I know most of the people who'd be interested. There are only two or three who really worry me."

Their hamburgers, complete with potato chips and a slice of limp pickle, had been delivered before the first of the two or three appeared.

"That's her!" Karen exclaimed, squeezing her greasy sandwich till mustard oozed out the sides. "Angelo."

"Really?" They bumped heads trying to look out. Peggy said incredulously, "That's a woman?"

The question was understandable. The figure approaching the bookstore was almost six feet tall and proportionately broad. Dark pants and flat shoes added to the androgynous look, and its head was hidden under a large black umbrella.

"That's her," Karen insisted. "Now what do we do?"

"She'll be a while," Peggy said. She popped the last of her hamburger into her mouth, chewed, swallowed, and wiped her mouth daintily on a paper napkin.

It was almost an hour before Angelo's massive form reappeared. She stood in the doorway struggling with her umbrella, and Peggy, face pressed against the window, exclaimed, "And I thought I was a tough-looking old broad! The meeting must not have gone well, to judge by that horrible scowl."

"That's her normal expression. The only time I've seen her smile was when she was harassing some helpless underling." Karen stared as intently as her friend. "She'd resent your description, though. She thinks she's irresistible to men."

Peggy was working on her second hamburger. "It's only one-thirty. Shall we hang around awhile longer? He may have scheduled two appointments this afternoon." Without waiting for an answer, she hailed the barman. "Hey, Dennis — how about a couple more beers?"

Dennis promptly obliged. "Any luck?" he asked solicitously.

"Not yet. The son of a bitch works a half day on Saturday, so he may not get here till mid-afternoon. I sure appreciate this, Dennis."

"So long as I don't get called as a witness."

Peggy winked at him. "I never told you a thing."

Dennis returned to his regulars at the bar. Karen decided any comment whatever would be futile.

Promptly at two o'clock the next suspect appeared, emerging from a taxi that halted in front of the shop. Karen pressed her face to the filthy glass.

"That's him!"

"Your grammar is deteriorating badly," Peggy remarked. "The bastard Bill, is it? He looks familiar. Have I seen him somewhere?"

"Oh, he's great at getting his face before the public," Karen said sourly. "He's hosted several public-television productions and written a couple of books on pop culture, with his photo splashed all over the back cover."

"Hmmm. He's not bad."

So far as Karen was concerned, the situation was too tense for misplaced humor. "How can you tell? You barely saw him."

"Tall, good shoulders, nice healthy head of hair . . ."

"He's losing it."

"No, he's not. That's just a noble, lofty intellectual brow. Is he married?"

"Honest to God, Peggy, I don't know what's come over you."

"I'm just considering all the possibilities. Maybe you can vamp him."

"He's not vampable," Karen said, unable to restrain a smile. "He's too damned conceited. God's gift to the frustrated females of the Modern Language Association. Peggy, he was carrying a briefcase."

"There's no law against it. Why are you so down on the guy?"

"He patronizes me. In print and in person. Once

he actually patted me on the head."

"I suppose you kneed him in the groin?"

"I wouldn't do anything so vulgar. I called him a rude name and walked away." Karen smiled complacently. "He's been known as Bill the Bastard in academic circles ever since."

Peggy's calm was the only thing that kept Karen in her chair. As the minutes dragged on, her impatience mounted; she didn't know what she wanted to do, but she felt a frantic need for action of some kind. When Meyer reappeared, after less than forty-five minutes, she couldn't stand it any longer. She jumped to her feet.

"He's got something in that briefcase! It's bulging more than it did."

"Follow him." Peggy's eyes gleamed.

"I can't!"

"What were you planning to do, grab his briefcase and run? He's looking for a cab," Peggy went on, as the tall figure with the good shoulders and nice healthy head of dark hair glanced up and down the street. "He won't find one in a hurry on a day like this. For God's sake, don't just stand there! Get to your car. Here, take my hat. We'll meet at the Sheraton. The first one to arrive books a room."

She tugged the hat down over Karen's forehead and gave her a shove.

"Is that him?" Dennis called. The other customers at the bar turned interested faces toward them. Karen decided it was time to go . . .

58

somewhere. Anywhere.

Face averted, she hurried toward her car. Meyer didn't notice her, he was too intent on flagging down a taxi. He was still standing in front of the bookstore, a look of exasperation tightening his long, thin face, when she drove onto Charles Street. She found an open space in the next block and pulled into the curb, ignoring the signs that prohibited parking, standing, and every other vehicular activity, and sat staring fixedly into the rearview mirror until Meyer finally succeeded in capturing a cab. After it had passed, she pulled out and followed it.

Meyer's ensuing activities gave her ample time to regret the insane impulse that had prompted her to fly into such frustrating and futile activity. She collected one ticket and a lot of invective from other drivers; there must be some trick to the business of following a suspect, and it was one she had yet to learn. Meyer visited two other bookstores and an antique shop before he ended up at a downtown hotel. When he paid off his cab at the door of the Holiday Inn, she decided the time had come to abandon him. He was not carrying a suitcase; he must have checked in and left his luggage earlier.

Which is what she should have done, Karen realized. She was in luck, however; the clerk at the Sheraton graciously admitted he had a room available. No, Dr. Finneyfrock had not checked in.

Karen cooled her heels for another half hour before Peggy appeared — long enough to arouse a considerable degree of apprehension on her friend's behalf. Peggy ought to have been there before her. Wild visions flooded Karen's imagination: Peggy getting happily drunk with Dennis, Peggy mugged and beaten as she tried to find a taxi, Peggy under arrest for lurking . . . When she heard the sound of a key in the lock, she flew to the door.

"Where the hell have you been?"

Peggy was wearing the rainbonnet. The balloons had run; pink streaks ran down her weathered cheeks. She yanked it off, dropped her coat, overnight bag and purse onto the floor, and collapsed onto a chair. Pushing her straggling hair away from her face, she grinned at Karen.

"Having tea with Simon. Is that a liquor cabinet I see before me? Thank God. Break out a bottle — I don't care what it is, so long as it's alcoholic. I need a drink."

"Having tea with . . ."

With a martyred sigh Peggy heaved herself to her feet. "You don't even have any ice. That's the first thing you do after you check in, get ice. Here." She shoved the plastic bucket into Karen's limp grasp. "The ice machine's next to the elevator."

When Karen returned, Peggy had invaded the cabinet and opened a bottle. Settling herself, she began her narrative, recapitulating, as any trained lecturer would do: "Having tea with Simon. He caught me in flagrante. Like the gent he is, he invited me in instead of calling the cops. Or the men in the white coats."

"I think I need a drink," Karen muttered, acting upon the idea. "Tell me."

"Well, after you left, it occurred to me that I didn't know any of the other suspects, so I decided I would take pictures of everyone who went into the shop." Peggy hooked another chair with her toes and pulled it close, so she could use it as a footstool. "I had to go outside and stand in the doorway, of course. I hadn't been there ten minutes when Simon opened his door and headed straight across the street toward me. He was carrying an umbrella, which he politely offered me, if I was determined to stand there in the rain, but he suggested that I might prefer a more comfortable and convenient ambience. Naturally, I accepted the invitation."

"Did he know we were in the bar?"

"So he claimed." Peggy sipped her Scotch with obvious relish. "He wasn't about to invite us in while his customers were there. Meyer was the last."

"You were with Simon for over two hours? How could you leave me in suspense so long? I was beginning to worry about you."

"I couldn't tear myself away. The man's got a mind like a razor — and a sense of humor too. Of course he's a hopeless male chauvinist — not surprising, considering his age and his background — but I think I set him straight on —"

"I know Simon's opinions better than you do," Karen interrupted. "I'm really upset about this,

Peggy. I spent two hours driving around in the rain, collecting tickets and making a fool of myself, while you were — uh — enjoying yourself with Simon."

"Flirting with Simon," Peggy corrected. "Not that I got anywhere. But it was entertaining. He's the first man I've met for ten years who was worth the trouble." Seeing Karen's expression, she laughed and shook her head. "Lighten up, Karen. Just because I like to kid around doesn't mean I don't take this seriously. The time I spent with Simon was very productive. He understands my interest in the historical aspects of the manuscript, and he has agreed to do us a big favor. He won't divulge the name of the original owner — quite properly, as I informed him — but he will forward a letter."

"I never thought of that," Karen said.

"No, you didn't." Peggy's eyes narrowed speculatively. "You ought to have thought of it. You're losing not only your sense of humor but your sense of proportion. I take it your pursuit of the bastard yielded nothing of interest?"

"I know where he's staying. We could call him and invite him to have dinner with us."

"Hmmm."

"I was kidding," Karen hastened to assure her.

"To convince me you haven't lost your sense of humor? The idea has its merits, you know. I could referee while you two fenced with one another; he must know you are a strong contender."
After pondering for a moment, Peggy said regret-

fully, "No, it would be a waste of time. He hasn't got it, you know. Simon assured me he wouldn't let it out of his hands. Since Meyer is staying overnight, he may be planning to come back for another look tomorrow."

"He can come and go unobserved, so far as I'm concerned," Karen said. "I must have been out of my mind to do something so undignified and so unproductive." Peggy's pensive, thoughtful expression aroused a horrible suspicion. Karen went on insistently, "We can't play the same silly trick again, Simon will be looking out for us. He knows about the bar —"

"There's a porn shop next to the bar," Peggy began, but the horror on Karen's face was too much for her. She burst out laughing. "You ask for it, Karen. You've got to stop being such a patsy. We'll have a nice quiet dinner à deux — without distracting male presences — and I'll spend the rest of the evening on a paper I was supposed to have finished last month while you write that letter."

The program was duly carried out. Peggy was still sitting at the desk, head bent over her work, when Karen finished the letter, and her concentration was so intense Karen decided not to interrupt her. She read for a while and then got into bed. "Will the light bother you?" Peggy asked, without looking up.

"No, not at all." Karen wondered what Peggy would say if she admitted she had been sleeping with a night-light for the past week — ever since the dreams began.

Sleep did not come quickly. The day's events kept running through her mind: the futile, infuriating pursuit of Meyer, the ridiculous charade they had performed in the bar. She would never dare show her face there again. Not that she had any inclination to do so . . . Who could have suspected Peggy would behave so childishly? Did everyone have a secret personality, a hidden self? The woman she had seen today was more like Peggy's evil twin than the distinguished professor she had known. Simon had apparently enjoyed her, though. Simon was somewhat schizophrenic himself. The practical joker meets the evil twin. Smiling, she drifted off.

Darkness like black earth pressing down on her face and flaring nostrils . . . She caught at the hands that held her, clinging as if to a rope offering escape from the dark abyss of sleep.

"It's all right." The voice recalled memories of other nights when she had waked crying in the night and found comfort at hand. "Just a bad dream. You're safe, you're okay."

"I'm sorry," Karen gasped. "Did I wake you?"

"I wasn't asleep." Peggy released her hands and sat down on the edge of the bed. "That must have been a bang-up nightmare. You sounded as if you were being strangled."

"Smothered."

"Oh, swell. Is this by any chance a dig at my smoking? I had the window open, but . . ."

"I've had the same dream before." Karen sat

up and raised shaking hands to her face. "It's the old buried-alive theme — a classic feminist nightmare. I know what brings it on. Frustration." Peggy's eyebrows rose and Karen snapped, "Not that kind of frustration. The dreams started after I saw the manuscript. Once I get my hands on it they'll stop."

"I hope so," Peggy said soberly. "You scared the bejesus out of me. I've never heard anybody, awake or asleep, make noises like that."

Chapter Three

I am obnoxious to each carping tongue
Who says my hands a needle better fits . . .
If what I do prove well, it won't advance,
They'll say it's stol'n, or else it was by chance.

ANNE BRADSTREET, 1650

A wet, cool April moved grudgingly toward spring.
The academic year was also moving toward its
close; the increasing press of work kept Karen too
busy to brood about her failure to hear from Simon
or the unknown recipient of the letter she had
written. She was still dreaming — the same dream,
almost every night — but she was learning to live
with nightmare. She slept with the window wide
open, whatever the weather, and left a night-light
burning. No problem.

Graduation was only a week away, and Bradford
pears, cherry and apple trees were scattering the
ground with white and pink petals when Karen
emerged from the library and saw a too-familiar
form bearing down on her. He knew she had seen
him; there was no way she could retreat without
rudeness, especially since he had broken into a
trot and was yelling her name at the top of his
lungs.

He hadn't run far or fast, but he was panting

heavily when he joined her. Joe Cropsey bragged about avoiding exercise, as if that were something to be proud of. In his case it wasn't. The folds of fat caressing his jaws and plump hands weren't pink and healthy; Karen always had the feeling that if she poked a finger into one of those bracelets of lard-white flesh, the indentation would remain indefinitely.

"And how is our Karen getting on these days?" he asked, trying to look down at her from a two-inch superiority in height.

"Fine, Joe. How is our Marilyn?"

He knew why she had asked about his wife. She always made a point of mentioning his wife. Not that it had the slightest effect. "A busy little bee as always," he said, smirking. "The kiddies keep her hopping, but we're planning a little party the week after graduation; you'll be receiving your invitation soon."

He made it sound like a royal summons. Karen moved away from the hand that was absently stroking her arm. "Well, give her my best."

"Don't run away. I want to talk to you about . . . about — uh — one of your students. Why don't we have a cup of coffee at the faculty club?"

That was all she needed — a tête-à-tête with Cropsey in full view of their colleagues, most of whom were only too well aware of his unsubtle attentions. She wasn't the first female faculty member he had pursued, and she wouldn't be the last. It was not difficult to understand why he picked on women who were younger and brighter than he.

"Sorry, I'm late for a lunch date," she said, moving away.

"It's only eleven-thirty."

"It's an early lunch."

Though they had arranged to meet at noon, Peggy was already there when Karen arrived. She had dismissed disgusting Joe Cropsey from her mind; her scowl had another cause, one Peggy interpreted accurately.

"No word from Simon yet?"

"No." Karen dropped into a chair. "I'm going to call him. It's been three weeks. He's doing this deliberately. Tantalizing me, making me wait —"

"Some men might do that. Some women, too," Peggy added fairly. "Not Simon. It takes time to talk universities into spending money."

Karen couldn't deny that. If it hadn't been for Peggy's offer, she'd be beating the hedges trying to raise money too. She waved away the menu the waitress offered her. "Taco salad," she said. "And coffee."

"You always have taco salad," Peggy said. "Why don't you try something different?"

"Taco salad is fine," Karen said abstractedly.

"Still brooding over the manuscript?"

"I've practically memorized the few pages I have. I've analyzed every sentence and studied every damn word, looking for parallels and references." Karen smiled sheepishly. "And, to be quite honest, I'm dying to know what happens next."

"It must be pretty good, then. How about giving me a synopsis?"

"You understand," Karen said, "that the beginning pages are missing. I don't know how many pages. She didn't number them."

"Cut the crap," Peggy said impatiently. "You've told me that a dozen times, and I am only too familiar with careful academic disclaimers. Consider me a potential reader, not a critic. I just want to know what's happening."

"Oh, all right. Ismene is telling the story. It's third person, but it is from her viewpoint, at least so far. She and her sister —"

"Name of Antigone?"

"Name of Clara. There are parallels with the play, though. The girls are orphans. Their father has recently died and they have been sent to live with their uncle, their only living relative. They've never met him. He and Daddy parted company years before, after a violent quarrel the cause of which has not yet been made clear."

Peggy's brow wrinkled. "I read a book like that once. Forget the title; something about wolves."

"It's a variation of one of the three original Gothic plots," Karen said impatiently. "Do you want to hear this, or don't you?"

"Go on."

"While the girls are traveling to their uncle's home, there is an accident. The coach is overturned, the coachman is killed or injured; I'm not sure exactly what happened, that's in the missing portion. When the text becomes legible, they are walking — staggering, rather — up the long muddy track leading to Ferncliffe, their uncle's house. It's winter. An icy rain is falling. The trees lining the way move and moan under the lash of the wind. Clouds hang low overhead, and as the twilight darkens, veils of mist gather like ghostly figures."

Peggy leaned forward, elbows on the table, lips slightly parted. Karen went on, "Ismene is supporting her younger, slighter sister, who is on the verge of collapse. Their thin slippers are soaked and torn, their skirts are heavy with water. Ismene's head is bare; the long, dank strands of her hair coil around her throat and over her mouth. She can't brush them away because her arms are around Clara. She knows that if Clara collapses she will not have the strength to raise her from the ground.

"Finally the trees fall back and Ismene sees the shadowy shape of the house ahead, darker than the steel-gray sky. There are no lights visible. Gasping words of encouragement to her fainting sister, she drags Clara up a flight of steps to a door. She can do no more; her grip loosens and Clara crumples at her feet. Ismene passes her cold, stiff hands over the wooden panels but fails to find a knocker. She pounds on the door with her fists, but the sound is lost in the wail of the wind, and she has the insane impression that her hands are sinking into the wood instead of striking against it. There is no response, no sound from within. Overcome with despair and a strange dread, she feels herself falling, and with the last of her strength gathers her sister's freezing body into her arms.

"She knows she is dying. The vision that imprints itself upon her failing sight is a vision of the world beyond death. The door that slowly opens, with a sound like muffled thunder, is the gate of Paradise; the figure its opening discloses is angelic, the head surrounded by a silvery nimbus. But where the angel's face should be, there is only an oval of darkness."

She paused, not for effect but to allow the waitress to serve the food they had ordered.

"Not bad," Peggy said. "I've read worse. Is that all you've got?"

"There's a little of the next scene. Ismene wakes to find herself lapped in warmth and in light. She meditates for a page or two on the transcendental but unexpected reality of heaven, and then the truth dawns. Someone is bending over her — a woman, wrinkled and kindly — obviously not an angel but a servant. Ismene realizes she is lying in bed, covered with blankets. Her first thought is for Clara. Rising up, she looks wildly around the room. It is handsomely appointed — I'll spare you the description — with a fire blazing on the hearth, but no sign of Clara. The servant reassures her. Clara is in the next room, where she is being tended with the same care. But 'there was no connecting door.' "

"That has a nice ominous ring to it," Peggy mumbled around a mouthful of enchilada.

"It's meant to sound ominous. She's got some nice descriptive touches," Karen admitted cautiously. "The storm-clouded sky and the moaning of the wind are typically Gothic, but the figure with the angelic halo and the blank face is quite well done. So is the transition from that horrific vision — was it hallucination or reality? — to the commonplace comforts of a warm, well-lighted bedroom and the smiling face of a kindly old servant."

"Sounds like . . . what's her name? . . . the housekeeper in *Jane Eyre*."

"Mrs. Fairfax."

"Right. Does that imply that Ismene had read Charlotte Brontë?"

"No." Karen's voice was sharp. The slightest suggestion that Ismene's work was derivative, anything other than brilliantly original, raised her hackles. "That's one of the things I've been looking for, of course — internal clues that could tell when the book was written. Right now I can only guess. Sometime between 1775 and 1840. That's another frustrating thing! I haven't heard a word from the original owner. Why the hell doesn't he have the courtesy to answer my letter? You don't suppose Simon —"

"No, I don't suppose Simon failed to forward it. The guy could be sick or out of town or just dilatory. It's all for the best, really; you've got a lot of work to do right now. Once the semester is over, you can concentrate on the manuscript."

Karen scowled at her. "I hate reasonable people. As a matter of fact, I could concentrate on my academic work a lot better if I knew there would be something else to concentrate on afterward. I don't have the manuscript, I don't have a name or an address — I don't have anything!"

"If it relieves you to make melodramatic speeches, go right ahead," Peggy said calmly. "But you know that's nonsense. You have Simon's word — and mine — that the manuscript will be yours."

"I wasn't implying —"

"And even if the owner doesn't respond to your letter we can probably track him down. It may take a while, but I can think of several methods." She glanced at her watch. "I've got a meeting at one-thirty. Hurry up, finish your salad."

Karen did as she was told, resignedly anticipating indigestion. It was easier to obey Peggy's orders than argue with her.

She stopped at the bank and the cleaner's, reaching campus in time to meet her two-thirty class. The students seemed particularly dim-witted that afternoon, and two of them asked for extensions on their semester papers. Karen's stomach was churning as she trudged up the stairs toward her office, and she cursed Peggy under her breath — unfairly, because her discomfort was due more to general frustration than to guacamole and sour cream. Turning the comer of the long corridor, she came to a sudden stop. Someone was standing in front of the door of her office. It was not one of her students. The outline was that of a man, abnormally tall and thin. Late-afternoon sunlight pouring through the window at the end of the hall framed his head in a golden halo, but his face was an oval of darkness.

Karen let out a stifled cry and lost her grip on the books she carried. The tall figure hurried toward her. It seemed to shrink and fill out as it approached, assuming normal dimensions; he was tall, but not monstrously so, lean but not as cadaverously thin as that first image had suggested, and when he spoke it was to utter the most banal of courtesies.

"I'm sorry, did I startle you?"

Karen knelt to collect her scattered belongings. She felt like a fool. That momentary impression of facelessness had been the result of her overactive imagination, assisted by the effect of the light. She could see him quite clearly now, even to the color of his eyes, as he stooped to help her pick up the books. They were grayish-blue, framed by lashes as light as his hair, which might have been silver-gray or sun-bleached blond. The latter, she thought, studying him covertly; though permanent lines had been etched into the skin of his forehead and around his mouth, she judged him to be in his mid-thirties. When he straightened, offering a hand to help her to her feet, she saw he was several inches over six feet, and dressed conservatively in a dark three-piece suit and white shirt.

He went on apologizing. "They said it would be all right for me to wait for you here. That is

. . . you are Dr. Holloway?"

He sounded as if he didn't believe it. She could see herself reflected in his look as in a mirror — round face and dimpled chin, snub nose and smooth pink cheeks. "Except for my hair I look like that damned moppet Shirley Temple," she had once shouted angrily at her mother, from whom she had inherited the characteristics in question. It was no consolation to know that when she was her mother's age, she would look fifteen years younger. Right now she needed those years. It was difficult enough for a woman to make men take her seriously. A moppet, even an adult moppet, didn't stand a chance.

"That is correct," she said coldly. "It was not your fault; my mind was on something else. We didn't have an appointment, did we?"

"No. I took the chance of stopping by, since I was in the neighborhood. My name is Cameron Hayes. You don't know me . . ."

She did, though — suddenly, surely, illogically. Her icy expression slipped; she beamed at him as if he had been a long-lost lover. Hayes's face relaxed into an answering, if tentative smile. "I'm the person you wrote to a few weeks ago, Miss Holloway. Or should it be 'Doctor'?"

"Ms. will do," Karen said. "I'm pleased to meet you, Mr. Hayes."

And that, she thought, was the understatement of the year. Somehow she managed to unlock the door without losing her grip on her books. Not until she had him settled in a chair did she dare

75

believe he was really there. "I'm so glad to meet you," she repeated. "I'd given up hope of hearing from you. It was kind of you to come."

Hayes leaned back, hands loosely clasped. They jarred with the white-collar businessman image, for they were callused and scratched — the hands of a manual laborer. He was much more at ease than she, Karen thought. She was babbling like a giddy student.

"I didn't get your letter until a few days ago," he explained. "I thought it might be better if we discussed the situation in person, instead of by letter or phone. But I don't want to interfere with your plans —"

"No, that's all right," Karen assured him, with the utmost sincerity.

Hayes nodded. "I had no idea that bundle of ragged papers would arouse such interest, but after I got your letter I checked with some people on the faculty at William and Mary. They said —"

"Oh, no!"

"I'm sorry. Shouldn't I have done that?"

"You had every right," Karen admitted, trying to remember if there was anyone in the English Department at William and Mary who specialized in early women's lit. Marian Beech. . . . It wasn't her field, precisely, but she would spread the word. Damn, damn, damn! Why hadn't it occurred to her to ask Hayes to keep her letter confidential?

"The thing is, I wanted to keep the discovery under wraps until after I acquired the manuscript," she explained. "From your point of view, it doesn't matter; you've already sold it, so you don't stand to gain anything by increased competition."

"How painfully true. Not that I'm complaining; Mr. Hallett paid a fair price, considering that neither I nor Jack Wickett had the faintest idea of what the thing was." He moved one hand in a gesture of dismissal. "Maybe we can still make a deal. Not on the manuscript, that's out of my hands. But I gather you are interested in other things. What, specifically?"

"Information. I did explain that I'm interested in the provenance of the manuscript?"

"Uh-huh. Well, I can tell you where I found it, but that's about all. I don't know how my great-uncle got his hands on it. You see, he . . . Are you sure you've got time for this? It's rather a long story."

"I've got the time," Karen assured him. "But, Mr. Hayes, I don't want to take advantage of you. You said something about a deal —"

"I'm a businessman, Ms. Holloway. Believe me, you aren't going to take advantage of me. But I don't charge for information — especially information you could easily acquire without my assistance. Shall I go on?"

Karen nodded. She was beginning to respect Mr. Hayes. He was shrewd enough to realize that now that she knew his name, she could easily trace him, and the family history he was about to relate was probably common knowledge in his home town.

"I'll have to go back a bit to give you the picture," Hayes said. "My family has been settled in the Tidewater area for a long time. A couple of centuries, to be precise. The old homestead is called Amberley. It's on the James . . . What's the matter? Did I say something wrong?"

"No," Karen murmured. This was too good to be true. This was what she had hoped to hear.

"My great-uncle had two sons; one was killed in World War Two, the other died, without issue, sometime later. Uncle Josiah turned into a recluse, shut himself up in the house and sat there brooding, while the place fell down around his ears. He was ninety-one when he passed away, leaving only daughters to inherit."

"Then Hayes is not the family name?"

"Correct. That's what sent the old boy into a decline — the fact that there were no sons to carry on the sacred name of Cartright."

"How long . . ." Karen turned the catch in her breath into a cough. She didn't want him to know how important the question and its answer were to her. "How long has the family lived at . . . Amberley, you said?"

"You won't have heard of it," Hayes said. "Unlike the famous James River plantation houses, it's never been open to the public. It has neither architectural distinction nor historical associations that would attract visitors. It is old, though. According to my mother, who used to amuse herself with genealogical research, the family has lived there since the beginning of the eighteenth century. They were definitely not one of the First Families of Virginia, though."

"You don't have a Virginia accent," Karen said — though why she said it she could not imagine. It was not only irrelevant, it was none of her business.

Hayes's expression suggested that he didn't think it was any of her business either. Karen got a grip on herself. To have him turn up out of the blue, after she had almost given up hope of hearing from him, had gotten her so excited she had not been able to think clearly.

"Perhaps we had better postpone our discussion," she said briskly. "I do have another appointment, and there's someone else involved — my partner."

"I see." Hayes had been rubbing his hands absent-mindedly. Some of the reddened patches might have been poison ivy, Karen thought. When he realized she was staring at them he folded his hands again. "I wondered about that. Mr. Hallett told me you had the right of refusal on the manuscript, and I got the impression that the price was going to be pretty stiff. No offense, Dr. Holloway, but I know what academic salaries are like. You have a backer?"

"A partner," Karen repeated. "A friend of mine."

He acknowledged the correction with a faint smile. "Fair enough. We'll meet later, then. Where and when?"

After he had gone, Karen ran to the window, which overlooked the parking lot, but he didn't appear. He must have parked on the street.

Or elsewhere. Why did she have the feeling that

he had kept something back? He had appeared candid enough, had spoken without apparent reserve, and yet . . . He wanted something from her, he wouldn't have come in person and agreed to another appointment solely in order to oblige a stranger. Money? That was the most obvious explanation. His curiosity about her financial status had been overt, and out of character for the Virginia gentleman role. He wasn't stupid. She had to be careful. Thank God some instinct had warned her to postpone the discussion until she had had time to calm down and think clearly about how to handle the situation. And confer with Peggy. Karen reached for the telephone.

"Well?" Karen demanded.

"Shhh." Peggy took her arm and pulled her away from the entrance to La Vieille France, Wilmington's most elegant and expensive restaurant. The food was supposed to be excellent, but Karen couldn't have testified on its behalf. She couldn't even remember what she had ordered, much less what it had tasted like. Glancing over her shoulder at the shadowy form retreating down the darkened street, she said irritably, "He can't hear us. What do you think?"

"He's not bad." Peggy unlocked her car door and shoved Karen inside. "Except that his eyes are a little too close together."

"For God's sake, Peggy!"

"Wait till we get to my place." Peggy slammed the car into gear and pulled away from the curb with a screech of tires. "We need to talk about this. The guy is up to something."

"If you had met me before dinner —"

"I couldn't. I had that meeting. If you had given me advance notice —"

"He didn't give me any."

"Right. I wonder if that was deliberate." Peggy pondered the question. "He wasn't too crazy about me being there."

"That's nonsense. You were the one he wanted to meet. You and your checkbook."

Peggy sighed. "They're always after my money. Even Simon. Someday I'll meet a man who loves me for myself."

Karen couldn't help laughing. "You don't come across as a susceptible, swooning millionaire, Peggy. That suit —"

"What's wrong with it? Years more wear in this suit." Peggy pulled into the curb in front of her house.

The house would have made a better impression than its owner. It was one of the old Victorians, lovingly restored. The glow of a nearby streetlight showed neatly trimmed boxwood behind an ornate wrought-iron fence and gate. The lawn was as smooth as a green carpet; flower beds were mulched and weedless. Peggy must employ a gardener, she couldn't keep the place in such impeccable condition by herself, and the house, with its ornate gingerbread trim and spreading porches, must cost its owner a fortune in yearly maintenance. Karen wondered why she hadn't realized before that Peggy had money. Well, the answer was obvious. It hadn't mattered to her before.

The interior, furnished with fine antiques, was as spotless as the exterior. Peggy must also employ a cleaning team. She had no live-in servants. It was an interesting contrast — Peggy's careless personal appearance and her impeccable house.

Peggy tossed her coat onto a chair. "Want a drink?"

Standing in the open doorway, Karen shook her head. "I really can't stay, Peggy. You know how those cats of yours affect me. My nose is already starting to itch."

"Oh, come on. I'll keep them away from you."

"You said that the last time. It's impossible; cats always head straight for me. Anyhow, it's the dander that sets off my allergy, and your house is full of it. Damn, there they come —"

Peggy scooped up the half-grown tabby that had plunged down the stairs and was indeed making a beeline for Karen. "Oh, all right, we'll sit on the porch." She tossed the tabby onto the stairs, fended off another admirer with a well-placed foot, and followed Karen out the door.

The night air was cool but not uncomfortably so. They settled into a pair of wicker chairs, and Peggy said, "Well?"

"I asked you first."

"So you did. Okay. The simplest and most obvious explanation for his behavior is that he wants to sell you something."

"What? He's already sold the manuscript."

82

"And regretting it. Not that he had much choice; as he candidly admitted, he had no idea that mess of papers was worth money. But behind his rueful, charming admission of fallibility, I sensed a certain smugness. He's got something else he wants to sell. Family documents? Maybe even the house itself. And now he knows it's worth money, at least to you. I'll bet used-car dealers love you."

"I'm not that gullible," Karen protested.

"Your appearance is against you," Peggy said, studying her critically. "Leaving off the makeup and wearing tailored suits doesn't help. Instead of an older, professional woman, you look like a kid trying to look like an older professional woman."

Karen scowled. "For your information, I handle used-car dealers just fine. I knew what he was doing. But when I started thinking about what he might have, I . . . so, okay, I lost it." She leaned forward, her eyes shining. "More poems. A diary. Letters. Even the missing pages of the manuscript!"

"The house has been cleared out," Peggy reminded her. "Simon already told you that."

"Yes, but the sale hasn't been held yet. They're waiting till May — the height of the auction season."

Peggy shook her head. "That sounds fishy to me."

"You're just determined to throw cold water on everything," Karen said sulkily.

"Somebody has to. You're flying high, honey.

If you fall, the crash is going to hurt like hell. You have no proof that Ismene ever lived in that house. The manuscript could have been acquired at a sale."

"There's only one way to find out."

"That's not true. There are a lot of ways. But," Peggy admitted, "we'll have a look at the place. Weekend after this, maybe. Or the following week."

Smiling, and outwardly calm, Karen nodded agreeably. It took all her willpower to keep that fixed smile in place, and to conquer the anger that knotted her stomach. She was sick and tired of being ordered around, treated like a child. Everybody did it. Simon, Peggy, her parents, her friends, her ex-husband.

Especially her ex-husband. Her decision to leave Norman had stunned her acquaintances. "But he adores you," one of them had said in obvious bewilderment. "He takes such good care of you."

His Baby.

Karen left town at ten o'clock Friday evening, after meeting all her classes, keeping several student appointments, attending a faculty meeting, and turning down Joe Cropsey's invitation to have a drink with him. Shortly after midnight she checked into a motel outside Frederick. It would have been irresponsible to drive straight through. Unproductive, as well; she could hardly go prowling around the grounds of a strange house in the small hours of the morning.

As she locked the door of the motel room and tossed her overnight bag onto the bed, a heady sense of escape filled her. No one knew where she was. No one could find her. There would be no knock at the door, no ringing of the telephone. This was the ultimate freedom — with no Grand Inquisitor lying in wait to drag her back to her cell.

Her slippered feet sank deep into mud that squelched and clung. The wet, matted weeds in the center of the rutted track were slick as ice. Interlaced branches formed a canopy overhead, a dark, twisted fabric through which the rain forced passage, now in trickles, now in heavier streams. Her wet hair writhed like a living thing, coiling around her throat. She reached up to pull it away, and saw the house ahead, looming dark against a storm-gray sky.

Karen stopped and rubbed her eyes. Her lashes were heavy with wet, but an overactive imagination, not impaired vision, must have produced those fleeting impressions. Her hair wasn't long; it was cut short, and plastered to her head by the rain that had soaked through her scarf. Her shoes were sensible brogues, not thin slippers. The skies were cloudy, but not menacingly dark; it was just past noontime.

The house still looked forbidding. It was no typical Tidewater mansion, beautifully proportioned and painstakingly hand-crafted (by slave labor, Karen reminded herself), but a graceless square block with narrow windows that gave it the appearance of a fort rather than a home. Chimneys on either end, disproportionately tall and slender, pointed skyward. Even the signs of long neglect and the weedy, untended grounds did not wholly account for its unprepossessing appearance. Hayes had been right; of architectural distinction there was none.

There were signs of recent attempts at renovation. The lawn had been mowed, though its green owed more to clover and variegated weeds than to grass. Some of the shutters had been painted. Others hung, gray and dispirited, from rusty hinges. Two of the windowpanes on the lower level were boarded up. Another set of panes had been recently replaced; the small paper stickers still adorned them.

So that was why Cameron Hayes's hands looked as if they had been chewed by a bear. He must be doing some of the work himself. The place certainly needed attention, it must have been neglected for decades. If the inside was as bad as the outside, Hayes's hope of finding a buyer were slim.

The house was for sale; she had seen the sign. The driveway gates were chained and padlocked, so she had been forced to leave her car outside. The small side gate, hung with "No Trespassing" signs, was padlocked too. She had climbed over it.

Karen gave herself a little shake. She couldn't stand here dripping and dreaming all day. Workmen wouldn't show up on a Saturday, especially in such weather, but Cameron Hayes might. She didn't particularly want him to find her here, but if he did, she would stand her ground — no sense trying to sneak away unseen, the presence of her car would tell him someone was inside — and make her excuses. "I just happened to be in the neighborhood . . ." She smiled wryly. Excuses be damned; she was hooked, and he probably knew it. Peggy had been right about that, at any rate; her eager questions had given her away.

Of course she ought to have called to tell him she was coming. She hadn't, though. It could be argued (she argued) that his willingness to answer her questions implied permission to visit the house, but that excuse was decidedly feeble. She hadn't called because she wanted to be alone on this first, secret visit.

Yet as she went on more slowly, slipping on the wet grass, uneasiness prickled along her spine. It wasn't a Gothic tingle, but rational, if belated, apprehension. Perhaps she ought to have approached Hayes directly, or at least told someone where she was going. She had not realized the place was so isolated. She had not seen another house or even another vehicle after she left the highway and turned onto the narrow back road, overhung with trees and studded with potholes. The only sounds that broke the silence were those made by wind and falling rain. She was over a mile from the highway, too far to hear traffic noises. Some such noise, some indication of life, would have been welcome just then. A bird chirping, a dog barking . . . Well, maybe not a dog. In her present mood a howling in the woods would conjure up images of wolves — or worse. More prosaically, this was the sort of place that would attract trespassers with less noble motives than hers — vagrants, poachers, hunters . . .

"Serial killers," she jeered at herself, and started at the sound of her own voice echoing in the silence. The rain had slowed to a drizzle. Wisps of fog drifted across the grass.

The steps leading to the front door were not gracefully curved, just slabs of stone mortared into place. They were a little too high, a little too narrow. She climbed them, treading carefully on the water-slicked surface. The door was a flat expanse of wood, with no window and no fanlight above. If ever a door had been designed to keep people out, this was it. Tentatively she raised her hands and pressed them against the panel. For a moment she had the unnerving impression that they had vanished. Everything was the same shade of pallid gray — her winter-whitened skin, the worn paint of the door, the surrounding air.

Karen stepped back, putting her hands in her pockets. They were ice-cold. Small wonder, she told herself. The air was cold — wet — chill. Even if the door were not locked, which it probably was, she had no business inside the house. Retreating a little too quickly, she followed a brick walk between low hedges of boxwood toward the west side of the house.

The windows on this side were lower than those in front, or the ground was higher; standing on tiptoe, she was able to look in. The view was discouraging — an empty room, swept clean of furniture and every other object. It might have been a library. The opposite wall, the only one she could see with any degree of clarity, had rows of shelves below a stretch of what appeared to be dark-paneled wood. The shelves were bare.

Her spirits plummeted. She reminded herself this was what she had expected.

The house was larger than it had appeared from the front. Instead of extending wings on either side of the main block, the owners had simply stuck another group of rooms onto the back when additional space was required. There was no attempt at architectural symmetry; the end product was a hideous hodgepodge of different materials and disparate shapes. There seemed to be no end to it, and the farther she went, the more apparent were the long years of neglect.

Finally the wings and extensions ended and she found herself in what might loosely be described as the backyard. The weeds there were not so high or so pervasive; they rose from what had been cultivated soil. She deduced that the area had once been a garden. A vegetable garden, no doubt; Great-Uncle Josiah wouldn't have bothered with flowers. Behind the plowed earth was a wall of tangled wilderness. The heavy stems of poison ivy and honeysuckle wound tight around tree trunks and hung in green curtains from dead boughs;

fallen branches interlaced with prickly thorns lay in tumbled heaps.

There was a single narrow opening in the barricade. As Karen approached, she saw it was the entrance to a path of sorts, low-roofed by leaves. An animal trail? But surely deer wouldn't come so close to the house, not when they had acres of wilderness in which to roam.

She had not seen any outbuildings, barn or sheds or the like. Perhaps that was where the path led. Ducking under a low branch, she followed it. After the first few yards it began to descend, gently at first, then at a steeper angle before it ended, abruptly, in an open space, sunken and roughly oval in shape. Hickories and white pines enclosed it, and a jagged outcropping of rock formed a natural wall along one side. The ground underfoot was thick with fallen needles that muffled her footsteps.

Except for the drip of water from the leaves, the air was utterly still. "A savage place, as holy and enchanted . . ." Not a comfortable verse to recall just then; but at least the moon wasn't waning and she was not tempted to wail for a demon lover. There was something uncanny about the place, though. Why should anyone beat a path to an empty clearing? And why wasn't it overgrown with weeds and brambles, like the rest of the woodland?

At first, when she heard the sound, she took it for the murmur of water — a stream tumbling over rocky rapids or the ripple of the river, which could not be far distant. Abruptly, shockingly, the murmur changed direction. It sounded as if it were coming straight toward her. It sounded as if it were just beyond the trees, closer, closer, under the ground at her feet, in the air itself, rising in pitch and volume until there was nothing else in the universe except that piercing undulating scream.

Karen ran blindly, arms across her face to shield it from the branches that stretched out as if to block her passage. By the time she broke out into the open, there was no sound except the drip of water and her own harsh breathing. As she stood struggling for control a shift in the direction of the wind carried a sweet scent to her nostrils. The bushes beside the enclosed back porch were lilacs. Though they needed pruning, the deadly vines had been stripped away and the branches were heavy with bloom. They were a reminder of normalcy and of beauty. Her breathing slowed. Stupid of her to be panicked by some unusual acoustical phenomenon.

The clouds overhead had darkened and mist veiled the wet ground. She knew she ought to go. Just one more look, she told herself. One more window. That one, to the left of the porch. The exquisite scent of lilac surrounded her as she forced her way between the bushes.

The sudden sound struck at her like a physical blow. It was a human voice — a man's voice, raised in a shout. "I know you're there! Come on out." He said something else, but she didn't hear the words; jumping forward, in an instinctive attempt at concealment, she felt the ground give way under her feet.

She did not fall far, but the jolt of her landing sent a stab of pain through one leg and took her breath away. She caught at the wall beside her for support. The rough surface rasped her fingers. The wall was of stone — large, roughly trimmed blocks. A single small window broke its solidity, a window heavily barred with rusted iron.

A yell of triumph from the invisible pursuer brought her reeling brain back to reality. The stone wall wasn't that of a prison cell, it was part of the foundations of the house. The grilled window, four feet below ground level, must open into the basement. Her weight had broken through the rotted covering of a window well. She stood ankle-deep in stagnant water.

The well wasn't deep; the top of her head was on a level with the ground. Left to herself, she could have climbed out, though one ankle had begun to throb. Too late for that. The crash of her fall had betrayed her presence and given him a clue as to her location. She heard the rustle of branches as he pushed them aside, searching.

Better to concede defeat, she told herself, instead of being dragged ignominiously out of hiding. He'd find her anyway as soon as he spotted the broken cover of the well. His peremptory tone suggested he had a right to be there, that he wasn't a wandering rapist or killer.

She took a deep breath and called, "I'm here."

He had already located her. Kneeling on the edge of the well he looked down, and the shadow of his body further darkened the gloom. The face that hovered close to hers was not the one she had expected to see, but it was only too familiar.

He recognized her too. Astonishment replaced his scowl, and an unpleasant smile widened his thin mouth. "Why, if it isn't my distinguished colleague Dr. Holloway! Fancy meeting you here."

"Hello, Bill." She managed to keep her voice under control. He sat back on his heels, studying her with that insufferable smile. "Would you be good enough to help me up?" she inquired.

"Oh, certainly. A pleasure. Give me your hands." Instead of grasping them he took hold of her arms just above the elbows. She clutched at his sleeves as he rose to his feet, lifting her without apparent effort. Her feet slipped on the wet leaves and she tottered, on the rim of the well. Meyer caught her in his arms and pulled her back onto solid ground. Instead of letting her go, he drew her closer. One arm circled her shoulders so firmly that she had to choose between resting her head against his chest or tilting it back at an angle that brought their faces into such close proximity that his breath warmed her cold lips.

Karen fought the temptation to struggle. Futile efforts to free herself would only amuse and exhilarate him, and she had a feeling he was well aware of how desperately she hated being held helpless. Maybe this was the moment to apply "conscious virtue," the last defense of beleaguered heroines who freed themselves from the villain's lustful embraces by forcing him to admit their moral superiority. Looking Meyer straight in the eye, she said coldly, "Thank you. You can put me down now."

According to the books, his eyes ought to have fallen and his cheek mantled with shame. He had read the same books, though, and he was infuriatingly quick at catching nuances. With a shout of uninhibited laughter, he quoted from one of the classics. " 'He stood for a moment the slave of virtue, though the votary of vice.' Fear not, innocent maiden, rescue is at hand."

"Have you found him?" The distant voice was a woman's, clear and anxious. "Be careful, William, he might have a gun."

"It's not a he, it's a she, and she is unarmed," Meyer answered. He backed out through the clustering lilacs, dragging Karen with him. A branch clawed at her face; another caught the dripping scarf and yanked it over her eyes.

Too depressed even to swear, Karen pushed the wet folds of cloth away and saw, as she might have expected, that the newcomer was young, attractive, and smartly dressed. Her spotless raincoat was pink, belted tightly around her narrow waist. A jaunty matching hat failed to cover a mass of blond hair — the kind of hair that curls bewitchingly with damp instead of subsiding into limp flatness. Neatly cut boots covered her calves.

"Mah Gawd," she said.

She then proceeded to complete Karen's humiliation by adding, in a less pronounced but prettily slurred Virginia accent, "You poor thing! There's a shelter for homeless people in town, it's really quite nice, Ah work there one day a week. William, let her go this instant minute, you're frightening her."

The effort Meyer made to keep from laughing made his voice crack. "I'm holding on to her because she seems to have sprained at least one ankle and I suspect she'll collapse if I let go. You are under a slight but understandable misapprehension, Lisa. Allow me to introduce Professor Karen Holloway of Calhoun College. Karen, this is Lisa Fairweather — the owner of this property."

The house wasn't entirely empty of furniture. Someone must camp out there from time to time; a small room next to the kitchen contained a cot and a table and chair. After Karen had been deposited on the cot Lisa said, "I'll just make some coffee, shall I? No, honey, it's no trouble at all, I do assure you. Cameron spends the night occasionally, to discourage trespassers, and he'd as soon face the mornin' without his trousers as without his coffee. It won't take a minute."

She trotted out, her face still flushed with embarrassment at her faux pas. Thank God I'm not that nice-minded, Karen thought. I don't blame her for mistaking me for a vagrant; I sure as hell look like one.

Meyer pulled up a chair and sat down, facing

95

her. "You'd better get those wet shoes off," he suggested, making no move to assist her in doing so.

"What are you doing here?"

"The same thing you are, obviously."

He crossed his legs and leaned back. "I was fairly certain you were the favored purchaser Hallett mentioned. You owe your reputation to Ismene; you'd do anything to gain possession of that manuscript. Just out of curiosity, how did you persuade the dear old gentleman to give you preference?"

Karen gave him a cold stare. "What a low-down filthy mind you have, Bill. You couldn't possibly understand the reasons why Simon approached me first; they have to do with trust, friendship, decency and other things beyond your limited comprehension. I wasn't referring to your reason for being here; I was inquiring how you found out where the manuscript came from."

"Oh, I see. You must learn to be more precise in phrasing your questions." He hadn't stopped smiling since he saw her, except when the smile broadened into a grin. Bastard, Karen thought. She had to keep calm. Yelling at him or smacking the grin off his face, as she yearned to do, would make her appear more of a fool than she already did. If that was possible.

"It wasn't difficult to trace the dealer from whom Simon Hallett bought the manuscript," Meyer continued. "Not for me, at any rate."

"For your graduate assistants, you mean," Karen retorted. "I suppose you had them reading the obituary columns."

For a moment he looked disconcerted, but he recovered quickly. "Among other things. I started with the assumption that the former owner was an elderly eccentric and that he had died within the past few months."

The whistle of a boiling kettle told Karen her unwilling hostess would soon be back. "Never mind telling me how clever you are," she said. "You're wasting your time, Bill. You won't get the manuscript."

"Hallett warned me my chances were slight to non-existent," Meyer said coolly. "I don't know where the hell you're planning to get the money, but that's none of my business, is it?"

"No. I assume you're going to run the price up, out of spite."

Meyer leaned back and brushed the damp hair away from his forehead. No one would have mistaken him for a bagman (if that was the right term), but neither did he resemble the elegant academician she had seen before. His jacket had to be Harris tweed, but his shirt collar was open and his well-tended hands were streaked with mud. The green, heartshaped lilac leaves caught in his tumbled dark hair looked like the remains of a wreath crowning a sylvan deity.

"No," he said.

"Why not?"

"I suppose you wouldn't believe me if I told

you I'm a swell guy who respects your expertise and acknowledges that in moral terms you are entitled —"

Karen laughed.

"I didn't think you would," Meyer said with a faint cynical smile. "However, I admit you have a certain claim on Ismene. I'd be perfectly willing to collaborate."

Karen gasped. "You are . . . You have the most . . . Words fail me, Bill, they honestly do! My vocabulary is inadequate to describe the sublimity of your conceit. What could you possibly bring to a collaboration that I can't supply myself?"

The insult didn't bother him a bit. His smile stretched wider. "Let's be kind, and say, 'A fresh viewpoint.' Two heads are better than one. And," he continued, over Karen's wordless sputter of outrage, "I have connections in the publishing world and in the media that might be very useful. If it were properly promoted, this book could be a best-seller."

"You would think of that."

"There's another thing." His smile vanished. In repose, his long lean face was as forbidding as that of an inquisitor. "You need a keeper, my girl, or a bodyguard. Are you out of your mind, coming here alone? Aside from the danger of running into some evil-minded trespasser, you could have fallen — as you did — broken a leg instead of spraining an ankle —"

"Your tender concern touches me," Karen snapped. "My ankle isn't sprained."

"Are you sure?" Lisa had returned carrying a tray. Meyer, bland and smiling, rose to take it from her. She thanked him with a sweet smile and went to Karen. "Do you mind if I look at it? I took a first-aid course . . ."

I'll bet you did, Karen thought. And courses in flower arrangement, yoga, and how to fold napkins into pretty shapes. Trying to emulate Meyer's sangfroid — though her cheeks were still hot with fury — she said, "Please don't bother. You've been more than kind, considering . . . considering the circumstances. I did speak to Mr. Cameron Hayes last week. I was under the impression that he was the present owner."

"He didn't mention me?" Lisa smiled and shook her head. "That's just like Cameron. A mean old male chauvinist at heart. The property was left to both of us, jointly. Naturally I agreed to let Cameron handle the business arrangements, but I didn't think he'd be rude enough to ignore my very existence."

"Lisa is Mr. Hayes's first cousin," Meyer said smoothly. "And he can't act without her consent. Right, Lisa?"

"I wouldn't want to cast the slightest doubt on Cameron's integrity," Lisa said with equal smoothness. "But I'd sure have to be a stupid little thing to give up my rights, wouldn't I?"

Her eyes weren't blue, as Karen had thought. They had a distinct greenish cast.

"Well, we can talk about business another time," Lisa went on cheerfully. "I hope you won't think me inhospitable, Dr. Holloway, if I suggest you get back to your hotel as soon as possible. It's starting to rain again and that ankle is going to swell up if you don't get some ice on it. Would you like me or William to drive you?"

"I can manage," Karen said, thinking she had never been dismissed with such courteous finality. "It's the left ankle."

They left as they had entered, via the side door.

Lisa insisted that she lean on "William," who obliged with a particularly infuriating show of gallantry. The last thing Karen heard, before she closed her car door, was his voice: "Take good care of yourself, my dear. I'll be in touch soon."

Chapter Four

To say in print what she thinks is the last thing the woman novelist or journalist is so rash as to attempt . . . Her publishers are not women.

ELIZABETH ROBINS,
first president of the Women Writers' Suffrage League, 1908

On a bright spring morning, with a chorus of birdsong filling the air and wildflowers blossoming among the coarse grass, the house didn't look menacing or sinister. It was just plain ugly.

Karen stopped behind the other vehicle and sat staring out the window, gripped by a feeling of flat anticlimax. The one positive feature of her disastrous visit the day before had been her conviction that she had found Ismene's house, the one described in the novel. Without the Gothic atmosphere, it looked like any other unattractive tumbledown old mansion.

After she had returned to the hotel the preceding afternoon, she followed Lisa's advice, wrapping her ankle in an ice-wrapped towel before she nerved herself to reach for the telephone. She wasn't looking forward to telling Cameron Hayes that she had trespassed on his property and been caught in the act by his cousin. But if she didn't tell him Lisa would, and by confessing before she was accused, she might preserve a few rags of her dignity.

He listened in silence as she stumbled through her explanation. The silence continued for several uncomfortable seconds after she stopped talking.

"I'm so sorry," he said at last. "I had no idea Lisa meant to be there yesterday. I ought to have told you about her."

You can take the boy out of the South, but you can't take the South out of the boy, Karen thought. It had been hard for him to find something for which to apologize, but he had managed it.

He had politely ignored her own apologies and heaped further coals of fire on her offending head by offering to accompany her to the house next day. "No, it's no trouble at all. I was planning to go myself, if the weather clears, as it's supposed to."

He had also insisted on taking her to breakfast. He apologized for that, too — or rather, for the early hour he suggested, explaining that he wanted to get in a full day's work.

That comment prepared her to some extent, but she had to look twice before she recognized him. The paint-stained pants and shabby windbreaker altered not only his appearance but his manner. Bareheaded, hands in his pockets and shoulders bowed, he seemed to shrink as he made his way through the crowded restaurant, acknowledging acquaintances with nods and murmured greetings.

Even his accent was softer and more slurred.

Apparently the Hungry Hog was the town's most popular rendezvous for the Sunday breakfast crowd. For the most part it was an elderly, welldressed crowd; a number of the women wore hats, and their gray-haired or balding escorts sported ties and three-piece suits. Not until one of the women (who would undoubtedly have referred to herself as "one of the ladies") asked Cameron whether she would see him in church did Karen understand why they were so dressed up.

Evidently the question was meant as a joke. The "lady's" companions laughed heartily. She laughed harder than any of them; all three of her chins wobbled and the violets on her hat shook alarmingly. Karen realized she was staring and wrenched her eyes away. But really, it was an astonishing hat; the violets heaped at random over the crown and brim had faded to a grayish lavender, and the purple veiling tacked over the ensemble had the cheap shine of nylon. It was not quite the same shade of purple as the "lady's" dress.

Cameron nodded and smiled but did not reply. Dropping into the chair across from Karen, he apologized for keeping her waiting.

"I just got here," she replied. Curiosity prompted her to add, "I hope I'm not keeping you from church."

"That was a joke," Hayes said seriously. "I'm not a regular churchgoer."

"Oh."

The glint in his eyes told her he was well aware

of her amusement. "A well-worn joke, in fact. I'm afraid that's typical of local humor. Miz Fowler and her friends believe that members of the gentry should follow the old traditions. They don't approve of me, but around here family connections count for more than behavior."

"An aristocratic ax murderer is more acceptable than a philanthropist of humble birth?"

"Exaggerated, but essentially correct." His tone told her he didn't care to discuss the subject any further. After they had ordered he said, "I talked with Lisa last night. She told me you hurt your foot. I hope it's better?"

"A little sore, that's all. You needn't be afraid I'll sue you," she added, smiling. "I had no right to be there."

"That wouldn't prevent you from suing. And possibly winning." He hesitated, and Karen braced herself for a kindly lecture about her impetuous and ill-considered behavior. Instead he asked, "Did you find what you were looking for?"

The question surprised her into an honest answer. "Yes. Not that I expected to find anything in particular, it was just a feeling . . . I didn't go in the house, of course. I'm anxious to see it, if you will allow me."

The waitress delivered Karen's croissant and presented Hayes with a heaped platter — eggs, sausages, bacon, and a heap of an amorphous white substance Karen recognized as the fabled Southern grits. "I gather Lisa explained the legal situation," he said, tucking into his breakfast with the appetite of a man who anticipates a long day of manual labor. "I have to have her approval before I act, but so far she's never differed with any of my decisions."

"Have you met Professor Meyer?" Karen asked.

"No. I'm surprised he went to her instead of contacting me. Have you any idea what he wants?"

"I know what he wants, but I don't understand what he's up to. He might think he could swindle a woman more easily than a man, but she couldn't sell anything without your consent, could she?"

"No. The converse is true, as well." Hayes finished his bacon before remarking, "You don't seem to have a very high opinion of your colleague."

"I wouldn't trust him with my garbage." Caught off guard by her candor, Hayes grinned, and Karen went on, "You know where I stand; Dr. Finney-frock and I explained the situation the last time we met. The manuscript is the most important thing. I have every expectation of getting it, and in any case it is out of your hands. What I hope to get from you is evidence that would enable me to identify the author of the manuscript — diaries, letters, family records. I think that's what Bill Meyers is after too. Knowing Bill, I assume he hopes to steal it or con someone into giving it to him."

"He's in for a shock then," Hayes said coolly. "Lisa may look like a cuddly little Southern gal, but I'd as soon bargain with a shark."

At his suggestion Karen followed him in her own car. "I'll be there all day," he explained. "You'll probably want to leave before I do."

His vehicle was an aged pickup that looked as if it were held together by wire and hope. As he preceded her along the rutted driveway, the truck shook so violently she feared one of the flapping fenders might fly off. Muddy puddles filled the sunken tracks, but the trees lining the way were gilded by sunlight; white blossoms of dogwood and pink sprays of redbud showed through the dark green of the pines. It was a far cry from the ominous landscape of the previous day.

She got out of the car before Hayes could open the door for her. He stepped back with a faint smile and a slight shrug and she knew he was thinking, "Another of those damned feminists." He took a set of keys from his pocket and led the way to the front door.

Though freshly painted and repaired, it gave the impression it ought to creak as it opened. There was no creak, but as it swung silently back, a wave of cold air poured from the opening and enveloped Karen like icy water. She let out a gasp of surprise. Cameron, beside her, hunched his shoulders and put his hands in his pockets. Neither of them moved for a moment. Then he said calmly, "The walls are two feet thick. Cool in summer, but you can imagine how much it costs to heat in winter. After you."

Sunlight did little to soften the stark emptiness of the entrance hall. At least it was clean. The walls had been freshly plastered and painted a pale cool cream. Doors on right and left, and at the back, were closed. A flight of stairs led up to a narrow landing. The only thing that satisfied an eye searching for beauty was the floor-wide boards of golden-brown wood, freshly sanded and varnished.

"Chestnut," Hayes said, following Karen inside. "One of the few attractive features the house can boast. Hideous, isn't it?"

"I wouldn't say," Karen began.

"Don't bother being polite." He shivered involuntarily. "I've always loathed the place. When I was a kid my mother used to drag me out here on duty visits. I'd pretend to be sick, but it didn't work; mothers catch on to those stunts, I suppose. As an adult I had to force myself to come here."

"Why did you?"

"Someone had to. He was old and increasingly helpless, and so badtempered he couldn't keep help even if he'd been willing to pay for it. I used to think it was his disgusting personal habits and foul mouth that made me dislike the house, but it still sets my teeth on edge."

Karen's teeth were on edge too. She had to clench them to keep them from chattering. The cold was pervasive, as palpable as a shroud of solid ice. "Maybe it's haunted," she suggested. "That might be a selling point; some people dote on ghosts."

The light touch didn't succeed. Hayes gave her a hostile look. "Most people don't," he said. "Do me a favor and don't suggest such a thing."

"I didn't mean it."

"I know. I'm sorry." His stiff shoulders relaxed. "It'll be hard enough to sell the place anyhow. Not even a sentimental Yankee looking for Tara would fall for this monstrosity. It's not just ugly, it's . . . unpleasant. I don't know why — but I don't believe in ghosts. No doubt there's something slightly off-balance about the proportions of the rooms — the reverse of the classic architectural golden section. Oh, well. Maybe I'll get lucky and find a buyer with no artistic perception whatever."

He opened the door on the right. The room was large and high-ceilinged, and, like the hall, oddly graceless. Dark paneling covered the walls. The narrow windows admitted little light.

"You don't have to show me the whole house," Karen said, as her host started toward the door across the hall. "You must be anxious to get to work."

"I always check after I've been away for a few days, for broken windows or signs of unauthorized entry. Anyhow, you'd better have an overall tour before you start wandering on your own. The place is an absolute maze, no plan, no coherence."

He wasn't exaggerating. The main block was simple enough, just a three-story square divided into square rooms, four on each level. From that point on, chaos intervened. The builders hadn't even attempted to keep the same floor levels; steps went up and down, corridors led into seemingly dead ends. Staircases had been inserted apparently at random; Karen saw at least four sets of them.

Hayes led her down the last set into the kitchen.

Like the rest of the house, it was impeccably clean; she was beginning to understand why her companion's hands were those of a laborer. He must have done most of the work himself, and a formidable job it had been, to judge from his description of its condition. Every room packed to the rafters with crumbling newspapers, rotting cartons, filthy clothes . . ."

"Well, that's it," he said. "Want to make me an offer?"

His tone made it a joke, but she wasn't deceived. Of course he hoped to sell her the house. He had watched her intently; he must have observed that her initial antipathy had faded as they went on. The most unpleasant part of the house was the central block; the rooms in the outspread wings were almost cozy by contrast, low-ceilinged and sunny, with big fireplaces.

All the same, it wouldn't be easy to find a buyer. The house was too big, too isolated, and still in need of extensive repairs. But if it was Ismene's house . . . If she could prove it, if the book turned out to be a critical success . . .

"There are the cellars, of course," Hayes went on. "But I would rather not show them to you; they're probably flooded, they always are after it rains, and I promise you, there's nothing down there. I cleared everything out of the house."

"What about the attic?"

"You don't want to go up there."

"Why not? Wasn't that where the manuscript was found?"

"That's right. In a trunk under a pile of old clothes. But there's nothing there now except dust and cobwebs. Everything is in storage."

"Everything?"

"Yes. Including," he added tantalizingly, "a few boxes of papers and photo albums and miscellaneous junk I kept out of the sale. Despite my greed I draw the line at putting family mementos on the auction block."

"You wouldn't get much for them at auction."

He gave her a knowing smile. "If you want to look through them we can probably come to an agreement."

"I do want to look through them, but not today. Just promise you won't sell them to Bill Meyer."

"Done."

"I'd still like to see the attic. You don't have to come with me, I know you must be anxious to get to work. Just point me in the right direction."

He didn't respond immediately. Then he said slowly, "I guess it's all right. A waste of time, as I said. You won't enjoy it. I haven't had a chance to clean the place, and there are mice."

"I like mice." Karen smiled sweetly. "Adorable little furry creatures."

He was not amused. "Come on, then, if you're determined."

He left her at the foot of the attic stairs, with a look that dared her to go on. The prospect was certainly not enticing. The narrow enclosed stairwell was a dusky dark, and she heard small scuttling sounds above. The mice were not visible, though, when she reached the top of the stairs. They must have run for cover when they heard the door open.

No wonder the place was so dark. There were windows high under the roof, but they were small and opaque with crusted dirt. The first board she stepped on sagged and groaned. She stopped, squinting into the shadows and trying to orient herself. The stairs she had climbed had been in the west wing. This space, though extensive, could not extend over the entire house; that wall of roughly mortared brick on her left must mark the end of the wing, with the central block beyond. As her eyes became accustomed to the gloom she saw the outlines of a door.

Slowly, testing each board before she put her weight on it, she moved toward the door. Creaks and groans accompanied each step, but the floor seemed solid enough. The door was solid too, a massive structure of rough boards. The heavy latch was of metal, red with rust that coated her palm and fingers when she took hold of it. The hinges screamed in protest when she forced the panel back.

Ahead lay a narrow passageway with closed doors along one side. That was all she saw before the cold leapt out at her like an imprisoned animal desperate for freedom. It was far more intense than that first wave of icy air, not the absence of warmth but a positive force, active and malevolent. Black cold, cold darkness, heavy with despair. It gripped her body like huge dead hands, weakening her limbs and stifling her breath.

She fled mindlessly, leaving the door ajar, and tentacles of icy air followed, trying to hold her back. Down the narrow stairs, stumbling and slipping, along the corridor toward the back of the house — and straight into the arms of Cameron Hayes. She clung to him, panting and shivering. But not with cold. Sunlight filled the corridor; the air was cool but perfectly comfortable.

"What's wrong?" His voice was low, the soft slurred accent more pronounced. He was a little taller than Bill Meyer; her head fit neatly into the angle of his neck and shoulder. Meyer was more heavily built, as she had good cause to remember. Now she was acutely conscious of the structure of Cameron's body, bone, sinew and muscle, under his thin shirt. He smelled of sweat and paint and turpentine, not expensive aftershave.

Karen stiffened, straightening the fingers that had clung to his shoulders, moving her hands to press against his chest. The ridges of his collarbones were hard and sharply defined against her flattened palms. "I beg your pardon," she said formally. "I didn't see you."

"My fault," Cameron said, in the same slurred voice. "I shouldn't have let you go up there alone. Did you see . . . Did a mouse run over your foot?"

She had not deceived him. She'd have to find some reasonable excuse for that mad rush, but pride kept her from accepting the one he had offered. "I am not afraid of mice. It must have been

112

a — a bat. Flying at me, flapping its wings."

"They don't get in your hair, you know. That's an old wives' tale."

"Would you mind letting go of me?"

"Oh. Sorry." One of his hands had cupped the back of her head. When he lifted it, a few hairs caught on the roughened skin. Karen pulled away, smoothing her tumbled locks.

"Bats can be rabid."

"Of course." He continued to watch her, his face unreadable. "They aren't usually active during the day."

"I must have disturbed it."

"Right. Well. I'd better get back to work. Sure you're okay?"

"Absolutely."

He nodded and walked away. Karen went in the opposite direction — primarily because it was the opposite direction. After getting lost once or twice in the twisting corridors of the west wing she found the stairs that descended into the kitchen. The old gas stove and painted cupboards were comforting reminders of ordinary domestic activities. Karen raided Cameron's supplies and made coffee. The room was warm, but she could still feel the chill deep inside.

Maybe there was a curse on the place, she thought wryly — something that doomed her to make a fool of herself every time she came there, something with a perverse sense of humor that pushed her into situations where she was forced to act like a helpless, hapless idiot of a Gothic heroine. Why the hell did Cameron have to turn up at that particular moment? He had known she was lying about the bat. Now he'd think she was a silly, hysterical idiot, especially after that joke about the house being haunted.

Karen didn't believe in ghosts either. She had never had an experience like that one, though. Was it possible that some places retained memories of past tragedy or desperate grief? Not the spirits of the dead themselves but emotions felt so strongly by the living that they had permeated the very fabric of the walls and the surrounding air?

It was just as likely that such experiences happened only to people with overactive imaginations and strained nerves. Especially people who had fattened their imaginations on horror stories like the one Simon had read to her. It had haunted her ever since. Darkness, cold and despair . . . Damn Simon anyway. That nasty story was probably the genesis of her dreams, too.

Time was getting on. She ought to start back soon, it was a long drive. For purely rational reasons she decided to go out the back door and around the house. She would then have explored every part of it. No need to pass through the main block again.

The enclosed porch she had seen only from the outside was cluttered with Cameron's equipment — rags, paint cans, tools. The door was unlocked; she opened it and cautiously descended the sagging steps. The scent of the lilacs was so strong it overcame the smell of paint and turpentine. Reaching across, she broke off a single spray of clustered bloom and sniffed it appreciatively as she followed the path toward the front of the house.

Someone else must have arrived; she could hear voices. One voice, rather. It was loud and aggressive and unfamiliar. Cameron's responses were inaudible until she turned the corner of the house in time to hear him say, "I said no, and I mean no. If you think you can —"

Seeing her, he broke off. The other man turned.

He was a few inches shorter than Cameron and a good many years younger. The unlined skin of his face was spotted with acne which he had tried to conceal with makeup and with artfully arranged locks of flaxen hair. He had dimples. He produced them when he caught sight of Karen and assumed a pose that showed an impressive display of muscles to best advantage.

"Morning, ma'am," he cooed. "I didn't know you was here. Hope I'm not interrupting."

Both statements were untrue. He must have known someone was there, he had seen the car. She was only too familiar with the look that had accompanied the second lie, she had seen it on other masculine faces.

With a brusque nod of acknowledgment she turned to Cameron. "You should have told me you had another appointment, Mr. Hayes. I wouldn't have detained you so long."

"My only appointment was with you," Cameron said in the same impersonal tone. "He's just leaving."

115

"Oh, is this lady a client? Well, I sure don't want to interfere with your business, Cam. Sorry, ma'am. Hope I'll see you again."

Karen did not echo the sentiment. Smirking and strutting, the young man returned to his pickup — a newer, brighter, fancier model than Cameron's — and drove off.

"Thank you," Cameron said, tight-lipped and red-faced.

"What for?"

"Preventing Bobby from beating the . . . from beating me up. That's how he'll tell it. And that's what you thought was going to happen — right? You assumed I couldn't handle him and you figured he wouldn't start anything while you were present."

"Was he about to start something?" Karen asked innocently.

Cameron let out a long breath. "I'm sorry. I shouldn't have said that. Have you finished for today?"

"Yes. But I'll be back."

His color had returned to normal. When he spoke, his voice was colorless and flat. "Any time, Dr. Holloway. Just let me know."

Glancing into the rearview mirror as she drove off, she saw him ascending the ladder. He did not look in her direction.

"Fifty-one five," Peggy repeated gleefully. "Hot damn!"

She didn't mean "fifty-one dollars and five

116

cents." She meant "fifty-one thousand five hundred dollars." Peggy's reaction to the price Simon had finally set assured Karen that Peggy was ready and willing to accept it, but the number sounded terrifying.

"It's a lot of money," she murmured.

"Cheap as dirt. You can thank the good old boy literary establishment for that," Peggy said cynically. "Men dominate the committees that determine how university money is spent. I could almost feel sorry for what's-er-name — Angelo — trying to convince a bunch of middleaged male chauvinists that a Gothic novel by an unknown woman writer is worth that much. I'm surprised she got them up to fifty thou."

"I'm surprised she didn't use her own money."

"Probably doesn't have it."

"How did you —" Karen stopped herself, but not quite in time.

"I write best-selling sex manuals under a pseudonym," Peggy said, in a tone which, though amiable, indicated she had said all she intended to say on that subject.

Simon's message had been waiting for Karen when she arrived home Sunday evening. There had been a number of other messages on her machine, including several from Peggy, increasingly irate in tone; Karen had called at once to tell her the good news and suggest they meet at the campus coffee shop next morning to discuss future plans.

The news had taken Peggy's mind off her grievance for a time. Now she turned a critical stare on Karen. "I hope you aren't planning to rush off to Baltimore today."

"No, I'm not."

"You hadn't planned to go to Virginia, either. You didn't tell me you were going. In fact, you deliberately misled me. Don't think you can sneak off without me today the way you did last weekend."

"I can't, can I?" Karen said quietly. "Not without the money."

Peggy's eyes shifted. "I didn't mean it that way."

"Yes, you did. I don't blame you." That was a lie too, but she made it sound convincing. "Let's get this out into the open, Peggy. I'm willing to accept your generous offer, but only as a loan. Strictly business. We'll go to a lawyer and draw up the necessary papers."

Peggy was silent for a moment. Voice and expression were neutral when she replied. "If that's how you want it."

"That's the only way I'll accept it." Another lie. She would have robbed a bank if there were no other way. She would have preferred to borrow from an impersonal source; a bank manager wouldn't lecture her about her personal habits and treat her like a two-year-old. But it would have taken weeks to get the money, even supposing she could persuade a bank to accept such doubtful collateral as a battered manuscript.

"Deal," Peggy said. "Now would you care to

tell me about your weekend, or is that none of my business?"

"You'll be happy to hear that without your restraining influence I managed to behave like a complete idiot," Karen said cheerfully. She had made her point, and Peggy, no fool herself, had understood. Whether she would continue to accept the implicit conditions was another matter, but Karen didn't want her to harbor hard feelings.

"Oh, yeah?"

Karen glanced at her watch. She had a class in ten minutes, so she made it brief, describing only her encounter with Lisa Fairweather and Bill Meyer. One admission of fallibility was enough; there was no need to mention that she had also made a fool of herself with Cameron Hayes. "It wasn't very smart of me to go out there alone," she admitted. "But I don't think I deserved such total humiliation."

Peggy was trying not to laugh. She lost. "Sorry," she sputtered. "But it's such a classic, banal Gothic plot! Being rescued by the dark handsome man you detest, in the presence of the beautiful Other Woman — a blonde, of course . . ."

"Meyer was thinking exactly the same thing, damn him. Conceited bastard . . . He isn't handsome. What made it especially entertaining was having the Other Woman take me for a bag lady." She consulted her watch again. "I'd better get going. Have you any free time tomorrow or Wednesday? I'll try to set up an appointment with my lawyer. We might plan to drive to Baltimore on Saturday."

"We?" Peggy repeated.

"Of course."

"Okay. I'm free tomorrow after three, and on Wednesday morning. Wait a minute," she exclaimed, as Karen rose to her feet. "You haven't told me what happened after you got caught."

"I managed to get in touch with Mr. Hayes that evening. He took me out to the house next day; he's trying to clean the place up so he can sell it. He was very nice," she added, with a meaningful glance at her companion. "He didn't lecture me about my rude, careless behavior."

Relations between them continued to be self-conscious, if not actually strained, for the rest of the week. Peggy was curt and businesslike during the meeting with the lawyer and left immediately afterward. There was no time for friendly conversation; it was one of the busiest weeks in the academic year, and Karen was pushing herself to finish her work as quickly as possible. She pushed her students too, scheduling exams at her convenience instead of theirs and rejecting all but the most compelling requests for extensions on papers and reports. Their response convinced Karen that they were the whiniest, most self-pitying bunch she had ever taught, and her opinion was confirmed when she found out some of them had complained about her to the departmental chairman.

"He had the gall to tell me I was obviously suffering from nervous strain, and that maybe what I needed was a more active social life," she reported bitterly. "Can you believe that guy?"

They were on their way to Baltimore. Peggy was driving — and smoking. Karen had not objected to either. Some concessions were necessary to reestablish friendly relations; Peggy's manner had been decidedly stiff when they met that morning.

Her efforts seemed to be succeeding. "Sure, I can believe it," Peggy said. "You'd better watch him, Karen. He's out to get you. Sexual harassment is a hot issue these days; he's not dumb enough to make a direct move or explicit remark, but he can drive you crazy without actually stepping over the line."

"He hasn't got anything on me. I haven't neglected my work; I'm completely caught up except for turning in final grades in two courses, which I will do on Monday. And once I've published the manuscript . . ."

"Fame and fortune will be yours." Peggy lit another cigarette. "If you found the right publisher, one with a little imagination and a lot of know-how, you could make a lot of money out of the book. Enough to buy me out."

"You won't be out unless you want out. I'm counting on you to help with the historical part. You can publish anything you like on that aspect."

"I wouldn't publish without consulting you."

"I know that."

Peggy tossed her cigarette out the window and

gripped the wheel so fiercely her knuckles whitened. "Then why the hell did you make such a fuss about the money? What difference does it make who has legal possession? It's your field, not mine; I wouldn't tackle a project like that, I have better sense. Did you think I'd sell the publication rights to someone else?"

"Don't be an idiot!" Karen's voice rose to match Peggy's. "God, I'm sick of apologizing for things I never did and explaining statements that ought to be self-evident!"

"Give it one more try," Peggy said in a strangled voice.

"I have absolute confidence in your integrity. I didn't think for a moment that you'd double-cross me. I just want to own it myself. I want . . . control. For the first time in my life I want to be the sole determiner of what happens to me."

"The first time? You've been an adult for several years."

"Somebody's always trying to boss me," Karen muttered. "My parents, my professors, my ex-husband, Joe Cropsey . . . They all treat me as if I were a child. It's this damned chubby-cheeked face of mine, I suppose. You wouldn't understand —"

"Whew." Peggy let out a long, relieved sigh. "So that's the problem. You think I don't understand? I'm five feet tall, for God's sake! You think it's tough being a chubby-cheeked woman, try being a short chubby-cheeked woman."

"I don't think of you as short," Karen said,

genuinely surprised.

"Neither do I. That's the trick. But it took me a long time to figure it out." Peggy smiled wryly. "Well, that cleared the air. At least I hope it did. We're more alike than you might suppose, Karen. I've been through it too — the patronizing smiles, the condescending remarks, the pats on the head. And although it was a long time ago, I was once as prickly as you are. Yes, you are — with some reason — but take it from me, my friend, being constantly on the defensive makes life a lot tougher than it has to be. I'll try not to boss you if you try to bear in mind that I boss everybody. It's one of the privileges of age. Nothing personal."

"I'll try," Karen agreed, still in a mild state of shock. Peggy was so mature, so respected, so completely in control of her life, it was almost impossible to believe she had ever been shy and insecure. With a violent effort of imagination Karen tried to picture Peggy as a timid young girl. She couldn't do it.

"So where do we go from here?" Peggy asked.

"To Virginia. I'm leaving on Monday, as soon as I turn in those exam scores and clear up a few odds and ends. I talked to Cameron Wednesday; he said he'd find me a room or an apartment. I can't afford to stay in a motel for weeks on end."

"Weeks," Peggy repeated. "That long?"

"I can work on the manuscript there as well as anywhere," Karen argued. "Maybe the ambience will inspire me."

"Be funny if it turns out to be the wrong house,"

Peggy said. "You still don't know for certain."

"I have a hunch."

"Oh, great. I can't go with you, Karen." She gave Karen a sidelong smile and added, "No, I'm not sulking. I really can't. I promised a friend I'd come for a visit. He's been ill and he . . . What's the matter?"

"Nothing."

"Now *you're* sulking. I'll be back in a week or ten days. Have you found out when the auction is to be held?"

"Memorial Day."

"The delay does makes sense, at that," Peggy said thoughtfully. "Memorial Day and Labor Day are the big weekends for country auctions. They're hoping to attract the city slickers. Well, I'll be back by then. I hope you won't take offense if I suggest that my experience could be useful."

"No." Karen decided she might as well admit the truth, before Peggy misinterpreted her frown. "I'm in trouble," she admitted. "Joan and I were supposed to go to Nag's Head for a week, right after graduation. To unwind. I forgot about it until you mentioned your friend."

" 'Were supposed,' " Peggy repeated. "You're going to cancel?"

"What else can I do? Don't answer that! I've been waiting for weeks already. Having to postpone it another week would make me crazy. I'll just have to think of some excuse for Joan."

"You could tell her the truth."

"I don't want her to —" Karen stopped. "Maybe

124

I should, at that."

"Truth is not only more virtuous, it's a helluva lot easier in the long run," Peggy muttered. "You can't keep the manuscript a secret much longer. Too many people know about it."

The accuracy of Peggy's assessment was brought home to Karen when they arrived at the bookstore to find that Simon was — reluctantly — entertaining a guest. His guarded look was sufficient warning; when the other man advanced to greet her, smiling amiably, his hand outstretched, Karen bit her tongue and kept her mouth closed. However, she could not bring herself to shake hands with him.

"I'm leaving," Meyer said, before she could speak. "Mr. Hallett has already explained you have a business appointment." He turned to Peggy, offering the hand Karen had rejected. "Dr. Finneyfrock? I don't believe I've had the pleasure of meeting you. I'm Bill Meyer."

"How do you do?" Peggy gave him her hand, and a smile as broad and hypocritical as his. "I've heard a lot about you, Dr. Meyer."

"How nice. Allow me to congratulate you, ladies. May I have the additional pleasure of taking you to lunch after you've concluded your business? Mr. Hallett too, of course."

"Why not?" Peggy said, before Karen could refuse.

"Good. I'll wait in that charming little bar across the street. Take your time."

The door closed behind him with a musical tinkle.

"I'm sorry," Simon began.

"It's not your fault." Karen gave the closed door a resentful scowl. "He doesn't know we were in that bar, does he? If that son of a bitch knew I was following him . . . He led me on a wild-goose chase that day, through the worst traffic in Baltimore, in the rain . . ." Rage choked her.

"Cool it," Peggy said. "So what if he did? You've won and he's lost."

"Perhaps he is only being a courteous loser," Simon suggested.

"Sure," said Karen.

Their business was soon concluded. As Karen's hands closed over the precious bundle she saw that Simon's eyes were fixed on her and that his expression was not that of a man who has just accepted a large check. She smiled at him. "Thanks, Simon. Thanks for letting me win."

Simon shook his head. "I hope I won't regret it."

"The check won't bounce," Peggy said cheerfully.

His dour expression brightened as he turned to her, offering one of the small glasses he had filled from a cut-glass decanter. "That was my chief concern, of course."

Peggy insisted they all accept Meyer's invitation. "He's up to no good," she declared with obvious relish. "But we may as well find out what he wants.

If the three of us can't outwit him we ought to be ashamed of ourselves."

Simon rolled his eyes heavenward. "I suppose I must join you. The superior intelligence of an older and wiser man is obviously needed."

Meyer had been watching for them. They took his car — Simon in front with Meyer, "ladies" in the back. Typical, Karen thought. Peggy let out a gurgle and poked Karen in the ribs when he pulled up in front of one of Baltimore's most expensive restaurants. "He's definitely up to no good," she mouthed.

They drank another toast, in imported Chablis. Peggy studied the menu with an anticipatory expression that made it difficult for Karen to keep her face straight. As she had expected, Peggy ordered the most expensive entrée available.

Meyer directed the conversation skillfully, sticking to neutral subjects until their orders had been delivered and the obsequious waiter had left. Then he opened fire.

"I hope your ankle is better, Karen?"

Simon didn't choke on his food or demand an explanation; he was far too well-bred. But the look he gave Karen assured her that she was due for a lecture when the truth came out, as Meyer intended it should.

"It's fine," she said. "Not a twinge."

"I'm glad we arrived when we did," Meyer mused. "I shudder to think what might have happened if you had been trapped in that filthy hole, unable to climb out, with the water rising and night coming on."

Simon did choke then, and Karen lost her precarious hold on her temper. "You've been reading too many Gothic novels, Bill," she snarled. "I stumbled into a window well, Simon. It was a basement window, and the hole was less than five feet deep. I could easily have gotten out by myself. My ankle was twisted, not sprained, and the water was three inches deep."

"All the same, you were taking a dangerous risk, going to such an isolated place alone," Meyer said. "I'm surprised you would let her do it, Dr. Finneyfrock."

"I'm not her keeper," Peggy retorted, while Karen sputtered speechlessly. "She doesn't need one, even if she is a woman. Seems to me you've got some explaining to do yourself, Dr. Meyer. What were you doing there? Mr. Hayes is the executor of the estate. You didn't have his permission."

"I was accompanied by Miss Fairweather, who is one of the heirs. Come to that," Meyer added gently, "Karen didn't have Mr. Hayes's permission either."

Simon's head had been turning from one speaker to the other. Now he said, "She was in touch with him, however. I didn't give you his name, Dr. Meyer."

"Karen is aware of that, Mr. Hallett. Your integrity has never been in question." Meyer leaned back, smiling smugly. "I reasoned it out myself."

"But you haven't any right," Peggy began.

"Ah, but I do. Let's be candid, shall we? Cards on the table."

"That," said Karen, "I would like to see. No, Peggy, let me speak for myself. Dr. Meyer is correct. We can't prevent him from pursuing his own inquiries. Publication of the manuscript is the main issue, but the identity of the author is also important. If my honorable colleague can figure that out before I do he diminishes my achievement and adds further luster to his distinguished career. A nice guy would give up gracefully and admit I have a moral, if not legal, right to pursue that search. But you're not a nice guy, are you, Bill?"

"Now, now, let's not be rude," Meyer said with a grin. "I was about to suggest a compromise. We can waste a lot of time and energy getting in one another's way; and I must warn you that Dorothea is also on the trail. She's even less interested in nice than I am, and she's furious at being outbid."

A brief silence followed, while they considered this information. It was Simon who spoke first. "That sounds to me like a threat, Dr. Meyer."

"A warning, not a threat," Meyer said smoothly. "I can't imagine why Karen is so determined to think the worst of me. You don't suppose I would be stupid enough — or unscrupulous enough — to do something illegal, do you? Dorothea might. She has a grudge against Karen, who is everything she'd like to be" — his eyes lingered on Karen's flushed face, moving deliberately from her eyes to her lips — "and whose career is on the rise

129

as Dorothea's is fading. Dorothea hasn't published anything significant for over a decade. I wouldn't like to commit myself as to what she might do to get that manuscript — or a copy of it. Think it over, Karen. I can be useful to you in a number of ways if you agree to my offer of assistance. If you don't agree . . ." He glanced at his watch. "Excuse me; I have another appointment. You'll want to discuss the matter with your friends, I'm sure."

"If he thinks he's going to stick us with the check," Peggy began, as Meyer made his way between the tables.

"He wouldn't be so crude," Simon muttered. "Good heavens, Karen, what have you gotten yourself into? This is beginning to sound like gang warfare."

Peggy patted his hand. "Poor Simon. You don't know much about the inner workings of the academic world, do you?"

Ismene woke to find herself wrapped in warmth and in light. Her thoughts were as diffuse and hazed as her vision; how strange, she mused, that Paradise should present itself in such familiar and homely images; not the dazzling brilliance of That Divine Visage, or the splendor of golden palaces, but a soft red glow like firelight. The softness that enclosed her might be that of blanket and comforter, rather than cloud or feathery wings.

The wings of the faceless angel? She shuddered at the recollection. So might Lucifer, the shining child of the morning, have appeared to the all-seeing Eye that observed in the shadowing of that angelic face the dread forecast of his inevitable fall from grace.

The face that presented itself to the field of her vision was no angel's visage, unless the Redeemer's promise to the oppressed was indeed fulfilled in a sense more literal than hope dared envisage. Wrinkled and kindly, dusky dark and crowned with a close-wrapped cloth of purest white, it smiled upon her and spoke in the soft accents of a living woman.

With a cry Ismene rose to a sitting position and glared wildly around the room. Flames flickering on a low hearth left the upper portions of the chamber in shadow. Its ceiling was high, its proportions ample. The bed on which she rested had a canopy of rich damask, gathered in folds. Curtains of the same fabric had been drawn back. The woman bent over her, pressing her back, murmuring words of reassurance.

"My sister!" Ismene cried. "Where is Clara? Oh, heaven, tell me she lives!"

Her eyes fixed on the servant, she did not observe the opening of the door nor note the person who approached till he stood next to the bed.

"Lie still," he said gently. "You were overcome by cold and wet when we carried you here, but all is well; and your companion, though in worse case than you, has taken no lasting harm. She lies in the adjoining chamber, tended with loving care. Let me bid you welcome, dear Ismene — for you can be no other than she whom we have long awaited."

Locks of palest silver-gilt framed the countenance now visible to her wondering eyes. It was as beautiful

131

as that of the angel her fainting mind had imagined, the perfection of the sculptured features unmarked by weariness or age.

"But surely," she began, "I am dreaming still, or wandering in delirium. Are you — you cannot be — Mr. Joshua Merrivale?"

"Alas." He took her limp hand in his and clasped it in a warm, comforting grasp. "It grieves me to greet you with such painful tidings, but I feel sure your fortitude is equal to the dread news. Poor girl, you have lost an uncle as well as a parent — and so have I. I am your cousin Edmund, and I give you my solemn promise that my affectionate care for you and Clara will be at least the equal of that my dear lost father would have rejoiced to provide."

Ismene sank back against the heaped pillows. Clasping her hand yet more closely, her cousin — her cousin! — exclaimed, "You are overcome. I blame myself; I should not have burdened you in your weakened state with this additional cause of grief."

Though still bewildered and confused, Ismene made an effort to respond. "Indeed I am sorry, but chiefly on your account, Cousin . . . Edmund. Forgive me if my speech falters; it echoes the confusion of my mind, for indeed I knew not that such an individual existed."

Gently, in soft accents, he replied, "The sad estrangement between our parents was deeply regretted by my father. You do not know its cause? Nor do I; he would never speak of it except with such sighs and signs of grief I could not in kindness pursue my inquiries. Let us forget the sorrows of the past and begin afresh. Think only that you have found a home and a brother; look to the future and prepare for happiness."

Chapter Five

This is an important book, the critic assumes, because it deals with war. This is an insignificant book because it deals with the feelings of women in a drawing room.

VIRGINIA WOOLF,
A Room of One's Own, 1929

Though the manuscript called out to her with a voice as seductive as the aroma of fresh-baked brownies, Karen tore herself from it after she discovered the identity of Ismene's faceless angel. That image had haunted her for weeks. Now that she had satisfied her curiosity, she could concentrate on the tasks that had to be completed before she could leave. Once settled in Virginia, her conscience at ease and all distractions left behind, she could turn her full attention to the manuscript and the equally engrossing question of its author's identity.

The correctness of her decision to skip town was confirmed by a rash of telephone calls on Sunday morning. The only one she responded to was from Peggy.

"It's in the *Times*," Peggy announced without so much as a preliminary hello.

"I know. Cropsey was the first to call, as you

might expect. I didn't pick up, even though he kept yelling, 'I know you're there, Karen; I know you're there!' "

"How'd he figure out it was you? The story didn't mention names."

"Damned if I know." Karen ran distracted fingers through her hair. "Bill might have told him, out of spite. He knows how much I despise the creep. What exactly did the *Times* say? I haven't had a chance to get a copy."

"It was pretty vague; just reported a rumor that an important manuscript had been found and sold to a professor at an eastern college. But if Cropsey knows or suspects it's you —"

"All the more reason for me to leave tomorrow. I'll call and give you a number once I'm settled. Look, I've got to hang up, I have a million things to do."

The most important of those things had occupied most of Sunday. She had copied the manuscript, page by slow page, on her own machine. The result wasn't as readable as a professional copy would have been, but Meyer's warning (or threat?) had worried her more than she liked to admit. She was afraid to let the original manuscript out of her hands — afraid even to venture out of the apartment with it. Three of the callers had hung up without leaving a message. Three — or the same one? Someone trying to find out whether the apartment was empty before attempting a break-in? Someone who would have responded to her "Hello" with an invitation that would induce her to leave the building? Not that she really believed Dorothea was mad enough to lie in wait for her, knock her down, snatch the manuscript . . . But why take the chance? The parking area in front of the apartment was relatively deserted on a gloomy, rainy Sunday afternoon.

The anonymous caller rang twice more during the evening. Scolding herself for timidity, and cursing Bill Meyer for causing it, Karen double-checked the locks on doors and windows before going to bed.

Next morning she left the apartment early, at the same time her fellow tenants were heading for work. No one was lying in wait. Relieved and embarrassed at her foolishness she drove straight to the bank and deposited the manuscript. She would have to refer to it before she published the book, trying to decipher blurred or illegible passages, but for a first read-through the copy would be good enough.

It would also be good enough for a would-be thief, Karen reminded herself. So long as the original was in her safe-deposit box a thief wouldn't gain the most important thing — exclusive possession of the text — but he or she could work from the copy and try to publish first. She'd have to guard the copy as closely as she had the original. Maybe she shouldn't have left it in the apartment. But it was safer there than it would have been in the car. She caught herself glancing frequently in the rearview mirror and gave herself a mental slap on the wrist. Taking reasonable precautions was one thing; becoming suspicious of every vehicle that followed her for more than a block was raging paranoia.

The campus was reassuringly well populated. Suspecting that Joe Cropsey would be lying in wait for her, she asked a passing student to take the final grades to the English Department office instead of delivering them herself. One more dirty job awaited her, and although it wasn't as unpleasant as an encounter with Cropsey would have been, she was not looking forward to it.

The trip to Nag's Head had been Joan's idea. She would probably scream like a banshee when Karen announced she couldn't go, and Sharon would probably support Joan. She had already expressed concern about Karen's growing "obsession" with her work, and her professional training made her only too ready to find hidden motives for every action.

They were waiting for her when she arrived at the restaurant. Joan was drinking wine, Sharon mineral water with a twist of grapefruit peel. At least it looked like grapefruit. The latest health fad, Karen supposed. Sharon followed every one.

She had decided to blurt it out and get it over with. "I have to cancel Nag's Head," she announced, sliding into a chair.

The other two contemplated her in stony silence. Joan's hair was so curly and of such a bright, improbable red that it looked like a wig. She was ten years older than Karen and several inches taller — a big woman, heavy-boned and imposing in appearance. Sharon was almost as tall, but she weighed fifty pounds less than Joan and her arms bulged with muscle. She worked out every day, attended aerobics classes several times a week, and ate like a Victorian lady. Currently she was on a low-fat, low-protein, vegetarian diet. Watching her eat always made Karen want to order the richest dessert on the menu. In her admittedly biased opinion Joan was much more attractive than Sharon. Joan looked like a woman, not an artificial model of one.

Joan looked at Sharon, who nodded at her. It was one of Sharon's significant nods. Karen knew what was coming.

"Aren't you being a teeny bit unfair to Joan, Karen? She can't afford to go by herself even if she wanted to, and it's too late now to find someone else."

"Weren't you the one who told me I had to stop being such a wimp and focus on my self-needs?"

"Not in those precise words, I hope," Sharon answered in assumed horror.

"That was a free translation," Karen admitted with a smile. "I know it isn't fair to Joan, but when you hear my reasons I'm confident you'll understand. I couldn't talk about it before the deal was concluded, not even to you."

She was a good lecturer, and she gave this one all she had, finishing with an animated description of the lunch with Meyer. "So you see I daren't waste time. Bill the Bastard is already nose-down

138

on the trail, and I'll be damned if I let him get ahead of me."

"Meyer," Joan repeated. "Didn't I meet him? Tall, good-looking guy with a supercilious sneer?"

"I don't think he's good-looking. But 'supercilious' is certainly accurate."

"It sounds like a wonderful find, Karen," Sharon said coolly. "Congratulations. But I don't see why you're finding such — may I say 'theatrical'? — implications in Dr. Meyer's behavior. He's a professional, a scholar. You seem to be suggesting he will engage in conduct that is unbecoming —"

"She's right," Joan declared. "Honest to God, Sharon, sometimes I wonder what ivory tower you've taken up residence in. I don't know much about literature, but if Karen's appraisal of the manuscript is correct it's a major discovery, enough to justify burglary, assassination, and blackmail. Scholars aren't any nobler than the next man."

"You're as bad as Karen," Sharon said fastidiously.

"Oh, I don't suppose he'd commit burglary or murder," Joan admitted. "But he'll cheat her of the glory if he can. You really don't have any idea of who this woman was, Karen?"

"Not yet. But I think I've located the house, and I'm pretty sure she was a member of the family that has owned it for over two hundred years."

"That's a good start," Joan agreed.

"You do understand, then," Karen said, relieved. "You're not mad?"

"I'd do the same thing if I were in your shoes," Joan admitted. "Tell me more."

Karen needed no further encouragement. It was a relief and a pleasure to talk about her big discovery to sympathetic listeners. Joan's field was sociology, Sharon was a psychologist; but both were intelligent and well-read. Karen had expected Joan would be the more responsive of the two, since her imagination was better developed, and she was right. Joan was enthralled; she kept interrupting with questions and comments. Sharon listened in silence, nibbling daintily at her vegetarian salad. However, she was unable to refrain from one professional caveat.

"I just hope you aren't going overboard on this, dear. Just remember, if you ever need to talk about it . . ."

"She means well," Joan said with a grin that bared most of her teeth. "Ignore little Ms. Freud, Karen, I'm on your side. This sounds like fun. When did you say you were leaving?"

Karen had been frowning over the check, trying to figure out how much each of them owed. Absorbed in abstruse calculations, she was slow to comprehend the implications of Joan's question. Her heart sank. Why hadn't it occurred to her that Joan, at loose ends after her defection, would want to join what she obviously thought of as a jolly kind of treasure hunt? She appreciated her friend's interest, but at this moment all she wanted was peace and privacy and a chance to work without enthusiastic interruptions.

"As soon as I finish packing," she said firmly. "I'll call you as soon as I've found a place to stay."

They had come in separate cars; Sharon took leave of the other two outside the door of the restaurant, but Joan insisted on walking Karen to her car, spouting questions as they walked. "How long are you going to be there? When do I get to read the book? Are you sure there's nothing you want me to do? How about that creepy Joe Cropsey? You want me to tell him you've gone to Antarctica?"

"Sounds like a great idea," Karen said abstractedly. "Joan, my dear old buddy, I really am in a hurry. I promise I'll call in a day or two."

"I can take a hint." Joan enveloped her in a mighty hug. "Take care of yourself, babe."

The driver of the car next to Karen's had parked so close she wondered whether she would be able to open her door wide enough to squeeze in. Cursing the thoughtlessness of others, she managed to unlock the door and open it. When the voice boomed out behind her, she started and dropped her keys.

She had recognized the voice; she had half-expected to hear it sooner or later; but she hadn't anticipated the sense of absolute, dry-mouthed panic that seized her when she turned and saw Dorothea looming over her. Dorothea was almost six feet tall and correspondingly broad. One might have described her as fat — a number of enemies had — but the word would have been inaccurate. She was big-boned and massive; solid flesh and

141

muscle evenly distributed from her broad shoulders to her thick legs and large feet. Bright-red lipstick and black eyeshadow gave a grotesque look of parody to her heavy features.

Karen told herself it was ridiculous to be afraid. What could Dorothea do to her, in broad daylight, with people all around? The answer was unfortunately too obvious. Dorothea's body completely filled the space between the two vehicles, and the open door behind Karen pinned her between two barriers, the one of flesh as impenetrable as the one of metal.

"You'll have to excuse me, Dorothea," she said breathlessly. "I'm in rather a hurry —"

"I want to talk to you." The other woman's eyes moved slowly over the interior of the car and then fixed on the briefcase-sized purse Karen held.

"I said I'm in a hurry." In order to slide into the driver's seat, she would have to turn her back on Dorothea. The very idea made her skin prickle.

"You have to listen to me." Dorothea's tongue crawled over her lower lip. "I don't want to do anything drastic unless you force me to."

Reason suggested she agree to anything Dorothea proposed, and wait for a chance to get away. Reason lost to rising outrage and the inability of rational people to believe other people can behave irrationally. "Damn it, Dorothea, are you threatening me? We have nothing to discuss. Get out of my way."

"Is this a private fight or can anybody join in?"

The cheerful familiar voice and the glimpse of

a mop of red hair made Karen go limp with relief. Dorothea turned, slowly and clumsily in the confined space.

"Who the hell are you?" she bellowed.

"A friend," Joan cried in a resonant shout. "Britomart, the warrior maiden, riding to the rescue! I think that was her name," she added, calmly. "I'm a sociologist, not an English major. And who the hell are you? And what the hell do you think you're doing, making a scene and threatening innocent people? There's a squad car pulling into the lot; I'll just give it a hail —"

She skipped nimbly out of the way as Dorothea beat a quick retreat. "Get in the car, quick," she called to Karen. Karen jumped in and slammed the door. She was just in time; the car next to hers was Dorothea's, as she ought to have anticipated, and it scraped jarringly along the side of her own vehicle as Dorothea backed out of the parking space. She took off with a screech of tires.

Karen got out to inspect the damage. "God damn that bitch! I'm going to have her arrested! Where's that squad car?"

Leaning against the rear fender, arms folded, Joan said, "There isn't one. I just made it up. It seemed like a good idea at the time."

"It was a very good idea," Karen said. She raised a shaking hand to her face. "God. Thanks, Joan. I mean — thanks a lot. I mean —"

"You all right?" Joan moved to her side.

"Yes, sure. This isn't the first time I've seen

143

her act that way, she's famous for it. It wouldn't have bothered me so much if I hadn't been worried about the manuscript."

"She's one of your rivals?"

"Dorothea Angelo. She's a full professor at Berkeley."

"And I thought sociologists were a crazy lot," Joan mused. "Well, I'm delighted to have been of assistance, ma'am. So long, and happy trails."

"So long, Britomart."

Though Karen felt sure even Dorothea wouldn't risk a second encounter, she did not relax until she had finished loading the car and had driven some distance without any sign of Dorothea's Chevy behind her. She had definitely made the right decision; Wilmington was getting a little too crowded for comfort. It would be nice to retreat to a small peaceful Southern town where no one knew her and no one wanted anything she possessed.

Karen's prospective landlady turned out to be Mrs. Fowler, the woman she had seen in the restaurant wearing the preposterous violet-trimmed hat. She was not wearing it that afternoon, but her dress was covered with nosegays of purple blossoms and the parlor into which she led her guests looked like a petrified garden. There were violets everywhere — on the wallpaper, on crewel-embroidered pillows, on the teacups and saucers. The tea set was plain silver, possibly because Mrs. Fowler had inherited it from an ancestor who didn't share her mania.

Cameron Hayes had tried to prepare Karen when she called him on Sunday to announce her imminent arrival. "She wants you to come to tea on Tuesday. Sorry about that, but the older folks around here insist on their little rituals. I think you'll find the place is ideal for you, if you don't mind letting her pretend she's doing you a big favor. She needs the money, but she'd never be vulgar enough to say so."

In the hope of making a good impression Karen had packed a dress she had bought in a fit of inexplicable insanity the year before — pink voile, with a gathered skirt and elbow-length puffed sleeves. She had been shopping with Sharon and Joan at one of the outlet malls, and they had assured her she looked marvelous in the dress. And, of course, it had been on sale — a perfectly good reason for buying it. She had never worn it until today, and as she studied her reflection she was tempted to tie her hair back with a big pink bow to complete the picture of girlish innocence. That would be going too far, she decided. Even an elderly Southern lady might detect a touch of caricature.

Mrs. Fowler's approving expression told her that her instincts had been correct. Cameron Hayes's expression had left her in some doubt as to his reaction.

His face was just as unreadable as he stood by Mrs. Fowler, waiting to hand the teacup she was filling to Karen, but she knew he didn't want to

145

be there. It was a necessary part of the ritual, the pretense that she was a friend of a friend, properly introduced, not a stranger engaged in a crass commercial transaction. He too had dressed for the occasion, in a coat and tie. He looked tired, Karen thought — or maybe just bored. On the surface the relationship between him and his hostess was friendly, but there were undercurrents — a sweetly barbed comment here, a meaningful glance there — that aroused Karen's curiosity.

Apparently she passed the test. After she had finished a second cup of tea and accepted a macaroon from the doily-covered plate Cameron passed her, Mrs. Fowler edged delicately toward the rude subject of renting her apartment. "Normally I wouldn't dream of such a thing, but since you're a friend of Cameron's, and a literary lady . . . Perhaps you'd be willing to speak to our little literary society sometime. We read only the classics, of course. Modern literature is so vulgar, don't you think?"

Karen said, "Mmmmm," and smiled. Not for any reward on earth, up to and including a free suite at the Ritz, would she have consented to address a little literary society. She could imagine what this one was like — a group of superannuated ladies and gents, like the ones she had seen breakfasting with Mrs. Fowler. They'd consider any writer postdating Charles Dickens vulgar and modern.

Mrs. Fowler led the way, tottering on her high heels and leaning heavily on Hayes's arm. The

146

place *was* ideal — an apartment over the garage, far enough from the house to give Karen the privacy she wanted, hidden from it by a high hedge. It offered garage space for her car and living quarters above — kitchen, bath, one bedroom and a tiny living room. The furnishings were shabby and there were definitely too many violets in evidence, but it was clean, and the price they agreed upon, with Cameron's tight-lipped assistance, was reasonable.

Mrs. Fowler said she could move in next day. "I'll get Belle in here to clean first," she remarked, with a disparaging glance at the spotless, dust-free room. "Around noon, my dear; is that all right with you?"

Karen would have preferred to move in immediately. The place had obviously been cleaned within the past twenty-four hours; Mrs. Fowler was still trying to maintain the impression that she hadn't had the slightest intention of renting the apartment. But it wasn't worth arguing about. She prevailed upon her landlady to accept a check for the first week's rent and Mrs. Fowler handed over a set of keys. "Don't you worry about me bothering you," she called, as they started down the path toward the front gate. "Cameron explained you were busy with some thrilling project. You'll be absolutely private if that's what you want."

Hayes waited until they were out of earshot before he spoke. "I hope you don't mind my mentioning your 'thrilling project.' I wasn't more specific."

Karen reached for the gate. His hand was there before hers; she let him open it for her. "That's all right," she said. "Anything that will fend off invitations to tea, literary meetings, and so on."

The lines in his face smoothed out into a faint smile. "I'm afraid you made too good an impression. If you give her an opening, she'll overwhelm you with unwanted hospitality."

"I understand." She let him open the car door too. When in Rome . . .

He dropped her at the motel, where she had left her car. "I'll meet you at Miz Fowler's tomorrow, at noon," he said. "Will you be all right this evening?"

"Of course. You don't have to help me move in tomorrow, I'm perfectly capable of carrying a few boxes."

"I'm sure you are. We ought to have a business discussion, though. A late lunch, perhaps."

"Yes, right." She wondered why he hadn't suggested dinner that evening, and then reminded herself the man might have a few other things to do than tend to her. "Thanks for taking the time to introduce me. I know you must be busy."

"Not at all." He was obviously impatient to be off, though. His hands were tight on the wheel. They looked even worse than they had the week before, scraped and cut and raw. Not the hands of a gentleman, as Mrs. Fowler's pained glance and raised eyebrows had made clear.

After he drove off Karen went to her car and opened the trunk. It was jammed full, as was the back seat. Her packing couldn't be called well organized. There had been so much to do and she had been so impatient to get away that she had thrown things at random into boxes and suitcases. But she hadn't forgotten the important things. Taking the briefcase from the trunk, she carried it to her room.

Once again Ismene's feet carried her to the rocky promontory from which Edmund had first displayed to her awestruck gaze the fearful solitude of the wilderness. That vision — the furious rush of the swollen stream, foam-flecked and dark, the savage woodlands stretching to the limit of vision — was imprinted in her memory as indelibly as if a celestial hand had pressed its stamp upon it, though sunlight and the soft airs of spring now supervened to wash the dark woods with green, and sparkle on the flowing water.

The tender duty she owed her sister (not bodily weakness, for the day following their arrival had seen her fully recovered) would have kept her at Clara's bedside had not Clara herself urged her to seek daily exercise. "I know your restless spirit cannot endure quiet long," she had said. "There is no need for you to sit dully beside me. No queen could ask for kinder attentions than I have received and am receiving."

Indeed, Ismene's fears for her sister's health had been relieved that first night when, penetrating the elegant chamber where Clara lay, she had found the younger girl sitting up in bed and partaking of a dish of soup. Edmund had even insisted on sending for a

149

physician, though by the time Dr. Fitzgerald arrived upon the scene he himself proclaimed his services unnecessary. The following days had seen steady improvement and no diminution of the attentions bestowed upon the invalid. Had it not seemed ungrateful, Ismene might have wished for such a diminution; Clara's only fault was a tendency toward laziness and a childish enjoyment of luxury.

It was on her first such walk that she had encountered Edmund; seeing her caped and hooded and ready for the out-of-doors, he had insisted upon accompanying her, claiming a brisk stroll was just what he wanted after a morning with his tedious ledgers and accounts. "In any case," he had added, "though it does not rain the skies are dark and the wind blows strong. The grounds are extensive and wilder than I would like; you might lose your way."

He had sheltered her with his cloak and supported her steps as they made their way through dripping shrubbery and along muddy paths; and yet he had led her to the unsheltered, windswept promontory, with its terrifying vista of untrammeled wilderness and its rocky precipice. Fearful yet strangely drawn, Ismene had stood balanced on the brink, leaning against the wind, until he drew her back into the circle of his arm.

"I knew," he had murmured, "that you would venture to the edge. Take care, Ismene, lest your courageous spirit lead you beyond daring into danger."

Had it been a test? And if so, a test of what? Ismene pondered the question as she stood marveling at the transformation a few weeks' passage had wrought.

Wildflowers blossomed shyly in the grass at her feet; the gently swelling curves of the distant mountains were modestly swathed in green; even the cruel rocks of the cliff below were softened by sprays of feathery green — a fernery created not by the hand of a gardener but by nature herself, rooted in adamantine stone and sheltered by it.

A nagging discomfort penetrated Karen's absorption. Her foot had gone to sleep. Looking up, she realized that the windows were dark, and that another source of discomfort came from her empty stomach. She had been working for hours.

She rose and stretched aching shoulders. A trifle repetitive, that last part, she thought critically. The flashback was handled fairly well, but there was no need for it; Ismene had filled several pages with a description of her cousin's "angelic" form and features, and her description of their walk to the windy promontory had been detailed and — as she clearly intended — vaguely ominous.

Still . . . The style was characteristic of nineteenth-century novels, and less effusive than many. When your readership demanded two- and three-volume novels, a certain amount of padding became necessary. And this was clearly a first draft. Changes and emendations were frequent, making the close-written lines even harder to read.

Enough for tonight; her eyes were tired, and she had made an exciting discovery. The ferns and the cliff . . . Ferncliffe? It wasn't proof, there were ferns and cliffs all over the place; but in this case it had to be more than a coincidence.

She decided to celebrate by calling room service instead of going to the trouble of changing out of her comfortable robe. After the waiter had delivered her sandwich and a pot of coffee, she stretched out on the bed and was soon deep in the exaggerated horrors of *The Castle of Otranto*.

The sight of this questionable masterpiece and the other books she had packed brought a surprised comment from Cameron Hayes. He had been waiting for her when she arrived at Mrs. Fowler's and had not only carried the boxes of books upstairs for her but helped unpack them. As he waited for her to arrange the stack he had handed her, he opened Horace Walpole's novel and read aloud. " 'I value not my life,' said the stranger, 'and it will be some comfort in losing it to free you from his tyranny.' Is this your favorite bedtime reading?"

Karen laughed and reached for the book. "Who could resist dialogue like that? As I recall, the heroine replies, 'Generous youth!'

"*The Mysteries of Udolpho, The Heir of Mondolpho, Melmoth the Wanderer* . . . Finally, here's one I know. I was beginning to feel like an illiterate. *Frankenstein*. Don't you have nightmares?"

Karen's smile stiffened. He couldn't know about the dreams; had that question been a sarcastic reference to the moment when she had flung herself into his arms like one of the timorous heroines of Gothic fiction? "Generous youth!" indeed!

He didn't mean anything by it, she told herself. He's being helpful and friendly, and he seems more at ease with me. Don't slap him down.

Cameron tossed the empty box aside and brought another. "They are research materials," she said. "I've read them all, of course, but not recently."

"Even this? 'Many were the wretches whom my personal exertions had extricated from want and disease . . . There was no face which lowered at my approach and no lips which uttered imprecations in my hearing.' "

Karen took the book from him. "Charles Brockden Brown's work is marred by touches of Godwinian didacticism, as one critic put it — in other words, he's a pompous son of a gun — but *Wieland* is a classic. It can scare the hell out of you once you get involved in the story."

"Hmmm," Hayes said skeptically.

"Did you ever read *Dracula*? Or *The Turn of the Screw*?"

"No. Should I?"

"They may not affect you the way they do me," Karen admitted. "Like *Wieland*, they were written by men. About women, as victims."

"I thought in *The Turn of the Screw* the kids were the victims." He added soberly, "I saw the film."

"Victims or villains? That's one of the great debates about the book. The governess was unquestionably a victim, whether from diabolic forces or growing insanity. In *Wieland*, Clara, the innocent sister, is the one terrorized, first by a villain whose only motive is love of emotional sadism for its own sake, and then by her own brother. The sexual threat in the vampire tales . . ." She broke off with an apologetic shrug. "Don't get me started."

"It's very interesting," Cameron said politely.

"Only to me and a few other pedants. Well, that's it. I may have to buy another bookcase," she added, looking at the filled shelves, from which she had removed the former contents — one shelf of *Reader's Digest* Condensed Books and a collection of ceramic animals. "Will Mrs. Fowler mind?"

"I don't see why she should. Aren't you going to need a desk?"

"That table will be adequate. I'll be transcribing by hand — that method seems to work best for me — and then making a typewritten copy."

There was no sign of life from the house, but Karen felt sure Mrs. Fowler was watching from behind the discreetly curtained front windows as they drove past. Hayes had suggested they take her car; feeling sure she knew why, Karen decided to settle that matter once and for all. "I've not only ridden in trucks that looked worse than this, I've driven them," she said firmly. "Let's skip the Southern gallantry, shall we? This is a business deal, not a date."

Hayes watched as she opened the door and climbed nimbly into the seat. "I'll give it my best shot," he said, and went around to the driver's

154

side, leaving her to close the door.

He took her to an unpretentious restaurant outside town. "The food is terrible," he said coolly. "But we're not likely to encounter any of my innumerable acquaintances or kinfolk. Is the manuscript in that briefcase you're clutching with all ten fingers?"

The abrupt question caught her by surprise. It was a logical deduction, though.

"A copy. The original is in a safe-deposit box."

His eyebrows lifted. "It's that valuable?"

"It is to me."

Indicating a booth, he slid into the seat facing her. "I have no right to ask this, but you've aroused my curiosity. What's it about?"

"The plot, you mean?"

Obviously that was what he meant. But asking the question and awaiting his response gave her time to consider his request. There was no reason why she shouldn't tell him, she supposed.

Cameron nodded. "Since you dragged all those boring books with you, I assume this is the same sort of thing. Gothic novels, isn't that what they're called?"

There was no reason why she shouldn't tell him.

Her summary of the plot didn't impress him. "So what's the point of it all? This woman — Ismene? — doesn't seem to have done much except wander around wringing her hands and finding sinister meanings in perfectly innocent activities. She's got a home and servants and friends and a kindly guardian —"

155

"I haven't gotten very far yet," Karen interrupted. "But the sinister overtones aren't just in her mind. You'll have to take my word for it."

"I guess I will. You're the authority. What would you like?"

Karen realized that the question was about food. The waitress was hovering. Without looking at the menu she ordered a tuna-salad platter; every restaurant of this type offered a tuna-salad platter.

"I don't want to sound any more ignorant than I can help," Cameron said, "but I'm trying to get this straight. You think the house in the book is based on Amberley, and that the author once lived there? That she is, in fact, an ancestress of mine?"

"It's a strong possibility. I can't prove it unless I find documentary evidence. That's why I need all the family records I can get my hands on."

"Uh-huh." He waited until the waitress had deposited their plates on the table. "You know those boxes of papers I mentioned? They're gone."

"What?" Karen gasped. "How? Gone from where?"

"They weren't in storage. I had them . . . in a place I considered secure. Especially," he added, with a wry twist of his lips, "since I had no reason to suppose they had the slightest value. The only person who could have taken them was Lisa. She must have done the job yesterday, when I was working at the house. I looked for them this morning, meaning to bring them to you."

"Can't you get them back?"

"I can try. She can't sell them without my consent, but she has as much right as I to have them in her possession. They aren't even listed in the inventory."

"Damn. You know what she's going to do with them, don't you?"

"I could offer a reasonably good guess. I've met your friend Meyer."

"He's no friend of mine," Karen protested. "Damn, damn, damn! When did he contact you?"

"Sunday. He spoke highly of you," Cameron said. "In fact, he was very civilized and above-board. Called to make an appointment, showed me his credentials, explained what he wanted and why he wanted it."

"Strictly business," Karen murmured.

"He indicated he would be willing to make me an offer. Depending, naturally, on whether the materials included anything of interest to him."

"What did you say?"

Cameron's smile didn't reach his eyes. "What any practical businessman would say. That I'd think about it. I didn't know then that Lisa had made off with the cartons. I suppose by now he's talked to her about them."

"Once he gets his hands on those papers he won't make either of you an offer. He'll take what he wants or copy it."

"I doubt Lisa would be gullible enough to hand the material over to him."

"But you were willing —"

"To go through the material with you. No offense, Dr. Holloway, but as you said, this is strictly business."

"Right." Karen thought furiously. It required all the self-discipline she possessed to make herself relax and give him a rueful, charming smile. "No offense taken, Mr. Hayes. I can only hope your cousin is as canny a businesswoman as you believe. I'd prefer to deal with you, though. I'll . . . I'll buy those papers, sight unseen. You set the price. I trust you."

He studied her thoughtfully. "You aren't a stupid woman, Dr. Holloway. Why do you —"

"Please call me Karen."

"Thank you." He wasn't stupid either. His expression indicated he was well aware of her reason for establishing a friendlier, more casual relationship, but there was no way short of rudeness that he could avoid responding in kind. "Some of my so-called friends call me Ron, or Cam, but I'm not fond of nicknames."

"Neither am I. I can't explain why this is so important to me, Cameron; only another crazy academic would understand. Bill Meyer's motives are the same as mine, except that he'd derive additional satisfaction from getting the better of me. It's a personal vendetta."

"Personal? Do you mean . . ."

Karen was tempted to confirm his assumption and spin a pathetic story that would arouse the old-fashioned chivalry she ordinarily scorned. Not that she had any scruples about using underhanded female tricks to gain her ends; fluttering lashes

158

and quivering lips only worked with men who underestimated women to begin with. But the idea
of claiming Bill Meyer as a rejected lover was too
repulsive. Ludicrous, too. Some of her colleagues
claimed he had made passes at them, but he'd
never indicated the slightest interest in her.

"No," she said. "It's just basic antipathy, I
guess. He's such a sneering, supercilious son of
a gun. He doesn't like competition, especially from
women. Look, I'm not asking you to take sides.
Just give me a fair chance."

"Certainly." He looked at her untouched plate.
"Is the food that bad or were you too distracted
to eat? Don't worry; all other things being equal,
I'd prefer to deal with you. I didn't much care
for Professor Meyer myself."

He dropped her at the apartment after promising
to speak with Lisa and let her know what had
transpired. Karen's first act was to find a safe hiding place for the manuscript — or try to. It didn't
take long to decide that the only options — under
the mattress, in the oven, behind the books —
were far from secure. She would simply have to
take it with her when she left the apartment.

After putting away a few odds and ends, she
stood looking around the small living room, uncertain as to what to do next. There were too
damned many things to do, and as she thought
of Bill Meyer doing them, one step ahead of her
all the way, she couldn't settle down. Damn Peggy,
she thought, conveniently ignoring the fact that

she had not exactly encouraged Peggy to participate. Why did she have to go rushing off on some meaningless social visit? She could be doing some of the research.

The most urgent matter was to find out all she could about the family that had inhabited the house during the years between 1775 and 1850. In fact, she was fairly certain the book had not been written before 1790 or after 1830, but even that was a broad time span. If only she could narrow it down! So far she had found no reference in the manuscript to a specific date or a specific event. Some such clue might yet turn up, but she couldn't count on it, and in the meantime Bill the Bastard was hot on the trail of the alternative sources. He knew how to go about it as well as she did, and she wouldn't put it past him to remove relevant material to prevent her from seeing it.

At this point she couldn't even be certain that Ismene was one of Cameron's progenitors. According to him the house had been in his family — one branch or another of it — from the beginning. According to Peggy, who knew her Tidewater history well, that claim was questionable. Many of the old families had died out. She'd have to trace the ownership of the property and construct a genealogy before she could make even an educated guess as to the identity of the woman who called herself Ismene. That was almost certainly a nom de plume; it wouldn't be mentioned in family records.

At least Karen hoped it wouldn't. Meyer was

probably looking through those papers at this very moment. Cursing, she picked up the briefcase and headed for the door.

Her best and nearest hope lay in the local Historical Society. Cameron had pointed out its headquarters — a handsome antebellum mansion on Main Street, which also served as the library. There were plenty of parking spaces. The shopping malls had drawn buyers away from the downtown area.

The interior of the mansion wasn't as handsome as the outside. Lack of space and meager funding had resulted in close-packed rows of metal shelves, a few worn tables and battered chairs. The young African-American woman behind the desk had her elbows on its surface and her eyes fixed suspiciously on a group of high school students gathered around one of the tables.

When Karen had explained what she wanted, the librarian shook her head. "I'm afraid we don't have anything here. The local history material is in the possession of the Historical Society, and they're only open three afternoons a week. This isn't one of those afternoons."

Figuring she might as well use all the weapons at her disposal, Karen introduced herself and threw in the names of Cameron Hayes and Mrs. Fowler for good measure. The librarian studied her with increased interest. "You're renting that — er — that apartment of Miz Fowler's? She can help you then. She pretty well runs the Historical Society."

"I can believe that," Karen murmured.

161

A discreet smile acknowledged the comment. "My name's Tanya Madison. I'd let you into the Society offices, but Miz Fowler doesn't trust anybody else with the keys. Anyhow, I don't like to leave the desk while those darned kids are hanging around. They tear pictures and maps out of the periodicals for their school papers if I don't keep an eye on them."

Karen left with proper thanks. Tanya Madison had lost interest in the darned kids; her dark eyes, bright with curiosity, followed Karen to the door.

All roads seemed to lead back to Mrs. Fowler. Karen had intended to probe the old lady's store of local legendry; she knew enough about historical research to know that oral tradition could offer useful clues. She wasn't in the mood that day for violets and Lapsang souchong, but the pervasive sense of a saturnine, dark man looking over her shoulder forced her to make the effort. After changing her jeans for a skirt and forcing her lower extremities into panty hose and pumps, she walked grumpily toward the house.

She could have sworn she saw the folds of the curtains flutter, but Mrs. Fowler allowed a decent interval to elapse before she opened the door, and her little squeal of surprised pleasure sounded authentic.

"Why, my dear, what a pleasure to see you. No, no, you aren't intruding one bit. I was just about to have tea, and I'd surely welcome company. It's been three years since my dear Harry passed on, but I still miss him. Living alone is so — so lonely, isn't it?"

Karen declined the tacit invitation to discuss her living arrangements; she felt sure Mrs. Fowler had already noticed her ringless left hand. After considerable fuss and bustle her hostess produced a second cup and what appeared to be the same plate of macaroons. They discussed the lovely spring weather for several minutes until Karen decided it was proper to ask the question that had brought her there.

"Why, surely," Mrs. Fowler exclaimed. "I'd be honored to show you our little collection, though a scholar like you probably won't think much of it. I can take you around tomorrow morning if you like. It will have to be early, I'm afraid; I have a luncheon meeting at noon. The Garden Club. I'm giving a paper on columbaria."

Karen had no idea what columbaria was — if Mrs. Fowler hadn't mentioned the Garden Club she would have assumed it had something to do with Greek architecture — and she didn't want to find out. Mrs. Fowler did not pursue the subject. In a deceptively casual voice she said, "It's the Cartright family you're interested in, I understand."

It did not seem likely that Mrs. F. was gifted with second sight. How much had Cameron told her? Or had she made an inspired guess after hearing of Karen's visits to the mansion?

"That's right," she admitted.

"I do hope you're not considerin' buyin' that old monstrosity of a house. Cameron's wasting his time, as I told him over and over. There's more than a little paint and plaster wanted; every piece of pipe and electric wire is at least fifty years old. Anyhow, you couldn't pay me to stay in that place. It gives me the cold chills to step inside."

Taken aback by the vitriolic tone, Karen could only murmur, "I haven't any intention of buying it."

"Well, I'm right relieved to hear that. Course I wish poor Cameron every success. That's all he's interested in, makin' money." She sighed. "But seems as if all the young people are that way. No respect, no interest in manners or in tradition. And Cameron has a lot of expenses. That private school for his little girl must cost a fortune, but you couldn't expect the child to go to public school, not in New Yawk, at any rate, where she'd have to mix with riffraff and colored folks."

Karen tried to conceal her surprise — not at Mrs. Fowler's assessment of the citizenry of New York City, which was typical of her class, but to the seemingly casual reference to Cameron Hayes's daughter. She knew the bright, unwinking eyes were measuring her reaction.

"He didn't mention he was divorced?" Mrs. Fowler inquired.

"There's no reason why he should," Karen said.

"Why, no, it doesn't make the least bit of difference these days . . . does it? And I certainly wouldn't say Cameron was to blame, though Maribelle was my own blood niece. They were too young, I expect. At least that's the excuse people give nowadays. I was only seventeen when I married my dear Harry, and we lived in unblemished happiness for forty-seven years." She dabbed at her eyes with the corner of her embroidered napkin. "Ah, well, it won't be long till we meet again, never to part. What was it you wanted specially to know about the Cartrights, my dear?"

By that time Karen was sorry she had introduced the subject, and she was not inclined to give Mrs. Fowler any additional information. Undeterred by her vague response, Mrs. Fowler continued to spout gossip — all of it malicious. It was rumored that the founder of the house, one Obadiah Cartright, had fled England a step or two ahead of the law. "He was a highwayman, or something romantic like that," said Mrs. F. with a sniff. "More likely a petty thief. He sure did act like one, hiding himself away in that remote region. Nobody living anywhere near, and he didn't encourage company. There's a streak of that in the family, always has been. Snobbishness. As if they considered themselves too good for other folks. There's a story that young Tom Jefferson passed by Amberley one time, and Obadiah wouldn't let him in the house. Made him and his men camp on the front lawn. Not that young Tom was anybody in particular then, but hospitality to strangers was a Virginia tradition. And another time . . ."

How long she would have gone on if Karen had not excused herself, the latter could not imagine. When she left the house and saw the sunlight golden on the lawn she felt as if she had escaped from prison — the dark cell of Mrs. Fowler's narrow little mind. What a malicious, hypocritical old bitch the woman was. If she was a friend of Cameron's, he didn't need enemies.

She was about to start up the stairs when she remembered the cupboard was bare. So was the fridge. She ought to have gone grocery shopping that morning, instead of finishing *The Castle of Otranto*. The chores of daily living took an outrageous amount of time. Bathing, brushing your teeth, acquiring and preparing the necessary nourishment, transporting yourself and your belongings from place to place . . . At least she wouldn't have to go upstairs. She had her purse with her, and the briefcase was in the trunk of the car.

Backing out of the driveway, she headed for the shopping center on the edge of town. There was a small convenience store closer at hand, but she might as well stock up and get it over with.

She had to mention Mrs. Fowler's name in order to cash a check. Another boring, necessary chore she had overlooked — establishing credit. The manager gave her a temporary card, which solved that problem, but his questions — prompted as much by small-town courtesy as by curiosity, she knew — annoyed her. She reminded herself that anonymity was impossible in such a small place. By now everybody in Mrs. Fowler's social circle must know who she was, and most of them would be speculating on why she was there . . . All at once a possible explanation for the old lady's malicious remarks about Cameron occurred to her.

She wondered why she hadn't thought of it before. Naturally a woman like that would assume another woman was in hot pursuit of a man.

By the time she had carried six bags of groceries and the briefcase up the wooden stairs that gave access to her front door she was hungry enough to eat anything that didn't bite her first. There was no microwave, so she chopped lettuce for a salad and opened a can of soup. As she sat at the kitchen table eating and reading, her thoughts kept wandering from the text she knew so well she could recite large portions from memory.

If Mrs. Fowler's interest in her love life was part of the deal, the apartment might be more trouble than it was worth. It had other disadvantages — having to carry everything up those steep steps, for one thing. Mrs. Fowler was probably violating a number of zoning laws; the plumbing and wiring were almost as antiquated as old Josiah Cartright's, and that staircase was the only exit from the apartment. Presumably it had been the chauffeur's quarters in the days when the town gentry could afford live-in servants. Nobody cared whether a chauffeur burned to death.

Karen tossed *Jane Eyre* aside and got to her feet. Reading Gothic novels was not good for the nerves, especially the nerves of a woman alone in a strange place after dark. Especially a novel that contained a horrific description of a burning house with a madwoman raging on the battlements.

From her windows she could see over all but the tallest trees. Lights shone comfortingly — from the street, from houses nearby, from one of the upper windows in the main house. The area immediately surrounding the garage was unlit, however. Odd that Mrs. Fowler, the fluttery Southern lady personified, hadn't taken the precaution of surrounding the house with floodlights. She must have a lot of confidence in her fellow citizens.

Karen wasn't worried about burglars, even a burglar named William Meyer. Anyone entering the apartment would have to climb the stairs and break down the front door. There was one window on that side, but it couldn't be reached from the stairs. She was more concerned about being able to get out than about someone else getting in. An ironic smile curved her lips as she continued her inspection. It was the classic dilemma, the contradictory threats faced by all the heroines of the traditional Gothic novel: fear of being imprisoned, unable to get out; fear of a deadly danger that could not be kept out.

However, the danger of fire was real. Garages were often used to store paint and other flammable materials, and her car was directly under her bedroom. There wasn't even a smoke detector in the apartment. Another violation of code, surely, but it wouldn't matter; by the time the detector sounded it might be too late.

Karen's lips parted in an exclamation of protest. What was the matter with her? Too many Gothics? All the same, she added another item to her mental shopping list. Taking sensible precautions was not neurotic. It was . . . sensible.

Having decided this, she closed the curtains and went calmly to bed. Nothing disturbed her sleep. She had not dreamed of enclosure and darkness since she arrived.

Mrs. Fowler was on the doorstep bright and early next morning — fifteen minutes early, to be precise. The intensity of the dislike that filled Karen at the sight of the pink, round, smiling face surprised her. She was forced to invite Mrs. Fowler in; as she hastily finished breakfast and got her things together, she felt sure Mrs. F. had wanted an excuse to inspect the apartment. Her beady little eyes missed nothing.

The Historical Society turned out to be another waste of time. The premises consisted of two rooms: an antechamber, formerly the upper landing of the mansion, which had high windows and a molded ceiling and no furniture except an antique rug and a mahogany desk; and a small cramped room behind it which contained all the society's records. Karen's hopes plummeted when she saw the piles of dusty papers heaped haphazardly on the shelves. The Historical Society was an ineffectual amateur organization — another of the games the old ladies of the town liked to play. Regally ensconced behind the handsome desk, they awaited visitors who never came and exchanged genteel gossip instead of filing materials.

It was impossible to work with Mrs. Fowler around. She was an accomplished ditherer, and she never stopped talking. Settling Karen at the single small table, she bustled from shelf to shelf shifting stacks of papers and murmuring to herself. "Now where has that box got to? I know I put it here; Flora Campbell must have moved it, she's always shifting things around . . ."

The box in question contained the correspondence of a late-Victorian Cartright lady. She had been a tireless traveler and letter writer; the letters had been sent to her friends from all over England and the Continent, and all of them contained a demand that the recipient keep the letter. "She'd go visiting and collect them after she got back," Mrs. Fowler reported with a giggle. "Quite an eccentric, Eliza was. Fancied herself an intellectual. She talks somewhere about having tea with Disraeli."

That particular letter was not to be found, though Mrs. Fowler spent fifteen minutes searching for it — to Karen's poorly suppressed fury. The other treasures eventually deposited on the table consisted of yellowed newspaper clippings, most of them obituaries of turn-of-the-century Cartrights, a collection of rust-stained caps, gloves and moldering fans ("I'm almost certain these came from Fanny . . . unless it was one of the Grants . . .") and seven volumes of Eliza's diaries.

"You can borrow those if you like," Mrs. Fowler said, with the air of one making an enormous concession. "I know you'll take proper care of them."

She had begun glancing at her watch. Karen didn't feel she could refuse the offer, though nothing on earth interested her less than Eliza

Cartright's reflections on travel. "I had hoped for something from an early period," she said hopelessly. "Or a genealogy. Surely one of the family must have belonged to the D.A.R. or the Colonial Dames."

"They were members of the Daughters of the Confed'racy, of course," Mrs. Fowler said.

"That's later in time than the period in which I am interested. It is necessary, isn't it, to submit proof that one of your direct ancestors served in the Revolution before you can join the D.A.R.?"

"Yes, naturally. My dear grandmama traced our family tree when she applied for membership; our ancestor was a Colonel Byrd, who served under Washington and Lafayette."

From what Karen had heard, there had been very few privates in the ragtag American forces.

"Now that's a very good question," Mrs. Fowler mused. "Seems to me there was a genealogy. We might even have a copy somewhere. I'll have a look for it another time."

Gently but inexorably she urged Karen toward the door. Lips compressed, Karen accepted the loan of boring Eliza's diaries. If she could persuade Mrs. Fowler to let her rummage through the shelves by herself, she might find something useful, but she doubted the remote chance was worth the effort. The D.A.R. was a better bet, even if it would necessitate a quick trip to Washington. They might have a copy of the Cartright genealogy, if one existed.

She dropped Mrs. Fowler at her front door and

then went shopping, picking up a number of odds and ends she had forgotten the previous night. After returning to the apartment she unwrapped the bundle she had bought at the hardware store. It was a heavy, unwieldy object, but it seemed to work as advertised. Karen stowed it away in the bedroom closet.

When she returned to the living room she saw something she had overlooked when she entered, her arms full of bundles. The envelope must have been slipped under the door. Her foot had kicked it farther inside.

The envelope was sealed but not addressed and the enclosure began abruptly, without salutation. "I spoke with Lisa. She assures me she will offer you the same opportunity she gave Meyer — a chance to examine the papers in her presence. Call her to make arrangements."

He had signed his full name. So much for her effort to establish a friendly relationship. Not even a "sincerely" softened the curtness of the note.

She went at once to the telephone and called the number he had given her. There was no answer.

Did Lisa's willingness to let her have a chance at the papers indicate that Bill Meyer had refused to make an offer, or that Lisa was looking for another bidder in the hope of running the price up? In either case, Karen felt she was already at a disadvantage. If there was anything of value in the collection, the first person to get a look at it would have a head start. Pacing from living room to kitchen and back again, Karen tried to reason with herself. She was behaving like a teenager on a treasure hunt. The worst possible scenario was the least likely, and even if the box contained what would amount to a signed confession by Ismene, that would only be the beginning of a long process. The winner would be the one who dealt most professionally with the material. Rushing into print, risking the chance of error, wouldn't add luster to a professional career. It might have an adverse effect. Meyer wasn't the only one of her colleagues whose idea of criticism was splitting hairs.

She called the number twice more before she persuaded herself to calm down and relax. She was eating a nutritionally balanced and carefully prepared lunch (a lettuce-cheese-and-tomato sandwich on whole-grain bread) when there was a knock at the door.

Hoping her visitor was Cameron, with good news, fearing it was Mrs. Fowler wanting to gossip, she was struck dumb by what could only be an answer to prayer. Lisa Fairweather wore a dress that had a strange resemblance to her despised pink voile. She also wore white gloves and a matching pink hat.

Lisa's first act was to remove the hat and toss it onto the sofa. Her second act was to strip off the gloves. "What a relief. I feel like a kid let out of school."

"The Garden Club?" I ought to have known, Karen thought.

"Uh-huh. The uniform is obligatory. I hate pink. And gardening."

"Why do you go?" Karen asked curiously.

"It's called good manners, honey. Also tact, respect for tradition, kindness to your elders. Would you think me rude if I begged for a cup of coffee — good strong coffee? The dear old ladies brew a beverage that looks like weak tea and tastes like warm water."

"Just instant, I'm afraid."

"That'll be fine."

She followed Karen to the kitchen and perched on a chair, chatting, while the kettle came to a boil. "I swear to you this is the first and last time I'll appear uninvited. But Cam said he'd been in touch with you, and I thought you might have called while I was out. I feel as if I owe you an explanation — an apology, even. I had no idea those papers would interest you."

Give her the benefit of a doubt, Karen thought. Aloud she said, "I suppose you couldn't have known. I haven't been exactly forthcoming about my reasons for being here. Reticence can become a bad habit with academics; I've known historians who sat on some obscure bit of research for twenty years, hoarding it like a miser."

"You don't have to tell me anything you don't want to," Lisa said, looking at Karen from under her lashes. "But I'm not exactly stupid, and if I knew exactly what you were looking for, I might be able to help. I know more about the family history than Cam does. He's never been interested."

Karen gave her a brief run-down. Lisa didn't appear to find the story interesting in itself, but the possibility of making money definitely aroused her interest. "I don't see why an old book is so valuable, but I'll take your word for it. So you want to find out who this woman was? Are you sure she was a Cartright?"

"Pretty sure. I may never know for certain." It was the first time Karen had admitted this to herself. The idea of failure was so appalling she had to swallow before she could go on. "At least I hope to come up with a strong possibility."

"Like, a woman who lived at the right period and who fits the other clues?"

"That's the general idea."

"Then some kind of genealogy might help."

"It certainly would." Karen's eyes opened wide. "Don't tell me you have —"

"I sure do. Bill practically fainted when he saw it, so I figured it must be important. He thought I didn't notice. Men never think women have right good sense, do they?"

Her smile invited Karen to share her amusement. Sisterhood was a word Lisa would probably reject, just as she would deny being a feminist. What she had invoked was the age-old secret understanding among women who manipulate men without letting the poor fools know they are being manipulated.

"You've got that right too," Karen said. "You

— you didn't let him have it, I hope."

"Course not. You want to see those papers?"

"As soon as possible."

"They're in my car." Lisa finished her coffee and rose. "What about right now?"

Chapter Six

America is now wholly given over to a d——d mob of scribbling women, and I should have no chance of success while the public taste is occupied with their trash — and should be ashamed of myself if I did succeed.

NATHANIEL HAWTHORNE,
Letters, 1854

Karen had never been particularly interested in tracing her, or anyone else's, ancestors. What was the point? Discovering that a remote predecessor had carried a musket or a pike in an old, pointless battle, or tracing a connection to a set of illiterate, bloodthirsty noblemen? Even if you could claim a distant relationship with Erasmus or Shakespeare, it didn't mean you had inherited their talents or were entitled to increased respect.

She had pictured the genealogy as a chart, a family tree with names and dates. Some of the ones she had seen had been designed to look like trees, with the names inscribed on leaves — more decorative than useful. When Lisa handed her a thick sheaf of papers her hopes soared. There might be more information here than she had expected.

She and Lisa had wrestled the heavy carton up the steps and into the living room. Lisa was stronger than she looked, and she didn't shirk her half of the weight. She sat watching in silence as Karen examined the papers.

The pages consisted of printed forms which had been filled in by hand. At the top right corner was the word "Generation." After puzzling over this for a moment Karen realized it referred to the number of generations since the original ancestor — in this case, the first settler in America. The form was fairly easy to decipher once she got the hang of it. A separate page for each individual listed the name, the names of father, mother, spouse and children, and the appropriate dates — birth, death, marriage — as well as the names of the spouse's parents. The spouse was always female, since (of course, Karen thought sourly) descent was traced through the male.

The Cartrights had been a prolific lot. The farther back in time she went, the greater the number of offspring. Six, eight, nine, twelve . . . Dates of death were not always given, but it was safe to assume that a good many of those children had died young. The infant mortality rate had been high.

She stopped at a page labeled "third generation." The name was that of Andrew Cartright, born February 26, 1771. One, two, three . . . eleven children. She felt a pang of pity for Elizabeth, Andrew's wife.

The birth dates of the children ranged from 1791 to 1810. Seven of them were girls: Catharine, Elizabeth, Maria, Sarah, Ann, Alexandra, Fanny. No dates of death were given, but there was an additional column, "Married to." The names of the husbands of Ann and Alexandra were listed. The others were described as "Never Married." Because they had remained spinsters or because they had died young? A vital question, that one, but the form did not answer it.

Karen turned back to the preceding generation, to Andrew's father Josiah. Andrew had had sisters, six of them. Some had married, some had not. The youngest of the girls would have been twenty years old in 1800, if she had lived that long.

The names fluttered around in her head, anonymous and without meaning. She hadn't expected to find a Cartright daughter named Ismene. Still, it was disappointing to discover they all had traditional, conventional names. Elizabeth, Sarah, Mary . . . Andrew's sisters and daughters were all possibles — those of them, at least, who had lived to adulthood. How did one go about finding the dates of their deaths? Was that information missing from the genealogy because it had not been available to the researcher, or because nobody gave a damn about females outside the direct line of descent?

For reasons she would have been hard-pressed to justify logically, Karen believed Ismene had been fairly young when she penned the novel. *Jane Eyre* had been written when Charlotte Brontë was thirty years old. She was dead before she was forty. Emily had been only thirty when she died, Anne twenty-nine. If genius didn't bloom early in those days, it didn't have a chance to bloom at all.

There was too much in those papers to absorb all at once. When Karen looked up she saw that Lisa was watching her with a faint cynical smile.

"Is that what you wanted?" Lisa asked.

"It's one of the things I wanted." Karen knew she had already given herself away; her passionate interest must have been plain to an intent observer.

"I can't sell it without Cam's okay."

Karen sat back on her heels and tried to marshal her arguments. "He told me he'd rather deal with me. I've already offered to buy the material, sight unseen. Now that I've seen it, I'll settle for a copy, if you don't want to part with the original."

"That's more than William was willing to do."

So Bill had seen the papers. Damn him, and damn Lisa for being such a sly, stupid, greedy little schemer. Karen said with great restraint, "Bill isn't the most scrupulous individual I've ever met. What did he offer you?"

"He wasn't willing to pay for a copy. The original or nothing, he said."

"What he was willing to pay for was sole possession of the information," Karen snapped. She fought to control her fraying temper. "He wanted to prevent me from seeing it. I don't suppose he mentioned that he has a fantastic memory? Not total recall, but damned close. He's already got what he needs to go on with. He won't give you a penny now."

"I don't understand."

"I'll try to explain. You see, all this gives me

is a list of possible candidates — women who lived during the right time period. From the literary style of the manuscript and my familiarity with the genre I can make an educated guess as to approximately when it was written. Bill probably can too; he had a chance to look through the manuscript. But I haven't found a terminus ad quem or a quo yet . . ." Seeing Lisa's smooth brow furrow, she explained. "I'll give you an example. Suppose there was a reference to the American flag and its . . . oh, let's say, fifteen stars. I'm no historian; I haven't the faintest idea when the fifteenth state was admitted to the Union. But I'd find out. And then I would know the book was written after that date."

"Why would she mention how many stars there were in the flag?"

"She didn't. She probably won't." Karen tried to control her exasperation. She had a feeling Lisa wasn't as dim as she pretended. "That was just an example. Suppose she mentions the name of a particular book she's been reading. I would know her manuscript was written after the date the book was published."

"Oh. I see what you mean."

"Good. So far I haven't found anything of that sort. At this point I'm looking at a time span of fifty, maybe seventy-five years. At least two generations. The genealogy gives the names of the Cartright women belonging to those generations, but that's all I know about them — their names. And now Bill Meyer knows those names too."

"So what do you do next?"

What Karen yearned to do was hand the whole thing over to Peggy. This wasn't her field. She tried to sound more authoritative than she felt. "The person who traced the genealogy was primarily interested in the people — the men — in the direct line of descent. There must be more information about the women in courthouse records and — and obituaries in newspapers . . ."

To her critical ears the speech displayed the abysmal extent of her ignorance, but Lisa nodded. "I get it. You'll have to go find out more about them."

"That's right. Actually, I — and Bill — could get the same information without the genealogy. It's only a short cut. By themselves the names are useless."

"That low-down hound dog," Lisa muttered. "He didn't tell me that. I suppose now that you've seen it you aren't —"

"I'd still like to buy it. Not only because I want to play fair with you but because . . . well, you never know what might turn out to be useful. Besides, I don't have that computer-style memory."

Lisa sat in silence for a while. Her face had smoothed out (Karen could almost hear a dear old mammy saying, "Frownin' leaves ugly wrinkles, honey chile.") but she was obviously thinking furiously. Finally she said, "You've been a lot more honest than he was. I'll check with Cam about the legal procedures, but so far as I'm concerned, the genealogy is yours. In fact, if you want to copy down those names right now . . ."

Karen definitely did want to.

An inspection of the remaining contents of the carton revealed nothing of interest. There were several photo albums and a box of snapshots, which Karen passed over; she might not be much of a historian, but she knew photography hadn't been in common use until the second half of the nineteenth century.

However, she indicated she was willing to stick to her original offer of buying the whole lot. Then she helped Lisa carry the carton back to the car. Lisa was favorably inclined toward her now, but she wasn't naive enough to hand over the material without payment.

In fact, Lisa wasn't at all naive. Meyer had succeeded in tricking her, not because she was stupid but because she was ignorant of the subject. Now that she had been warned she'd be on her guard. Against me, too, Karen thought. But she didn't regret her candor. In this case at least, honesty was probably the best policy. She must remember not to underestimate Lisa, or assume that the other woman was necessarily an adversary.

Leaning on the table, she studied the list of names. Elizabeth, Sarah, Maria; Georgiana, Louisa, Rebecca . . . None of them struck a chord. She straightened, with a derisive little smile at her own folly. Had she expected some inner voice would shout, "That's the one!"?

She had promised to report progress and give

183

Peggy her new address, so that evening she called the number Peggy had given her. It turned out to be a hotel. Karen was surprised; she had assumed Peggy would be staying with her friend.

Peggy answered the phone on the second ring. At first Karen didn't recognize her voice. "What's wrong?" she asked. "Are you sick?"

"Just tired." Peggy cleared her throat. "It's been a long day. How are things going?"

By the time Karen finished her report Peggy was sounding more like herself — that is, critical. "You're still not certain Ismene was a Cartright. Have you done anything about tracing the manuscript itself?"

"I've been a little busy," Karen said sarcastically. "But I think that's a hopeless cause. From what I've heard about Josiah, he was not only a pack rat but a scavenger; he'd cruise the streets picking up newspapers and other junk people left out for the trashmen. There's a better way of proving the manuscript originated at Amberley. The more I read, the more convinced I am that it's semi-autobiographical. Oh, not the plot, of course; it seems to be your standard Gothic melodrama. However, the setting — the house and the grounds — closely resembles what I've seen of Amberley. I'm going out tomorrow to look for — for a particular landmark Ismene mentions."

"For God's sake, be careful. If the place is as wild and isolated as you said —"

"I won't be alone. Cameron is out there every day, working on the house."

"Oh, so it's Cameron now, is it?"

"Don't start that," Karen said in exasperation. "Just give me the benefit of your expert advice. The genealogy wasn't as useful as I hoped. I haven't the faintest idea what to do with it."

"Don't do anything. I can be there Saturday. If you still want me to take over that part of the job . . ."

"I thought we'd settled that. Don't get huffy and self-conscious on me; I can't do this without you."

"Oh. All right, then. You might find me a hotel. I presume there is one?"

"One," Karen agreed. "I'll make a reservation for you. Unless you'd rather stay here; there are twin beds."

"You wouldn't care for me as a long-term roommate, dearie. I have too many filthy habits, none of which I intend to give up."

She sounded more like her old self. Sitting with a sick friend had to be depressing, Karen supposed; Peggy had probably had more than enough of it. And she was looking forward to Peggy's company — not only to her help, which was going to be more useful than she had anticipated, but to her sense of humor and bluff common sense.

She hadn't told Peggy the best part. Eagerly she returned to the manuscript and reread the section that would undoubtedly intrigue her friend as much as it had excited her.

The composition of the household at Ferncliffe

had changed with the arrival of Edmund's sister, who had been visiting friends on a plantation farther south. Edmund explained, in answer to Ismene's exclamation of surprise, that Isabella was in fact his half-sister, the only child of his father's second wife. The fate of Edmund's mother and the cause of the break between his father and Ismene's were still obscure to Karen and, as far as she could tell, to Ismene herself. (The dread family secret was a stock element of Gothic fiction; no doubt the horrible truth would be disclosed as part of the denouement.)

"I have missed her sadly," Edmund explained. "My own disposition, as you have no doubt observed, tends toward the reflective and melancholy. Her smiles and high spirits bring sunshine to me and to this dreary old house, as you and Clara have done. She was delighted to hear of your coming, and now that she has companions of her own age and sex, I hope I can prevail upon her to spend more time at Ferncliffe."

Like the laughing daughter of Ceres returned from her sojourn in the dismal regions of Hades (as Ismene put it), Isabella brought the spring with her. The old house was transformed; windows were thrown open to the soft breezes. The singing of birds was no more musical than Isabella's laughter, and her golden curls shone like sunlight. She and Clara instantly became bosom friends. Ismene found herself spending more and more time with her books, or in the company of Edmund. Like his, her disposition was reflective and withdrawn;

but she admitted her jealousy of Isabella even as she struggled to overcome it. Until now she and Clara had been closer than sisters. It was not pleasant to be supplanted.

Isabella's was not the only new face. Her circle of acquaintances was extensive and her nature open; there were visits, callers, social gatherings. So idyllic and light-hearted were the scenes Ismene described that the narrative would have turned into a social novel — an American *Pride and Prejudice* — had it not been for the hints of dark family secrets and one scene of pure Gothic sensationalism that didn't seem to have any bearing on the plot. It was effective, though, all the more so because of the contrast with what had gone before. To retire after an evening of cheerful social intercourse and encounter "the dark form, swathed in shadows and silence, its arm raised in somber warning," was a shock to the reader as well as to the startled Ismene. She caught one horrifying glimpse of a withered face, a toothless gaping mouth, and a blind eye covered with a white integument, before the apparition retreated into the shadows from which it had emerged. Convinced that unhealthy imagination, stimulated by too much reading — "dangerous to the delicate brains of females" — was responsible for this horrific vision, Ismene had not mentioned it to anyone in the household. Not for worlds would she have frightened Clara or roused Edmund's kindly contempt.

That had been rather stupid of Ismene, Karen thought critically. Such behavior was typical of romantic heroines, however; if they didn't conceal information and hide their feelings, there wouldn't be a plot. This was not the part of the text that had aroused Karen's fascinated interest.

A group of travelers arrived at Ferncliffe next day. They were on their way to "the city," and, as was customary in those days of poor roads and slow transportation, had decided to break their journey at the home of friends.

These visitors were not strangers to Isabella, though her brother had never met them. He welcomed them, of course; but Ismene fancied, from the ironical glance he gave her, that he was no more taken with them than she had been. Her description of the family was wonderfully satirical: the pompous, puffing father, whose waistcoat strained across his middle; the meek, faded wife; the swaggering sons and the giggling daughters. Ismene's temper was not at its best; the increasing intimacy between Isabella and Clara was difficult to bear, and the ghostly encounter the previous night had added weight to apprehensions she was reluctant to confess even to herself. But she controlled herself throughout dinner. Afterward, when the gentlemen joined the ladies for tea, the conversation took a turn that roused her to wrath. It concerned the "late unpleasantness" and the joyful success of "our forces."

Aware of her sister's imploring glances, Ismene had restrained her speech, though she felt that the words filled her mouth and pressed against her tight-closed lips to such an extent that breath was stifled. One of the young gentlemen — whose military service, it appeared, had been limited to riding around the family estate in a handsome uniform — spoke glowingly of loosing the bonds of tyranny; raising his cup, he proposed a toast to freedom and independence.

Ismene could contain herself no longer. With an impetuous movement she sprang to her feet. "And why should we women join in your self-congratulation? You gentlemen have indeed freed yourself — and from what frightful burden? Already you enjoyed the rights you still deny to half your race. What have females to celebrate in this new nation of yours? We are bound by the same unfair laws, the same stifling convention, that held us prisoner before. And what of them?"

Her gesture indicated the dusky maiden who had entered with a fresh pot of tea. "She, of course, is only a woman," Ismene continued bitterly. "But her father, brothers, sons share her servitude. Are they not men? Are they not endowed with the same rights you claim from the Creator?"

She could not go on. Emotion stifled speech. Clara's brimming eyes, Edmund's look of gentle surprise affected her more than the shocked expressions of the ladies or the flushed, infuriated countenance of Mr. Hampton. The only face that showed no trace of emotion was that of Rebecca. Mute and emotionless as an automaton, she carried out her duties.

Pressing her handkerchief to her lips, Ismene fled. Once in the sanctuary of her chamber she flung herself onto her bed and gave way to violent weeping. She

189

was unaware of Clara's presence until a gentle hand pressed hers.

"Dear sister," Clara began. Her soft voice and loving gesture broke through Ismene's defenses as no reproach could have done.

"Forgive me!" Rising, she caught Clara in a tight embrace and blotted her tears on her sister's shoulder. "How often and how rightly have you counseled me to control my passionate temperament! But, oh, Clara — to what avail is moderation? Silence is no better than cowardice and hypocrisy! If safety were to be ensured thereby, the temptation to remain silent would have practical if not moral justification. I cannot believe this is so! I cannot believe the meek inherit the earth, except for that small portion of it in which they rest at last. The same fate awaits us all, our common inheritance is the grave; why should we not demand the same happiness mankind enjoys during its brief sojourn upon this planet?"

Clara gazed upon her with a troubled brow. "Are you not happy here, Ismene? I had thought . . ."

Again Ismene caught her in a fond embrace. Even as she murmured agreement and reassurance she knew, with a cold and chilling despair, that Clara would never understand; that the one dearest to her heart was a stranger to her thoughts.

Karen let out a sigh of pleasure. What a discovery — a hitherto unknown Early American woman writer who was also a feminist and an abolitionist! She wouldn't have to plead for grants to enable her to work on the book; foundations would be lining up at her door, fighting to give her money.

In practical terms the passage gave her the terminus a quo she had hoped for. The book must have been written after 1780 — after the Declaration of Independence, the decisive Battle of Yorktown, and/or the final peace treaty between Britain and her rebellious American colonies. That didn't tell her anything new; she had already concluded, on the basis of the literary style, that a date after 1800 was most likely. Still, the reference to the Declaration of Independence and the end of the Revolution were solid facts that would look good in her introduction.

Closing her notebook, she gathered the papers together, put them in the briefcase, and stowed it away under the bed. She felt foolish doing this, like a nervous old lady hiding the family silver before retiring, but what the hell, she thought defiantly. There was nobody watching her.

One more chore before she could go to bed. She had promised Joan and Sharon she'd call when she got settled. Joan would still be up, she was a night owl.

Not only was Joan still up, she had guests. They sounded very happy. Joan was feeling no pain either, but when Karen apologized for interrupting the party and tried to cut the conversation short, Joan would have none of it. "It's just the usual bunch of my drunken, boring friends," she shouted. "They're composing limericks. I hate limericks. Wait a minute, I'll take the phone into the other room . . . Okay, that's better. I'm glad you called, I wanted to warn you. Cropsey telephoned me yesterday. He's looking for you."

"I hope to God you didn't tell him where I am!"

"What kind of lousy rat fink do you take me for?"

"Thanks," Karen said sincerely. "Did he tell you why he's trying to find me?"

"Oh, sure. You know Joe. He's got this delusion that he can persuade or bully people into doing whatever he wants. He needs to talk to you about the manuscript you found. He is at a loss to understand why you did not confide in him. You have put him in an impossible position. People keep calling and asking him about it and it is humiliating to be forced to confess he knows nothing. He is deeply hurt. He is also pissed. He didn't say that, but I figured it out."

"It'll do him good."

"I couldn't agree more. How did he find out? I swear to God I never said anything."

"I believe you. Warn Sharon, though, will you? She's so damned conscientious she might fall for his whining."

"Fear not, fair maiden, your secret is safe with us. So tell me what you've been up to."

Karen obliged with a spirited description of her encounters with Mrs. Fowler and Lisa. "I've got the genealogy," she finished. "But Bill the Bastard is on the trail and on the spot. Fortunately he was his usual detestable self and managed to piss off both Lisa and Cameron."

"It sounds like fun," Joan said wistfully. "Plots and counterplots, mysteries and treasure hunts. Maybe I should join you. I could seduce the Bastard and distract him while you —"

"No, thanks. I don't need femmes fatales, I need help in ordinary boring research. Peggy is coming on Saturday. Without wishing to denigrate your talents I think she'll be more useful than you could be."

"Oh, yeah? Is the house haunted?"

The question was so unexpected, Karen couldn't think what to say. Joan went on, her voice quite serious, "You shouldn't ignore folklore and oral tradition. The old lady with a fixation on violets sounds like a hoot, but she and her buddies could tell you some good stuff. I wasn't kidding about the ghosts, either. So-called psychic investigators crow when they find out somebody really was murdered in a house whose occupants have seen bloody specters and heard horrible screams. They don't realize it works the other way around. A tragedy inspires legends and makes nervous, imaginative people see things."

Nervous, imaginative people. She had seen nothing. But there were other senses among the normal five. The blast of cold air, palpable as a plunge into an icy river, the voice calling from empty air . . . "There aren't any ghosts," she said firmly. "Nor a tragedy."

"How do you know? Life is full of tragedies and in those far-off days . . ." The murmur of voices in the background suddenly rose in pitch,

193

and Joan said, "Oh, hell. The party's getting noisy. I'd better see what they're doing before the neighbors start calling the cops. What's your number?"

Before she got into bed Karen went through her evening routine. Going from window to window, she looked out into the darkness. Mrs. Fowler must be asleep; no light shone from her window. There was movement out there, though — branches swaying in the breeze, a shadowy shape gliding silently across the driveway. The shape was that of a cat; its eyes glowed eerily, reflecting some unknown source of light, before it vanished into the shrubbery.

All the same, Karen decided to take a sleeping pill.

The morning skies were as gloomy as Karen's mood. She hated taking sleeping pills; they took too long to wear off, leaving her grumpy and groggy. She was finishing her second cup of coffee and feeling slightly less inclined to slash her wrists when a faint sound got her onto her feet and into the living room. Someone at the door? The sound had not been a knock. Then she saw a white triangle next to the door. It moved toward her, growing larger, turning from a triangle into a rectangle.

Karen opened the door. Cameron Hayes got to his feet. "I was just leaving a note for you," he explained unnecessarily.

"So I see." She wasn't inclined to ask why he favored this means of communication. Maybe it was an old Southern custom. Realizing that her voice had been less than welcoming, she added, "Would you like a cup of coffee?"

"No, thanks." He stepped back. "I just wanted to tell you that you can have that box of papers. Does fifty bucks seem fair to you?"

"I'd have paid more," Karen admitted, her mood miraculously improved.

"So I gathered. I'll deliver it this evening, if you like. Or you can call Lisa if you want it earlier."

"This evening will be fine. Come in and I'll give you a check."

He retreated again until he was backed up against the wooden rail that enclosed the landing. "That's okay, you can pay on delivery. I want to finish up some things at the house. It's supposed to rain tonight."

"I'll follow you there if I may."

"Sure." He hesitated; she could see courtesy and curiosity vying for precedence. Curiosity won. "Anything in particular you're after?"

"I was hoping I could have a look at the cellar."

He obviously didn't like the idea, but after a moment he said, "I guess this would be as good a time as any. The water should have subsided by now, and if it rains again tonight . . . It's a filthy mess, though. Wear — uh — something old. And boots, if you have them."

He hadn't looked directly at her except for the first startled acknowledgment of her sudden appearance. Amused, Karen went to her room and exchanged her lace-trimmed pale-blue, rosebud-embroidered robe for jeans and sweatshirt. The robe was another of the follies she had committed under the influence of Joan and Sharon; she wore it, in private, because it would have been a waste of money to buy another, more practical garment. It must have given Cameron a false impression, especially after the pink frilly gown she had worn to tea. He had been embarrassed, bless his innocent little heart. Or perhaps he had feared Mrs. Fowler would see them in what she would certainly interpret as a potentially compromising position. If she could see Mrs. Fowler's window, Mrs. F. could undoubtedly see the apartment from that same window, and it wouldn't surprise her to learn that Mrs. Fowler kept a pair of binoculars on the windowsill.

Her present ensemble ought to convince Cameron her wardrobe was not limited to business suits and frilly frocks. She studied the effect in the mirror as she applied lipstick. The jeans had a patch on one knee and the color had faded to a blue almost as pale as that of the robe, with streaks of yellow paint still showing from the time she had redecorated her apartment. The sweatshirt featured the President of the United States, in glowing blue neon, playing a blue saxophone. How was that for making a statement? She slid her feet into sneakers, pulled her boots from the closet, collected her purse and the briefcase, and went out. She could have sworn she saw the curtains of Mrs. Fowler's bedroom window twitch.

The air was heavy with moisture and warm

enough to make the sweatshirt unnecessary. She might be glad of it later, though, if the cellar was as damp and chilly as cellars often were.

Cameron had left the gate open. Not until she reached it did Karen realize the pillar of smoke she had seen came from the vicinity of the house. Apprehension dried her mouth as she pushed her car along the drive at a speed that endangered the muffler, the tail pipe and a few other important appendages. Had her premonition of fire been born of concern, not about the apartment but about the house? Subconsciously she must have noted its vulnerability — the time-dried wood, the paint cans and other flammable materials . . . Not the house, she prayed silently. Please, not the house. Not yet. I'm not through with it.

The fire was outside the house, not inside. A column of flame rose skyward from a blackened pile in the cleared space before the steps. Karen slammed on the brakes, and Cameron Hayes came around the corner of the house carrying an armful of broken branches. He stopped and stared, and then ran toward her. She was already backing away. When she stopped the car, at a safe distance from the blaze, he thrust his head in the open window.

His expression led her to expect a blistering reprimand. Instead he took a deep breath and said, "Sorry. I should have warned you I intended to burn trash."

"My fault, I was driving too fast. I was afraid the house had caught fire."

"And that you'd see me on the roof, screaming out curses, like the first Mrs. Rochester?"

Karen's face grew warm. She hadn't even considered danger to him, she had been too concerned about the house. Apparently he took the blush for maidenly confusion, for he went on, "Your lecture on Gothic novels aroused my curiosity. As you have probably deduced, I've been reading *Jane Eyre.*"

So had she. In her present mood she was abnormally sensitive to coincidences — if that was what they were. "Why that book?" she asked.

"Because it was there, I suppose. In the bookshelf."

The answer was so obvious she was ashamed she hadn't thought of it. Brontë's masterpiece was a classic, often assigned reading for high school or college English courses. Cameron hadn't struck her as the sort of man who kept his old schoolbooks, but one never knew.

"I hope you enjoyed it."

"More than I expected," he admitted. "The first part was kind of boring, but it livens up after Rochester appears on the scene. Though what she saw in him —"

"He represented freedom, escape from the narrow confines of a woman's world, communion with an original, expanded mind —"

" 'Original' is right. He pretends he's in love with another woman, lies to her about his crazy wife —"

"Nobody's perfect."

He gave her a startled look; then his face dissolved in laughter. "That's an original, expanded way of looking at it, I suppose. Okay, I can take a hint. Ready to explore?"

Karen got out of the car. "Yours is an enlightened, liberated viewpoint, actually," she said demurely. "A lot of male critics consider Jane a prissy, priggish pain in the butt."

"I didn't say she wasn't." His eyes inspected her from the top of her head to her sneakered feet. "Didn't you bring boots? You're going to need them."

"They're in the car."

"Good. The water's gone down, but there's a lot of mud on the floor. And other things."

"I'm not afraid of snakes, if that's what you mean. Or mud."

"Snakes, spiders, rats. Very Gothic." He smiled. "I'm sure you could tackle a tiger single-handed, but I'd prefer to come with you. Can you wait half an hour or so? I want to let the fire die down before I leave it."

He had phrased it as a request, but he had every right to insist on her compliance. It was his house, and his liability, if she accidentally injured herself. She told herself that that was why she acquiesced — not because she was afraid to go alone. But only the need to search for what might be the final proof of her belief that Ferncliffe had been Ismene's home could have forced her to suggest the visit to the cellar. If an empty attic and a harmless woodland path had sent her imagination into overdrive, how would it react to a dank dark underground cavern, the quintessence of Gothic nightmare?

It wouldn't misbehave in his presence, she assured herself. Sheer pride would inhibit another expression of "womanly" squeamishness.

After Cameron had returned to his fire she leaned against the car and studied her notes. In passing, Ismene had mentioned a number of the features of the fictitious house. If they matched the features of the real house, the identification would be strengthened, even if she didn't find what she hoped to find in the cellar.

One difficulty was the question of how much had changed since the early nineteenth century. Karen decided she wouldn't worry about that now. It was a complicated question that might necessitate consulting an expert in architectural restoration. Some parts of the house were obviously relatively late in date; others, like the main block and the long wing jutting out behind it, were just as obviously very old. The house Ismene had described had two such wings. One might have been destroyed, in a fire or otherwise, but there ought to be some traces of it remaining.

She was stalling, and she knew it. Sooner or later she would have to face that cold hallway. Squaring her shoulders, she went to the door.

It wasn't as bad as she had feared. Knowing what to expect helped. So did her memory of the dreadful blast in the attic. By comparison, this was like a balmy afternoon in Bermuda.

Still, her fingers were stiff and clumsy with cold when she heard the front door open and Cameron called to her. "Ready when you are."

He studied her clipboard curiously, but said only, "You'd better leave that and your purse in the kitchen. You'll need both hands."

"For climbing the walls in case I'm attacked by a tiger?" Karen inquired. She followed him through the maze of corridors that ended in the kitchen. No question about it, the temperature in this part of the house was a lot more comfortable. "What on earth have you got down there?"

"You'll see. Here." He handed her a flashlight and took another from the same drawer before leading her back toward the front of the house.

She had not noticed the narrow wooden door. It was in a deep alcove under a staircase — not the one in the front hall, another, even narrower, flight that might have been the servants' stairs of the original house. The hinges shrieked when Cameron pulled the door open. Reaching inside, he pressed a light switch.

Why the flashlights? Karen wondered. She started down the steps. They were only boards nailed onto a support, with no risers between. She took hold of the railing and felt it give; Cameron's hand closed firmly over her arm. "It would be a grave error to depend on that," he said. "I haven't got around to replacing it yet."

He held her arm until they reached the bottom of the steps. She was beginning to see why he had told her she would need both hands free. The

201

floor was slimy with a mixture of mud and the crumbled mortar that had fallen from the stone wall. The roughly shaped stones had once been painted. Little of the paint or the mortar remained; the latter substance wasn't modern cement, but a pale-brown, crumbling mixture. It must be part of the original foundations, but only one wall was old. The others looked like partitions of wood or plasterboard. A single bare bulb dangled from the ceiling, which was crisscrossed with a maze of pipes. The only objects visible were an oil tank and a huge antique furnace.

"Where are the tigers?" she asked. "This is no worse than my parent's basement before they installed a sump pump."

"That was one of the useful items Uncle Josiah refused to buy," Cameron said dryly. "He decided it was cheaper to seal this room off and let the rest of the place rot. I presume it's the picturesque part you want to see."

Without waiting for an answer he headed for a door opposite the stairs. It screeched horribly across the floor as he wrenched it open. Karen stepped carefully across a hole in the floor that must act as a drain, and went to Cameron's side.

The stench that issued from the open door, compounded of mold, damp, and other elements she did not want to identify, was so strong it made her gag. Her companion gave her a sardonic look. "Sure you don't want to change your mind? Come on, then. Mind the steps."

He took her arm again and turned on his flashlight. Karen followed suit. The pale-yellow beams were lost in the cavern of darkness ahead. There were three steps, rickety and slippery with wet. Cameron hadn't exaggerated about the mud. It squelched disgustingly under Karen's booted feet when she stepped down onto the floor.

Cameron's voice was eerily magnified by echoes as they moved slowly forward. "This part of the cellars was never electrified. When they installed central heating — around the turn of the century, it must have been — they raised the floor of that one section in order to make the furnace more accessible. I suppose the old boy's decision to shut the rest of it off makes some sense; there was ample storage space, in outbuildings and in the house, and it would cost a fortune to renovate this area. It should be of interest to historians, though; some parts are original, and over two hundred years old."

Karen was becoming accustomed to the odor now; it was nothing worse than damp and decay. She was relieved to find that her discomfort was entirely physical. The air was no colder than that of any other underground region, and although she would have preferred to be elsewhere she had no feeling of mindless panic.

"Stop a minute and have a look around," Cameron said.

It was sensible advice. She had had to concentrate on keeping her footing; the mud was as slippery as ice, and the idea of falling into it, getting the noxious stuff on her clothes and skin, was not attractive. Settling her feet firmly, she sent the beam of her flashlight slowly around the room.

The image of the cave was irresistible — limitless caverns, natural prisons of windowless stone, deep in the bowels of the earth, lightless and inescapable — the classic metaphor of confinement and burial alive. The stone walls shone greasily green with lichen. The indescribable substance underfoot covered her feet; pools of sickly iridescence marked its surface. Somewhere, under the slime, was a solid surface. Stone, brick? She was not tempted to investigate.

The wall on the right was blank except for a barred opening high against the rough wooden boards of the ceiling. A window well, she thought, but not the one into which she had fallen; this one was dark, its covering still intact. On the walls ahead and to her left, some of the stones had been shaped into arches. If there had been doors, they were gone; darkness as solid as wooden paneling filled the openings.

"There are two more rooms like this straight ahead," Cameron said. "One opening out of the other. The arch on the left leads to a passageway with two rooms on either side and another at its end. I made a rough plan; if you'll accept a copy of that in lieu of further exploration, you will do me and yourself a favor. The rest of the place is just like this, only worse."

He was trying to control his voice, but she heard the strain in it. "Are you claustrophobic?" she asked, without stopping to think that it might not be a tactful question.

"Doesn't it affect you that way?"

He wouldn't admit it, of course. "I'm not a happy person," Karen said frankly. "But the smell and the slime and the mud bother me more than the sense of enclosure. We can go. I'm sorry to have inflicted this on you."

"Not at all." But his movement was a little too abrupt; turning, he slipped and had to take a few quick running steps to keep from falling. The mud sloshed and splashed. Viscous drops struck Karen's hand and clung like glue.

"Sorry," Cameron said breathlessly.

"Oh, stop apologizing!" Karen resisted the impulse to scrub her hand against the seat of her jeans. The mud stank horribly. It would be easier to wash her hands than her pants.

She moved cautiously toward the steps, where Cameron joined her. His breathing was too quick and too loud, though he was obviously fighting to control it. Men, she thought contemptuously. Why hadn't he admitted he suffered from claustrophobia? An impulse she was soon to regret prompted her to say cockily, "No tigers, no snakes."

She heard his breath catch. The beam of his flashlight swung to one side. Greenish black, thick as her wrist, scales shimmering with wet, it was framed clearly in the light before it slithered out of sight, with a wet sucking sound.

As she stumbled back, feeling her feet sliding out from under her, Cameron's arm caught her and pulled her against him with a force that drove the breath from her lungs.

"Just a water snake," he said. "Perfectly harmless. There are copperheads in the woods, though, so if you go exploring watch where you put your feet and hands."

He did that on purpose, Karen thought furiously. He knew the damned thing was there; he must have heard or seen something I missed. Of all the silly, childish tricks — getting back at me because I witnessed his moment of weakness . . .

"You can let go of me now," she said through clenched teeth.

"As soon as you get up those stairs safely."

"Thank you so much."

"Not at all."

Karen made no attempt to free herself. She had found what she wanted. Every detail matched Ismene's description of the cellars — including one particular detail that gave the final proof of her hypothesis. The capstone of the arch that opened into the passageway had been shaped, by nature or a sculptor's hand, into the shape of a monstrous head.

Chapter Seven

Alas! A woman that attempts the pen
Such an intruder on the rights of men,
Such a presumptuous Creature is esteem'd
The fault can by no vertue be redeem'd.

ANNE FINCH,
Countess of Winchelsea, 1713

It is whispered, by those whose memories (though dimmed by the passage of time and warped by the influence of pagan superstition) extend into the distant past, that the stone was discovered by workers clearing the fields for cultivation. It was one among many such boulders; but it alone had the appearance of having been shaped by deliberate intent. The poor ignorant workers fled, screaming in terror, when this diabolic countenance glared up at them from the soil from which they had freed it; and threats (and worse — for those were harsher times than ours) were required to induce them to carry it to the site where the mansion was even then in the process of construction. Its builder was a man of grim and sardonic humor, yet not unlearned; it suited his fancy to incorporate the grimly visage into the foundations of his home. The "genus loci," he called it; the demon of the house.

"Yet," Edmund went on reflectively, "no sensible individual could credit the wild legends that attribute

this stone to an abandoned and forsaken temple: the site of frightful pagan rites. Old Obadiah may have intensified its features by design; but surely the original face was accidental: the work of nature, which as we know sometimes produces such anomalies."

"I have no doubt you are right," Ismene replied, studying the carven surface. Its sunken eye pits and gaping mouth, the suggestion of fangs rimming that scream and the stony protuberances on the brow were hideous in the extreme; but the shiver that ran through her body was not produced by superstitious terror. What sort of mind, she wondered, could admire, much less preserve, such a horrid travesty? "The aborigines of this region," she continued, "did not, I believe, build in stone, or carve graven images of their gods. Moreover, the features recall to mind the demonic visages sometimes found in medieval cathedrals, or even the rude local godlings of the ancient Greeks."

"Your reaction is as reasonable as I had hoped and expected," Edmund said approvingly. "You do not fear the task I ask you to assume, then? The keys to storage vaults and wine cellar should be in the hands of the mistress of the house, but my sweet sister will not come here; it resembles too closely the haunted monasteries and demon-ridden caverns featured in her favorite novels; and she swears sheeted forms gibbered and rattled chains at her on the sole occasion when she ventured here. She is of a sensitive nature and reads too much."

It was not difficult to understand why a sensitive nature would shrink from that ambience, Ismene thought. The smell of mold and damp, the rough-hewn stones of the enclosing walls, the darkness that filled the passageway ahead and the chambers beside and behind her did indeed conjure up the worst excesses of sensational fiction. The candelabrum held by the silent servant only intensified the shadows beyond the reach of the light. The man stood rigid as an ebon statue, as bereft of animation as the object of furniture whose function he served.

Karen closed the manuscript. Ismene must have seen that carved stone, there could not be two such unusual ornaments in old American mansions. And what woman other than a member of the household would have the opportunity to see it? Delicate lady visitors were not taken on tours of the cellar.

She had come straight back to the apartment, leaving Cameron to his labors — and thankful, probably, to see the last of her. Though she had rinsed her boots and her hands before leaving, the smell of the dank cellar filled the car like a fog of poisonous gas. She could almost believe a faint whiff of it still lingered, though she had changed and showered.

Perhaps Ismene's description of the cellar had prompted the impression. She had felt compelled to reread that part of the manuscript, even though she knew her memory was accurate. Picking up a spoon she began to eat the soup she had heated. No wonder she was hungry; it was later than she had realized. Leaning back in her chair she savored the pleasure of self-congratulation. She could hardly wait to tell Peggy of her discovery. That detail clinched the identification. Peggy would probably insist on finishing the job of comparing the actual house to Ismene's description, but there was no longer any doubt in her mind.

The skies had darkened, though the rain still held off. She could, with a clear conscience, devote the rest of the afternoon — what was left of it — to the manuscript. She had gone to the stove to put the kettle on for coffee when she heard a sound at the front door. Surely it couldn't be Cameron with the papers he had promised to bring. He would work till rain or darkness forced him to stop. And surely this time he wouldn't poke a note under the door instead of knocking.

The note was there, rustling as it moved across the floor. Karen flung the door open.

Not Cameron — Mrs. Fowler in all her glory, violet-crowned and triple-chinned, like a Hogarthian caricature of a Greek goddess. She started back with a little scream. "Oh, dear, I've disturbed your work. I had no intention of doing that, I was just leaving you a little note."

"That's quite all right," Karen said untruthfully. What the devil did the woman want? Checking up to make sure her tenant wasn't entertaining a male visitor? "Won't you come in?"

"Oh, no, I've been nuisance enough already." But she continued to stand there, feet firmly planted, face beaming. "It's the Literary Society, you see. Our next meeting is Wednesday and I hoped you'd be able to give your little talk then.

I know it's short notice, but I'm sure that won't be a problem for a scholar like you, and your nice friend assured me you'd be real hurt if we didn't ask you."

The series of bland, unfounded assumptions — that she had promised to speak, that extemporaneous lectures were no problem, and that she would be hurt if she were ignored by the Literary Society — left Karen momentarily speechless. Then she managed to focus her confused brain on the last part of Mrs. Fowler's speech.

"My nice friend," she repeated.

"Yes, that nice Professor Meyer. He certainly does admire you." Mrs. Fowler gave her a meaningful twinkle.

"When did . . . I didn't realize you knew him."

"Why, I didn't, till he telephoned me yesterday evening. He was courteous enough to invite me to lunch today. Such a pleasure, talking to an intellectual gentleman like that. He said all sorts of sweet things about our little literary group; I didn't realize we were so well known." Her pause invited a corresponding compliment from Karen, but the latter was still too dumbfounded to produce it. With a deprecating chuckle Mrs. Fowler continued, "You can just blame him for encouraging me to ask you. I wouldn't have dared otherwise."

A sudden gust of wind set the violets on her hat to dancing madly. "Please do come in," Karen said. "I can't quite . . . I'll have to check my schedule."

"Certainly, my dear, I know how busy you are.

That's why I was going to leave my little note, so you would have a chance to think about it."

Karen thought about it. She'd have to accept — or leave town for a few days. Bill had done his usual expert job of setting her up. As he was capable of doing when he chose, he had charmed the socks off Mrs. Fowler; she'd never believe he had acted out of malice, and she would be deeply offended if Karen turned her down without good and sufficient reason. Nothing less than a death in the family would suffice; despite her modest disclaimers, she obviously had a high opinion of her "little literary society."

"I guess I can manage it," Karen said. "Next Wednesday, you said?"

"How lovely! I'll notify the members right away; I'm sure such a famous speaker will attract a large group. Now as to your topic . . . Something along the lines of 'Lady Writers'? Or perhaps 'Lady Writers of the Nineteenth Century'? That's your specialty, I know."

Karen wondered whether the topic was Mrs. Fowler's idea, to make certain she wouldn't offend the audience by quoting from current "unladylike" writers. It was more likely that the topic had been Bill Meyer's idea of a joke. Oh, well, she thought resignedly, I can always talk about Jane Austen. She should be ladylike enough. The literary mavens of Blairsville wouldn't notice Jane's delicately barbed comments about male-female relationships unless someone pointed them out.

Mrs. Fowler retreated in triumph, holding

tightly to the rail as she descended the steps. She had tiny feet; at least they looked small compared to the mass of the body they supported so dangerously. And of course she was wearing dainty high-heeled shoes. Karen closed the door and clumped, flat-footed, back to the kitchen.

When the rain began she hardly noticed it, except as a soothing background noise. She was fully absorbed in Ismene's story.

As she had expected, there were more visits to the grim cellars. They formed a dark counterpoint to the descriptions of sunny spring days and cheerful social engagements, and symbolized Ismene's unhappiness as she watched her sister's increasing fondness for Isabella. It was not an attachment Ismene could approve; Isabella seemed to her frivolous and heartless, and under her influence Clara's corresponding faults of character (reluctant as her sister was to admit them) were encouraged, to such an extent that she came to resent openly Ismene's gentle remonstrances. Increasingly isolated, by her own temperament as well as by Clara's coldness, Ismene wandered the wild acres of the estate, seeking solace, as she put it, in the immutable charms of nature. It was while she was engaged in one of these rambles that she came upon the little stone house.

A knock at the door interrupted Karen at this thrilling point in the narrative, and she came back to reality with a start, realizing that the sound she had scarcely noticed was that of rain beating on the roof and that the room was filled with a cavelike gloom, except for the single lamp that illumined her work. She hurried to open the door.

Cameron looked as if he had gone swimming in his clothes. Rain had darkened his hair and plastered it to his head. The box he carried had been covered with a tarpaulin, but water had collected in its folds and ran down onto the sagging floor of the porch, from which a miniature waterfall poured down the steps.

"Good God," Karen gasped. "Come in — hurry up, don't just stand there. Is this a flood or what?"

"Just a good old spring rain," Cameron said, depositing the carton on the floor and removing the tarpaulin. "It's all right — the box isn't wet. The same can't be said for your rug, I'm afraid."

"It's not my rug," Karen said callously. "Stand still; I'll get a towel, or . . . or two. "

He brushed the wet hair back from his face and grinned. He looked unreasonably cheerful for a man whose clothes clung wetly to his body and around whose soaked shoes a puddle was forming. "Your entire supply would be inadequate for the job. I got pretty wet out at the house, so I decided I might as well deliver the carton before I changed clothes. Sorry about the mess."

"Wait, I'll write you a check," Karen began.

"The sooner I get out of here the less damage I'll do to your — Miz Fowler's — carpet. You can pay me later. I trust you."

He was out the door before Karen could reply. She shrugged. If he was that determined to avoid even the appearance of a social relationship, that was okay with her. Had there been a suggestion of sarcasm in his final comment? She decided there had been, and went in search of a cloth to wipe up the puddle. He'd been right about the towel situation. The ones Mrs. Fowler had supplied her tenant were extremely threadbare.

There was something rather soothing about rain if you didn't have to go out in it. And if it didn't come in. A smaller puddle on the kitchen floor told her that Mrs. Fowler needed to have the roof repaired. Karen put a saucepan under it and went in search of additional leaks. She found two more, one in the bedroom — not over the bed, fortunately — and another in the corner of the living room.

She only had three saucepans. Rummaging under the sink, she found a couple of empty coffee cans, rust-stained from, she suspected, similar usage in the past. The *plink* of raindrops onto metal made a particularly pervasive, annoying sound.

The rain wasn't as soothing as she had thought. She roamed restlessly through the apartment, unable to settle down. There were a number of things she could turn to: the manuscript, with its evocative, exciting reference to a house of stone; the genealogy, which she hadn't examined in detail; her notes on the discovery she had made in the cellar. They ought to be copied and expanded while the incident was still fresh in her memory.

She wasn't in the mood for any of those things. Instead she set to work preparing supper, hoping the mechanical, domestic chore would settle her nerves. A good healthy supper — broiled fish fillets, salad, brown rice with herbs, and chopped vegetables. She had finished this repast and was feeling more cheerful when the phone rang.

Hoping it wasn't Peggy announcing she would be delayed, she was pleased to hear Joan's voice.

"I'm bored," the latter announced flatly.

"You, the party animal?"

"No party tonight. I'm alone, I'm slightly hung over, and it's pouring down rain. Dreary."

"Ditto."

"Is it raining there too?"

"Yes, it is. This is long distance," Karen reminded her. "Did you call to talk about the weather? Have you heard anything more from Joe Cropsey?"

"No to both. I called to find out what thrilling new discoveries you made today. My life is so dull I derive vicarious excitement from listening to the adventures of my friends."

"I'm sorry about the beach house," Karen said. "If you had to pay a cancellation fee —"

"You've got to stop being so defensive. I wasn't even thinking about that."

"Oh, yeah?"

"Yeah. I didn't have to pay anything, they had a waiting list a mile long. In case your conscience is still bothering you, I'm going to spend a glorious week in the mountains instead. With Sharon."

"Doing what?"

"I said, with Sharon. You know what her idea

216

of a vacation is. It's some kind of spa. Riding, hiking, tennis, golf. And when we tire of those amusements there's a completely equipped exercise room."

Karen laughed. "Is Sharon bullying you? You don't have to go, you know."

"It won't be so bad, I guess," Joan said gloomily. "I could stand to lose a few pounds. Now tell me about your unhealthy, dangerous — dare I hope fattening? — life."

Karen described her supper. Joan groaned. "It sounds disgusting. Not even a glass of wine? A chocolate-chip cookie? You're inhuman. What did you do today?"

"I explored a dark, muddy, odorous basement with a guy who went out of his way to show me rats, snakes and spiders."

"You lucky devil. Who was the guy? Bill Meyer?"

"If you ever catch me in a dark basement with Bill Meyer, I'll agree to let Sharon psychoanalyze me." She gave Joan a lurid description, including one of the snake, but did not mention the carved stone face. That information and other confirmatory evidence of her theory were best kept to herself until she was ready to spring the finished work on an admiring world.

"If you won't let me distract Bill, how about this other guy? You can't handle both of them."

"I have no intention of handling either one of them." Hearing a ribald chuckle from the other end of the line, she added, "Don't say it. Thanks for calling, Joan. I was in a rotten mood and you've cheered me up.

"Is that a hint I should hang up?"

"This is costing you a fortune."

"Too true. Okay, I'll say nighty-night. Take care of yourself."

Her frame of mind considerably improved, Karen was able to get some work done. She forced herself to type up her notes on the exploration of the cellar, so she could present Peggy with a neat workmanlike report, before she went back to the manuscript. It proved to be disappointing; after her first description of the stone house ("windowless and squat, like an extrusion from the rocky skin of the earth, held fast by giant vines that crawled across roof and walls") Ismene went into a long digression about the rights of man and Rousseau's theories of the noble savage. Pious moral soliloquies were common in novels of that type, and it wasn't the first time Ismene had succumbed to the pleasure of preaching to the reader, but Karen had to fight to keep from skipping ahead — reading the narrative instead of transcribing it, line by slow line. She knew the futility of that, however. The writing was too cramped and faded, the text too obscure. It had to be deciphered rather than read.

Sheer boredom finally forced her to call it a night. Tucking the manuscript and her notes into the briefcase, she stowed it away and got ready for bed. The drip of water into the coffee can had slowed, which made it even more annoying; she found she was waiting for the next plink and counting the seconds that elapsed between them. Muttering irritably she wadded up a few paper towels and put them in the coffee can. It seemed to work.

The rain had slackened. It fell slow and steady on the water-soaked ground, glistening on the leaves of the shrubs under Mrs. Fowler's window, dimming the glow of the streetlight. No other lights were visible. With moon and stars hidden by clouds, the night was very dark. Nothing moved in the blackness, not even a prowling cat. Cats had better sense than to go out in the rain.

So do I, Karen thought. Joan's mention of wine and chocolate had made her wish she had stocked up on both, but she hadn't wanted them badly enough to go looking for them. Tomorrow she'd get a bottle of Scotch for Peggy, and pick up something for supper. Peggy probably wouldn't arrive until late afternoon. Rather than go out for dinner they could settle in for a prolonged Show and Tell session. They had a lot to catch up on.

Mrs. Fowler's bedroom window shone steadily through the rainy night. Rather late for the old lady, Karen mused. Perhaps she was refreshing her memory of "lady authors of the nineteenth century."

Karen made a face and closed the curtains. Why hadn't she refused that invitation? It would kill an entire day. What a wimp she was! At least I won't have to worry about fire tonight, she consoled herself, as she got into bed. Everything is too waterlogged to burn.

Fire and water and earth were three of the basic elements of Greek science. The fourth was air. Earth, in the form of the primeval cave, was a recurrent motif in Gothic novels. How would the other elements apply? Fire was not so common. There was the horrific blaze in *Jane Eyre*, of course — the terrible but cleansing force that had removed the barrier to Jane's happiness with Rochester and destroyed the house that symbolized enclosure and imprisonment. And the blast of supernatural lightning that had burned the elder Wieland to a nasty crisp. There must be other examples, as well as examples of the other pair of elements. Hadn't she read somewhere that two were considered masculine and the other two feminine? Fire would be masculine, of course. It was aggressive, active, destructive. And by the standards of those super–male chauvinists, the Greek philosophers, earth could only be considered feminine — passive, acted upon instead of active. It would make an interesting article: "The Aristotelian Elements in the Gothic Novel." Happily distracted by useless speculation, Karen drifted off to sleep.

She woke after another dreamless night to find sunlight filling the room. Mrs. Fowler's curtains were as thin as her towels, and they didn't quite cover the window.

Glancing out the uncurtained bathroom window as she brushed her teeth, she saw that the ground was steaming. It was going to be a hot, sticky day.

Poor old Cameron, she thought contemptuously; he's probably out there right now, wading through soggy leaves and trying to find something dry enough to paint or burn. The man seemed absolutely driven. He must need money very badly to work so hard, but if he was expecting to recoup the family fortunes by selling the family mansion he was unduly optimistic.

After a hasty breakfast she made a mental list of errands. Liquor store, grocery store, Laundromat. She hadn't brought many clothes, and the ones she had worn the day before retained a faint but disgusting smell. There was a huge puddle outside her door; the floor of the landing wasn't just uneven, it was absolutely caving in. Larger elongated puddles filled the ruts in the graveled driveway. It must have rained hard. The cellars at Amberley would be flooded again. Lucky she had examined them already. She'd never have had the courage to wade through several feet of filthy water.

Locking her briefcase in the trunk of the car, she backed out of the garage and headed for the shopping center. The Laundromat first, she decided. The windows of the car were open, but it seemed to her that a faint unpleasant odor emanated from the bundle of clothes in the back seat.

The place was doing a brisk business. She had to wait for a machine. As she stood tapping her foot impatiently, she saw a familiar face. It was bent over a book, but she recognized the tight-clustered black curls and heavy horn-rimmed glasses, despite the fact that the body to which it belonged was clad in jeans and an enveloping loose shirt instead of a tailored dress. The librarian — what was her name? Tanya something. The glasses must be an affectation, an attempt to look older and more authoritative. Most women of that age wore contacts. Karen edged closer, trying to see the title of the book and failing, since it was covered with brown paper. She ought to have brought something to read. She hadn't used a Laundromat for a long time; she had forgotten she'd probably have to wait.

The book was obviously absorbing. Tanya didn't look up until her machine had stopped spinning. She started to remove the contents and then saw Karen.

"Good morning. I hope you weren't waiting for this washer. I have another load to do."

"I'm waiting for my turn, as is proper," Karen said with a smile. "To be honest, I was trying to see what you're reading. I'm one of those compulsive people who is driven to read book titles."

Tanya peeled back the brown paper and displayed the book — the new Toni Morrison. "Have you read it?"

"I admire her work a great deal, but I haven't read that one. I usually wait till they come out in paperback," Karen admitted. "I can't afford to buy hardcovers."

"Neither can I. This is from the library. It's one of the few perks of the job, getting first crack at the best-sellers."

Karen's number came up then. She tossed her armload of clothes into the machine the woman had indicated and sat down on the bench next to Tanya.

"I hear you're addressing the lit'rary society next week," the other woman said, giving the word a sardonic accent.

"I got railroaded into it. How did you know? I only agreed yesterday."

"Miz Fowler was in bright and early this morning with a handful of artistically hand-lettered posters. She stuck one on the bulletin board and another on the front door."

"That must have been what she was doing so late last night," Karen muttered. "Damn!"

Tanya laughed. She was much more relaxed than she had been at the library. "Don't you court publicity?"

"Not when I'm speaking on 'Lady Authors of the Nineteenth Century,'" Karen said wryly. "I'll never live it down."

"You weren't the one who selected the subject, then."

"Good God, no. I suppose Mrs. Fowler wanted to make sure I wouldn't shock the audience by quoting from Morrison, or Sylvia Plath, or some other 'unladylike' writer."

"It would shock them, all right."

"Don't tell me you're a member."

"Good God, no," the other woman repeated, grinning. "I just might attend this meeting, though. Unless you'd rather I didn't."

"I may be in need of one sympathetic listener. Promise you won't laugh or make faces."

"It's a deal." Tanya got to her feet. "I've got to get back; my so-called assistant is manning the desk. She's a volunteer, about a hundred years old, and the kids drive her crazy. The manager here is pretty reliable; if you don't want to stick around she'll put your load in the dryer and have it ready when you get back."

"Thanks for the suggestion. I'll do that."

They parted at the door. Tanya stripped off her shirt as she crossed the parking lot; under it she wore a tailored white blouse and knotted tie. Back into uniform, Karen thought, studying the other woman's slim hips and long legs. The jeans fit like wallpaper. If I had a body like that I'd probably wear them too, she acknowledged to herself — despite all my feminist principles. And I'd cover it up in public, as Tanya had done, with a long shirt. The jeans wouldn't show if she stayed behind the desk.

She visited the liquor store and the grocery store and then went back to pick up her laundry. The interior of her car felt like a steam bath, though it was only a little past noon. She rolled down the windows, wrinkling her nose as she caught a whiff of that sickening swamp odor. It must be her imagination. Only a few drops of the foul mud had splashed her clothes, and they now reeked of some commercial scented softener.

She had to pass the library on her way home; seeing a bright-pink placard on the front door, she pulled into the curb and stared. Mrs. Fowler had outdone herself. Not only was the poster pink, it featured a sketch of a lady in full skirts simpering from under a frilly parasol.

It did not improve her mood to find someone waiting for her when she arrived home. He was perched on the steps leading up to the apartment, legs stretched out, head thrown back as if enjoying the sunshine. Karen brought the car to a stop and began counting under her breath. She got to forty-seven before she felt calm enough to face him without yelling.

Meyer rose and came toward her. "Can I give you a hand with those bags?"

There was a running joke in the profession about Bill Meyer's three-piece suits and expensive Italian ties — and how he could afford them on a professor's salary. He was more casually dressed this morning; the striped shirt had to be from Brooks Brothers or some establishment of similar prestige, but it was open at the throat and the sleeves had been rolled up to display tanned forearms. A modest amount of dark hair showed at the open neck of the shirt. He flashed white teeth in a broad smile. "No, thanks," she said. "I can manage."

"Sure you can." Before she could stop him he took the grocery bags from her. "But why should you? I'm perfectly harmless, you know. I just want to have a friendly chat."

Lips compressed, Karen started up the stairs. He was a master at maneuvering people into untenable positions. Short of wrestling the groceries away from him — which would be not only undignified but probably fatal to the vegetables — she couldn't prevent him from following her at least as far as the door. When she put down the bundle of laundry in order to search for her key, Meyer scooped it up, one finger under the string.

"Give me a break, Karen," he said quietly. "I know we've been on bad terms. It's my fault. I don't have much talent for social relationships, and for some strange reason I put my foot in my mouth every time I talk to you. I have a great deal of respect for you, you know. I think we could be friends, if I can stop acting like an arrogant jackass. Let me try."

"Humility is a new approach for you," Karen said. "I suppose it works with some people."

"What have you got to lose?"

Karen glanced over her shoulder. The briefcase was in the trunk of the car. There was nothing in plain sight that had any bearing on her present work, except the cardboard carton of papers — and he had already seen those.

"Come in," she said, stepping back.

He went straight through to the kitchen, without looking at her worktable or the box of papers, and deposited the grocery bags on the table. "Go ahead and put the groceries away if you like. We can talk while you —" He clapped a hand over his mouth and then removed it to display a sheepish smile. "There I go again. That's the trouble with teaching, you get in the habit of ordering

226

people around. Can I sit down?"

"I suppose so," Karen said ungraciously.

He watched without offering to help, while she unloaded the groceries. "I don't suppose you'd consider having lunch with me," he said gloomily.

"No, thanks." Karen pulled out a chair and sat down. "This is all very pleasant and polite, Bill, but I haven't seen any signs of you changing your spots. I suppose you thought it was a huge joke to set me up for a lecture on lady writers."

The corners of his mouth quivered. "Oh, come on, Karen, lighten up. You'd have thought it was funny if it had happened to me. It was the old lady's idea, honestly. You don't have a dialogue with that one; she makes statements and interprets whatever you say as agreement."

Karen had to admit there was a grain of truth in that. Meyer went on, "I was trying to get in her good graces, sure. I assumed you were doing the same. Addressing her ghastly little group gives you an in. That's where you're going to get your evidence, Karen — from old fogies like Mrs. Fowler. She and her contemporaries live in the past, wallowing in memories of dead heroes and old glories."

Joan had said something along the same lines, Karen thought. Oral tradition, family legends.

"It's one source," she admitted. "But it's highly speculative. I've got better evidence, Bill."

"The manuscript is the essential item, I agree. As for the genealogy, you know as well as I do that it's only the first step. I counted no fewer than fourteen women who are possible candidates. There's absolutely no way of knowing from the genealogy which of them was Ismene." He didn't give her time to reply, but went on, "Have you thought — hell, there I go again, of course you have — about the implication of the name? She must have read *Antigone*. That's astonishing in itself; a classical education wasn't available to many women at that time."

"It weakened their brains."

"And drove them insane," Meyer agreed in the same sardonic tone. "The house of stone — in the poems and in the novel — must have been inspired by Antigone's 'place of stone,' her 'vaulted bride-bed in eternal rock.' But why did she choose to call herself by the name of the weaker of the two sisters? Antigone was the heroine; defying a tyrant at the risk of her own life, she is more admirable than any of the men in the play, even her lover."

It wasn't the first time Karen had considered the question of Ismene's nom de plume, but it was the first time she had had the opportunity to discuss it with someone who knew the literature as well as she did and whose interest was as keen as hers. "He died too," she pointed out. "He killed himself for Antigone's sake."

"But in a fascinating reversal of conventional male-female roles. Usually it's the hero who nobly sacrifices his life for a principle, and the heroine who refuses to go on living after the sole light of her life is gone. As for Antigone's sister . . .

Admittedly she does offer to join Antigone in death, but only after she has tried to persuade her sister to accept the tyrant's refusal to give their dead brother honorable burial. And in the end, Ismene doesn't go through with it. She lives and Antigone dies."

"Antigone talks her out of sacrificing herself. She doesn't want to share the glory."

"That's one interpretation." Meyer raised his eyebrows. "But I didn't expect you to be so cynical about female heroes."

"Why should they be any different from male heroes? Do you think it was love for her sister that moved Antigone, then?"

"Why not? Ismene had offered the highest proof of her love; she was willing to die for a cause she obviously considered foolish. Their brother was already dead and rotting. What use is honorable burial to a corpse?"

"That's a modern viewpoint. The Greeks didn't share it."

"True," Meyer admitted. "Nor did some of our not-so-distant ancestors. I doubt the parallel between the drama and the novel extends beyond the similarity of names, however, so I wouldn't bother searching for a pair of sisters and a dead brother in the Cartright genealogy. I have, however, found Ismene's house of stone."

The words were like a slap in the face of a swooning heroine. Karen had been leaning forward, elbows on the table, chin in her hands, forgetting her dislike of Meyer in the rare and unmatched pleasure of shop talk. There weren't many people who knew her field so well, and whose intelligence was as quick as Meyer's. Or as crafty. He had caught her completely off guard.

"You sneaky son of a bitch," she exclaimed. "How much of the manuscript did you read?"

"And then he said, with one of those nasty grins of his — I quote exactly — 'I'm quite a fast reader. And I know how to skim the cream off a text.'"

She was speaking to Peggy, who had called to report her arrival shortly after Meyer left. She was earlier than Karen had expected, but Karen hadn't commented on that or on Peggy's drawn, tired face. The perfidy of William Meyer still rankled. As she drove to the motel to pick up her friend she carried on a profane monologue with herself, but it was an even greater catharsis to express her rage to a sympathetic listener.

"Have a drink," Peggy suggested. She already had one; her first question, after they reached the apartment, had been, "Where's the booze?"

"Maybe I will." Removing the cork from the bottle of wine relieved a little of her spleen. While she worked at it Peggy said mildly, "So what's the beef? He didn't have to tell you. Did he describe the location of the place he had found?"

"Well . . . yes. I'd have found it anyway. I had already located the clearing in the woods."

"But not the house."

Karen shifted uncomfortably. She didn't like to remember the attack of panic she had felt in that clearing, and she had no intention of admitting it to anyone — not even Peggy. "I only found the reference to it last night," she said evasively. "Up till that point I had no reason to suppose Ismene's house of stone was anything other than figurative."

"I wasn't criticizing you. You've accomplished a hell of a lot in only a few days." She watched Karen pace back and forth and then added, in a sharper voice, "For God's sake, sit down and relax! I don't know why you let Meyer get to you. What else did he say?"

"Not much. He didn't have a chance to say much — I more or less kicked him out." Karen slumped into a chair and sipped her wine. "Calling him a son of a bitch didn't exactly improve matters."

"What . . . did . . . he . . . say?" Peggy repeated.

"He didn't return the compliment." The wine, or Peggy's presence, or both, had had a soothing effect. Karen smiled faintly. "In fact, he laughed. He said he'd given me the information as a token of his good intentions, and that he'd continue to pass on anything of interest, without expecting me to reciprocate. Not that I believe it."

"It could be he's on the up-and-up," Peggy mused. "Cherishing a secret passion for you, unable to express it because you are a professional rival as well as a beautiful, desirable woman . . ."

"Very funny." But the idea had its appeal. It would certainly be a triumph to have Bill Meyer, the Don Juan of the Modern Language Association, kneeling at her feet. Karen savored the image:

Meyer submissive and stammering, like some bucolic swain, with her foot planted firmly on his bowed neck.

The picture was as absurd as it was unlikely. "Maybe I did overreact," she admitted. "I doubt my rudeness fazed Bill, though. He'll be back. Want another drink before I start my report?"

"Yes." Peggy rose and followed her into the kitchen. "I wouldn't say no to a cracker and a crumb of cheese, either, if you have them. I haven't had anything to eat since this morning; stopped off at the house to change clothes and pick up the car, and then drove straight through."

"No wonder you look so tired." Karen went to the refrigerator. "I'm sorry; I should have asked. How is your friend?"

"Dead," Peggy said. "The funeral was yesterday."

Chapter Eight

We paused before a House that seemed
A Swelling of the Ground —
The Roof was scarcely visible —
The Cornice — in the Ground —

EMILY DICKINSON, 1863

The package of cheese slipped from Karen's hand. She bent over to retrieve it. "I'm so sorry," she mumbled, painfully aware of how inadequate the words must sound. "What . . . I mean, was he . . . What I really mean is, do you want to talk about it?"

"Not at length." Peggy had already helped herself to the Scotch. "But I don't mind answering the questions you were courteous enough not to ask. 'What' was AIDS. He's been sick a long time, and it was not a merciful death. He was a close friend, I guess you'd say. I was married to him."

Karen's hand slipped again. The cheese fell onto a plate this time. "I didn't know you were married," she gasped, forgetting tact in astonishment.

" 'Was,' I said. We split up fifteen years ago, after he found the courage to admit he preferred his own sex. I had," Peggy said without expression, "suspected that earlier."

"But you went to be with him when . . ."

"When he asked for me. Sure I did. I got over my anger and hurt a long time ago. He didn't want to hurt me. He was a nice guy; we could have been friends if he'd been able to face the truth. It wasn't as easy to do that twenty years ago."

"It still isn't easy, I guess." Still reeling mentally from the barrage of revelations, Karen offered a plate of cheese and crackers like a burnt offering. "Are you all right?" she asked.

Peggy grinned. She still looked tired — small wonder, Karen thought remorsefully — but it was her old smile. "I'm not infected, if that's what you mean. He called me as soon as he found out, even though he was sure it hadn't happened until after we separated."

"That was a decent thing to do."

"He was a nice guy," Peggy said again. "As for my mental state — well, it hasn't been a pleasant week, but I'll survive. When you're my age, you become more accustomed to losing friends." She stuffed a cracker into her mouth and added indistinctly, "The intellectual challenge you are about to offer will distract and divert me. Tell me all."

The distraction proved effective; it was Karen who called a halt to the discussion, though the hour was still early and they hadn't covered all the possible ramifications.

"You must be exhausted, Peggy. I'll take you

back to the motel. Unless you want to stay here tonight."

Peggy admitted she was ready for bed, but she refused the invitation with all her old acrimony. "I'll bet the mattress is almost as thin as the towels. The old lady didn't exactly knock herself out furnishing this place, did she?"

"It's adequate. Are you sure you don't want company? I'll stay with you if you like."

"The only company I want is this genealogy." Peggy tucked it and the notes she had made into her bag. "Don't get sentimental and mushy, Karen, I don't need a shoulder to cry on. You needn't pick me up tomorrow. I know how to find the place now. Suppose I get here about nine? I'll bring doughnuts or something equally unhealthy. We'll finish planning our campaign, and then drive out to have a look at the house. Do you suppose your friend Cameron will be working there tomorrow?"

"Probably." Karen located her keys and opened the door. "Watch the steps, they're steep. Why do you want to see the house? I told you —"

"I am not questioning your data," Peggy said, determinedly patient. "I just want to see the damned place, okay?"

"Okay, okay." Karen unlocked the trunk and put the briefcase inside.

"Cautious little creature, aren't you?" Peggy said. "Do you haul that manuscript with you everywhere you go?"

"Yes, I do. There's no safe hiding place in the

apartment. It wouldn't take much strength to force the door."

"That was not a criticism, just a simple question." Peggy settled herself with a grunt and reached for the seat belt. "I have to admit I keep losing sight of how valuable the damned thing is. Not in monetary terms but —"

"I wouldn't lose sight of the monetary terms," Karen said grimly. "How much do you suppose Bill would pay for a copy?"

"Please don't say things like that," Peggy pleaded. "The idea opens up too many horrible possibilities. Bill's not the only one who would pay for a copy, you know. You shouldn't have called him a son of a bitch."

"He is a son of a bitch."

"Who knows?" Peggy murmured. "Life is full of surprises. That is what makes it so interesting."

Cameron was descending a long ladder when they caught sight of him. Karen deduced he had been painting the shutters or woodwork of an upper window, and had left off when he heard the car.

"Who's that?" Peggy demanded, staring. "Not the prim and proper business gent we had dinner with? Wow! Who'd have thought he had such a good-looking pair of —"

"Shhh! He'll hear you."

"He can't possibly hear me. Anyhow, what's wrong with expressing admiration of a shapely body? Men do it all the time. The rest of him isn't bad, either. Except for his expression. I don't think he's happy to see us."

"Peggy, if you don't shut up . . ." Karen hastily got out of the car and hailed their obviously unenthusiastic host. "Good morning. I'm sorry if we disturbed you. You remember Dr. Finneyfrock?"

"Call me Peggy," said Peggy with a broad smile and an outstretched hand.

"Uh — thank you." In some astonishment Cameron studied the small figure, dressed like a miniature commando in khaki shirt, baggy pants and heavy boots. Karen realized he hadn't recognized Peggy until she mentioned the name.

Recovering himself, he displayed a palm liberally smeared with green paint. "It's nice to see you again, Dr. — Peggy. You'll excuse me for not shaking hands."

"It would be easier to paint them if you took them off," Peggy said.

"What . . ." He blinked at her. "Oh, you mean the shutters. I can't get them off without using a hacksaw on the hardware, it's rusted solid. This job is purely cosmetic; I haven't time for . . . But you don't want to hear about that. What can I do for you?"

The question implied he didn't want to do much and that he hoped they would go away. Karen said, "Peggy wanted to see the house. There's no need for you to go with us."

"The cellar's flooded again," Cameron said.

"Good," Peggy said. "That gives me an excuse to decline a visit. I come all over queer in dark,

237

dank, enclosed spaces. We'd like to explore the grounds, though, if that's all right with you."

"There's poison ivy, brambles, snakes —"

"Honey, I'm a country girl at heart. I know all about snakes. As you can see, I dressed for the occasion."

Hands on her hips, feet planted firmly, she tipped her head back and gave him a cheerful grin. Cameron still appeared a trifle dazed by the transformation, but his lips relaxed in an answering smile.

"Yes, I see. Be careful."

"Same to you," Peggy retorted. "That ladder doesn't look very sturdy. You shouldn't be working out here alone. If you fell —"

"I won't fall. But I appreciate your concern." He sounded as if he meant it.

Karen had been curious to see how Peggy would react to the chill in the front hall. It struck her as forcefully as it had on the other occasions, but if Peggy felt anything she didn't mention it. Muttering to herself and scribbling notes, she tramped from room to room with Karen trailing after her.

"What are you looking for?" the latter finally asked.

"I'm trying to get some idea of how old the main house and its appendages are, and whether there are visible signs of alteration. For instance —" she pointed with her pen — "that could be a bricked-up doorway. It's in the right location for an entrance to another wing."

"Ismene mentions two wings."

"Don't tell me what she mentions. You saw the house after you'd read the manuscript. I want to do it the other way around. Not that I doubt your conclusions," Peggy added quickly. "This is by way of being a crosscheck."

"That's why you refused to read it last night?"

"That and the fact that there wasn't time. The manuscript . . . We can't keep calling it that. What's the title?"

"It hasn't got one. I told you, the first pages are missing."

"You'll have to give it one when you publish."

"I already have." Karen hunched her shoulders and tried not to shiver. Peggy had actually unzipped her jacket. Didn't she feel the cold? " 'Houses of Stone.' "

Peggy considered the name, and then nodded. "I like it. Why the plural, though? You said she mentions only one such place."

"It's figurative. Like the poem. Enclosure, the imprisonment of women's minds."

"Uh-huh. Well . . ." Peggy brandished her pencil. "Let's get on with it. Figurative or not, I want to locate that stone house before we leave."

Karen led the way up the stairs. "It's a weird place," Peggy said thoughtfully. "There was no attempt at architectural beauty or symmetry, just shelter — an enclosed block with small windows and thick walls. More like a fort than a house."

"There were Indians," Karen began.

"Native Americans, please," Peggy corrected. "By the beginning of the eighteenth century the

239

local tribes had been pretty well pacified — driven out or slaughtered, that is. The other plantation houses in this area are beautiful mansions, as elegant and sophisticated in design as their English counterparts, and some of them were begun as early as the 1720s. I wonder when this house was built."

"What difference does that make? I'm only concerned about what it looked like in 1787 and after. Ismene couldn't have written her book before then."

"Just another little anomaly," Peggy said vaguely.

Finally she announced that she had seen enough of the house. She had not asked about the attic, and Karen didn't remind her. "What do you say we make sure Cameron isn't splattered on the driveway? We might invite him to join us for lunch."

However, Cameron, still on the ladder, declined to join them in the sandwiches and soft drinks Peggy had brought.

"You could faint from hunger," Peggy yelled.

He answered more patiently than Karen had expected. "I want to finish the shutters first. It's not worth the trouble of cleaning up."

"How about an hour from now?"

"For heaven's sake, Peggy, leave him alone," Karen whispered, pulling at her sleeve.

Peggy shook her off. "An hour and a half?" she shouted.

"An hour should do it." There was amusement

as well as resignation in his voice. After a moment he added, "It's very kind of you."

"Kind, my eye," Karen muttered, as they headed along the path toward the back of the house. "For heaven's sake, take it easy, Peggy; he's even pricklier than I am, and if you keep hassling him he may refuse to let us come here again."

"No, he won't. He thinks I'm cute."

"Cute!" Karen couldn't help laughing. "Like a barracuda."

"He doesn't know me very well yet," Peggy said complacently.

Karen abandoned the argument. "What do you want to do now?"

"It's obvious, isn't it? We have to find the stone house."

Peggy took the lead. Pulling a pair of gloves from one of her bulging pockets, the older woman said critically, "You aren't dressed for this. Why didn't you bring gloves? At least roll down your shirt sleeves."

"I didn't know you were planning a trek into the jungle," Karen grumbled.

"You knew it was a jungle, you've been here before. I only surmised as much. Oh, well, all right, I'm sorry. I should have reminded you."

She had also brought a pair of heavy clippers, which she used briskly and effectively to cut away brambly branches and vines that blocked the path. No country girl herself, Karen was astonished to see how much the weeds had grown in only a few days. The moisture left by the last rain had had no chance to evaporate under the enclosing shade; the ground was slick and the leaves glistened wetly.

She tried to concentrate on finding solid footing and on avoiding the branches that, despite Peggy's efforts, swiped at her face and caught in her clothing. She had not dared object when Peggy proposed the expedition. Any excuse she could have invented would have sounded suspicious, for under normal circumstances she would have been on fire to locate the structure Meyer had told her about. And under no circumstances would she have mentioned the voice she had heard. The auditory hallucination, she corrected herself.

When the distant murmur of sound — of water, just water, nothing else — reached her ears she burst into speech. "How did you know it would be like this? It really is like a jungle, hot and steamy. You can almost see tendrils shooting out and weeds growing, like a speeded-up nature film."

"Oft have I wandered Virginia's woods," Peggy said, stooping under a dangling branch. "Watch your head . . . And North Carolina's woods and so on."

"Bird-watching? Or are you interested in wild-flowers? What are those pretty little pink things that look like tiny bells, on very thin stems?" She knew she was babbling, but she was afraid to stop talking. Silence might not be . . . entirely silent.

"What pretty little pink things?" Peggy stopped

to look. "You mean spring beauties? I don't see any."

"I must have seen them someplace else." She had run out of conversation, and Peggy was staring at her curiously.

The sound was like the wordless babble of an infant, rising and falling in the imitation of human speech patterns that leads doting parents to claim unusual precocity in their offspring.

"Do you hear it?" she asked.

"Hear what? Oh — running water. Can't be coming from the river," Peggy said calmly. "More like your standard poetic babbling brook. Sounds close. Do we have to cross it?"

"No."

"Your face is the funniest color," Peggy said, chuckling. "The way the sunlight filters through the leaves makes it look almost greenish."

She turned and went on walking. Karen took a deep breath. Water running over stones. Right.

By the time they reached the clearing she had dismissed her fears. Imaginary horrors hadn't a chance with Peggy around; she was too matter-of-fact, too rational. And — Karen noticed — in much better condition than she. Peggy's face was wet with perspiration, but she hopped over puddles and fallen branches with youthful agility and her breathing wasn't even quick. She let out a crow of discovery when they came out of the trees into the sunlight.

"This must be it. I wonder why this one spot is so open? There's water enough, and sunlight.

243

Something in the soil, maybe." Her tone dismissed the question even as she raised it. "I don't see any structure, do you? Wait a minute — what's that?"

Karen had seen it too — a heap of tangled vines, intertwined like green snakes. There was an animal-like ferocity about them, as if they were fighting for survival, seizing and strangling their weaker fellows; and a kind of triumph in the way they had overcome and buried the ephemeral works of man. She recognized the signs now — edges of stone, too regular to be fallen boulders — and the raw breaks in the vines where someone had cut and pulled them away.

Peggy trotted briskly toward the tangled mass, clippers at the ready. Karen followed more slowly. Peggy had been right, she wasn't dressed for this project. Her sneakers were soaked, and it would have been reckless to attack the vines bare-handed; blackberry brambles and poison ivy mingled with flexible canes of honeysuckle, strong as rawhide. She watched with rising excitement as Peggy tugged cut branches aside, gradually exposing a stretch of fitted stones. Only a few courses remained intact, but they obviously formed part of a wall. The upper portion must have collapsed into the interior of the structure along with the roof, which had probably been built of more perishable materials, to form a tumulus-like mound.

With a grunt of satisfaction Peggy stepped back. "This is it, all right. At least it's an enclosure of some kind; I just found a corner. Have a look."

Her face was bright red and streaming with perspiration, but she looked extremely pleased with herself. As she had every right to be, Karen thought. She ought to have spotted that mound of vegetation herself. It didn't take an archaeologist to realize that vines wouldn't form a pile that high unless they had something to build on. If she hadn't let her imagination get the better of her . . . There was nothing unusual about the sound of the brook. It was just a pleasant musical murmur.

She reached the wall and leaned forward to examine it more closely. If there had been mortar between the stones, none was visible now. The longer she studied it, the less certain she was that it had been a house — or a dwelling of any kind. Surely stone was an unusual building material for that region and that period. Clearing the land for planting provided the settlers with a wealth of hardwood for construction . . .

It came without warning. There was no darkening of the sky, no rising wind, no change in the murmurous sound of water. This was a different sound entirely. It came from behind her, shrill and distinct, rising in volume as if it came from the throat of someone or something that hurtled toward her, racing along the path, across the clearing and . . . And died. The air shivered with silence.

Peggy was the first to break it. They had reached out instinctively to clasp hands; Karen's fingers ached from the pressure of Peggy's grip.

"Jesus H. Christ," Peggy gasped. Her face was

a sickly shade of gray. "What the hell was that?"

"You . . ." Karen's throat was dry. She had to swallow before she could go on. "You heard it too?"

"I'd have to be deaf not to hear it. There was nobody — nothing — there."

"But you didn't feel the cold . . ."

"What cold?" Peggy peered into her face. "Let's get the hell out of here. Can you walk?"

"Of course."

Karen took a deep breath and forced herself to look again at the tumulus. That was all it was, a heap of fallen stone. Sunlight filled the clearing. The only sounds she heard were bursts of birdsong and the soft voiceless murmur of running water.

"Let's go," Peggy said.

"Don't you want to —"

"No. Start walking."

They had to go single file. Peggy followed close on Karen's heels. Neither spoke again until they had emerged from the woods. "I'd like to wash up," Peggy said. "Is it okay if we use the kitchen sink?"

"I don't see why not. We can go in the back way."

Peggy's face had regained its healthy color, but the bar of soap slipped from her hands when she started to scrub them under the tap. She recaptured it and handed it to Karen. "I don't suppose there's anything to drink around here."

"The cans we put in the refrigerator —"

"That wasn't what I had in mind. Oh, well. It's

a bad habit I ought to control." Leaning against the counter, she folded her arms and stared at Karen. "I never heard anything like that in my life. Can you think of a rational explanation?"

"Animals make funny noises," Karen said feebly.

"Very true. Siamese cats in heat, mating porcupines — you can understand why a female porcupine might object to that process — bobcats . . . I've heard 'em all, at one time or another. That was not an animal. And it was *there,* only a few feet away, when it stopped."

"What are you suggesting?"

"Not what you're thinking." Peggy rubbed the bridge of her nose reflectively. "That doesn't fit either. I've never had a psychic experience in my life, but I'm familiar with the literature. Your traditional ghosts don't appear in broad daylight without suitable accompaniments — frissons of terror, chilling cold . . . Wait a minute. What was that you said about cold?"

She'd never have had the courage to confess if Peggy had not shared the experience. After she had described the feeling of ghastly cold in the hall and in the attic, she added, "Cameron felt it too — in the hall. He tried to hide it, but I could tell. And although he took me through the rest of the house, he let me go alone to the attic."

"Hmmm." After a moment of cogitation Peggy shook her head. "There's no pattern that I can see. To me the hall felt chilly but it wasn't abnormal — just the ordinary cold of an unheated

247

house. You weren't aware of anything unusual in the cellar, yet he was uncomfortable there."

"Claustrophobia. I don't have that problem."

"It's possible to find pseudo-scientific explanations for everything," Peggy muttered. "Claustrophobia, sensitivity to incompetent architectural measurements, collective auditory hallucination . . . Well, you'll be relieved to hear that I am not going to suggest a séance or a visit to the attic. In a way I wish I could buy the ghost story; it would be so much easier to summon Ismene's spirit from wherever the hell it is and ask her what we want to know instead of doing all this boring research."

Karen was prevented from replying by the arrival of Cameron Hayes, who entered by the door leading to the front of the house. "Sorry," he said. "I didn't realize you were here."

"I don't know what you're apologizing for," Peggy said coolly. "It's your house. Ready for lunch?"

"Soon as I get some of this paint off my hands." He went to the sink. "Find anything interesting?"

"Yes, as a matter of fact. Do you know anything about that tumbledown pile of stones in the clearing?"

His hands stopped moving. After a long second he reached for the can of paint remover. "I'm not sure what you mean," he said.

Peggy took the can from him and removed the top. "Hold out your hands. I'll pour, you scrub. There's a path — you must know which one I mean, it's the only one — leading downhill toward the river, and an opening in the woods about — oh, quarter of a mile from here. The stones are almost hidden by vines, but they once formed a structure of some kind."

"A wall . . ." Cameron began.

"Not a wall. This is a discrete mound, not an elongated structure. I can't figure out what it might have been," Peggy went on, half to herself. "The stones are massive; they wouldn't build an animal pen or storage shed out of such solid materials. Slave quarters and the other outbuildings that were part of a plantation wouldn't be located so far from the house. Any ideas?"

Cameron reached for a ragged towel and dried his hands. "Sorry. You might ask Lisa; she spent more time with our uncle, listening to his boring stories, than I did. It does sound like a strange place to find a stone building; I hadn't thought about that until you —" He broke off, his eyes widening. "Is that what you're thinking? A house of stone . . . Hers?"

"How do you know about that?" Karen demanded suspiciously.

Cameron raised his eyebrows. "I read the poems, after you explained your interest in the lady. I was . . . curious. Maybe I'm missing something, since I'm just a dull-witted reader instead of a literary critic, but I thought the house of stone was a figure of speech."

"So did I," said Peggy, before Karen could reply. "So did everybody else who read the poems. But if that pile of rubble was a literal, physical stone house, it opens up all kinds of interesting speculations. Sit down, Cameron. Our menu today includes ham-and-cheese sandwiches, with a choice of soda or cola, and for dessert a tempting array of supermarket cookies."

He insisted on helping her. Karen didn't offer; arms folded, she watched them move from the refrigerator to the table, exchanging witticisms about the elegance of the waxed-paper and foil serving dishes and the gourmet menu. She suspected Cameron was fully aware of the reason for Peggy's corny jokes and motherly concern about his sore, scraped hands. She was flirting with him, literally batting her lashes and letting him lift everything that weighed more than half a pound. Not only did he know exactly what she was doing, he enjoyed it. Meekly he allowed her to bully him into eating two of the four sandwiches and half a box of cookies, but when she offered to help with the painting, he laughed and said, "Don't overdo it, Peggy."

Unabashed, she smiled back at him. "I'm a damned good painter."

"I'm sure you are damned good at everything you do," Cameron said pointedly. "Thanks just the same. What can I do for you?"

"I'm going to need some help excavating that pile of stones. Not from you," she added quickly. "You have enough on your hands with the house. Can you recommend some kids with strong backs who'd work for minimum wage?"

"Are you serious?"

"Quite serious. There's no hurry, I probably won't get around to it for another week or so. We can come to an arrangement about a short-term lease —"

"That won't be necessary," Cameron said. "If you find anything, it might be an inducement to prospective buyers. I can tell them the place is of great historical interest."

"It is," Peggy said.

She was unusually silent during the drive back. "I'll be back about six, if that's agreeable to you," she announced, when they reached Karen's apartment. "I want to shower and change. Who knows, I might even spend some time thinking."

Karen didn't argue. She wanted some time to think too.

When she unlocked the door she saw the square envelope on the floor. The pale-violet color told her who her correspondent must be. In darker violet ink Mrs. Fowler presented her compliments and an invitation to tea on Monday, for Karen and her distinguished friend, of whose arrival she had heard. She didn't say from whom she had heard it.

Karen was tempted to call and refuse — or stick a little note under Mrs. F.'s door, to the same effect. She had a pretty good idea of how Peggy probably felt about tea parties. However, with Peggy one could never be certain. She might be able to get more information from the old lady than Karen had managed to do.

Preoccupied with the annoying habits of Mrs. Fowler, she was halfway across the room before something struck her. Something . . . but what? After a moment she realized that the books she had left lying on the table didn't look quite right. She was in the habit (a neurotic habit, according to Sharon) of stacking them with the spines aligned. Had she neglected to do it that morning? They were definitely not aligned now.

She could not be certain about the books, but a look around the apartment convinced her that someone had searched the place during her absence — even the kitchen cupboards. Another (neurotic) habit of hers was to separate the canned goods: all the soups in one group, all the vegetables in another. Now the mushroom soup rubbed shoulders with the canned peas and the chili was next to the tomato juice. In the bedroom she found the final proof: the worn chenille spread had not been tucked under the pillows but pulled clumsily up over them.

Mrs. Fowler was the most obvious suspect. She was the only one who had a key, and bored old ladies were notorious snoops. Such a harmless-sounding word, snoop. Snooping was prompted by idle curiosity, a harmless if socially indefensible habit, with no particular end in mind.

She could have been looking for "dirty" books or more titillating objects indicative of sexual activity. A little old lady would be certain to look under the mattress, since that was where she would hide the evidence of her own secret vices. But a little old lady would know the proper method of making a bed.

Bill Meyer? He was the most likely suspect from another point of view — that of motive. Karen opened the front door and examined the lock. There were no signs of forced entry. No, he wouldn't risk that, and it was unlikely that an academic — even a louse like Bill Meyer — knew how to pick a lock without leaving traces. But he might have charmed or tricked Mrs. Fowler into lending him a key, or stolen hers for long enough to have a copy made.

Lisa Fairweather was no little old lady; Karen doubted she was in the habit of making beds, hers or anyone else's. She was on good terms with Mrs. Fowler and could have borrowed a key, with or without the old lady's knowledge. Not all snoops were elderly women; but there was another reason, stronger than idle curiosity, that might have inspired Lisa to search the place. She knew, thanks in part to Karen herself, that certain people would be willing to pay a lot of money for a copy of the manuscript.

The same motive could apply to Cameron. He had had no idea what the manuscript was worth when he sold it; some people in his position would feel they had been cheated, and were, therefore, entitled to whatever extra they could pick up. Only a sick, warped individual would feel that way, but there were a lot of sick, warped individuals running around loose. And it was a safe bet that Cameron had never made a bed in his life.

Considering various methods of laying a trap for an intruder, she showered and changed into clean clothes. Several methods occurred to her, but none of the ones she had read about would provide a clue to the intruder's identity. Offhand she couldn't think of an excuse for asking to take the suspects' fingerprints.

With an irritated shrug she dismissed the matter. There had been no harm done, and as long as she kept the manuscript with her at all times she didn't risk losing anything she valued. Most likely the snoop had been Mrs. Fowler.

The distraction had come as a welcome relief; it prevented her from thinking about the clearing in the woods, so open and empty and so filled with voices.

Could there be a simple physical cause for the feeling of cold — something as harmless as low blood pressure, or a vitamin deficiency? Her last physical had given her a clean bill of health, but people dropped dead every day from conditions that hadn't shown up in physical examinations.

A happy thought. She would have embraced that theory, though, had the feeling of cold been the only unusual phenomenon. Peggy had heard the scream too. It had scared hell out of her, and she wasn't a nervous woman.

So, find another rational explanation for that occurrence. An acoustical peculiarity of the hollow? A police or ambulance siren on the highway, thrown like the voice of a ventriloquist away from its source? There were places like that, she had read of them — the Whispering Gallery at St. Paul's, for one.

Peggy had apparently forgotten about Karen's nightmares. She had almost forgotten them herself; they had not occurred after she got hold of the manuscript. They were the easiest of all to explain away. Dreams of darkness, enclosure, burial alive. Frustration. A classic feminist nightmare.

Three different rationalizations for three different phenomena. Well, why not, Karen thought. They weren't connected in any other way.

When Peggy arrived she was carrying a brown paper bag. "Hope you like Chinese," she announced. "There aren't a lot of food options in this burg. The alternatives were hamburgers or hoagies."

"I take it we are not going out," Karen said.

Peggy looked surprised. "I thought you might be too tired."

"I'm not tired. It doesn't matter," she went on, before Peggy could reply. "We have a lot to discuss."

"Right. I made an agenda." She had put her clipboard in the bag with the cartons of food. Muttering, she reached for a paper towel and scrubbed at a greasy spot.

"Before you get started on it, I have some new business," Karen said. "Someone searched the apartment while I was gone."

Peggy trailed after her while she pointed out the evidence, which she had not disturbed. The badly made bed provoked Peggy's first comment. "I haven't made a bed in twenty years. You sure you don't suspect me?"

"I might, if you hadn't been with me all afternoon." Karen faced her. "You don't believe me, do you?"

"It's not what a cop would call conclusive."

"You're not a cop. You're supposed to be a friend."

Peggy exhaled deeply. "What do you want from me, tactful acquiescence or honest criticism? In my book friends can disagree and still be friends. In fact, honesty is the only possible basis for lasting friendship. Oh, I know I'm a bossy, opinionated, irritating old bitch; I should have asked you whether you wanted to go out to dinner, and what kind of takeout you preferred. So tell me when I step out of line, okay? Talk, don't sulk. And tell me when you think I'm wrong. I am wrong occasionally. Not often, but occasionally."

"You're wrong," Karen said. "Someone was here."

After a moment Peggy's scowl turned to a sheepish smile. "Right. I stepped out of line. Sorry."

"I was out of line too," Karen said. "I guess I'm a little scared. It's a nasty feeling, having your space invaded — the classic nightmare of beleaguered heroines, come to think about it. Having forced upon you the knowledge that you aren't safe even in your own home."

"It's any woman's nightmare," Peggy muttered. "Any person's, male or female, these days. I was a little scared too; why do you suppose I yelled at you? Okay, where's my clipboard? New business: burglar. Would-be burglar, rather; nothing is missing?"

"There's nothing a burglar would bother with, not even a TV. I don't have valuable jewelry and I don't leave cash lying around."

"I just mentioned that in order to cover all the bases," Peggy said. "It's unlikely that your ordinary sneak thief would bother with a place like this, in broad daylight and practically under your landlady's nose. I agree with you that she's the most likely suspect. I must meet the old dear."

"You can meet her tomorrow if you like." Karen gave her Mrs. Fowler's note. "Another piece of new business I forgot to mention."

"We'll accept, of course," Peggy said. "You wouldn't happen to have any pink notepaper, would you? Preferably something with little flowers on it. Don't bother answering," she added with a smile. "The question was rhetorical. I'd also like to meet Lisa Fairweather. You might offer to take her to lunch. There's nothing like food and drink, especially the latter, to inspire confidences."

"All right. What sort of confidences are you hoping to inspire?"

"Cameron mentioned 'boxes' of family papers, didn't he? Lisa only gave you one box."

"Damn, that's right. Do you think she's holding out on me?"

"Could be the plural was just a slip of the tongue. It's worth asking about, though."

"Certainly." She watched Peggy check off an item on her list. "I'm not criticizing you or being overly sensitive, but it seems to me you're going over the same ground I've already covered — and expecting me to trail along. There are so many other things we could be doing —"

"And will do. This is going to be a long, complicated process. What's the hurry?"

"Bill Meyer has already beaten us to the punch once. God knows what other clues he found; he bragged about knowing how to skim a text. And he's seen the genealogy."

"You think of it as a competition, do you?"

"It is."

"Maybe so. Relax, he can only do so much with what he's got, and if I may be permitted to brag a trifle, I know better than he does how to go about it. Your discoveries strongly support the presumption that Ismene lived in that house, but was she a Cartright? The property may have changed hands, not once but several times. In this case we can't rely on people's memories, we need documentary proof. I'll hit the county courthouse tomorrow morning and begin tracing the deeds. You ought to — this is just an opinion, of course —"

"Don't be so damned tactful."

"Me, tactful? Please, don't be insulting." They smiled at one another, and Peggy went on, "As I was saying: Now that I've seen the manuscript, I realize how difficult it is to decipher. I'm amazed you've got through as much as you have. For heaven's sake, don't let Bill get to you with his boasts about skimming a text. You can't risk doing that. The text has given us our best leads so far, and a single blurred word or phrase could be crucial."

Karen spent the next day on the manuscript, not skimming. Peggy had said she would show up in time for the tea party and she was as good as her word. It lacked several minutes till four when Karen heard the pounding on her door. The emphatic, peremptory noise would have identified her caller even if she had not been expecting Peggy, but when she opened the door she had to look twice before she was certain. Her jaw dropped.

"Hurry up and change," Peggy ordered. "It's not polite to be more than ten minutes late."

Karen recovered herself. "I'm going as I am. I'm neat and clean and my pants are modestly loose. For God's sake, Peggy, don't you think you went a little overboard? She'll know you're making fun of her."

Peggy picked up her flowing skirts and curtsied. The wide-brimmed straw hat fell over her eyes. "Damn thing," she muttered, shoving it back into place. "You wouldn't have a hat pin around, would you?"

"I'm as short of hat pins as I am of pink note-paper. Honestly, Peggy —"

"She won't see the joke, believe me. It's important to make a good first impression."

She looked so pleased with herself, and so charmingly, consciously absurd, that Karen burst out laughing. "Peggy, you light up my life — to quote a distinctly minor poet. I suppose the least I can do is comb my hair. Come in, it will only take me a minute."

Mincing on high heels, one hand clutching her hat, Peggy watched her return the manuscript to the briefcase. "Any luck?"

"Not in the sense I had hoped. The love interest has turned up. At least I think he's going to be the hero; he's dark and gruff and taciturn. He's also a doctor, which I gather makes him a social inferior."

"Not necessarily. But unless he's also landed gentry he probably wouldn't be considered a suitable suitor. You ought to change your blouse at least; that one looks rather grubby."

"Oh, all right. Is this one acceptable?"

Peggy stuck her head in the closet. "This one. Little flowers and a Peter Pan collar."

"How about you?" Karen asked, slipping into the blouse.

"So far it's all Cartright. But I'm only back to 1830. It's slow work, especially when you're reading script instead of print. Hurry up, can't you?"

She did not comment when Karen carried the briefcase downstairs and locked it in the trunk of her car. They followed the driveway to the front of the house and knocked at the door.

Karen had anticipated Mrs. Fowler's reaction

with a certain amount of pleasure. She and Peggy would have made an absurd couple even without the hat, which was so wide-brimmed it made Peggy look like an animated mushroom. However, she underestimated Mrs. Fowler's breeding. Only the faintest flicker of criticism crossed her face when she saw them, and it was directed at Karen. Hearing voices from the living room, the latter realized she had committed a social error. They weren't the only guests. This was a party, not a casual visit.

There were four other guests, all male. Two of them had been with Mrs. Fowler at the restaurant: a heavy, pudgy-faced elderly man with an expression of insufferable self-satisfaction, and a wizened little scarecrow of approximately the same age. The third man was also someone she had seen before — trying to "start something" with Cameron, as he had expressed it. The fourth . . .

Only Peggy's shrill cry of greeting stopped Karen from making a profane remark. "Why, Dr. Meyer, what a pleasure to see you again. I had no idea you'd be here today."

"It's my pleasure. But please, won't you call me Bill? Hello, Karen."

"Such an honor to have three such distinguished visitors," exclaimed Mrs. Fowler. "Dr. Finney-frock, Dr. Holloway, allow me to present Colonel Bishop and Mr. Blair, two of our leading citizens. Both of them are prominent in civic and intellectual affairs. And this young man is one of those to whom our failing hands will pass the torch of learning and culture — my nephew, Robert Mansfield."

"Just call me Bobby," said Robert Mansfield, flashing his teeth, flexing his muscles, and seizing Karen's limp hand. "Old Cam took care I didn't get introduced last time we met, but I told you I'd see you again."

After shaking hands all around Karen sank into the nearest chair. She was the only one who wasn't dressed to the nines. Even Bobby had put on a coat and tie; his hair, stiffy and shiny with gel, had been shaped into upstanding curls. Meyer's charcoal-gray suit would have been appropriate for a wedding or a funeral, and the other men matched him in formality if not in shape. The Colonel's stomach strained the buttons of his waistcoat. Somehow Karen wasn't surprised when he modestly admitted to being an authority on Civil War battles — referring to that conflict, of course, as "The War of Southern Independence." Settling into a chair next to Peggy, whom he was kind enough to acknowledge as a fellow-historian, he started talking and, so far as Karen could tell, didn't stop until they were ready to leave.

His voice boomed a background accompaniment to the genteel conversation of the others. Mrs. Fowler did most of the talking. Bobby arranged his face in a smile and fixed pale-blue, white-lashed eyes on Karen. With his hair standing up in gluey tufts, he reminded her of an albino rabbit. Mr. Blair said very little, but he nodded a lot. He asked Karen one question: "What do you think

262

of the work of Mr. James Fenimore Cooper?" Karen's surprised reply — "I try not to think about it" — upset him to such an extent that he didn't try again. It also wrung an explosive noise from Bill Meyer, which he managed to suppress before it developed into a laugh.

Sandwiches (crustless, paper-thin and spread with various indeterminate substances) had been added to the inevitable macaroons. The Colonel and Bobby ate most of them. Since there was no hope of escape from the Colonel, Peggy was relieving her boredom by making fun of him. "How fascinating," Karen heard her say. "Really? Why, I never knew that. Do tell me more."

Karen tried not to look at her watch. How long, oh Lord, must she endure this agony? Bobby's fixed stare was driving her up the wall. He obviously expected she would be flattered by it. She couldn't pump Mrs. Fowler for information with Bill Meyer sitting there, ears pricked. Damn him, she thought, smiling sweetly at him as he proffered the plate of macaroons; he knows I'm about to explode with frustration and he's loving it.

After an hour and twenty minutes, Peggy jumped to her feet with a girlish giggle, her skirts billowing wildly. "My goodness gracious, just look at the time! I've been enjoying myself so much I couldn't tear myself away. Thank you so much, Mrs. Fowler; it's been a pleasure meeting you gentlemen — and seeing you, Bill dear —"

Bill dear left with them. The other men remained; Karen felt sure they were looking forward to a good gossip about the visitors, with special attention to her tactlessness and improper attire. The Colonel's parting remark was addressed to her. "We're all looking forward to your little talk on Wednesday, young lady."

As soon as they were out of earshot Peggy asked curiously, "What little talk is that?"

"I am addressing the literary society," Karen snapped. "Thanks to Bill here. He set me up."

Meyer caught Peggy's arm as she staggered. The hat fell off; he fielded it with a deft left-handed catch. "I said I was sorry," he said with an unrepentant grin. "You all right, Peggy?"

"It's these damned shoes."

Meyer shook his head sympathetically. "Martyrdom of that magnitude deserves a reward. Can I buy you a drink? Or a thick steak? Or both?"

"Sure," Peggy said, before Karen could reply. "Let me change my shoes first. My sneakers are in my car."

They turned into the driveway, Peggy still holding Meyer's arm. Karen followed, kicking at pebbles to relieve her feelings. Whatever Meyer's motive for inviting them to dinner, it would have been childish to refuse — but that didn't mean she had to like what she was doing.

"Who's that?" Meyer exclaimed, coming to a stop.

"Where?" Thrown off-balance, Peggy clutched at him. He thrust her at Karen and started to run.

Karen managed to stay on her feet and keep Peggy from falling. By that time Meyer was out of sight. Cursing female fashions, specifically foot-wear, Peggy tottered toward her car. She was changing into her sneakers when Meyer reappeared, pushing through the bushes at the back of the garage. He was disheveled and short of breath when he joined them.

"She got away. Must have parked in the alley; I heard a car start up and take off."

"She," Peggy repeated. "Who?"

Meyer hesitated. He had unbuttoned his coat and vest and loosened his tie. "I should have asked if you were expecting a visitor. She took off in such a hurry —"

"I didn't see anyone," Karen said.

"I only caught a glimpse of her, coming down the stairs. Did you?"

He spoke to Peggy. She shook her head. "I was too busy concentrating on walking. What did she look like?"

Meyer ran his fingers through his hair, dislodging a shower of twigs and leaves. "Almost my height, built like a tank. Sound like anyone we know?"

"Dorothea!" Karen exclaimed. "It can't be."

"I'm afraid it could," Meyer said.

Chapter Nine

"Nothing here but kitchen things," he said, with a little laugh for the insignificance of kitchen things.

SUSAN GLASPELL,
"A Jury of Her Peers," 1918

" 'The lamplight falling full upon him brought into strong outline a physiognomy more notable for strength than comeliness. Strands of silver glittered in the sable locks which were swept back to bare a brow forbiddingly high and prominent. The jutting nose and thin lips set in a habitual downward curve, the harsh modeling of the bone structure over which the skin stretched tightly: all his features combined recalled to Ismene a desolate landscape shadowed by low-hanging clouds. Yet when he smiled it was as if the same scene were illumined by a flood of sunlight breaking through the clouds; what had been shadowed was now bright and fresh, what had seemed a solitary wilderness was now animated by life.' "

Peggy looked up from the manuscript. "Remind you of anyone you know?" she asked.

"No," Karen said curtly.

"How about this? 'The gentleness of his countenance was the product of expression rather than structure. Those soft blue eyes could harden with anger or flash with noble indignation, and on such occasions the golden locks framing his brow seemed to glitter with a supernal fire.' "

Karen swung around in her chair to look at Peggy, who was curled up on the sofa.

"What are you talking about?" she demanded. "You're supposed to be looking for clues. I'd be the first to admit that Ismene's literary style lags at times, but those descriptions are typical of the genre — the Byronic hero-villain, dark and gloomy, and the fair-haired hero —"

"No doubt. But that's not what I meant."

"I know what you meant, and no, I can't picture Bill Meyer as a Byronic hero."

"Hero-villain, you said. That's one of the problems, isn't it? Is he for us or against us?"

"Come on, Peggy. Surely you weren't naive enough to believe those protestations of his. He put on a good show tonight, I admit. I told you he can be charming when he wants to be."

"He does have a nice smile. 'A flood of sunlight breaking through the clouds . . .' "

Karen made a wordless sound of disgust. Peggy chuckled, and then sobered. "I'm not saying you're wrong about Bill, Karen, but you're too intelligent to let prejudice influence your judgment. So far he hasn't done anything wrong — except tease you a little — and he's done several helpful things. Look how he rushed chivalrously in pursuit of your shy visitor. Got his nice neat hair all messed up."

"I didn't see anyone. Did you?"

"I thought I caught a glimpse of someone ducking into the shrubbery. But I'm very suggestible," Peggy admitted calmly. "Are you accusing him of inventing the whole thing?"

"Possibly. On the other hand, it wouldn't surprise me to learn Dorothea was still on the trail. I only hope to God Joe Cropsey doesn't track me down. What did you think of Bill's offer to help excavate the stone house?"

"That's another of those wonderfully enigmatic Gothic touches," Peggy said gleefully. "Is he genuinely anxious to assist you, or does he have an ulterior motive? We may not know the truth until the denouement, when he saves you from a hideous fate or threatens you with same. In the latter case it will be Cameron who rushes to your side in the nick of time, risking his life to —"

"An even less likely scenario. Did you find anything I missed?"

With a shrug and a smile Peggy accepted the change of subject. "Can't say that I did. There's no question about the ambience — the terrain she describes, the flora and fauna, the presence of slave-servants . . . It's American, and Southern American at that. From her description of the house we can make a very strong case for Amberley being the specific locale — in fact, the carved stone you described makes the identification virtually certain."

"Virtually?"

"That's the standard academic qualifier," Peggy said ironically. "There's no doubt in my mind.

The time period is post-Revolution, but I haven't found anything that would pin it down more precisely, not even references to specific articles of costume. Cloaks and mantles and hoods and trailing skirts could apply to any time in the century. You'd think a woman would describe clothes in more detail."

"I hope you're not implying Ismene was a man. That's the old male-chauvinist syllogism: Women's books have no literary merit; this book has literary merit; hence this book could not have been written by a woman. Some idiot even claimed that *Jane Eyre* and *Wuthering Heights* were written by Branwell Brontë."

"The town drunk of Haworth?" Peggy grinned. "Did he ever publish anything? Surely not even an idiot would make that claim unless he had something indisputably written by Branwell with which to compare the novels."

"That would be a logical procedure, wouldn't it? Branwell's own work, such as it was, proves beyond a doubt that he couldn't have written a salable Silhouette romance, much less *Wuthering Heights*. But the syllogism is hard to fight. What the hell do you think feminist critics are complaining about?"

"Don't yell at me, I'm on your side." Peggy pretended to cower. "I never doubted Ismene was female. Neither does Bill Meyer."

"Who gives a damn what Bill Meyer thinks? I don't want to talk about Bill Meyer. Or Cameron."

"Fine with me. But didn't it strike you, as it struck me, that Ismene's characters are more ambiguous than conventional Gothic heroes and villains? I haven't read that many of the damned things, but usually the dark brooding villain and the fair-haired rather vapid hero are more distinct. Heathcliffe and what's-'is-name — Edgar — in *Wuthering Heights*, the dark browed-Baron and the insipid youth in *Castle of Otranto* —"

"Heathcliffe isn't a typical hero or villain, any more than Emily's novel is a typical Gothic. It's unique, unclassifiable. In *Jane Eyre*, Rochester is dark and brooding, but he's the hero. Jane rejects St. John, the saintly blond, because his icy detachment and denial of normal human emotion threaten her very sanity. He's not a traditional villain, though. Like Rochester, and even poor old Edgar in *Wuthering Heights*, he is far more complex. Like real people."

"There is certainly a degree of ambiguity about Ismene's male characters. I don't trust that angelic cousin of hers," Peggy muttered. "He's up to something."

"So you're enjoying the story?"

"I'm hooked, if that's what you mean, despite the archaic language and the interminable moralizing. How much longer is it going to take you to —"

The ringing of the telephone saved Karen from a reply, which would have been too vague to satisfy Peggy. The voice at the other end surprised her so, she forgot her manners. "Simon! What's wrong?"

His deep laugh reassured her. "That reaction is more characteristic of my generation than yours, Karen. I thought you had substituted telephone calls for letters as a means of social communication. I hope all is well?"

"Yes; things are going very well. We've found the right house, Simon! There's no doubt about it. I'm a third of the way through the manuscript; it's wonderful . . ."

He waited until she had run down and then said politely, "I'm looking forward to reading it. And to hearing the story of your adventures. You said Peggy was working on the genealogical aspect. Is she there, by any chance?"

"Yes, she is." Karen began to have a deflating suspicion that she was not the object of Simon's interest. "Do you want to talk to her?"

He did. Karen handed the telephone to Peggy, who was looking particularly bland and innocent. She retreated to the kitchen and started to make tea, but it was impossible not to overhear Peggy's end of the conversation. It was not especially informative, however.

"Yes, fine, thank you . . . Really. . . Oh? . . . Yes, certainly. That's a good idea . . . Yes, I think so. And you? . . . Good . . . Yes, of course . . . Good night."

The kettle shrieked. Karen snatched it off the stove and poured water into the cups. Looking up, she saw Peggy standing in the doorway, watching her with an amused smile. "What tact. Did you think I was going to murmur sweet nothings?"

"No, I expected to hear ribald remarks that would offend my ladylike sensibilities. That was a very businesslike conversation."

Peggy sat down at the table and spooned sugar into her tea. "I've talked with Simon a number of times," she said. "I hope the relationship will continue to develop."

"Do you mean you and Simon are . . ." Surprise loosened Karen's tongue. She stopped herself. "I'm sorry. That's none of my business."

"No, it's not," Peggy said coolly. "I only mentioned it because I don't want you to suspect me of plotting with him behind your back. Tonight's conversation, in contrast to others we've had, was strictly business; he got a call today from the dealer from whom he bought the manuscript. While preparing for the auction — which is on Saturday, in case you've forgotten — the guy found more papers at the bottom of a box of linens. He wanted to know if Simon was interested."

"What did he say? What kind of papers? How much did he —"

"Calm yourself, please. I will give you the information in an orderly manner. Simon, moral giant that he is, refused the implicit offer; interest having been aroused, the seller stands to gain more in an open auction than in a private deal. He doubts the papers are important. All the dealer could tell him was that they look old — which as Simon knows, and you ought to know, doesn't mean a damned thing."

"Does that mean we have to bid for them on Saturday, in competition with everybody else attending the auction?" Karen demanded.

"Not without having a look at them first." Peggy tugged thoughtfully at her ear. "I'd planned to attend the auction, of course. There may be other things we'll want."

"What?"

"I won't know till I see them," Peggy said, maddeningly vague. "Usually there is a preview the day before, to give potential buyers a chance to examine the merchandise. We could attend that, but I'd prefer a private viewing, without a lot of auction freaks breathing down my neck. Do you think Cameron could arrange it?"

"I could ask."

"Do that little thing." Peggy gulped down the last of her tea and rose. "I'm off. I want to get to the courthouse as soon as the offices open tomorrow. I'll turn up here in time for Happy Hour, okay?"

Karen followed her to the door. "Be careful on the stairs," she warned. "It's awfully dark."

"It is, isn't it? Be sure and lock up."

Karen stood in the open door until Peggy had started the engine and turned on the headlights. The glare of their beams shattered the darkness and shadows turned familiar objects into grotesque caricatures. A shiver shook Karen's body as she remembered the last sentence she had read before Peggy interrupted her that afternoon. "Sometimes," Ismene had written, "it is better not to know what lies hidden in the dark."

She was hard at work the following morning when a pounding at the door interrupted her. Automatically Karen covered the manuscript with a blank sheet of paper, and got stiffly to her feet, wondering who it could be. Not Mrs. Fowler, unless she had run out of violet notepaper and was employing clenched fists instead of ladylike knuckles to the door. Karen hesitated, struck by a sudden thought. Could the person demanding entrance so peremptorily be Dorothea Angelo? She had feared that Dorothea would track her down sooner or later, and she wasn't keen on facing that large angry individual alone.

I'll be damned if I'll let the woman intimidate me, she told herself. Squaring her shoulders, she reached for the doorknob.

Despite her bravado it was with considerable relief that she recognized her visitor. Joan's red hair was windblown, and she was wearing a bright. green T-shirt covered with feminist mottoes and insignia. The least provocative of the mottoes read, "A woman needs a man like a fish needs a bicycle."

"Hi," Joan said brightly.

"What are you doing here?"

"I'm a refugee from a rowing machine. Can I come in?"

Brushing past Karen, she rattled on, "I had to get away from that place. If I don't get my teeth into a hamburger or a taco within the next few hours I may turn cannibal. Everything on the menu over there is low-fat, low-cal, low-protein, and low-taste. I've consumed so goddamn many bean sprouts I keep feeling my head to make sure things aren't growing in my hair."

"Where's Sharon?" Karen asked, looking out the door.

"Lunching on vegetable consomme and fat-free yogurt, after a morning on a treadmill. Didn't they used to sentence vicious criminals to the treadmill? Aren't you glad to see me?"

Karen indicated a chair. "Yes, to both questions. But don't think you can make a habit of this. It drives me crazy to have people think they can interrupt my work just because I'm sitting in my living room instead of in somebody else's office."

"I know. I get that all the time too. I'll call next time, I swear. This was one of those sudden, irresistible impulses Sharon keeps talking about." Her repentant frown turned to an unrepentant grin. "She doesn't even know I'm gone. I sneaked out. Come on, let me take you to lunch."

"Lunch?" Karen looked at her watch. "I didn't realize it was so late. I can't take the time, though. I could make us a sandwich —"

"It probably wouldn't be greasy enough. I came prepared to bribe you if necessary." Joan reached into her bulging purse and whipped out a paperback book. "Look what I found yesterday, during a brief moment of recreation Sharon allowed me at a bookstore."

"*Haunted Houses of the Tidewater?*" Karen read

the title aloud. "No, thanks. I've got enough reading material on hand."

"Ah, but there's one chapter in this that may
interest you. You remember what I suggested the
other night?"

"Oh. Is there something about Amberley?"

She reached for the book. Joan returned it to
her purse. "I'll read aloud as we eat. There's a
place down the road that serves half-pound burg-
ers with chili and bacon and cheese and onions
and —"

"Oh, all right." Karen grinned reluctantly. "An
hour and a half, not a minute more."

"Make it two hours and I'll give you the book.
I have to start back by three anyhow; it's a two-
hour drive, and we're having a special treat at
Happy Hour. Six whole ounces of tomato juice."

The hamburgers weren't quite greasy enough
for Joan, but she compensated by devouring a pile
of french fries. A little moan of pleasure escaped
her lips as she leaned back, replete.

"You missed one," Karen said, indicating a lone
French fry.

"Oh, yeah. You've done your good deed for the
day, dearie. You have just saved a life."

"Sharon's, I suppose."

"She may yet survive the week. I promise I
won't bug you again, but I trust you have no objection to my attending the auction this weekend."

"How do you know about that?"

"There was an ad in *Auction Weekly*."

"Oh, so you're an auction freak. Why didn't I know that?"

"It's a secret vice. I only share it with fellow addicts. This looks like a good one — Saturday and Sunday both."

The information was new to Karen. She wondered why Peggy hadn't told her. Probably because she hadn't asked.

Joan went on, "The prison gates open at noon on Friday, so I plan to drive down and attend the viewing that afternoon. We might have dinner if you can spare the time."

"I'll see. Is Sharon coming with you?"

"She'll have to, unless she wants to rent a car," Joan said calmly.

"It could be quite a jolly little reunion," Karen said. "Peggy is here too. Did you know that?"

"I thought she might be. You'll get nasty wrinkles if you frown like that. What's the matter with you? Sure I'm curious about what you're doing. That's what friends are for — to share your interests and help out when they can."

"I wasn't frowning, I was thinking," Karen explained. "I appreciate the offer, Joan, but I don't see how you can help, unless Dorothea turns up again. You loom threateningly almost as well as she does."

Joan grinned. "I did enjoy that. However, I possess other talents besides the ability to loom, talents which I will now demonstrate." She took a book from her purse, and shook her head when Karen reached for it. "I insist on reading aloud. The literary style is absolutely delicious." Clearing her throat, she pronounced the words with unctuous enjoyment.

" 'Though the handsome mansions of the region abound in apparitions of infinite variety, none boasts the collection that haunt a grim old house not far distant from the bright lights and cheerful society of Fredericksburg. The visitor who approaches this domicile, overhung with untrimmed trees, on a gloomy winter day feels certain that a curse does hang over the place as the dark clouds hang down over its roof.

" 'No one knows when the house was built. It is one of the oldest in the region, but history and local legend remain silent as to the precise date of its origin. Those same legends tell of the builder's horrible history; fleeing his native England after some unspeakable crime, he selected a spot in the wilderness remote from civilization, and many an unfortunate slave died in its building. And not slaves only. For he brought a companion with him, a beautiful young girl whose face bore the stamp of sorrow and was never heard to utter a word.' "

Joan paused for a drink of water, and Karen said, " 'Appalling' is more appropriate than 'delicious.' How much more of this drivel is there?"

"I haven't gotten to the best part. Listen. 'Was she mute by birth or had some cruel hand deprived her of her tongue? Was she his daughter, as he claimed, or his hapless, helpless paramour? Whatever, she went with him into the forests and was never seen again — in life. But she has been seen since, by many a terrified trespasser and poacher, her white garments floating as she runs, and in pursuit the dark, hooded shape of the man she flees. In vain! For if the watcher has the fortitude to remain and see the drama out to its end, the pursuer wins the race, falling upon the tragic victim and swallowing her up in his cloak and stifling, with repeated blows, the agonized shrieks that at last quiver into silence. Yes; in death the poor creature found the voice life had denied her, but too late! The Screaming Lady is one of the Tidewater's most tragic ghosts.' "

Joan looked up from the book. "Honestly, Karen, you're staring like a stuffed owl. Isn't it hilarious? I thought you'd get a kick out of it."

"Oh, yes. It is. I do."

"There's a pack of spectral hounds too," Joan said happily. "And a rocking chair that rocks when nobody's sitting in it, and footsteps that thump up and down the back stairs, and cold spots in various rooms — the author claims she heard the footsteps and felt the cold — and bloodstains that can't be cleaned off, and other good stuff."

Karen nodded dumbly.

"The people who produce these books are usually local wanna-be writers," Joan explained. "I collect them from all over the country. The same basic themes are repeated over and over — lights going on and off, funny noises in an empty house, furniture moving — and White Ladies aren't uncommon. This one is a little off-beat, though. You see what that could mean."

"It's an interesting idea," Karen said slowly. "But it's pretty farfetched. What else does he say about Amberley?"

"Such chauvinism. It's a she, not a he. Violetta Fowler."

Peggy was fascinated by the Screaming Lady. "You're absolutely certain you never heard or read that story before today?"

"Of course I'm not certain," Karen said wearily. "I have no conscious recollection of it, but I might have run across it at some time or other. As a child I reveled in fairy tales and ghost stories."

"So did I. I don't remember this one, but we all have a lot of buried memories. The sound we heard . . . It could have been a woman's scream, couldn't it?"

"In broad daylight? You were the one who said it, Peggy — the ambience was all wrong."

"Maybe she figured she'd have to risk it, since we weren't likely to wander around the woods after dark." Karen's expression indicated she didn't appreciate the light touch, and Peggy said, "Just kidding. It's a common theme in your feminist criticism, isn't it? Women being silenced, mute — no one listening?"

"Oh, sure. Mary E. Coleridge's poem about the image in the mirror: 'She had no voice to speak her dread.' There are also many references to being deprived of the most powerful 'voice,' that of literature. Even demure little Jane Austen points out that men have succeeded in slandering women because the pen has always been in their hands. She . . . Oh, shit!"

"Good gracious. What brought that on?"

"I just remembered. I promised I'd talk to that damned Literary Society tomorrow."

"About Jane Austen, I cleverly deduce."

"She's safe, don't you think?"

"If you don't mention that she was a brilliant social satirist. Stick to Elizabeth and Mr. Darcy, as played by Greer Garson and Laurence Olivier."

"Most of them probably haven't even read the book," Karen grumbled.

"It's a good opening for you to quiz Mrs. Fowler about ghosts, though,"

Peggy said. Her voice was quite serious. "Go early, take her book along and ask her to sign it."

"You really think it's important?"

"Could be. Not just the ghost stories. Scandal is what I'm after. I'll bet she knows a lot she hasn't told you." Peggy glanced down at the page she had been reading. " 'So long as that ancient crime is not expiated, so long will the curse, it is said, pursue the descendants of Obadiah Cartright. Despair and failure have marked the fortunes of the family down the centuries. When will the Screaming Lady be avenged? When will the soul of her tormentor find punishment in the eternal flames of damnation?' "

"Spare me," Karen said wryly. "Her literary style is as appalling as her theology."

"You're missing the point," Peggy insisted. "Don't you see the malice in those vague hints of failure and crime? She obviously detests the Cartrights."

"That's because Cameron divorced her niece. Of course Mrs. F. implied it was the other way around — that his cruelty and neglect drove the poor girl to leave him."

"You never told me that."

"It struck me as profoundly uninteresting."

"Gossip is always interesting. So that smirking pimply youth we met at the tea party is Cameron's brother-in-law?"

"I guess so," Karen said, surprised. "That would explain why he was hassling Cameron the other day."

"You never told me that either. What happened?"

"I only heard a few words. Cameron said something like 'I said no and I mean no,' and then I showed up, and Bobby Boy left."

"Probably wanted money," Peggy mused.

"Cameron's personal problems are none of your business," Karen said impatiently. "Or mine."

"How do you know? Gossip and trivialities, so-called, affect people's daily lives far more than the great events of history."

Karen had been about to object. Peggy's final comment struck a nerve; thoughtfully she said, " 'The insignificance of kitchen things.' "

"What?"

"It's from a short story — 'A Jury of Her Peers.'

There's been a murder. A man has been found lying in bed with a noose around his neck. The chief suspect is his wife. Two women go back to the lonely farmhouse with their husbands — the sheriff and his men — to get clothes and other necessities for the imprisoned wife. While the men are searching for clues that would explain the motive for the murder, the women look around the kitchen. 'The insignificance of kitchen things,' derided and ignored by the men, tells the women why the wife was driven to murder her husband. All the things he did to her were little things: making her cook on a broken stove; keeping her shabby and ill-clothed so that she was ashamed to go out and make friends — another form of imprisonment; and finally destroying, wantonly, the only thing she loved — her canary. The dead bird is the vital clue — and the women suppress it. They understand, as the men cannot, that the killing was justifiable homicide."

"Ha," Peggy said triumphantly. "That's exactly what I was talking about. Vital trivialities. I'll bet Mrs. Fowler knows a lot of useful dirt about the Cartrights, for six generations back, and she'd be delighted to spread it. All she needs is a little encouragement. You might confide to her your growing romantic attachment —"

"That will happen on the same day the eternal flames of damnation freeze over. I'm sorry I ever showed you this stupid book. What luck did you have today?"

"Let's sit on the steps. I want to smoke."

"I told you you could smoke in here — if you insist. Just sit next to the window."

"I want to smoke a lot and I'm a very considerate person. Come on, it's a nice day."

The declining sun cast shadows across the lawn and deepened the green of young leaves and new grass. Around the sundial in the backyard a circle of lavender hyacinths bloomed bravely — except for the ones that had been flattened by the body of a gray-and-white cat, sprawled in a patch of sunlight.

"That's a handsome cat," Peggy said. "Your landlady's?"

"I don't know who it belongs to. I doubt it's Mrs. Fowler's; you've seen that finicky neat house."

"Right. I hope it's not a stray."

"Control yourself. You have enough cats. And I am not adopting one."

"You can take shots for those allergies, you know."

"I could, but I'm not going to. Stop wandering off the subject."

Peggy continued to stare. As if aware of admiration, the cat rolled over and stretched. "It's wearing a collar," Peggy said, relieved. "Okay. My luck ran out today. The title search dead-ended in 1778. There was nothing before that."

"That's far enough. The book couldn't have been written before then. Why are you so set on tracing the ownership of the house?"

"I don't like unfinished business. However,

there's not much I can do about it unless I spend a lot of time and effort trying other sources. So I spent the rest of the day looking up birth and death certificates. I managed to fill in a number of blanks on the genealogy."

She stubbed out her cigarette and turned so that she could unfold the papers. "Don't worry, I made copies before I started scribbling on them," she said, anticipating Karen's objection. "Here's the second generation. As you might expect, a lot of the poor little devils died in infancy. Three of the girls survived, one to the ripe old age of seventy-four. She must have been a tough old bird; she managed to outlive three husbands, and produced — are you ready for this? — sixteen children."

"My God," Karen breathed.

"You said it. I doubt she's Ismene. Show me a woman who finds time to write while birthing and raising sixteen kids, and I'll introduce you to a real superwoman. One of the other women — Alexandra — died at seventeen. Too young?"

"Almost certainly. But she could be Clara."

"Clara . . . Oh, Ismene's sister. I think you're leaning too heavily on the autobiographical idea, but . . . The other, Ann, was older by two years. She lived to be thirty-seven. Had only two children."

"She was married?"

"That's what women did in those days. Got married. Period." Peggy lit another cigarette and stared thoughtfully out across the garden. The cat had gone, leaving the broken corpses of several hyacinths. "Don't get fixated on a picture of Ismene as a carefree unattached spinster. It happened, but not very often. Most women achieved economic independence by surviving a well-to-do husband. Ismene could have been a widow or even a happily married woman with a husband who was sympathetic to her literary aspirations."

"Fat chance," Karen said cynically. "Even Tom Jefferson, who gave his daughter a classical education, told her she had to learn to sew in order to direct the servants' work." She picked up the papers and leafed through them. "You've only covered one generation."

"The farther back you go, the more fragmentary the records," Peggy explained patiently. "I don't see the sense of spending time and effort on unlikely possibilities. What's your informed, expert opinion on a probable date? You must have some idea by this time."

"I was afraid you were going to ask me that."

"I know you can't be precise within a year or two —"

"Year, hell. I can't even pick a likely decade." Karen shifted position; the wooden steps were hard. "There are too many variables. You've got to allow for originality and individual talent. The style of 'Houses of Stone' is much less artificial and stilted than that of the eighteenth-century Gothics, but the type had almost disappeared, at least in America, by 1800. It was replaced by the sentimental or domestic novel, whose plot elements are entirely different from —"

"Spare me the lecture," Peggy interrupted. "And never mind the cautious academic qualifiers; I'm not one of your critical colleagues. Pick a decade."

"Well." Karen thumbed through the pages of the genealogy. "I'll commit myself to this extent: the women of the second and third generations are the most likely. You can concentrate on them."

"That's some help," Peggy grumbled. "All right, I'll tackle the third generation tomorrow; at least I should be able to eliminate the ones that died young. But bear in mind that there's a limit to what I can do with original historical sources. Some of them just aren't there. I have some hopes for the auction, and for those possibly apocryphal boxes of papers Cameron mentioned. How I'd love to find a family Bible — one of those big heavy tomes with pages for births and deaths. And I intend to have a nice long gossip with your landlady. If I can — Well, well, speak of the devil."

Mrs. Fowler had emerged from the back door. She wore a wide-brimmed hat, tied under her chin with a coquettish bow, and a pair of gloves. At first she appeared not to see them. Hands behind her, she strolled slowly along the walk, pausing from time to time to sniff at a blossom or inspect a clump of what appeared to be violets. When she approached the sundial she let out a squeal and knelt stiffly, fingering the broken flowers. Her agitated monologue was audible, but Karen could not make out the words. Rising, she stamped her foot and turned, looking around the yard.

"I pity the cat if she gets hold of it," Peggy said with a chuckle. "She's seen us. Hi, there, Mrs. Fowler!" She waved.

Mrs. Fowler waved back, but was apparently too ladylike to imitate Peggy's yell. Crossing the grass she stopped at the hedge that bordered the drive and looked up. "Did you see a cat?" she demanded.

"Why, yes," Peggy answered. "It was lying by the sundial."

"I knew it!" Mrs. Fowler's chins quivered. "I've told the Millers over and over they must keep that beast out of my yard. It digs in the flower beds and — and — uses them as a litter box, and leaves dead moles on my back steps and kills the sweet little birds."

"Sweet little birds my arse," Peggy muttered out of the corner of her mouth. "They make as much mess as a cat — droppings, and piles of seed hulls . . . You notice there's no feeder visible."

She raised her voice and called back, "It's hard to confine cats, Mrs. Fowler. But it's a shame about your pretty flowers. We have been admiring your garden."

"Such a lot of work," Mrs. Fowler sighed, inspecting her gloves, which appeared to be unstained by vulgar dirt. "But worth every bit of it. I derive spiritual sustenance from these lovely blooms. 'One is nearer to God in a garden, Than anywhere else on earth,' you know."

"I'll bet that's the motto on the sundial," Peggy said, in the same ventriloquist's murmur.

"I mustn't stand here shouting," Mrs. Fowler shouted. "That's the sort of vulgar thing the Millers do. But I'm glad I happened to see you, Dr. Holloway; I wanted to tell you the Colonel has kindly offered to drive us to the meeting tomorrow. He'll pick us up at eleven-thirty."

Karen had been enjoying the double-edged conversation; consternation replaced amusement when she heard Mrs. Fowler's offer. She could imagine how the Colonel drove — straight down the middle of the road, through red lights and stop signs. "That's very kind, but unnecessary," she called. "I'll drive you. The meeting isn't at your house, then?"

"Oh, no, my dear, there wouldn't be room. We're expecting a large crowd, with such a distinguished speaker. Our monthly meetings are always at the restaurant. A private room, of course."

"Creamed chicken on toast and petrified peas," murmured Peggy. "Lucky you."

"Are you sure you want to drive?" Mrs. Fowler called. "The Colonel will be happy —"

"Absolutely sure," Karen said firmly. "Can you be ready by eleven? I'd love to have a little chat before we go." Out of the corner of her mouth she mumbled, "How was that?"

Peggy raised her thumbs.

After Mrs. Fowler had retreated, Peggy got to her feet. "My stomach is making noises Mrs. F. would consider vulgar. Where shall we eat?"

"I don't care. Someplace quiet. I have a treat for you — an excerpt from the manuscript. The

289

stone house was Ismene's — a room of her own. The book was probably written there."

The small structure drew her to it. She could think of nothing else. What had been the function of that strange house of stone? Why she thought of it as a house she could not say; the word was inappropriate, with its connotations of a dwelling place, a source of homely comfort. It preyed on her mind to such an extent that one evening, when she and Edmund sat in the library, she spoke to him of it.

They were alone. Clara and Isabella had gone the day before to visit friends of the latter; they would remain, in all probability, for at least two weeks. Ismene had refused the invitation; the alacrity with which her excuses were received, without urging or repetition, assured her that only courtesy had prompted the offer. She did not repine; Clara was lost to her now, unless some sudden change of fortune or of heart should lead her sister back to the love that would never fail. Much more to her taste than empty chatter and laughter were those peaceful hours of companionable silence with one who shared her interests and sympathized with her feelings.

For a time she watched the play of lamplight through his golden curls as he sat with head bent over the volume he was perusing. Not for worlds would she have disturbed his communion with the poet; but at last he closed the volume and turned in his chair. "I feel your eyes upon me," he said with an affectionate smile. "Are you musing, in your own thoughtful way, on the passages you have read, or does something trouble you? Surely you know you need not hesitate to confide in me."

Thus encouraged, she told him of her discovery and confessed the inexplicable urge that drew her to the structure. It seemed to her that his brow grew troubled as he listened; yet when she had finished he answered with ready grace. "I knew of it, yes; but I cannot tell you what its function may have been. It has been long abandoned. A grim, unsightly place; I confess I do not understand your attraction. But," he went on, "that very attraction is sufficient cause to arouse my interest. We will inspect the place together, shall we? Tomorrow."

This duly ensued; though summer's stifling breath had oppressed the earth for the past weeks, this day might have been stolen from May. Soft breezes caressed their cheeks, and the luxuriant greenery, the fascination of nature brought a smile to Edmund's face as they strolled.

"This is a pleasure, indeed; I am grateful to you, Ismene, for forcing me out of my office. I have been bent over my ledgers too long."

"I observed that." She hesitated, unwilling to display vulgar curiosity, but affection conquered delicacy. "I trust, Cousin, that there is nothing in those ledgers that causes you concern. If I can assist in any way —"

He pressed the hand that rested on his arm and smiled at her. "You need not assure me of your goodwill or your affection, Ismene. Let me forget the deadly dullness of business for a time. What a heavenly spot! Those grim stone walls are like a blot on a master painting."

Yet to Ismene there was beauty and meaning in the contrast of rocky harshness and twining greenery. The delicacy of the honeysuckle softened the stone, smothering it in a soft veil of green. That slow, patient growth would triumph in the end over man's intrusion. Here was a living illustration of the Divine promise that the meek should inherit the earth.

"Strange indeed," murmured Edmund, studying the structure with a puzzled frown. "Let us see what is within."

With a strength his slender form did not suggest he put his shoulder to the sagging door and forced it open. "You had best stay back," he warned. "A regiment of spiders guards the interior."

Nevertheless she came to his side and looked inside.

Only dust and cobwebs met her eyes. The interior, windowless and dark, had been swept clean of visible objects. At first it seemed to her that the floor was of earth, but then she realized that under the dust lay a carpet of cut stone, blocks as massive as those in an antique temple, closely fitted.

"It is like a pagan temple," said Edmund, echoing her thoughts as he so often did. "The innermost sanctuaries of the shrines of Greece and Egypt were made thus: darkness shrouded the mysteries of those ancient cults."

"It could not have served such a purpose here."

"Surely not. There is a mystery, however, and it would amuse me to solve it. I will have the place cleared out; perhaps some clue as to its function lies buried under the dust."

Ismene had not intended to speak, unless to express approbation of his intent. She heard her voice as if it had been that of another. "May I, thereafter, claim it as my own? A private place in which to write and read and reflect?"

Astonishment shaped his features as he drew her away. "This grim, lonely place? There is much to admire in the uncultivated expanses of nature, but it is wild, uncontrolled —"

"So must Eden have been," Ismene said. Her hands were clasped so tightly they pained her. "I would be alone."

"I see." Thoughtfully he repeated, "Yes, I see. If this is your desire —" But then he broke off with a cry, and caught her up in his arms, swinging her aside; and she heard a rustle of foliage and beheld a sinuous footless form glide through the open doorway into shelter.

"There is a serpent in your Paradise, Cousin," Edmund said with a strange little laugh. "If it offers forbidden fruit, will you resist the tempter?"

Karen rolled over onto her back. She had tried every other conceivable sleeping position, and she was still wide awake. She couldn't blame the weather; it was, as Peggy had said, a perfect night for sleeping, cool and crisp as autumn, with a soft breeze stirring the curtains and rustling the leaves.

Nor was it the thought of her "talk" next day that prevented her from sleeping. Stage fright no longer bothered her and she had delivered countless lectures on the immortal Jane, to her own classes and elsewhere.

Could the Screaming Lady be a distorted, romanticized memory of a woman silenced not by nature but by her society? Karen would have liked to believe it — what a subject for an article that would make! — but she couldn't. The symbolism was too subtle, too far-fetched. Did the weird story contain the seeds of some actual past event, or was it only another version of a common folk legend? Peggy's admission that she had reached a dead end in tracing the ownership of the house implied a corollary Karen hated to admit. This might be the first of many dead ends. She might never know who Ismene really was.

She forced her tense muscles to relax; she had been lying stiff as a board, fists clenched. Historical research seldom presented neat, unanswerable solutions to problems. Scholars were still arguing about whether Richard III had slaughtered his nephews in the Tower, and how much Mary Stuart knew about the plot that had taken her despised husband's life. She had been unreasonable to expect that a few days or weeks of investigation would provide an answer to the question that had become an obsession. Sharon would probably say she needed counseling. It wasn't "healthy" to care so much about a dead woman.

I don't need a psychologist to explain why I feel that way, she thought, turning onto her side. That same sense of helpless rage, of voicelessness, was familiar to her too, though — thank God and Betty Friedan — not to the same extent. She understood Ismene's need for a place of her own, even a place as forbidding as the abandoned house in the woods. It was desirable because of its very desolation; no one else would claim it.

Did everyone feel that same need for solitude, she wondered, or was it an aberration, experienced by only a small percent of the human race and incomprehensible to the rest? And why was it so difficult to attain? Modern life had added various forms of mechanical intrusion into one's privacy; the very ringing of a telephone was a demand for attention, even if one had enough willpower to ignore it, and automobiles made it easier for friends to drop in and purveyors of goods and services — including purveyors of salvation — to reach one's door. Resentment of intrusion provoked not apology but indignation and hurt feelings. That had been true even in Jane's day, when she sat writing in the parlor, covering her papers when she was interrupted as she so often was. Some people found that picture charming — cute little Jane, curls tied back and slippered feet dangling, looking up with a smile whenever someone popped in to chat. It had always made Karen's blood run cold.

She yawned and stretched and wondered drowsily whether that had ever been used by a mystery writer as a motive for murder: the frantic, frustrated need to be alone. Snatching up the first weapon that came to hand — shotgun or knife, frying pan or baseball bat — striking out in a frenzy, seeing faces turn from smiles to blood-streaked, ruined horror.

Perhaps it had been a motive for murder more frequently than anyone suspected — uncomprehended even by the killer.

Chapter Ten

The sniffs I get from the ink of the women are always fey, old-hat, Quaintsy, Gaysy, tiny, too dykily psychotic, crippled, creepish fashionable, frigid, outer-Baroque, maquille in mannequin's whimsey, or else bright and stillborn.

NORMAN MAILER,
Advertisements for Myself, 1959

Karen had spoken at a number of luncheon meetings. This wasn't the first time she had toyed with the idea of starting a protest movement. Serving the food before the speech might suit the audience, but it was sheer hell for the speaker. If she didn't dribble salad dressing down her front or spill coffee onto her skirt while making genteel conversation with her neighbors, she might get a scrap of lettuce or spinach caught between her teeth, with no hope of extracting it genteelly before she was introduced. If she ate too much she ran the risk of emitting what some Victorian writer had called "an unseemly sound of repletion" in the middle of a sentence.

In this case Karen wasn't tempted to overeat. The entree was creamed chicken and peas, just as Peggy had predicted. The gluey mass rested in and on a patty shell so flaky it exploded like a grenade whenever she cut into it. At least she wasn't pilloried on a podium, in full view of the audience. There had not been time for the "little chat" with Mrs. Fowler. The old lady hadn't been ready at eleven; she had dithered and fussed and misplaced hat, gloves, and purse for over forty-five minutes. They had barely made it to the restaurant on time.

Mrs. F. sat at Karen's right; the Colonel, in his capacity of vice president of the organization, was on her left. Peggy was across the table. She had not mentioned her intention of attending, no doubt because she knew Karen would object; she had simply turned up, in full uniform — gloves, heels, fluttering skirts — except for the hat, which, she admitted, was more trouble than it was worth.

Bill Meyer was not at their table. He was present, however. "I wouldn't miss it for the world," he had assured Karen, when they met by chance outside the door of the restaurant. She had managed not to call him a rude name.

Dessert consisted of cheesecake with cherry topping. Glancing at Karen's serving, from which she had taken two small courtesy bites, Mrs. Fowler smiled and patted her hand. "Don't be nervous, dear. This is quite an intellectual audience, but I'm sure you'll do just fine."

The kindly reassurance might have been partially responsible for what happened, but at the time Karen wasn't aware of feeling anything except mild irritation and amusement. Bored and impatient, but not at all nervous, she sat through Mrs. Fowler's introduction — which described her as a distinguished lady scholar — and took her place at the reading stand amid a spatter of applause. Then, as was her habit, she looked over the audience before beginning to speak.

A few familiar faces: Peggy's, set in a sardonic but sympathetic smile, Bill Meyer, grinning in a way that made Karen want to slap him, Lisa Fairweather . . . What was she doing here? She hadn't returned Karen's calls. Catch her before she leaves, Karen thought, and introduce her to Peggy . . . Tanya, the librarian. There were only four dark faces in the room, all at the same table.

The faces of Mrs. Fowler and the Colonel blended into the mass. With a few exceptions most of them might have been blood relatives, not because of a particular physical resemblance but because they bore the same stamp of complacency. Well-fed, well-dressed, warm and comfortable, they now awaited the confirmation of their own self-satisfied sense of intellectual superiority. Half of them would doze off before it was over. The other half wouldn't understand what she was talking about.

It felt like a sudden rush of water pouring into a container, filling something that had been empty before, rising from feet to body to throat till it overflowed her parted lips — anger, cold as melted snow, consuming as flame. It was unlike anything she had ever felt before, but it was not alien. It felt . . . right. Clearing her throat, she said, slowly and deliberately, "The Pen as Penis."

She paused, expecting a gasp of collective outrage from the audience. There was no sound at all. The faces that stared back at her were like masks, unblinking, frozen. She saw Peggy clap her hand over her mouth.

"In 1886 Gerard Manley Hopkins — he was a poet, by the way — wrote, in a letter to a friend, 'The Male quality is the creative gift.' Ruskin — I'm sure you've all heard of Ruskin — was more direct. He described the 'Penetrative Imagination' as a 'piercing mind's tongue.'

"This image of the male quality, symbolized by the male member, as the only true source of literary and artistic creativity permeated nineteenth-century criticism and nineteenth-century attitudes.

"It is such an obvious pun, such a childishly irresistible symbol, that modern critics have been unable to abandon it. A book review that appeared in *The New York Times* in 1976 remarked that women writers 'lack that blood-congested genital drive which energizes every great style.' Well, of course they do, don't they? Castrated by nature, lacking that essential instrument, they are by definition incapable of originality or a great style. Another critic, writing a decade later, employs an even more emphatic metaphor. Creativity, he says, arises from 'the use of the phallic pen on the pure space of the virgin page.' That metaphor certainly excludes women writers; it makes literature a variety of rape."

Two women at a table near the door pushed their chairs back and stood up. Their faces were crimson with rage or embarrassment, or a blend of the two. Karen half expected they would rush at her, swinging their big black purses like clubs. Instead they turned as one and stamped out of the room.

Karen's eyes moved coolly over the faces of the audience. Most were the same angry shade as those of the defectors, and their expressions were equally outraged. No one else left the room, though. They're waiting to hear more dirty words, Karen thought. I mustn't disappoint them.

"But what, you may ask," she went on, "does all this have to do with Jane Austen? According to certain giants of criticism, her novels are not worthy of inclusion in the lofty canon of true literature. They lack — and I quote — 'a strong male thrust.' "

The paralysis that had held the Colonel immobile snapped; his face swelled like a big red balloon and he leaned toward Mrs. Fowler, muttering in her ear. Across the table Peggy sat quietly, hands folded, eyes fixed on Karen's face. Meyer's face was equally impassive, but the corners of his mouth were quivering.

The lecture was one Karen had given on several occasions, tailoring it, as experienced speakers do, to the particular audience. The only concession she made to this audience was that of simplification. They wouldn't have recognized the names of the modern critics she had quoted, so she didn't mention them. She gave them Jane from a feminist perspective — the subtle digs at male vanity, the cynical resignation of women who were passed from one male guardian to the next, without independence or legal identity — and ended by quoting one of Jane's few overt protests against masculine domination. "Men have had every advantage of us in telling their story . . . The pen has been in their hands."

She didn't have to belabor the point. Dirty old man, she thought, smiling sweetly at the Colonel, whose complexion had darkened from crimson to purple. With a polite "Thank you, ladies and gentlemen," she gathered up her unused notes.

An isolated outburst of applause drew her eyes to Bill Meyer. He was on his feet, clapping enthusiastically.

"I can't imagine what came over me," Karen repeated for the tenth time.

They were in Peggy's room at the hotel — "hiding out," as Peggy put it. Karen had collapsed onto the bed, her head in her hands.

Peggy got her amusement under control and wiped her eyes. "Well, you sure took care of Mrs. Fowler. She won't be sticking any more cute little notes under your door. And you gave me the thrill of a lifetime. I haven't enjoyed myself so much since . . . Never mind. Stop berating yourself; it was worth it, even if you did antagonize the old lady."

"Oh, I don't regret giving them a taste of feminist criticism." Karen raised her head and gave Peggy a defiant look. "Those quotations speak for themselves; all you have to do is hear them to realize how absurd and unfair and *silly* they are. It isn't what I said that bothers me — it's the way I said it. Not only was it counterproductive, it was rude! Those poor stupid pompous people can't help being the way they are. They were trying to be nice to me. And what gives me the right to assume they are all stupid and pompous? Am I turning into a damned intellectual snob? I could have got the point across without going out of my way to offend them."

"You could have, but it wouldn't have been as much fun."

Karen groaned and hid her face in her hands. "I sounded like Bill Meyer," she mumbled.

"He loved every word," Peggy said. "I was watching him."

"Thanks, that's just what I needed to hear."

Peggy said nothing. Karen sat up with a sigh. "Ah, well. I made a mistake. I regret it, I'll try not to repeat it, but I'm not going to brood about it or go into hiding."

"Are you going to apologize to Mrs. F.?"

"No. That would imply that I'd done it on purpose. Seems to me my best defense is innocent unawareness of wrongdoing. They claim to be a literary society, don't they? I paid them the compliment of speaking to them as if they really were."

"You're probably right," Peggy said. "It's a

minor tempest in a very small teapot, after all. There was no lasting harm done." Smiling, she added, "Look at it as a symbol of how far women have come. A hundred years ago they'd have ostracized you. Two hundred years ago —"

" 'Tarred and feathered and carried in a cart, By the women of Marblehead.' "

"Is that a quote? Sounds familiar."

"It's a poem, by Whittier," Karen said abstractedly. "It was old Floyd Ireson they tarred and feathered — for his hard heart."

"They didn't tar and feather uppity women, even then."

"No, they just exiled them into the wilderness, like Anne Hutchinson, or hanged them as witches, or ducked them till they drowned, or —"

"Enough of this," Peggy said firmly. "I'm going to change out of this ridiculous outfit and then we are going to pay a business call. Lisa Fairweather has agreed to let me inspect the rest of the family papers."

"Lisa?" Karen repeated in surprise. "When did you talk to her?"

"Before your speech. Bill introduced us, and then tactfully withdrew. I'm beginning to think he really has reformed."

"The hell with him, I don't want to talk about him. That's good news, Peggy."

Peggy pulled a blouse and skirt off their hangers and headed for the bathroom. "I'm not counting on any great discoveries, but it's a loose end we have to tie up. Be with you in a minute. Have a drink while you're waiting."

"No, thanks."

Karen sat unmoving, her hands limp in her lap. Peggy was one hundred percent right; the incident had been a tempest in a teapot. Even if Bill Meyer reported it to their colleagues, it would arouse mild amusement in some quarters, and enthusiastic commendation in others — the quarters whose approval meant most to her. So why did it bother her so much?

There had been no alien intrusion into her mind that day, no eerie sense of another voice speaking with her tongue. The voice had been her own, amplified . . . by what? Anger, vast and uncontrolled. And hate. For an hour-long interval she had hated those poor silly people. And she had felt the hatred hidden behind their smiling masks, even before she started to speak.

She couldn't get the image out of her head — the image of a mob, out of control and bent on violence. Peggy was mistaken. Women — fallen women, prostitutes — had been tarred and feathered and run out of town as recently as a hundred years ago; Mark Twain mentioned it in *Huck Finn*. Huck had seen the King and the Duke being ridden out of town by such a mob. "They didn't look like nothing in the world that was human," he had said, adding, "Human beings can be awful cruel to one another."

Lisa's apartment was in a new development on the outskirts of town. The buildings looked like

305

thousands of others in thousands of other towns across the country: rectangular blocks of brick, with minuscule balconies and neat conventional landscaping. Karen knew the style; she lived in a building very much like Lisa's. Even in this peaceful country town security had become a problem. They had to ring from the lobby before the inner door unlocked.

Neat and slim in well-cut pants, her hair tied at the nape of her neck with a bow, Lisa greeted them at the door of the apartment. A blast of cold air issued from the living room; she had the air-conditioning on full. The living room looked just about as Karen had expected: a few hanging plants, a few good prints, a conservative muted color scheme of oatmeal and brown. The only unexpected feature was an Oriental rug, its blend of peacock blues and greens exquisitely faded by time.

"That came from Amberley," Lisa explained. "It's not very attractive, but I needed something on the floor; it's in my lease. And carpeting is so expensive."

"It's Turkish or Kashan," Peggy said. "Antique."

"I haven't decided yet whether to put it in the sale," Lisa said. "I'm told it's rather valuable and it sure doesn't go with my other things. But I'm forgetting my manners. Please sit down. Could I offer you a cup of tea or a glass of wine?"

Peggy accepted the latter and Karen followed her lead. She wondered whether Lisa would mention her speech. She had no intention of introducing the subject herself.

After they had discussed the weather and admired the apartment, Lisa said politely, "I enjoyed your speech today."

"Thank you," said Karen politely.

Peggy's method of breaking the ice was to use a club. "I'll bet that reaction wasn't universal," she said with a laugh.

Lisa's faint social smile broadened. "Not hardly. The Colonel was fit to be tied. I heard him tell Miz Fowler she ought to evict you."

"That would be a nuisance," Karen said calmly. "But I can always find another place."

"Oh, she won't." Lisa's pretty lip curled. "She's like all the other old folks, always talking about honor and dignity, but when her principles come up against cold hard cash, guess which loses. She needs money. Like all the rest of us."

Peggy's methods seemed to be effective; Lisa was speaking more candidly than she ever had to Karen. "Including Cameron?" Peggy asked.

"Especially Cam. He's as anxious to get out of this hick town as I am. Why do you suppose he's dirtying his nice clean hands fixing up the house? The minute he gets enough money to stick his mama in a nursing home, he'll be gone."

"Oh, is his mother ill? I'm so sorry," Peggy exclaimed.

"She's not sick, she's just old and senile. The only places that will take people like that cost a bundle." Lisa dismissed the subject with a shrug.

"But I'm boring you with all this gossip —"

"No, not at all," Peggy said sincerely. "I hope the auction is a great success and that you make lots of money."

"So do I," Lisa said with equal sincerity. She gestured. "There are the boxes of papers you wanted to see. Cam refused to put them in the auction and I didn't argue, because I didn't suppose they were worth much. Have a look if you like. I trust you to do what's fair."

She sat watching, ankles crossed and hands primly folded, while the other two inspected the contents of the two cartons. It was a dirty job; the envelopes and albums had been given a superficial dusting, but they were encrusted with the mold and grime of decades. Karen didn't doubt that Lisa had already inspected them thoroughly.

It took Peggy less than half an hour to reach a conclusion. She sat back on her heels and shook her head.

"Nothing that interests you?" Lisa asked.

"I'm afraid not. There doesn't seem to be anything earlier than the turn of the century. This century. There's no reason why you should take my word for it —"

"There's no reason why I shouldn't." Lisa uncrossed her ankles and put her feet primly together. "I could see by your expression that nothing hit you. Mr. Meyer's reaction was the same."

Peggy began returning the dusty bundles and

old photo albums to the cartons. "The old boy was certainly a pack rat, wasn't he? He even kept newspaper clippings and advertisements. Some people collect those things, I believe. And old photo albums."

Lisa nodded, but did not reply. When the cartons had been repacked, Peggy rose stiffly to her feet. "Damned arthritis," she muttered.

"I'm sorry you didn't find anything," Lisa said. "Would you like another glass of wine?"

"No, thanks, we've taken up enough of your time."

Karen had remained silent, feeling it was better to let Peggy handle the matter. She wasn't as good as Peggy at hiding her feelings, and at the moment her feelings for Lisa were not especially friendly.

Lisa escorted them to the door. "Will I see you at the auction?" she asked.

Peggy nodded. "I don't suppose there was a family Bible?"

They were like a pair of duelists, Karen thought, thrusting and parrying. Lisa pursed her lips and looked thoughtful. "I don't remember offhand. It might be among the books. They'll be sold Saturday."

As soon as they were outside, Peggy let out a crow of triumph. "One up for me. She's a tricky little devil, though. By this time she must have a pretty good idea of what we're after, and she's going to milk us for all she can get. And I doubt she'll share with Cousin Cameron."

"You think there is a Bible?"

"Yes. And I don't think it is among the books that will be sold."

They got in the car, and Peggy looked distastefully at her grubby hands. "I need to wash. I'd have asked Lisa if I could use her bathroom, but somehow I got the impression she wasn't crazy about having us hang around."

"Maybe she's got a date tonight — with another prospective customer. I still think she and Bill are in cahoots."

"But she doesn't trust him, so she's getting a second opinion from us? Could be. She didn't expect us to find anything in that lot. I'll bet she's got more enticing material squirreled away."

"Those boxes were full," Karen said. "There wouldn't have been room in them for much else."

"But how many boxes were there?"

After a moment Karen said, "There's one way to find out."

"Cameron."

"Right." She turned onto Main Street. It was lined with handsome, carefully restored old houses. Some were antebellum, with the classical porticoes and white columns of that era; others displayed the sprawling extravagance of Victoriana, with towers and verandas and yards of gingerbread trim.

Karen brought the car to a stop at a traffic light. Peggy wiped the perspiration off her face with the back of her hand. "Haven't you got air-conditioning?"

"There's no point in turning it on. We're almost there."

Peggy grunted critically but did not pursue the point. "Is that the main library?"

"The one and only. And that," Karen said, "is the librarian."

The light changed and traffic began to move, but not before Tanya had seen them. She bared all her teeth in a broad grin and raised a clenched fist. Karen waved.

"One supporter," Peggy said. "Do you know her?"

"Slightly. I checked out the library first thing. There's nothing there."

"You sure you don't want to go to my place?" Peggy inquired delicately.

"No. I want to change out of this ladylike ensemble. And I'm not going to sneak in after dark."

Mrs. Fowler was sitting on the porch. She held a piece of embroidery, but when they caught sight of her, her eyes were fixed on the street. Karen had slowed to make the turn into the driveway; moved by an irresistible impulse, she put her arm out the window and waved vigorously. She slowed even more, waiting for a response, but there was none; Mrs. Fowler sat like a statue and glared like Medusa.

"That is not a happy person," said Peggy, chuckling. "But I guess she doesn't intend to confront you directly. Maybe she's left you one of her little notes."

"Or sent an emissary?" Someone was sitting on the bottom step, his head bent over a book. Hear-

311

ing the car he looked up and rose to his feet. Karen went on, "He arranged for me to rent the place; if she wants me out, she'd likely get him to do the dirty work."

Cameron didn't look like the bearer of bad news. After greeting Karen he hurried to open the car door for Peggy, who had remained in her seat looking particularly demure. "I hope you haven't been waiting long," she murmured, accepting the hand he offered and stepping more or less gracefully out of the car.

"Only a few minutes. I was just about to leave a note." He flourished the object he had been reading — not a book, a thick sheaf of papers. "I thought you might like to see the auction catalog. I just got a copy myself."

"And you brought it straight to us? How sweet!"

"I do appreciate it," Karen said. Cameron seemed to be enjoying the byplay, but Peggy was inclined to overdo her performance. "Come in, if you have time."

He accepted readily. As she preceded the other two up the stairs, Karen wondered if it was the presence of a chaperone that had made him agree to an invitation he had been reluctant to accept before. Peggy would love that idea. She'd probably go all out for the role of duenna, nodding and smiling in a rocking chair, with a wad of knitting on her lap.

Propped against the door was a large white box. For one insane moment Karen thought Mrs. Fowler had been there to leave, not a note, but a bomb or some less theatrical demonstration of disapproval. Peggy identified it at once. "Someone's sent you flowers," she exclaimed, lifting the top to display a bouquet of tulips, daffodils and ferns nestled in green tissue paper.

"Not I," Cameron said, frowning. "I didn't even come up the stairs."

Leaving Peggy to carry the flowers, Karen got her key out and opened the door. She had a strong suspicion as to the identity of the sender, so she let Peggy lift the container out of the box and search for a card. "Well, well," said Peggy. "Guess who."

"Bill Meyer, I suppose."

"Right on the mark. He says, 'With heartfelt admiration and deep respect.' "

"I take it," said Cameron, "that you and Dr. Meyer are no longer at odds?"

Wooden and stiff as a cigar-store Indian, he stood in the doorway.

"We are certainly not collaborating," Karen said. "I don't know what he hopes to gain by . . . Oh, never mind. Come in, Cameron, and sit down. Please."

"How about a drink?" Peggy asked. "All we've got to offer is Scotch, I'm afraid; Karen's no drinker. It's one of the few flaws in her character. Oh, come on, you wouldn't let a lady drink alone, would you?"

Cameron lowered himself cautiously into a chair and Karen excused herself. When she returned, cleaner and cooler in loose shirt and slacks, the others were looking over the auction list. She was in time to hear Peggy exclaim in tones of deep disgust, "Silver dollars, Indian-head pennies, stamp collection, Meissen figurines . . . Was there anything he didn't collect?"

"Not if it was cheap. You should have seen the place; every room was crammed with junk. There were stacks of old magazines and newspapers, from the present time all the way back to the twenties. Most worthless, unfortunately, because they are in such poor condition." Absently Cameron rubbed a patch of red, roughened skin on his cheek. It looked like poison ivy. "On the other hand, he kept everything he'd inherited, which included some good things. The Meissen was his mother's, and there's a lot of old silver."

"Some wheat among the chaff," Peggy muttered, scanning the list.

"A lot more chaff than wheat. That's why I handed the whole mess over to Jack Wickett. He's reputed to be honest, and it required more expertise than I possess to weed out the junk. I was surprised he kept so much of it, but he tells me some people collect anything."

"Correct. Barbed wire, soft-drink bottles, license plates . . . Yep, here they are on the list, along with old clothes, linens, paintings, books." Peggy turned over the last sheet. "I want to have a look at this stuff, Cameron. At my leisure, before the public viewing."

"I could arrange that, I guess. Jack is giving other people the same privilege."

314

"Including Bill Meyer?" Karen asked.

"If he requests it, there's no reason why I should refuse, is there? It's to my advantage to have you two bidding against each other."

So that was why he had appeared annoyed at the suggestion that she and Bill were on good terms. "You're right," she said, in a voice as cool as his had been.

"I'll call Jack and let you know." Cameron got up. "Keep the list if you like; I can get another. Oh — I almost forgot. I've found a couple of guys who will dig out that ruin in the woods if you're still interested."

"I'm interested," Peggy said. "Not before next week, though."

"Let me know the day and I'll have them there."

"What's your hurry?" Peggy asked amiably. "We're going out to dinner before long; care to join us?"

"I'm afraid I can't. Thanks anyway."

"Scared to be seen in public with the person who scandalized the haut monde today?"

Again Peggy's sledgehammer tactics had the desired effect. Cameron's face registered shock and then reluctant amusement. He leaned against the door, hands in his pockets. "I hope you don't think I'm that much of a social coward."

"You heard about the speech, then," Karen said.

"Miz Fowler was on the phone as soon as she got home," Cameron admitted. "I found three messages on my answering machine."

"So you rushed over here to defuse the situation," Peggy said. "How gallant."

Cameron shifted his shoulders and looked uncomfortable. "I was going to bring the list over anyhow. Miz Fowler was lying in wait for me. She gave me an earful, all right. But she never had any intention of kicking you out, if that's what you're afraid of."

" 'Afraid' is hardly the word," Karen said sharply.

"I beg your pardon." He straightened and took his hands out of his pockets. "It was the wrong word. As I pointed out to her, you can easily find another apartment, and I have a feeling that her disapproval isn't going to worry you much. That's all she can do — disapprove."

"I know."

"Good. I'll let you know about the viewing."

He closed the door very quietly behind him.

"Why do you have to do that?" Peggy demanded.

"Do what?"

"Just when I've got him nice and relaxed and making friendly gestures, you respond with a verbal slap in the face."

"I'm tired of people reassuring me and protecting me. I'm a grown person, who is perfectly capable —"

Peggy interrupted with an emphatic Anglo-Saxon expletive. "Why don't you drop-kick those flowers across the room while you're at it? I don't give a damn how you feel about men in general and those two in particular; but from a practical

316

point of view your behavior is, to say the least, counterproductive. What's the sense of antagonizing people — male or female — who could be useful to you?"

"I don't dislike men in general! Simon —"

"Is old enough to be your grandfather. Safe, in other words. What are you afraid of?"

"The conventional answer is, 'Of being hurt again.' " Karen's lips curved in a self-derisory smile. "That's what Sharon thinks; that the failure of my marriage made me wary of 'intimate relationships.' "

"She could be right."

"That's too simplistic," Karen said, sighing. "Norman didn't hurt me. He honestly believed, and believes to this day, that treating me like an adorable dim-witted child was what I needed and wanted. That didn't hurt me; it just drove me crazy! Compared to many women who have been abused physically, mentally and emotionally, I got off easy, but I'm not ready to jump into another potential disaster. Why the hell should I be in a hurry? But you are absolutely right, it's stupid to antagonize Cameron and even stupider to let Bill get to me. I'm sorry. This has not been one of my better days."

Peggy's sour face relaxed. "It's been quite a day, all right. Have a drink and then we'll go someplace for dinner. Someplace far, far away."

Before they left, Karen had a chance to practice what she had promised. When the telephone rang

317

she went reluctantly to answer it; she had braced herself for reproaches from her landlady, but she wasn't looking forward to the conversation. It was almost a relief to hear Bill Meyer's voice.

"Thank you for the flowers," she said, in a sugary-sweet voice, making a face at Peggy. "They're lovely."

"You got them? I just wanted to be certain. And to reiterate my admiration. I wouldn't have had the guts to stand up in front of that crowd and stick to my guns."

"Yes, you would have," Karen said. "You're an inspiration to us all, Bill."

Peggy frowned and shook her head, but Meyer wasn't annoyed by the sarcasm. He laughed. "I don't suppose you'd let me take you out to dinner."

"Sorry, we've made plans. Some other time?"

After she had hung up she turned to Peggy. "How was that?"

"Not bad. I take it he asked you out tonight?"

"Uh-huh. I suppose you'll say I should have accepted, but I just couldn't face it. Not tonight."

"Honey, I'm not suggesting you go to bed with him. Just be polite."

There was another call as they were preparing to leave.

"Lisa?" Karen repeated, surprised. "No, you're not interrupting anything. We were just about to go out to dinner, but there's no hurry . . . Really? Yes, of course. When? . . . Fine, we'll see you then."

"She's just happened to run across something else we might want to see?" Peggy said, as Karen replaced the phone.

"Good guess."

"It wasn't a guess, it was almost a certainty. She's going to produce her wares a little at a time, you just watch."

"She's going out to dinner; suggested we come by around nine-thirty. I assume that's all right."

"Sure. Though it will probably be a waste of time. She's not ready to produce the good stuff yet."

Peggy was, as she pointed out, absolutely right. Lisa's offering consisted of a few books, which she doled out one at a time.

"They're old," Lisa pointed out. "You said you wanted old things."

The comment was unnecessary; it was obvious that the books were old, and most were in wretched condition. The bindings had once been handsome, fine morocco and calf heavily tooled in gold, but the leather was crumbling and the transparent tape patching the pages had only worsened their condition.

After leafing through one of the volumes, Peggy handed it to Karen: "This is your specialty, not mine."

Karen opened the book to the title page. " 'Oeuvres diverses de M. Pannard,' " she read. " 'Tome deux, Opéras-comiques.' Obviously Pinnard was a playwright, but I've never heard of him. French lit. is not my field."

"It's dated 1783," Lisa said eagerly. "It's the oldest, but some of the others are almost as old."

They were also almost as obscure — collections of essays and sermons. "Salutary reminders of the ephemeral nature of fame," Peggy remarked. "Two hundred years from now, will collectors come across a book by Stephen King and wonder who the hell he was?"

"Modern books won't last that long," Karen said abstractedly, leafing through the yellowed but intact pages of a volume of Sheridan's plays. "The paper is made of wood pulp and treated with acidic compounds. Old paper was handmade from cotton and linen rags. At least Sheridan's name and fame have survived. I honestly don't know whether this is worth anything or not. It's one volume of a set, and in poor shape, and it's certainly not a first edition . . ."

By accident or intent, Lisa had saved the best till last. Peggy insisted afterward that she did it deliberately, after observing that her initial offerings failed to attract them. She also bawled Karen out for reacting with a gasp and an exclamation.

"You've got to develop a poker face! Antique dealers pray for customers like you."

"I couldn't help it," Karen protested. "Ismene must have read *Children of the Abbey*, it was a best-selling early Gothic. This could have been her own copy."

The books — all the books — were in the back seat of the car. Stars shone dimly through the misty night. Darkness had not brought much relief from the heat, however, and Karen had turned on the air-conditioning without being asked. Meekly, she added, "Thanks for buying the rest of them. They may not have been hers, but they're old enough to have been in the library of Amberley during her lifetime. One of the points I'll want to discuss is what she might have read —"

"Yeah, right." Peggy lit a cigarette. There had been no object resembling an ashtray in Lisa's apartment, and even Peggy hadn't had the gall to ask if she might smoke. "They probably won't set us back that much," she admitted, in a less aggressive voice. "I'll check with Simon as I promised I would, but I doubt these are rare books. It is an error to assume that a book is valuable just because it's old."

"So you're becoming an authority on rare books now. Is that what you and Simon talk about?"

Teasing Peggy was wasted effort. She chuckled richly. "That and other things. Shall I tell you what other things, or are you still young enough to think it's disgusting for people over fifty to be interested in sex? He knows more erotic poems than any man I've ever met. Which reminds me, maybe you could make some suggestions."

"I'll think about it," Karen said.

Peggy had left her car at the restaurant; after Karen had dropped her off she drove down the street toward the apartment. It was not late by her standards, but small Southern towns rolled up the sidewalks early on weeknights; only the restaurant and a convenience store had lighted windows. Mrs. Fowler's house, like most of the others nearby, was dark.

The mist had thickened, dimming the starlight. Karen left the car lights on while she opened the trunk and took out the briefcase, but after she had switched them off she was blinded by darkness. Groping, she found the banister and the first step, and felt her way up, cursing Mrs. Fowler's penuriousness. She might at least have provided an outside light. I ought to fake a fall and sue the old witch, Karen thought. After this I'll leave a light on inside. Or take a flashlight. I wonder what happened to that flashlight that used to be in the glove compartment? No use going back to look for it; even if it's still there, under the maps and other junk, the batteries must have died long ago.

It took forever to get the key in the lock. Once inside, she fumbled for the switch to the right of the door, and pressed it up and down several times before she was willing to admit the truth. Every light in the damned place was out. It wasn't a single burned-out bulb; the switch controlled all the lamps in the room.

Karen swore and kicked the door shut. It was not much darker inside than it was outside, and for once she preferred enclosure to open air. The significance of accessories she had failed to understand now came home to her. Those cute little candle holders, glass kittens and ceramic flowerpots and whatnot, weren't ornamental. There must be some problem with the electricity — an antiquated fuse box, perhaps — that caused frequent failures.

Muttering profanely, she felt her way across the room toward the bookshelves. She barked her shin painfully on a chair before she reached them and knocked half a dozen books off the shelf groping for the candle. It wasn't until she had located it that she realized she had neither matches nor lighter.

Taking a firm hold on her temper she stood perfectly still and tried to think sensibly. She certainly didn't intend to wander around in the dark looking for a fuse box; it might even be downstairs, in the garage. Why hadn't she thought of buying a flashlight? The stove was gas. She might be able to light a candle from the burner flame . . .

A puff of hot air from the open window stirred the curtains and made her start. The heat and humidity seemed to have increased since the sun went down; perspiration slid down her face and into her eyes, making them smart and water. Her discomfort wasn't entirely physical. The darkness pressed against her. Every inch of exposed skin tingled. It wasn't panic, in the strict sense of the word, for she had no desire to fling herself out the door in mad flight, as those unfortunates pursued by the god had done. She wanted to crouch under something, curl herself into the smallest possible space, remain motionless and unbreathing, like a mouse hunted by a cat.

The hell with the stove. She might as well go to bed; she couldn't work by candlelight anyway, the faded script of the manuscript was hard on the eyes even with adequate light. Crouch in bed, under the covers, hidden by darkness . . .

She had located the open bedroom door when a violent sneeze erupted from her and she suddenly understood why the analogy of the cat and the mouse had come into her mind. She stopped short, thrown off-balance by the explosion, supporting herself against the doorframe.

The symptoms were unmistakable. The cat was here, inside the apartment, probably in the bedroom. But how had it gotten in? The answer was just as unmistakable. Cats couldn't pick locks or pry open windows. And if the cat was still inside, the person who let it in, deliberately or inadvertently, might also be inside.

Another sneeze rocked her body. She turned very slowly and began to pick her way back across the room, pressing a finger under her lips and praying she could control the explosion that threatened until she was outside the apartment. A faint rustling sound from the bedroom made her stomach contract. There weren't many places in the small apartment where an intruder could hide, even in that convenient darkness. He must be in the bedroom, waiting till she was in bed or asleep, before he emerged.

It never occurred to her that she might be in danger. She knew what he wanted. He had searched the place once before and failed to find it. It was a logical assumption that she must carry it with her. Breaking in after she was already in the apartment, even asleep, would have involved some noise and some risk. This plan was simpler and safer; if it hadn't been for the cat, and her convenient allergy, she would never have suspected anyone was there. Looking under the bed before retiring wasn't a habit of hers.

The pressure inside her head was so intense she felt her skull would explode. She was almost at the door; stooping, she picked up the briefcase. Just a few seconds longer . . . No use. The sneeze echoed like a bomb blast. As the echoes died, she heard footsteps. He must have realized that she was retreating, that she knew someone was there; there was no use trying to conceal his presence now.

A thin beam of light struck across the room with the impact of a missile, darting from the table to the door and stopping on her right hand. The hand that held the briefcase.

Left-handed, Karen fumbled for the doorknob. She didn't turn around; she wouldn't have been able to see him, he was behind the light that would blind her. She was still fumbling when a hard shove sent her sprawling. By sheer luck she missed hitting a piece of furniture, but the impact was hard enough to knock the breath out of her. Something dark and shapeless bent over her; an odd, musky scent tickled her agonized nostrils and she burst into a fit of sneezing. Even the violence of the paroxysm didn't distract her from the grip that seized the briefcase and tried to pull it away. She wrapped both arms around it and rolled over.

She discovered to her surprise that she had enough breath left to scream, and then realized with even greater surprise that the outraged sound had not come from her mouth. It was a horrible noise, piercing, inhuman, unending. There was a flurry of movement behind her and a low-voiced, muffled exclamation. The door opened and closed again.

Karen lay still for a moment, listening. Had that been a trick? No; footsteps ran down the steps and faded into silence. Still clutching the briefcase, she located the candle and made her way to the kitchen. The glow from the lighted burner made her blink. Carrying the candle she ventured back into the living room.

The cat was sitting by the door. It stared pointedly at her over its shoulder and meowed. Karen stared back at it. Her eyes were streaming. She sneezed.

Chapter Eleven

No sigh relieved her speechless woe,
She had no voice to speak her dread.

MARY E. COLERIDGE,
The Other Side of the Mirror, 1908

"Why didn't you call me?" Peggy demanded. Her voice had the tight, controlled tone of someone who wants to yell but is determined not to.

"I did call you." Elbows on the table, head propped on her hands, Karen stared blindly into her cup of coffee. She was still in her nightgown and robe. Even though she had stuffed herself with antihistamines, it had taken her a long time to get to sleep, and she was still drowsy and stupefied. "Your line was busy."

"I was talking to Simon. Damn it, you could have told the hotel operator it was an emergency —"

"But it wasn't, not by that time. The police had arrived —"

"Oh, you called the police, did you?" Peggy caught hold of her head with both hands and shook it violently. "Damn, there I go again. If I didn't care about you so much I wouldn't yell at you."

"I know," Karen said, smiling.

"It's no excuse, though. I'll work on it. What

did you tell them?"

"I didn't mention the manuscript."

"Hmmm. You think that was wise?"

"I couldn't see that it would do any good," Karen argued. "There are already too many people who know that it's worth stealing; why advertise the fact to the rest of the town? I couldn't give them the names of the people I suspect, since there's no evidence. I think the person was wearing gloves."

"Any crook who can read or watch TV knows enough to wear gloves," Peggy agreed. "He didn't leave a cast-off garment or a packet of matches, or any other useful clue, I suppose."

"No." Karen yawned. "The officer called this morning, to say they'd keep the case open, but since they had no leads . . ." Another earsplitting yawn interrupted her; she went on indistinctly, "Mrs. Fowler told them she didn't see or hear anything. She also mentioned that nothing of the sort had ever occurred until I got here."

"Nice," Peggy muttered. "Well, I guess it could have been worse. You saved the manuscript."

"It was the cat that saved it." Karen laughed feebly. "She must have stepped on its tail. I never heard such a sound. It was as loud and as effective as a burglar alarm."

"She," Peggy repeated.

"She was wearing perfume. I didn't recognize the scent, I hardly ever use the stuff because of my allergies."

"Men use cologne these days. And after-shave."

"None of the men I know use anything that pervasive. It was musky and heavy, the kind that has names like Passion Flower and Jungle Lust."

"Mrs. Fowler douses herself with some sickly flower scent," Peggy said. "Supposed to be violets, I guess."

"Lisa too. Now don't suggest it was a casual burglar with exotic tastes. She was lying in wait for me and the first thing she grabbed was the briefcase."

"I'm not going to suggest any such thing. Your reasoning is logical. The lights?"

"The master switch had been thrown. The fuse box is in the garage; it's one of those old-fashioned types with fuses instead of breakers. The whole damned electrical system probably violates some housing code."

"I expect this place violates a lot of codes," Peggy agreed. "She got in through the front window?"

"Yes. The screen had been replaced, but not secured. She must have left it open long enough for the cat to jump in. It was under the bed, curled up in a box of sweaters." Karen rubbed her nose. The itch was strictly psychosomatic; the sweaters were in the car. She'd have to have them cleaned before she could wear them again.

Peggy opened the front door and went out onto the landing. When she returned Karen said snuffily, "I know, I looked too. It was stupid of me to suppose that just because I couldn't reach that window from the steps, nobody could. All the same she couldn't have managed it without hammering in a spike to stand on while she slit the screen and unlocked it."

"You think that's it? There's no spike now, just a hole."

"Had to be." Karen yawned. "The whole thing was neatly done. She came back out after she'd unlocked the door, and removed the evidence. The cat could have slid past her then, while the door was open. She might not have seen it."

"Maybe it wasn't only the racket the cat made that scared her into leaving. Visible scratches, on hands or face, would be a dead giveaway if . . ."

"If it's someone I know," Karen finished. "It could have been Dorothea Angelo. She's big and husky and unscrupulous, and she douses herself with perfume. But it could also have been someone big and husky and unscrupulous who had doused himself with perfume to pin the blame on Dorothea."

Peggy sucked in her breath. "Bill?"

"It would be so easy," Karen said. "In the dark, my sense of smell was the only sense available for purposes of identification, so long as the intruder didn't speak. Which he didn't. Would Dorothea be stupid enough to overlook that distinctive aroma?"

"She might," Peggy muttered.

"Oh, sure, she might; you can get so accustomed to a particular odor that you don't notice it yourself. But there are other suggestive points. Hammering in that spike to stand on, for instance — isn't that the sort of thing a man would think of, rather than a woman?"

"Now you're being sexist," Peggy said critically.

"True. And you are prejudiced. You don't want to suspect Bill."

"True." Peggy's smile was half hearted. "But we'll inspect him for cat scratches. Hell, we'll inspect everybody."

Soon afterward they went their separate ways, Peggy to the courthouse and Karen to the table in the living room to work on the manuscript. Peggy paused in the doorway to remark gruffly, "I don't have to tell you to keep that window closed and locked, even if the temperature in here gets to be a hundred."

"You don't have to tell me." Karen wiped perspiration off her forehead. "It's almost as hot outside anyhow."

"Looks like rain." Peggy studied the low-hanging clouds. "A good thunderstorm would clear the air."

"Be careful driving."

"Ha! You be careful."

After a second cup of coffee and a cold shower Karen got to work, but the oppressive weather made her sleepy and she was rather too full of coffee when Peggy returned late that afternoon carrying two brown paper bags.

"Deli," she announced, unpacking cold cuts and cheese, rolls and salad. "It's too hot to cook and

I don't feel like going out."

"You mean you don't want me going out and coming back to what might not be an empty house." Karen leaned against the door, arms folded. "Did you bring your jammies?"

"No use suggesting I stay the night, huh?"

Peggy stood with feet braced and arms folded. She looked like a belligerent elderly child. Touched and amused, Karen managed not to smile. "I appreciate the offer, Peggy, and I'm sure you'd be a match for Bill and Dorothea combined. But it's not necessary. She won't try this again."

"She's not registered at the motel." Peggy stowed the food in the fridge and took out a tray of ice cubes.

"How do you know? They surely wouldn't let you look at the register."

"Of course not. I told the clerk I was expecting a friend, a famous and eccentric author who gets a kick out of surprising her buddies. She's so famous she always registers under a pseudonym."

"That is the most preposterous story I've ever —"

"The clerk bought it." Peggy chuckled. "She thinks it's Alexandra Ripley."

Karen began to laugh helplessly. "Peggy, how awful of you! I've seen pictures of Ripley; if she ever finds out about this — this masquerade she'll sue you for slander."

"I'll worry about that tomorrow," Peggy said, chuckling. "I do wish we could locate Angelo, though. It would be a load off my mind if she

332

turned out to have an alibi."

"Why? I thought you didn't want to suspect Bill."

The amusement left Peggy's face. "Because, whatever Bill's other failings, he isn't likely to commit physical assault. For one thing, he's too smart. For another, he — now don't get mad —"

"I probably will if you say what I think you're going to say."

"Dammit, Karen, I know the signs! He may be a consummate actor, counterfeiting increasing — let's say 'affection' — so you'll admit him to your confidence; but unless I miss my guess he's becoming genuinely — let's say 'fond' — of you. Either way, he's not going to hurt you. She might."

"Whoever it was didn't hurt me," Karen pointed out. "Or try to. He or she could have hit me or choked me; he or she — English needs another pronoun! — was taller and heavier. Instead, I was pushed aside. Does that tell us anything about the burglar?"

"Not a damned thing," Peggy said gloomily. "Bill and Dorothea aren't the only candidates, you know. The entire academic community must know about the manuscript by now. Creepy Joe Cropsey certainly does. Lisa or Cameron, or some third party, might try to steal it in order to sell it to any of the above. Oh, hell, this isn't getting us anywhere. Let's drop the subject."

They went back to the living room with their drinks. "I hope you had a productive day," Peggy said. "Mine was a bummer. I couldn't find birth or death certificates for anyone in the third generation. Whoever concocted that genealogy must have had private sources."

"If it was submitted to the D.A.R. or some other such organization —"

"I don't know what kind of documentation they require. It's worth checking, I agree, but I want to cover all the local possibilities before I leave town. There's one we haven't mentioned. Gravestones. You don't happen to know where the family plot is located, I suppose?"

"The subject didn't come up," Karen said dryly.

"Raise it, then. We might even luck out and find that the parish church has records."

Karen made a face. "I'll leave that job to you. Crawling over gravestones in some weed-infested old churchyard doesn't appeal to me."

"You know not whereof you speak. It's a very soothing activity on a summer afternoon. Old cemeteries are shady and quiet. Very quiet," she added in sepulchral tones.

A rumble of thunder sounded, like a musical score from a horror film underlining the suggestion of menace. Karen laughed uneasily, and Peggy said, "Maybe we'll finally get that storm. If it's raining hard, can I spend —"

"No. Thanks."

"So how's Ismene getting along?"

"Not too well. She and Clara have had a fight. Not that Ismene used such a vulgar word, but Clara accused her of ruining her — Clara's — chances of an advantageous marriage because she — Ismene

— has aroused the antagonism of their well-bred neighbors by orating about the rights of women, slaves, and other inferiors. Ismene, thus provoked, retorts that Clara won't have any problem catching a husband because she's got every quality a man wants in a wife — money, good looks, and a complete absence of brains. After she blows up she bitterly repents her unkind words and tries to apologize, but Clara walks off in a huff and gets her revenge by flirting furiously with both Edmund and the doctor, who has become a frequent caller. Edmund is brooding about some mysterious problem, which he won't explain, and which necessitates frequent absences from the house. Ismene spends more and more time in the stone house, writing gloomy poems, and . . . oh, yes, she has another encounter with the mysterious figure in black, but when she attempts to follow it she finds her path barred by a locked and bolted door, from behind which she hears sounds of agonized weeping."

"I hope you never try to write a novel," Peggy said critically. "That's about as boring and flat a narrative as I've ever heard. Don't tell me any more of the plot, I'd rather read her version. She knows how to pile on the Gothic atmosphere."

"I'm getting impatient with her," Karen admitted. "There's plenty of atmosphere and no useful information whatever. It's as if she were deliberately trying to hide from me. Why won't she let me in?"

The silence that followed was broken by another, louder roll of thunder. "That's a strange way of putting it," Peggy said. "Into what?"

The room darkened as the storm drew nearer. The wind was rising. The curtains at the side windows lifted and fell.

"Into her mind, of course," Karen said. "It's closed to me. How much of what she wrote is the 'I,' the identity, the real thoughts of a real woman? She's shut people out just as her society tried to shut her in. A house of stone can be either a refuge or a prison."

"Or a grave," Peggy said. "As it was for Antigone."

The storm broke just as they were sitting down to supper. It was a humdinger, as Peggy put it — torrential rain, lightning and thunder. After a few preliminary flickers the lights dimmed and went out, and Peggy, with loud self-congratulations, produced a pair of flashlights from the other bag she had brought. They were large, heavy torches, and Karen suspected her friend was hoping for another invasion so she could hit the burglar over the head. Nothing of the sort occurred, of course, and when the storm had passed over and the electricity had gone on again, Peggy had no excuse to linger. She wanted to make an early start; Cameron had left a message telling her she could view the merchandise any time after nine.

Stars had begun to show between banks of thinning clouds and the air felt sweet and cool. The flashlights were definitely useful, though. Karen kept hers focused on Peggy until the latter had reached her car.

For all her bravado she didn't sleep well that night. The drip of water from the sodden leaves sounded like footsteps, and just as she was drifting off, a series of spitting, piercing howls jerked her back to wakefulness. They faded as she listened; one of the combatants had thrown in the towel and fled. She hoped the winner was her unwitting defender. Peggy had wanted to reward it with a lavish spread of delicacies, but Karen had talked her out of it. She didn't want to encourage the cat to hang around. Maybe, before she left town, she could deliver a basket of cat goodies to its owners.

The break in the weather was brief. It was raining again next morning, a slow, dismal drizzle that enlarged the puddles on the sodden ground. Karen was ready and waiting when Peggy arrived. She blinked in surprise at the apparition standing on her threshold. Crimson umbrella, scarlet raincoat, snappy matching cap . . .

"Very cheerful," she said.

"I'm sprucing myself up," Peggy explained shamelessly. "Simon likes bright colors. No, I won't come in, if you're ready to go; no sense dripping all over your carpet. I'll drive, I'm parked behind you. We can lock the manuscript in my trunk."

She had it all figured out. Karen shrugged into

her old raincoat, feeling very drab next to the dapper little figure in scarlet.

"Do you know where the place is?" she asked, getting into the passenger seat.

"Cameron gave me directions. Now listen good, I am going to give you a run-down on procedure. The first thing you do is practice an expression of impenetrable disdain. Like this." She curled her lip and wrinkled her nose. "Plaster it on your face and leave it there. Don't look excited or squeal in delight even if you run across a diary labeled 'Jane Jones, aka Ismene.' Since we don't know exactly what we're looking for, we'll have to go through every box. A pile of what appears to be old magazines might have other papers within. If you do find anything you want, take careful note of its location. Got that?"

"I guess so," Karen said uncertainly. "It sounds much more complicated than I'd realized."

"My dear, bidding is an art form that requires not only natural talent but years of practice." Peggy squinted through the streaming windshield. "I think we turn here. Can you read that street sign?"

Karen obliged. With a grunt of satisfaction Peggy swung right. "Two and a half miles to Old Forge Road. Watch out for the auction sign. Yes, dearie, I'm an old hand at country auctions. I used to hit one every weekend, before my house got so crammed full. I've cut back lately, but Joan and I —"

"Joan!" Karen exclaimed. "I forgot about her.

She said she was coming. Suggested we all have dinner tonight."

"We'll see." Peggy was concentrating on business. "Ah, there's the sign."

The road was a narrow two-lane stretch of macadam. Water flowed through the ditches on either side. Peggy slowed and pulled to the right as a pickup approached, taking up more of the road than was its due. "Damned farmers always think they own the road," she grumbled. "Why have you got your hands over your eyes? Relax, I know what I'm doing." The auction house was a rambling, flat-roofed structure set among fields green with growing crops. A big tentlike structure flanked one side of it, and a graveled parking area the other. More parking was available across the road, in a field that had been mowed but not paved. It was a sea of mud and flattened weeds that morning; since they were early, there was space available in the graveled lot.

Peggy cast a professional look over the other vehicles. "Look at the license plates. New York, Pennsylvania, Florida . . . Dealers. I was afraid of this. He must have advertised in antique papers clear across the country. Get your sneer in place."

Karen followed her into the building. When she saw the interior she stopped and stared in consternation. Peggy had not overstated the size of the job. The large room was crammed with objects in haphazard array, tables piled on top of bureaus and sideboards, cardboard cartons heaped atop one another, long tables covered with stacked quilts and linens and china. There were more cartons under the tables. To the right of the entrance was a small platform with a desk and high stool — the auctioneer's podium, Karen assumed. Glass cases on either side held smaller, choicer objects; the overhead lights glinted off silver and crystal. At the back of the room, opposite the podium, a stout, aproned woman was dispensing coffee and doughnuts to several men who leaned on the counter talking and laughing.

"Old, favored customers," Peggy muttered, indicating the men. "They've been here before. Let's get some coffee and do a preliminary survey together."

She had stripped for action, leaving her coat and umbrella in the car, and was professionally attired in dungarees, denim shirt and heavy laced boots. Karen was glad she had been warned to wear old, comfortable clothes; the bare cement floor of the building was already marked by wet, muddy footprints.

Carrying a Styrofoam cup, she trotted obediently after Peggy as the latter walked along the rows of merchandise. Before they had gone ten feet, everything began to blur in Karen's mind. She understood why Peggy had insisted she bring a clipboard. Several of the dreaded dealers carried them too.

They finished their circuit of the room and their coffee simultaneously. Tossing her empty cup into a stained oil drum outside the door, Peggy flexed her arms and spoke.

"They save the big stuff like furniture and silver till later in the day. They'll start with the miscellaneous objects they don't expect will bring much — like those cartons. I'll let you excavate the ones on the floor, if you don't mind. My knees are giving me hell in this wet weather. Drag things out and dig to your heart's content, but be sure to put everything back in the same box you got it from."

Abject panic gripped Karen. "Suppose I miss something. I don't know what I'm looking for!"

"Neither do I." Peggy grinned broadly. "Have fun."

Karen didn't have to feign an expression of distaste as she dropped to her knees. Not only was the floor far from clean, but the contents of the boxes were thick with grime.

There were — she counted — thirty-seven cartons under the tables. She had finished inspecting them and moved on to another pile of boxes when she felt a hand on her shoulder.

"Ready to take a break?" Peggy asked. "It's eleven-thirty."

"So late?" Karen carefully replaced a collection of soft-drink bottles and rose to her feet. "This was a wasted morning. You wouldn't believe the junk! Why on earth would anyone buy a stained, chipped, ceramic bedpan?"

"I hear people use them for planters," Peggy said, and grinned at Karen's horrified expression. "Chacun à son goût. Come on. There's a powder room of sorts; we'll wash up and then have a spot of lunch. The food's usually good — homemade soup and pie and sandwiches."

They had to wait for service; several others had decided on an early lunch in order to avoid the crowd that would appear at one o'clock, when the viewing opened to the public. Seating herself in one of a row of chairs that lined the wall, Peggy unwrapped a country ham sandwich and took an enormous bite.

Karen sipped her soup and looked around the room. "There are more people here now. I don't see any familiar faces, though."

"Bill will turn up, never fear. And you are going to be very sweet and polite."

"Oh, right. Do you suppose Dorothea will have the gall to make an appearance?"

"If she does, you'll be polite to her too," Peggy said firmly.

"I'll distract her with witty conversation while you inspect her for cat scratches." Karen laughed. "I don't know why, but I'm beginning to enjoy this."

"I thought it would get to you."

"It has a weird fascination," Karen admitted. "The treasure-hunting instinct, I suppose."

"Mmm-hmmm. One never knows what gem may lie buried under the dreck. There are stories — most of them apocryphal, I admit, but some true — of people who've found a diamond bracelet in a box of costume jewelry, or a rare bit of porcelain jumbled in with cheap cups and saucers."

"There wasn't any rare porcelain among that

lot," Karen said decidedly. "How about you? Any luck?"

"Some of the furniture is rather nice. A cherry lowboy, with original brasses, a carved fruitwood buffet with a marble top —"

"You haven't got room in your house for any more furniture."

"No." Peggy's eyes took on a faraway look and she murmured the phrase that, as Karen was to learn, is the motto and the heartfelt prayer of the dedicated auction buff. "But if it goes cheap . . ."

"Is furniture all you looked at? There's a hell of a lot of stuff here, Peggy, and we don't have time —"

"I looked in every drawer and opened every door, kiddo. People sometimes overlook small objects. But no, that wasn't all I looked at. Finished? Come on, then, I want to show you something. And keep your face under control!"

She led Karen behind the podium. The wall was hung with paintings, many of them in ornate gilded frames. "I may bid on a few of these," she said, without troubling to lower her voice. "Isn't the lady in the bonnet divine?"

She glowered at them from the canvas, her lined, unsmiling face framed by white frills. The fingers of the hands folded on her knee looked odd; there appeared to be more of them than there ought to be.

" 'Divine' is hardly the word," Karen said dubiously. "How could you stand to have that face

343

glaring at you? The artist's knowledge of anatomy wasn't exactly . . ." She stopped with a catch of breath, and Peggy jabbed her hard in the ribs.

"The dog's anatomy is even more peculiar," Peggy said. "But I love him. Look at his imbecile expression. These are primitives, you ignoramus, and they'll probably fetch high prices. Too high for me, though I'll take a crack at them. Did you see the frames?"

She drew Karen behind the podium, where a stack of frames stood leaning against the wall. "If you can't do better than that I'll leave you home tomorrow," she whispered, stooping. "Didn't you even think about family portraits?"

"I never dared hope for anything like that," Karen whispered back. "God, wouldn't it be wonderful? A frontispiece for the book — a jacket cover . . . But the portraits don't seem to be labeled, and we don't even know her real name!"

"So we acquire everything from the right period," Peggy said cheerfully.

"That nasty-looking old woman can't be she."

"Oh, God give me patience! We'll discuss your romantic prejudices tonight, in private." Lowering her voice even more, she continued to sort through the frames. "Get ready for this. If you so much as gasp, I'll slug you."

The frame she extracted from deep in the pile was a cheap, mass-produced affair, of a type that can be still purchased in any drug or department store — narrow strips of light wood in a standard

344

eight-and-a-half-by-ten size. It was not new; the grain of the wood was stained with grime and the nails at one corner had come loose. The picture it enclosed was defaced by straight lines, one perpendicular and one vertical, and it was so dark Karen couldn't make out the subject.

"What is it?" she asked.

"Does it remind you of anything? Keep looking."

As she stared, shapes emerged from the background. Human figures, or the upper parts of them. Two people? Husband and wife, perhaps? A pity about those defacing lines . . . Then the connection Peggy had tried to evoke struck her, and she understood the meaning of the lines across the painting. It was an oil painting, not a print or a watercolor. The old paint had cracked off when the picture was folded.

"Branwell Brontë's portrait of his sisters," she whispered. "It was folded too. I can't make out who —"

"I've already had it out in the light, and I don't want to draw any more attention to it. You'll have to take my word for it — there are two women, not the usual portrait of a husband and wife. That's about all I could tell, but if it were cleaned and restored . . . Shall we go for it?"

"My God, yes! This is incredible!"

Peggy returned the portrait to its original place. "Don't get your hopes up, this is probably two other people. I figure it's worth a try, though, and if you can keep your big mouth shut and your

345

big brown eyes from shining, we might get it cheap."

"I will. I swear. I —"

"Shut up," Peggy said amiably. "Back to work now. We haven't even looked at the books."

They spent the next half hour examining the contents of the glass cases — just in case, as Peggy said. The cases had to be unlocked by the woman in charge, and she kept a watchful eye on the objects, some of which were small enough to be slipped into a pocket or handbag. Her imagination fired, Karen examined every piece of jewelry and every ornament. It was a deflating experience, however; some of the old jet and garnet jewelry was attractive and, according to Peggy, fairly valuable, but the oldest dated, according to the same expert, to the mid-nineteenth century.

"I'll bet this was jumbled together in a box in the attic," Peggy muttered. She had whipped out a jeweler's loupe and gave an appearance at least of professional competence as she squinted through it. "A lot of the stones are missing, and some are chipped."

"You got it," said the custodian, visibly impressed by the loupe. "The good jewelry, if there was any, must've been sold a long time ago. Guess the old guy forgot about this collection. If you'd seen the place, you'd see how he could. Took us two months just to sort through the stuff."

"You'll get good prices for some of these, though," Peggy said consolingly. "Antique jewelry is skyrocketing. I might have a try for this garnet necklace; it's in pretty good shape."

Karen had lost interest. "Are you almost through here? The place is filling up, it must be after one."

"A few more minutes," Peggy said, indicating a pile of jet pieces to the attendant. "You don't have to hang around."

Karen headed like a homing pigeon for the boxes of books. They had called to her all morning; only a stern sense of duty had enabled her to resist. She hadn't rummaged among old books for a long time. It was like breaking your diet.

Some of the Cartrights had been readers. As she moved on from box to box, she began to see a pattern. Few books were as early in date as the ones Lisa had acquired — "pilfered," most likely, Karen thought. One large group dated from the late eighteen hundreds — an eclectic collection of novels and essays, poetry and drama, biographies and travel books. Another sizable lot had dates in the teens and twenties of this century. She recognized some of the best-selling authors of that period. Could they have belonged to the old man who had recently died? If so, he had stopped buying books in the early thirties. The Great Depression? Possibly. A pile of condensed books, much later in date, gave her pause until she realized they must come from Uncle Josiah's scavenging period. The books were worthless, people couldn't give them away — except to pack rats, collectors of junk, like the old man. A shiver of pity ran through her. What a horrible thing to happen to someone. His had not been a house of stone in the literal

347

sense, but he had shut himself up in a prison as impenetrable — that of his lonely, suspicious mind.

She was rummaging through a box of ledgers and recipe books when Joan appeared, sinking cross-legged to the floor beside her. Giving her friend an abstracted "hi," Karen continued to rummage.

"Finding goodies?" Joan plucked a tattered paper-covered book from her hand. It bristled with clippings and scraps that had been stuck between the pages. "*Best-Loved Poems of the World.* This doesn't look very enticing. She's cut poems out of the paper too. 'A Mother's Lament for her Dead Infant.' 'Thy tiny brow now marble-cold in death . . .' Yucko."

She tossed the book back into the box. "Have you been here all day? Then you need a break. Come on, I'll buy you a cup of coffee."

Karen returned the other books to the carton. "Oh, all right," she said abstractedly.

Joan hauled her to her feet. "The warmth of your welcome touches my heart. Where's Peggy?"

"Somewhere around." Karen scanned the room. "Where's Sharon?"

"She hates auctions. After she dropped me she went to the motel. I figured I'd hitch a ride back with you and Peggy."

"Son of a bitch," Karen exclaimed.

"If it's that much trouble, never mind." Following the direction of Karen's intent stare, she let out a gurgle of laughter. "Oh, I see. It is the son of a bitch. You've upgraded him from bastard, have you?"

Meyer was watching them. He smiled and raised a hand in greeting. Karen smiled and waved back and went on walking.

"I'm making nice, following orders from Peggy," she said. "That doesn't mean I've changed my opinion."

"If you don't want him, how about introducing me?"

"It may come to that," Karen muttered. "Excuse me. I'm going to wash my hands."

When she returned, Joan was waiting, guarding two cups of coffee and two pieces of pie. Karen realized she was starved.

"One of the reasons I come to auctions is the food," Joan announced, scraping her plate. "I think I'll have a piece of red devil's food cake next. I need nourishment. Do you know what I had for lunch?"

"I don't want to hear about it."

"No, you don't. What can I do to help? Tell me what you're looking for and I will work my fingers to the bone."

"Early papers and books," Karen said vaguely. "But you needn't sacrifice yourself. We've covered most of the stuff."

"Including the barn?"

"What barn?"

"The barn out in back. The stuff for Sunday's auction is there. They won t move it in till tonight or tomorrow morning."

Karen gaped at her in horror. An entire barn, packed from roof to rafters . . .

"That's probably where Peggy is," Joan said. "I'll go look for her. You've still got a couple of hours," she added consolingly.

"See you later." Karen fled back to the books.

By the time she had finished with them it was after three-thirty. A suspicious survey of the now crowded room told her Meyer was not there. He was probably in the barn too, damn him.

It had stopped raining, but pools of water spread over every dip in the ground. As she picked her way through puddles and patches of mud toward the barn, her spirits slumped. It was a barn, all right. A big barn. A very big barn. Patches of the original red paint were still visible upon the faded boards, and the wide doors stood open, showing a scene like the one she had just left — crowds of people moving slowly through close-packed furniture and high-piled tables. She stopped in the doorway, tense with a feeling that was new to her, but only too familiar to the old hands in the business — the feeling that somewhere in that barn was the one object she most desired and that someone else would see it first.

Joan's mop of red curls appeared over the heads of lesser mortals as she straightened from examining something Karen could not see. Squirming through the other bodies, Karen finally reached her, and saw that Peggy was there too.

"What?" she demanded, catching Peggy's arm.

"What what?" Peggy was maddeningly calm.

Joan let out one of her raucous whops of laughter. "It's got to her. See what you've been missing all these years, babe?"

"Will they make us leave at five?" Karen demanded feverishly. "We can't cover all this in an hour."

"Fear not. I've been making notes." Peggy displayed the catalog, now disfigured with cryptic symbols. She rubbed her forehead, adding another smear of dust to her grimy face. "It does get confusing," she admitted. "I haven't seen an auction this big and this disorganized for years. We'll go over the notes tonight."

"You're tired." Karen knew she ought to make Peggy stop for the day, but that degree of nobility was beyond her strength at the moment. "Go have some coffee and rest, why don't you?"

"Maybe I will. Here, you take the list — and for God's sake don't lose it! There are several items I haven't been able to locate. I've marked them with a star."

Karen watched her walk away, shoulders sagging, steps slow. "Is she all right? I shouldn't have let her do this."

"You couldn't have kept her away with a club," Joan said cheerfully. "Don't worry about Peggy, she's a tough old broad. I've seen her in worse shape. Hell, I've been in worse shape myself; and if you think you're tired now, just wait till tomorrow night."

Karen inspected the list. "Why do you suppose she's interested in an overstuffed chair and a collection of pillows?"

"Ours not to reason why. Let me see that. Uh-huh . . . I'll look for the furniture, you do your thing, whatever that may be. See how useful I can be? Aren't you glad I came?"

She trotted off. After a hopeless survey of the clutter Karen shrugged and knelt by a carton of books. It wasn't self-indulgence, she told herself; this was her field, after all.

She was still at it when Joan came for her. "It's after five," the latter announced. "Peggy's ready to go, and so am I."

"I haven't finished —"

"If you don't leave of your own free will, the auctioneer and his staff will kick you out. They've had a long day, with worse to come." She put out a steadying hand as Karen staggered to her feet. "Tired?"

"Exhausted," Karen admitted.

When they left the barn they saw Peggy standing near the door of the main building, talking with several men. Her animated gestures and broad smile reassured Karen; the rest had obviously revived her.

One of the men was Bill Meyer. He had kept strictly away from her all day; give him credit for manly modesty, Karen told herself. On the other hand, he might have had other things to do.

The other men politely faded away as they approached. Karen acknowledged Meyer's greeting with a smile and a concentrated stare. His face was unmarked. His hands were in his pockets.

Joan coughed and jabbed an elbow into Karen's ribs, and the latter performed introductions. Joan put out a grubby hand; Meyer took it in his. No scratches on the right hand . . . Or the left.

Feeling her eyes on him, Meyer turned to Karen. "You look tired," he said solicitously.

"Always tactful, Bill." Karen brushed a lock of hair away from her cheek.

"Always on the defensive, Karen." He smiled at her. "What's wrong with admitting you're tired? I am. I had no idea this was such hard work."

"You aren't an auction fan, then?"

"I've done book auctions occasionally — can't resist the damned things, even though I've run out of bookcases and walls on which to put them — but this is a whole new experience."

"It grows on you," Peggy said. "But I admit I'm ready to put my feet up. Do you need a lift, Bill?"

"No, thanks, I've got my own car." They started toward the road. Somehow — Karen wasn't sure whether it was deliberate or accidental — Joan and Peggy drew ahead, and she found herself several feet behind them, with Meyer beside her. "Wanna make a deal?" he asked, smiling.

"What kind of deal?" Karen asked suspiciously. They had reached the road. There was a considerable amount of traffic, as the late-leavers pulled out of the lot and headed home. Meyer stopped.

"Nothing underhanded. There are some lots I'm interested in, but I don't want to bid against you. Tell me what you want and I'll back off."

Karen bit her lip and managed not to say what she was thinking. "That's very nice of you. Right now I'm so confused I couldn't tell you exactly."

He laughed soundlessly, baring his teeth and throwing his head back. "I don't blame you for suspecting my motives. They are pure as the driven snow, however."

Peggy and Joan had crossed the road. "I'll think about it," Karen said. "Excuse me, Bill —"

"Discuss it with Peggy," Meyer urged. "I suppose you'll be here early tomorrow? So will I. We can talk then."

"Fine. I really must go, I don't want to detain Peggy any longer."

She waited till a van had passed and then started to cross the road.

Sound, movement and impact slammed together in a single blur of sensation. A human cry, a mechanical scream, a heavy object striking and lifting her. Mud and weeds cushioned her fall; it was shock rather than pain that kept her motionless, curled in upon herself like a small animal fearing further attack. Then hands, unsteady and gentle, moved over her head and arms and she saw Peggy kneeling beside her.

"Anything broken?" Peggy's voice wasn't too steady either.

"No." Slowly Karen rolled over and sat up. "I'm all right, really. Just surprised. It happened so fast . . ."

Peggy let out her breath and sat back on her heels. "I guess the car didn't hit you. It was a near thing, though. If he hadn't pushed you out of the way . . . ."

Several people had gathered around something that lay on the ground nearby. He lay face down, unmoving, but she recognized the white shirt, now stained and wrinkled, and the dark head half hidden by the weeds.

Chapter Twelve

Female writers should only aspire to excellence by courageously acknowledging the limitations of their sex.

SIR EGERTON BRYDGES, 1928

"It was not some smart-ass kid," Joan insisted. "The driver was a woman."

"How do you know?" Peggy demanded. "You didn't see any more than I did. I didn't turn until I heard Bill shout, and by that time there was nothing to be seen except bodies flying through the air. For a few interminable seconds I thought . . . Excuse me. I need another drink."

At the time she had been the calmest person on the scene. After ascertaining that Karen was unhurt except for bumps and bruises, she had dragged her to the car and driven her straight home, leaving Joan to tend the other victim. She and Sharon had arrived shortly afterward. Sharon was trying to be the cool voice of reason, but she hadn't made much progress; everyone else was shouting and interrupting and contradicting one another, and a cool voice of reason is not supposed to yell.

Joan followed Peggy, presumably on the same errand, and Sharon finally got her chance.

"The important thing is that no one was seriously injured," she said in her measured professional voice. "Though I do think you ought to have taken Dr. Meyer to the emergency room, Joan."

"He wouldn't go. So far as I could see there was nothing wrong with him except a few square inches of missing skin and a possible sprained wrist." Joan returned to her chair and collapsed with a martyred sigh. Karen detected a certain gleam in her eye, however. "Every cloud has a silver lining, as they say. This gave me an excuse to insist on driving him home. Isn't it lucky he is staying at the same motel?"

"There is only one," Sharon pointed out. "You were quite right, Joan, he shouldn't have tried to drive immediately after a shock of that sort, but for heaven's sake don't say things like — like that remark about silver linings. People who don't know you might misunderstand."

"What's to misunderstand? I like men, and I'm not ashamed to admit it. I'm afraid I'm out of luck with Bill, though. All he'd talk about was Karen. He asked if I meant to stay a few days and my little heart started to go pitter-pat, and then the adorable son of a bitch said he knew he could count on me to look after her."

"I don't need looking after," Karen said automatically.

Peggy's lips parted. Catching Karen's eye she coughed and said nothing.

"It was a horrible shock for everyone, of

course," Sharon said. "But I'm sure we all agree that further discussion would be counterproductive. No one managed to get the license number of the truck —"

"Our attention was elsewhere," Peggy said sarcastically.

"— so the police could not possibly identify the driver," Sharon went on, ignoring the interruption with professional coolness. "I hope none of you believe this was anything more sinister than a case of reckless driving. Many of these young men drive too fast and drink when they drive. There is a sharp curve in the road and the surface was slippery with mud —"

"I still think it was a woman," Joan said.

"Some women drive too fast and drink when they drive," Sharon began.

"And there was a sharp curve, et cetera," Peggy said. "You've made your point, Sharon. Further speculation would be a waste of time — and God knows I'd prefer to accept your interpretation."

"Good." Impeccably groomed, every hair in place and every article of attire crisply pressed, Sharon studied the others with a critical frown. "Are you going to change before we go out to dinner? Karen is clean, at least, but if you'll excuse me for saying so, Peggy —"

"Joan looks worse than I do," Peggy said sullenly.

"I wanted her to change before we left the motel, but she was in a wild rush to get over here. Why don't you and she —"

"The hell with changing." Joan lifted her feet onto a hassock and reached for her glass of beer. "Let's go someplace quick and casual. I might wash my hands and comb my hair if you ask me nicely."

"I agree," Peggy said. "Nobody feels like dressing up. I suggest we eat here. We've got a lot of work to do on that auction list and we ought to get to bed early."

Peggy prevailed, as she usually did when she had her mind made up. Joan volunteered to go forth in search of portable food; Sharon volunteered to go with her, in search of socially acceptable healthy food.

After they had gone, the other two sat in silence for a few moments. Then Peggy said, "It must have been Bill who told Joan the driver was a woman. She's convinced herself she really saw her, but she couldn't possibly have gotten a good look."

"Could he?"

"He's the only one who might have. Joan and I were walking away, he was watching you. He said the car just appeared around that sharp curve, coming much too fast."

"I didn't even see it. Or hear it."

"You wouldn't have heard anything. There were too many other cars revving up and driving out. If he hadn't pushed you out of the way . . ."

Karen rubbed her sore shoulder — her only souvenir of that potentially fatal incident. "So I have to be grateful to him for saving my life?"

"Tsk, tsk," said Peggy, lips pursed in a wicked

imitation of Sharon. "Don't let other people hear you say things like that, they might misunderstand. 'Saving your life at the risk of his own,' is how Joan would probably put it. She's such a damned romantic." Her face grew sober. "But she could be right. What he did took not only guts but very quick reflexes. That's not to say that it wasn't an accident. The road was wet; if the driver hit the brakes too hard, he — or she — could lose control."

Karen's nerves were not at their best. "Of course it was an accident! I know what you're thinking, and it's ridiculous. Dorothea Angelo may not be Miss Congeniality but she wouldn't try to run me down for the sheer fun of it. What would she gain by killing or maiming me?"

"Hmmm." Peggy rubbed her chin. "If this were a Gothic novel she'd turn out to be your birth mother and nearest heir."

"That's not funny."

"Only mildly amusing," Peggy conceded. "I guess you're not in the mood for bad jokes. I agree, I can't see any obvious motive. But it would be interesting to find out whether she's in the area."

She got up, glass in hand, and went to the phone.

After a brief conversation she hung up and turned to Karen. Obviously she was no longer in the mood for jokes either. "She's here, all right. At the motel. Checked in around noon."

Karen feared she would be too keyed up to sleep, but physical exhaustion won out over mental agitation. The persistent ringing of the telephone — Peggy's promised wake-up call — dragged her out of deep sleep and she had to rush in order to be ready when Peggy pulled into the driveway fifteen minutes later. The trunk was open; she tossed the briefcase in, slammed the lid, and scrambled into the front seat.

"I still don't see why we have to get there so damned early," she grumbled.

"I told you. Some of these crooks move things from one box to another. We'll have to run a last-minute check to make sure the things we want are in the same place they were yesterday."

"Joan and Sharon are meeting us there?" Karen asked, not really caring.

"Uh-huh." Peggy looked infuriatingly bright and cheerful. She had tied a red ribbon around her head; the ends of the bow stuck up like miniature horns.

If Karen had not been so sleepy, the red ribbon might have warned her. The first person she saw in the auction room was Simon.

He looked out of place, like a Mittel-European count paying a duty visit to a social gathering of serfs. The man with whom he was conversing might have been the overseer — short and red-faced, in shirt sleeves and denim pants, with a cap perched atop a balding head. In fact he was the owner of the auction house; Karen had seen him the day before. He and Simon were chatting and laughing like old friends, but Simon broke off when he saw them and lifted a hand in greeting.

"What the hell is he doing here?" Karen demanded.

"Buying books, of course. Where do you think he finds them?"

"He hasn't had time to look at them."

"He's been in this business a long time, Karen. I think you can assume he knows what he's doing."

Simon came toward them. "Good morning, ladies. Ready for action, I see."

He bowed over the hand Peggy offered him and then put his arm around Karen's shoulders and gave her a brief, affectionate hug. Despite the perky red bow Peggy was in no mood to waste time in social activities. "Did you ask about the safe?" she demanded.

"Yes. He is willing to oblige us."

"Good. I'll go and get it. Give her some coffee, she's barely conscious."

She went trotting off and Simon led Karen toward the refreshment counter. Though the auction was not scheduled to begin for almost an hour, several early birds were already there.

"I didn't know you were coming," Karen said. "What else have you and Peggy arranged behind my back?"

His eyes narrowed in amusement, wrinkles fanning out at the corners. "You do need coffee," he said, proffering a cup. "From what I've heard you are in no position to be surly with your allies. A mensch you may be, but Superwoman you are not. No ill effects after your accident, I trust."

He indicated a chair. Karen sat down with a

sigh. "Is there anything you don't know?"

"Very little." Simon deposited himself in a rocking chair next to hers. "Peggy has kept me up-to-date. I hope you don't object?"

"It wouldn't do me any good to object, would it?" She tucked her hand through his arm and smiled at him. "I'm so glad to see you, Simon. Bless you for coming."

"My dear, my motives were completely selfish. There are a number of items in which I am interested."

"I don't care what your motives are, I'm just happy you're here. I've missed you." She added, with a meaningful sidelong look, "So has Peggy. You know she has designs on you, don't you?"

Laughter transformed his face. "How delicately you express yourself. In deference to my old-fashioned sentiments, I suppose? Yes, I do know. I haven't enjoyed myself so much in years." Then his smile faded. "I'm not at all happy about the situation, though. Had I but known —"

"You wouldn't have told me about the manuscript? That's nonsense, Simon. You had to let me see it and I had to have it." She turned the cup in her hands, trying to find the right words. "I can't believe I am in physical danger, if that's what is worrying you. None of the people involved in this business are capable of violence."

"I would agree with you," Simon said, "if I had not received a telephone call the other day from Dr. Angelo. She sounded almost unbalanced."

"Oh, she does that all the time," Karen said

reassuringly. Glad as she was of another ally, she didn't want Simon to worry about her. "Dorothea's threatening phone calls are notorious. And please don't mention menopause."

"That is not a subject I care to discuss," Simon said fastidiously.

Karen laughed. "In her case it's certainly not menopausal. She's always had a foul mouth and a nasty temper. What can she do to me except call me bad names?"

"Aside from the fact that she would make two of you . . . Ach, never mind, I am being a nervous old man. Here is Peggy coming. It was her idea, not mine, that the manuscript should be in a safe place today, but I am in complete agreement with her. It would be too easy to break into a car parked in the lot, with so many people coming and going."

After they had seen the briefcase placed in the safe in the auctioneer's office, they separated for final inspections.

"Simon saved three seats for us," Peggy said, indicating the tent, which was now filled with rows of wooden chairs.

"What about Joan and Sharon?"

"They'll have to fend for themselves. Joan's an old hand, she's probably brought folding chairs. Let's register and get our numbers. Remember, you are not to bid on anything, and I mean anything, without asking me."

Karen realized her heart was beating faster than usual. As they stood in the line waiting to register, she scanned the thickening crowd. It was beginning to look like a high school reunion — everyone seemed to know everybody else, and she saw several familiar faces. Lisa Fairweather, clipboard in hand — to keep track of how much money she was going to make; Mrs. Fowler, complete with violets and with the Colonel in devoted attendance; a squat, pasty-faced man whom, for a heart-stopping moment, she took for Joe Cropsey; Bill Meyer . . . She gasped aloud.

The square inches of skin he had lost were on his face. The left side of it, from cheekbone to jaw, looked like raw meat. A single patch of white was visible on the same side of his forehead, near the temple.

Peggy had seen him too. "Wow," she said, impressed. "He must have hit a patch of gravel on his way to a final landing. He was so coated with mud, I didn't realize how extensive the damage was. Don't you think a polite thanks might be in order?"

Karen was forced to agree. She was able to postpone the gesture, however, for by the time she had finished registering, Meyer had disappeared and it was time for them to take their seats.

As they crossed the room they found themselves face-to-face with Mrs. Fowler. Her smile froze. She acknowledged Peggy's cheerful "Good morning" with a nod, and then proceeded to cut Karen dead. It was the first time it had ever happened to Karen, but she had read about it. When someone looks straight through you and then deliberately turns her back, the point is hard to miss.

Peggy took Karen's arm and drew her away. She was shaking with silent laughter. "You're supposed to shiver and say, 'Brrrrr,' " she pointed out.

"If she weren't an old lady and I were not . . . well . . . a lady, I'd slap her silly face," Karen muttered.

"She's a welcome touch of comic relief. Now remember what I said. If you raise your arm without permission, I'll break it."

They took their seats. Peggy arranged herself comfortably, clipboard and auction list on her knee, pen in her hand. Karen turned, looking for Simon. She couldn't see him; the chairs were all filled and people were roaming around.

"Peggy!"

Peggy jumped. "What?"

"I forgot. The papers Simon told us about — when he called the other night —"

"Oh." Peggy relaxed. "Don't hiss at me like that, I thought you'd seen something important. The auctioneer showed me the papers yesterday. They aren't important, just a lot of late account books and miscellaneous junk. I may bid on that box, though; there were a couple of elegant lace-trimmed petticoats —"

"You're as bad as Uncle Josiah," Karen said critically. "Is there anything you don't collect?"

"Lots of things. License plates and antique Coke bottles, among others. Shhh, he's about to start."

Things didn't get interesting until late morning. It took that long to sell the miscellaneous box lots and what Peggy described contemptuously as "col-

366

lectibles." Most of them went cheap, except for the license plates and one box of books. Karen was allowed to bid on it, but dropped out after the price reached twenty dollars. It was finally knocked down at two hundred, and Karen turned to stare at Peggy. "What in heaven's name was in that lot?"

"God knows. And Simon."

"You mean he . . . I didn't see him bidding."

Simon was wandering back and forth, sometimes sitting with them, sometimes strolling around the room.

"You're not supposed to. There are a lot of book people here. They're all watching him and each other." Peggy chuckled and hugged herself. "Wheels within wheels within wheels. Are you having fun? I am."

She had bought two boxes of old clothes and the painting of the dog. Karen stiffened as one of the auctioneer's helpers carried in another painting. "There's the old lady. Are you —"

"No. And neither are you."

"But —"

"Hush up." Peggy reached up and straightened her hair bow.

The bidding was brisk. When the painting was finally knocked down, Peggy let out a satisfied sigh. "Got it," she whispered.

"You didn't even . . . You mean someone else is —"

"Shhh." Peggy relaxed. "They're starting on the

lamps and fixtures. That'll take a while. Let's get some coffee."

They squeezed past knees and bundles, and Peggy said warningly, "I told you to leave this to me. If you've got rivals who might bid against you, you get someone else to bid for you. Simon and I made arrangements last night."

"Oh. You didn't believe Bill either?"

"Bill is not the one I'm worried about. You haven't spotted her, I take it."

Only Karen's interest in the proceedings would have prevented her from seeing someone so conspicuous. Dorothea stood at the back of the tent, her arms folded. Penciled brows raised, lips tight, she did not attempt to disguise the fact that she was watching Karen. Catching the latter's eye, she nodded brusquely but did not smile or wave.

"See any scratches?" Karen muttered.

"Hard to tell from here, she's got so much makeup plastered on her face. Is she wearing gloves?"

"I can't tell . . . Yes, by golly, I think she is! That's suspicious, isn't it?"

"Not necessarily. She may not want to dirty her elegant hands. She bid on everything either of us did," Peggy went on, drawing Karen away.

"Even the dog?" Karen asked incredulously.

"Yep. Ran it up fifty bucks extra." A look of evil anticipation transformed Peggy's face. "I'll get back at her before the day is over. That's encouraging, actually; it means she doesn't have the faintest idea what she's looking for."

Karen was not surprised to find Joan at the refreshment stand devouring pie. "Sharon is getting bored," she announced. "She'll probably leave pretty soon. Have you seen Bill? Poor baby, doesn't he look terrible? I hope you told him how noble he is."

"I haven't had a chance," Karen said defensively. "Anyhow, he's probably gotten enough gushing admiration from you."

"He wants it from you," Joan said. "Not that he actually said so; it was my sensitive feminine intuition that enabled me to discern his shy yearnings."

"You do have a way with words," Karen said with a reluctant grin. " 'Shy' is not the one I'd apply to Bill, but maybe I have been unfair to him; I have to give him credit, he hasn't swaggered up demanding appreciation. I'll work up a good gush, I promise. Peggy, shouldn't we be getting back?"

"Everything is under control." Peggy dumped sugar into her coffee. "I haven't seen Cameron, have you?"

"I haven't been looking for him."

"I have," Peggy said calmly. "I expected he'd be here to see how prices were running."

"If he shows up I want to meet him," Joan announced. "Since I don't seem to be making any progress with Bill."

They left her still eating pie.

It was late in the afternoon before Cameron made his appearance. Karen spotted him first; the auctioneer had been selling furniture for well over an hour and her interest had flagged. She nudged Peggy, who was chortling because she had conned Dorothea into buying a box of old *National Geographic* magazines for an outrageous price.

"There's Cameron."

"Oh, good." Peggy gathered up her belongings. "I'm ready to take a break. Let's go talk to him."

When they arrived Simon was talking to Cameron. Simon's elegantly casual attire and aristocratic features made Cameron's rolled shirt sleeves, faded denim pants and heavy work shoes look even shabbier. He had shaved that morning, however, and made some attempt to clean the ingrained grime from his hands. They were raw and red and crisscrossed with angry scratches.

That didn't mean anything, Karen thought. Cameron's hands always looked that way.

Simon said, "I was telling Mr. Hayes that prices seem to be running high. He should do well."

"Thanks in part to us," Peggy said, grinning at Cameron. "I squeezed an extra twenty bucks out of Angelo for that awful flower painting." Her smile fading, she added gloomily, "She's run me up on a few things too."

"I'm sorry to hear it," Cameron said politely.

"You shouldn't be. Where've you been? Your cousin has been here since dawn, adding up prices. Aren't you anxious to find out how rich you're going to be?"

Simon rolled his eyes and exclaimed, "Really,

370

Peggy, you have the manners of a battering ram."

"That's all right." Cameron's face relaxed into a smile. "I'm accustomed to Peggy's — er — candor. Lisa has more leisure than I, Peggy. As you can probably tell from my appearance, I was working. I think I have a buyer for the house. That won't affect your plans," he added, anticipating her reply. "The deal won't be finalized for several weeks, so you'll have time to finish what you want to do at Amberley."

"I'm glad to hear it, for your sake." Peggy's brow furrowed. "It could affect our plans, though, if the buyer intends to make extensive alterations. Is he going to develop the land, or —"

"For pity's sake, Peggy, this is neither the time nor the place for such a discussion," Simon said, scandalized at her bluntness. "We'd better get back to the bidding. Nice to have seen you, Mr. Hayes."

Amused and unashamed, Peggy let him draw her away. Karen was about to follow when Cameron said, "If you have a few minutes, Karen, I'd like to talk to you."

"All right. Let's go outside; it's stifling in here, and I could use a breath of fresh air."

Picnic tables and chairs had been set up in the shade of the trees near the barn. All the seats were occupied, however, so Karen leaned against a tree. Cameron stood facing her; she could tell from his expression that he wasn't looking forward to the conversation.

"I heard about your . . . accident last evening," he began.

"From whom?"

"Dr. Meyer. He didn't volunteer the information; I met him when I arrived today and asked what had happened to him." Cameron hesitated for a moment, as if uncertain how to phrase his next statement. "He doesn't believe it was an accident."

"He doesn't?"

"Is that all you have to say?" Cameron's cheeks darkened. "You might have been killed."

"Oh, I doubt it." Karen folded her arms and tried to look unconcerned. "It was some kid, driving too fast and losing control. The near miss probably scared him as much as it did me."

"Dr. Meyer thought not. He pointed someone out to me — a woman named Dorothy Angelo —"

"Dorothea." Karen laughed, and saw the flush on his cheeks deepen. She wasn't sure why he was so angry, but she was rather enjoying the spectacle of Cameron the imperturbable about to lose his temper. "She's a little crazy, but she wouldn't do anything so stupid. Bill is just being melodramatic. And overprotective."

"I see." After a moment he said, in a voice as cool as hers had been, "In that case I won't belabor the point. I wanted to assure you, as I assured Dr. Meyer, that Ms. Angelo has not approached me. I never saw her before today."

"I appreciate your telling me," Karen said formally. She turned away. "I'd better get back now; Peggy buys the most extraordinary things if I'm not there to restrain her."

Cameron followed her in silence.

Turning the corner of the barn, Karen suddenly found herself again face-to-face with her landlady. This time the encounter was even more direct; they would have run into one another if Mrs. Fowler had not fallen back, with a shriek and a look of such horror, one might have supposed she had come in contact with a leper. Her abrupt movement set off a chain reaction; she bumped into the stomach of the Colonel, who was following on her heels, his arms loaded with miscellaneous objects — presumably her purchases as well as his own, since Mrs. Fowler's hands were empty. The Colonel staggered, lost his grip, and a rain of small items fell to the ground. Mrs. Fowler swayed wildly back and forth until Cameron caught her arm and steadied her.

"Sorry," he said. "My fault. Are you all right, Miz Fowler?"

Karen stooped to pick up the fallen treasures — chipped cups and miscellaneous saucers. "Lucky the ground is still soft," she said pleasantly. "They don't seem to be damaged."

Since the Colonel's arms were fully occupied, she offered the objects to Mrs. Fowler, with what she hoped was an ingratiating smile.

Mrs. Fowler could retreat no farther. She was pressed up against the Colonel, whose red round face hovered over her like that of a gargoyle. Hers

373

was almost as colorful.

"How dare you?" she gasped. "Cameron, you planned this, I know you did. Well, you can just get her away from me and keep her away. I will not lend my countenance to such a person."

"Now, Miz Fowler —" Cameron began.

"She made a laughing stock of me! She deliberately, cold-bloodedly set out to humiliate me. You knew what she was when you brought her to meet me." She proceeded to describe what Karen was, using words her astonished auditor had encountered only in Victorian novels. "Brazen hussy" and "trollop" were two of the mildest terms.

If she wanted to avoid publicity, Mrs. Fowler was going about it the wrong way. The noise level had risen — her piercing soprano voice, the Colonel's bass rumbles of indignant agreement. People were staring and edging closer. Cameron's face was brick-red and he was having trouble controlling his mouth, but Karen couldn't decide whether anger, amusement or embarrassment was responsible.

Mrs. Fowler finally ran down; either her breath or her vocabulary had given out. Cameron's voice was soft, but there was an edge to it. "You can't say things like that, Miz Fowler. Take her home, Colonel. She's making a fool of herself."

The Colonel swelled like a crimson toad. "Sir, if I were a younger man and you were a gentleman, I would . . . I would . . ."

Karen had found the business mildly entertaining thus far, but things were getting out of hand. The old man looked as if he were on the verge of a stroke, and Cameron was on the verge of losing his temper. She would have enjoyed seeing that phenomenon, but not under these circumstances; it was too ludicrous, like a travesty of a Southern romantic novel. The two men squaring off in defense of their ladies . . . Some ladies!

"I think we've had enough of this," she said. "I'll move out on Tuesday, Mrs. Fowler. I've paid my rent till then, if you remember."

She couldn't resist the last dig. It had an effect she had not anticipated. The angry color faded from Mrs. Fowler's face and a look of calculation narrowed her eyes. "That won't be necessary. Unlike some people, I keep my word once I've given it. Our business arrangement still stands. Just don't you expect me to take notice of you on a social level. No, Colonel, not another word; they aren't worth it."

Realizing that Karen had no intention of retreating she did so. The Colonel followed, growling like a very large dog.

"I'm sorry," Cameron began.

Karen turned on him. There were a lot of people watching them, so she kept her voice soft and the smile fixed on her face. "For the love of God, will you stop apologizing for everything everybody does? If anyone is responsible for that poor crazy old creature's foul mood, it's me!"

He studied her in silence — counting to ten, Karen thought. Why didn't he let himself go? Such self-control was abnormal — unhealthy, Sharon would probably say. And why, Karen wondered, did she give a damn?

Fascinated by the twitching of the muscles around his mouth and jaw, she did not see Peggy until the latter spoke.

"Wonder how she got at the booze this early. Carries a flask, maybe."

"What are you talking about?" Karen turned. Simon, at Peggy's side, smiled sardonically.

"It needn't have been alcohol talking, Peggy. You've encountered people like that, I'm sure. The world revolves around them, and they interpret everything in terms of their narrow little egos."

Cameron's rigid shoulders relaxed. "She drinks, all right," he said wearily. "She thinks no one knows, but . . . How did you know, Peggy?"

"I recognized the signs," Peggy said curtly.

"I'll find you another apartment, Karen," Cameron said.

"That's kind of you, but you needn't bother."

"Why not? It's my job."

"You're a realtor?"

It had never occurred to her until then to wonder what he did for a living. His eyes shifted away from her curious gaze and he said brusquely, "Real estate, insurance, sales rep, you name it. Anything to make a buck."

Karen couldn't tell whether he was jeering at himself or her. Her question hadn't been meant as a snub or a sneer, but she could not altogether blame him for taking it that way. Apology or explanation would only make matters worse, she decided ruefully.

"I've no intention of moving out," she said. "Why should I waste time apartment hunting? It's only for a few weeks."

"If that's what you prefer," Cameron said. "Just let me know."

He started to turn away. Peggy, who had followed the exchange with a poorly concealed smile, said quickly, "One question, Cameron. Where are your folks buried?"

"What?" Then his scowl turned to the smile Peggy could usually induce. "Oh, I get it. Peggy, that old cemetery is as wild and overgrown as the estate. I assume you want the old one? Nobody has been buried there for fifty years. You don't want to go out there."

She grinned back at him without speaking. Cameron laughed and took a notebook from his pocket. "You do want to go out there. All right. I'll draw a map for you. You want Gothic ambience, you'll get plenty."

Simon leaned against the tree and reached for a cigar. He looked as neat and relaxed as he had eight hours earlier. Karen glanced down at her wrinkled, dusty pants and decided a few grass stains couldn't worsen their appearance. She sat down cross-legged at Simon's feet. "I assume everything is under control or you and Peggy wouldn't be loitering here."

"Oh, yes. We carried a few of her miscellaneous purchases out to her car and were on our way back when we saw you. Relax and enjoy the fresh air. Would you care for coffee, or something to eat?"

"No, thanks."

Sunlight sifted through the leaves in a scattering of gold. The shadows deepened as the sun sank lower. The air was very warm, but a breeze ruffled Karen's hair and cooled her cheeks. From inside the tent she could hear the drone of the auctioneer's voice. People wandered in and out, carrying boxes, stopping to chat or resting in the shade. A large brown dog of indiscriminate breed wandered around looking for scraps, its tail wagging hopefully. One young woman pushed a stroller; the towheaded child within lay in a sprawl of arms and legs, its mouth gaping in infantile slumber. There were other children in the crowd; most of them were whining and tugging at parental skirts. Bored out of their skulls, poor little things, Karen thought sympathetically.

She saw Joan first; that redhead was hard to miss, especially when it dazzled with sunlight. She held a sandwich in one hand; the other hand had a firm grip on Bill Meyer's arm.

"Here he is," Joan announced. "I told him you wanted to thank him."

In the bright light his face looked even worse than Karen had realized. He started to smile and winced, almost imperceptibly, as the muscles around his mouth stretched.

"That's not why I let Joan drag me here," he

378

said quickly. "I thought you ought to know I saw Dorothea heading for the parking lot just now. She'd left her jacket on her chair and she wasn't carrying anything, so I couldn't help wondering —"

"Aha!" Peggy cried. "Simon, she saw us taking those boxes to my car. Hurry, maybe we can catch her in the act."

"Come now," Simon protested. "There is nothing she can do. The car is locked. And you have no reason to suppose —"

"I just thought I'd mention it," Meyer said humbly.

Peggy was already on her way. "I'll go after her," Simon said with a sigh.

"I'd better go too," Karen said, glad of an excuse to leave. She felt uncomfortable — not angry or wary, as she usually was with Bill Meyer, just . . . uncomfortable. He appeared to be as embarrassed as she, and Joan was beaming at them like a marriage broker.

Karen cleared her throat. "I did want to thank you, Bill. I haven't had a chance before this. I hope you feel better than you look."

"Don't make me laugh," Meyer begged, raising a hand to his cheek.

To her annoyance, Karen felt herself flushing. "I suppose I could have expressed it more gracefully. If you hadn't acted so promptly I might be nursing something nastier than a scraped face. I'm very grateful."

"I'll settle for that," Meyer said softly. His eyes

379

lingered on her face. "In the hope of better things to come."

Cameron cleared his throat. "Do you want me to go after Peggy and Mr. Hallett?"

Meyer said easily, "Oh, hello, Hayes. I didn't see you. Thanks, but I don't believe your assistance will be necessary."

"Now he's offended," Karen muttered, as Cameron walked away without another word. "Excuse me, if I'm going to catch Peggy, I'd better hurry."

"What did I say?" Meyer demanded, trotting after her.

"Nothing. Forget it." She broke into a run.

She had no difficulty finding the people she sought. The sound of voices could be heard a long way off. There were only two voices — Dorothea's booming and loud, Peggy's higher in pitch, but no less penetrating. They were standing at the back of Peggy's car and when Karen first caught sight of them she feared armed combat was imminent. Peggy, her back to Karen, held what looked like a crowbar. Dorothea needed no weapon; if she had flung herself on the smaller woman she would have covered her entirely and left not a square inch showing.

"Oh, there you are, Meyer," Dorothea said, without moderating her voice. "Take this crazy dwarf away before I murder her, will you? I caught someone trying to break into her car, and this is the thanks I get."

"You were the one who was trying to break into the trunk," Peggy shouted, brandishing the heavy piece of metal. "You threw the tire iron under the car when you saw me coming."

Simon stood a few feet away, his hands in his pockets. Catching Karen's eye, he shrugged. "I tried, Karen. Perhaps you can do better."

"Is this cretinous midget a friend of yours, Holloway?" Dorothea demanded. "I might have known."

Meyer reached out and caught hold of the tire iron. "Let me have it, Peggy. Dorothea loves to sue people."

Peggy relinquished her hold. "If anybody sues anybody, it will be me suing her. Look at the lock!"

"Just try it," Dorothea sneered. "It'll be your word against mine. With the rest of you backing her up, no doubt."

"Do try to control yourself, Dr. Angelo," Simon said frostily. "No one is going to sue anyone. You surely don't mean to imply that I would perjure myself on behalf of Dr. Finneyfrock here. I may have my suspicions, but I didn't see anything."

"You're all against me," Dorothea muttered. "But I don't give a damn. I can take care of myself. I'll take on the lot of you."

She stalked away. The others stared after the monolithic form.

"She's really lost it," Peggy said. "Thanks for playing peacemaker, Bill. I thought for a few minutes she was going to jump me."

"She's never actually struck anyone," Bill said doubtfully. "At least I never heard of her doing so."

"She doesn't have to," Karen said. "She looms over people and screams at them. It's a fairly effective technique."

Simon nodded agrement. "Most people are reluctant to make a scene in public. That was a most distasteful exhibition. And I must say, Peggy, your behavior —"

"She called me a cretinous dwarf!"

"Not until after you had waved the tire iron at her." Simon laughed and took her by the arm. "Come along. You can revenge yourself by getting her to spend more money on useless junk."

Karen followed them, Meyer falling in step with her. "If I'd realized Peggy was such a firebrand I wouldn't have told her about Dorothea," he said ruefully. "Sorry about that."

"Don't you start apologizing, Bill. It doesn't suit you."

The roughly plowed ground was uneven. She stumbled over a clump of weeds. Meyer caught her by the shoulder and swung her around to face him.

"What does it take to get you to lower those barriers?" he demanded. "I've done my damnedest to prove I can be trusted —"

"I said I was grateful," Karen began.

"Oh, that. I don't expect gratitude for that; it was sheer instinct, anyone would have acted the same. What you should appreciate is the strenuous self-control I've displayed over the past couple of weeks. At this precise moment I am fighting the urge to kiss you till your stubborn head swims."

His fingers bit into her shoulder. She cried out, more in anger than in pain; with an incoherent mumble of apology he wrapped his arm around her and pulled her close. One of the scratches on his cheek had broken open; a bright drop of blood shone against the tanned skin. She leaned against him, off balance in several ways, and tried to steady her voice. "That would not be a good idea, Bill."

"Don't you think I know it?" After a moment the hard muscles of his arm relaxed; he set her politely on her feet before he stepped back and put his hands in his pockets, as if imprisoning them. "I can wait." Karen tried to think of an appropriate response. No doubt something witty would occur to her about two in the morning. At the moment her head was as empty as a sieve. She turned away.

He fell in step with her, hands still in his pockets. "If you really want to get rid of me you might try a little reverse psychology," he suggested amiably. "Try throwing yourself into my arms and see what happens."

"Some other time. Just what the hell are you up to, Bill?"

"Falling in love with you, I suspect." His voice was so gloomy she glanced at him in surprise, and again stumbled over the rough ground. He let her recover herself unaided this time. "Or maybe I'm hopelessly attracted to women who despise me. Damned if I know. I never felt this way before."

"Oh, really? What way is that?"

He pondered the question, his brow furrowed.

"Worrying about you. Maybe I've just turned philanthropist in my middle age. Whatever it is, it's keeping me awake at night. What harm would it do you to let me hang around and help out? For God's sake, Karen, you've already got everybody in on the deal but the Marx Brothers. Why not me?"

They stopped at the edge of the road. Karen looked carefully in both directions before crossing. "I trust them," she said over her shoulder. "They're helping me, not competing."

"If you let me collaborate I won't be competing," Bill said patiently. "With all due respect to your friends they aren't the stoutest of champions. Simon is an old man, Peggy is — er —"

"Don't call her old. Or short."

"I think she's terrific. Let's say she is no longer young and not extraordinarily tall. Wait a minute before you go rushing off. I've one more thing to throw into the pot. You saw the portrait."

An unpleasant sinking sensation seized Karen. "There were a number of portraits," she said warily.

"Oh, come off it. You know the one I mean; I know Peggy saw it because I saw her pull it out and take it into the light."

"So that's why you left me alone all day Friday. You were trailing Peggy!"

Bill was unrepentant. "Of course. She's the historian. I'd already spotted the painting, actually. The resemblance to the Brontë portrait was coincidental but eye-catching. I didn't bid on it."

"How do I know that's true?"

"Give me a break, will you? You should know no other interested party was bidding, you got it damned cheap. At least I assume it was one of your agents that acquired it. You and Peggy weren't bidding on anything interesting, so you must have had someone else doing it for you. A smart move."

"Peggy is a smart lady."

"But not very tall."

Karen tried not to laugh, but failed. He was wearing her down, not with his absurd declaration of love — it was much more likely that, as he himself had suggested, he was drawn to women who resisted his charms — but by his sense of humor and his intelligence. Whatever his motives, he was trying hard, and humility wasn't easy for a man of his arrogance. Or was pride a more accurate word? Karen smothered a smile. Bill's pride and her prejudice against him — another classic plot! Bill had a better sense of humor than Darcy, though.

"All right," she said. "I'll discuss your offer with Peggy. But not until after the auction."

"Fair enough. See you later."

By the end of the second day Karen's head was spinning and she was so tired she could have gone to sleep in the hard wooden chair. Anxious to finish, the auctioneer picked up the pace as the day wore on; objects were knocked down so quickly she had a hard time keeping track of what was up for sale. Somehow or other she had acquired a pile of things she had not intended to buy, including a box of crocheted doilies and a lamp made out of an old whiskey jug. When Peggy nudged her she started and turned a dazed face on her companion.

"We can go now," Peggy announced. She looked better than Karen felt, but the red bow hung limp over one ear and her face was gray with dust and fatigue.

"Thank God," Karen said sincerely. "Where's Simon?"

"He left an hour ago. We're meeting him for drinks, so get a move on."

Sharon had abandoned ship much earlier, but Joan refused to leave. "This is when you get the bargains," she muttered, glazed eyes fixed on the auctioneer. "Go away, you're distracting me."

Simon was waiting in the bar when they got there. "I know I look terrible," Karen declared, dropping onto the sofa beside him. "But I'm too tired to care. I did wash my hands."

She held them out. Simon took them in his, turned them over, and gravely inspected her palms. "They'll do. It is a tiring procedure. I'm a little weary myself."

"How'd you do?" Peggy asked. As a kindly gesture to her bedraggled companion she hadn't changed either, but the red bow rose triumphant and she had put on fresh makeup.

"Very well," Simon said.

Karen knew that guarded tone. "What did I miss?" she asked. "I swear I looked at every book in the place."

"You didn't miss anything. We weren't looking for the same things. What will you have, ladies? Champagne would be appropriate but not perhaps at this hour."

"That well, huh?" Peggy beamed at him. "Congratulations. I think I'll have Scotch, though."

"Is anyone else joining us?" Simon asked.

"I don't know where Sharon's got to, and Joan is still hanging in at the auction," Peggy said. "The way things were going they may not finish till late." She glanced at Karen. "I invited Bill Meyer, but he said he wouldn't come unless you asked him."

"How touching." Simon was visibly amused.

"Childish, you mean," Karen retorted.

"No, no, you misinterpret his intent. He is not sulking, he is allowing you to decide when and if you wish to see him. It is a most delicate attention," Simon added approvingly.

"Why not let him come to the cemetery?" Peggy suggested. "There's nothing to stop him from investigating the place anyhow; we could use a little muscle."

"Well . . . All right. When?"

"Tomorrow. Want to join us, Simon?"

"I had planned to return to Baltimore," Simon said slowly.

"How can you resist such a treat? Crawling around in the weeds, nose-to-nose with snakes and other critters, getting scratched and covered with poison ivy."

"It does sound enticing. I'll think about it." He glanced toward the doorway. "There's Geoffrey. He has your purchases, I presume?"

"Right. I'll have to settle with him." Peggy finished her drink and stood up. "Want to come along and see the goodies?"

Karen had already helped Peggy carry her other purchases to her room. After the amiable Geoffrey had brought the rest upstairs Peggy scribbled a check and sent him on his way. Then they surveyed the loot. It covered both of the twin beds and several square feet of the floor.

"Good God," Karen breathed. "I didn't realize you'd bought so much."

"Neither did I," Peggy admitted. "I tend to get carried away."

"You certainly do. Why did you buy this trunk?" Karen wrestled with the tight-fitting lid and finally managed to lift it. A pervasive, pungent odor rose from the interior. She turned her head aside. "It's full of old rags!"

"Those aren't rags, those are vintage clothes. Very collectible, unfortunately; I had to pay a stiff price for this." Peggy lifted a mass of dark fabric from the pile and shook it out. Dark sparks shimmered in the lamplight. Peggy swung the black, jet-beaded cape around her shoulders and pirouetted in front of the mirror, wrinkling her nose against the strong stench of mothballs. Or was it camphor? Some preservative, Karen supposed.

"Very becoming," Simon said with a smile.

"I might actually wear it someday," Peggy said, studying her reflection complacently. "After it's been aired, that is. Whew, what a smell! We can thank whatever that stuff is for the survival of the manuscript, though."

Under a pile of old clothes in a trunk in the attic . . . "You mean this is that trunk?" Karen exclaimed, digging both hands into the remaining fabric. "Why didn't you tell me? Why didn't I think —"

"You've had a lot on your mind," Peggy said. "Don't bother excavating it now, there are no more papers there. I bought it for purely sentimental reasons."

"I'm glad you thought of it." Karen held up a strange construction of tape and wire. "What on earth is this?"

"A bustle," Peggy said, laughing. "That I won't wear. But some of the dresses are in good shape. Want to try them on? I think they're all too long for me."

Karen tossed the other clothes back into the trunk and closed the lid. "Not now. Where's the portrait?"

She exclaimed in outrage when Peggy dragged it out from under a collection of tarnished silver pieces. "Be careful! You'll scratch it."

"Honey, one more scratch won't even show. Have a look, Simon. What do you think?"

She spread it out on the bed and turned on both lamps.

Simon inspected the sad object in silence. "It could be two women. It could also be a woman and a man wearing a wig. Or two men wearing wigs. Or a couple of dogs with long ears. I hope you didn't pay a great deal for this master-piece."

"Don't be such a killjoy," Peggy said. "It will have to be cleaned, of course. And restored."

"Dogs!" Karen exclaimed, aghast.

"He's just kidding," Peggy assured her.

"The dogs were indeed a jest." Simon stepped back and squinted professionally at the canvas. "However, I think the casual resemblance to the Brontë portrait — which results primarily from the fact that this canvas, like the other, was folded — has given you false hopes."

"Probably," Peggy said cheerfully.

"On the other hand . . . If you like, I'll take it back with me. Paintings are not my specialty, but the people at the Walters can probably rec-ommend someone. Now this . . ." He lifted the framed portrait of the grim old lady onto the bed and studied it approvingly. "This has a certain appeal. The technique is poor, of course, but the painter has certainly caught a personality."

"But it's not Ismene," Karen exclaimed.

Simon turned to look searchingly at her. "How do you know?"

"Why, she . . . She's not . . . Well. The clothing, for one thing. It's Victorian — late Victorian. This is in much better condition than the other, it can't be as old."

"That doesn't necessarily follow," Simon said. "As for the date . . . Let's say this was painted in 1870 or 1880. The subject appears to be elderly. She may have been born in 1800, give or take ten years. You believe the manuscript could have been written as late as 1840.

"Earlier, I think," Karen mumbled, returning the old lady's painted frown.

Peggy pulled up a chair and straddled it, arms folded on the back. "We may as well settle this, Karen. I've seen it coming, and it is going to prejudice your judgment. Just how do you picture Ismene?"

Karen didn't answer. Peggy chuckled. "There's a scene in one of the Alcott books — *Jo's Boys*, I think — which takes place after Jo, like her creator, has become a famous author with doting fans pursuing her. In those days they didn't just write fan letters, they dropped in, uninvited and unheralded."

"What are you talking about?" Karen demanded belligerently. Simon was smiling too. She might have known he had read Louisa May Alcott. He was probably the only male in the world who had.

"Wait, this is not irrelevant. One such party of admirers corners Jo, although she has disguised herself as the cleaning lady in the hope of avoiding them. She is by now the mother of grown sons and not by any stretch of the imagination a beautiful woman. When the visiting lady turns to one

391

of her daughters and says, 'Don't you want her autograph,' the honest child replies, 'No. I thought she'd be about seventeen, with her hair done up in braids.' "

Simon's shoulders were shaking with laughter. After a brief internal struggle Karen threw in the towel. "You're right, damn it. I wasn't picturing a seventeen-year-old with pigtails, but my image of her was certainly influenced by irrational romanticism. Someone young, sensitive, slight . . ."

"A typical heroine, in fact," Peggy finished. "Even heroines get old, Karen. Or . . . they don't. The first alternative may not be romantic, but take my word for it, it's the lesser of the two evils."

Chapter Thirteen

Most of these books are about women who just can't seem to get out of the house.

E.C. DeLaMOTTE,
Perils of the Night, 1990

Half-raising herself from the bed, Ismene drew aside the curtain and looked toward the door. Sleep and the confusion attendant thereon weighted her eyelids; but it was soon replaced by the liveliest sensations of apprehension, for the sound was repeated: a soft scraping or scratching, like that which would have been produced by the claws of a beast. She had extinguished the lamp upon retiring; the fire, no more than a bed of red coals, gave not enough light to enable her to see the portal clearly; it was hearing, not sight, that allowed her to solve the mystery, for when the sound came again she recognized it for the turning of the handle.

So uncertain, so sly and slow was that movement that her heart sickened within her. The hour was late; the cold moon sank toward the horizon. Not even Clara would creep to her door at such an hour; Clara's hands would not fumble and slip, pause and renew the effort.

She forced her trembling limbs to abandon the deceptive shelter of the bed and the enclosing curtains.

Once on her feet, a little of her courage returned; but what could she do to save herself? There was no fastening on the door, no other exit from the room save the high window. Every fiber of her being cried out for light. To locate tinderbox and candle, and force her tremulous fingers to perform the necessary motions, would take too long. The door was opening.

She rushed to the fireplace, seized the bellows, and with the strength of terror fanned the embers to new life. The flames were low and feeble, but they gave sufficient light to illumine the dark figure advancing toward her. She saw the outstretched hands first, pallid and knotted like roots long underground. The form itself was indistinct, squat, shapeless and dark. With a slow writhing movement a face thrust itself forward, into the light.

Ismene had known who it must be, but the sight of that withered countenance with its one blind white eye reflecting the firelight in a crimson glare and its features horribly shadowed was so shocking she fell back against the wall with a stifled shriek.

The dreadful face turned in her direction. "Is it she? Is she the one?" a hoarse voice mumbled. Twisted fingers groped through the dark, writhing like white worms. Ismene shrank back. "Where is she? She must be warned. It must not be. Is she the one?"

Karen had dreamed of that face, luridly lit by flames. The portrait of the old woman and Peggy's morbid commentary must have recalled to her sleeping mind the last scene she had transcribed from the manuscript. It was still unpleasantly clear in her mind as she got dressed and made coffee.

She wished she hadn't agreed to join the expedition to the cemetery. It had been three days since she had been able to work on the manuscript, and she was anxious to find out what was going to happen next. She had finished almost two-thirds of it now, and her familiarity with the conventions of the Gothic novel had inspired several hunches — educated guesses, rather — as to how the book would end. In one sense she hoped she was right, for that would prove how clever she was; in another sense she hoped Ismene would prove cleverer than she, scorning the old Gothic traditions in favor of a more original solution.

It would have to wait a few more hours. She had been too tired the night before to work, and there wasn't time now; she had promised to meet the others at the motel and she was already late. She called Peggy, announced she was on her way, grabbed her purse and the briefcase, and ran out.

Absorbed in literary speculation — was the dark, surly doctor the hero, or were the dark hints about Edmund only red herrings? — she didn't notice the ominous thumping sound until she turned onto the highway and put her foot down on the gas. By the time she reached the motel it sounded as if there were a rock ricocheting back and forth under the hood.

They were waiting for her: Peggy in her commando outfit; Bill equally businesslike in jeans and denim shirt; and Simon, whose only concession to the rough work ahead had been to leave off his cravat.

Peggy trotted toward the car. "What's wrong with it?" she yelled, over the thunderous knocking.

"I don't know. It just started." Karen turned off the ignition.

"Sounds like a rod," Bill said, sauntering up. "Want to take it to a garage? I'll follow you —"

"Follow her where?" Peggy demanded. "We haven't got time to locate a reliable mechanic. I'll drive. Pull over next to my car, Karen."

"How much is that rod going to set me back?" Karen asked, once they were on their way.

Bill, in the back seat with Simon, replied, "Try not to think about it."

"Damn. All right, I won't think about it." She turned, arm over the seat. "I thought you were going back to Baltimore, Simon. You aren't dressed for this, you know."

"I mean to supervise," Simon said coolly. "And take a few photographs, if you are fortunate enough to find anything worth photographing."

"You brought a camera? Good thinking, Simon."

"It's mine. I brought tools, too." Peggy indicated the shopping bag at Karen's feet. "Clippers, shears, trowels."

Karen's first thought, when she saw the cemetery, was that a power mower and a few scythes would have been more useful. Except for the rusted iron fence that surrounded it and the ruins of the church, she would have taken the place for a meadow or an unmowed pasture. A few monuments reared stained marble heads above the waving grass, but there was no sign of an ordinary tombstone.

Bill was the first to break the pained silence. "We could just set fire to it."

"I'd be tempted, if I thought the damned stuff would burn," Peggy muttered. "Oh, well. Let's get organized."

Rummaging in her bag she produced an aerosol spray can and advanced purposefully on Karen. With a resigned shrug, Karen submitted. "Is this necessary?" Bill demanded, watching the evil-smelling mist surround Karen. "Surely it's too early for ticks."

"No, it's not," Peggy said. "Hold out your arms."

When she turned to Simon he backed away. "No, thank you."

"You want Lyme disease?"

"No, but —"

"Hold out your arms."

The gate sagged on rusted hinges. One by one they squeezed through. "Disgraceful," Simon murmured. "Even the church has fallen into ruin. They show no respect, these people."

"They probably don't have any money for restoration," Peggy said. "Fan out now. We're looking for the Cartright place. There should be a monument or mausoleum in the center of it, and maybe a low fence around it. Watch out for that, if it's metal you could trip and impale yourself."

The grass was knee-high. Lush and green, sprinkled with the delicate blooms of weeds and wildflowers, it was as pretty as a piece of embroidery, and Karen decided not to think about why it flourished with such extravagance. She stumbled over an unseen obstruction, and felt a supportive arm catch her around the waist.

"Fan out, Bill," she said.

"Then start shuffling" was the amused reply. "It's the only safe way to walk in this terrain; there are fallen tombstones every foot or so."

Shuffling, Karen headed for the nearest of the visible monuments, a tall marble column horribly stained by weather and bird droppings. Whatever object had surmounted it was now gone; the jagged shaft had cracked clean across. The lettering had been deeply incised; she could make out enough of the name to be sure it was not the one she wanted. A face leered up at her from the grass at its foot; dimpled cheeks and the stubs of wings at its shoulders identified it as some variety of angel.

Bill and Peggy had fanned out, Peggy to her right and Bill to her left. True to his promise, Simon was supervising. He had found something to sit on, but she couldn't see what, because it was hidden by the tall grass. He looked uncannily like a Hindu mystic perched cross-legged on empty air, his face as blandly impassive as that of an idol, his fine hands folded loosely on his lap.

It was Bill who found the Cartright monument

— a miniature mausoleum shaped of dark stone, square and unadorned except for a simple cavetto cornice. In response to his hail they converged upon him; even Simon climbed down off his tombstone and joined the others.

"As a family, the Cartrights display an admirable consistency of bad taste," Bill remarked, studying the unprepossessing structure. "It's a simple rectangle; hard to go wrong with a form like that, but there's something about the proportions . . ."

"Granite," Simon murmured. "Dark as night, hard as adamant. Could one conceive of resurrection from such a habitation?"

"Don't be fanciful," Peggy said. "This is where the fun begins. Take your clippers, ladies and gentlemen."

Karen had to force herself to kneel. The grass enveloped her as it had the stones, pressing in on either side, bending in over her head to form a green canopy.

It took over an hour for them to clear the plot, and all three were hot and perspiring by the time they finished. Studying Peggy's flushed face, shiny with sweat and speckled with green grass clippings, Simon decreed a pause for rest and refreshment. The bottled water was lukewarm, but they gulped it down, leaning against the car and catching their breaths.

"Did we find them all?" Karen asked.

"No." Peggy swabbed at her face with her sleeve. "I don't think so. Some have sunk under the ground. And they, as you might expect, are the oldest ones."

"Hence the trowels," Bill said morosely. "Let's get at it, then."

"Sorry you came?" Undaunted, Peggy grinned at him.

"No." He gave Karen a soulful look.

"I will be recorder," Simon announced, corking the bottle. "Call out to me the inscriptions as you find them. In that way you will not have to carry writing materials with you."

"Glad you came?" Peggy asked.

"I would not have missed it for the world."

His suggestion saved a good deal of time. How long they would have been at it — and how she could possibly have survived the ordeal — without Simon's assistance Karen could not imagine. Not only did he record the inscriptions but he produced a neat plan, with numbers keying the stones to the inscriptions. The plan also enabled them to see gaps in the placement of the graves; following that lead, Bill dug out two of the missing stones. The inscription on one was so worn it was illegible. The other bore a name Karen recognized; it had been in the genealogy. Poor little Jacob Cartright, born 1796, died 1798; the firstborn son of that generation, he had been given a more elaborate stone than most of the dead infants.

The majority of the remaining tombstones were of a later date than the ones with which they were concerned. One of these caught Karen's attention, and she lingered long enough to clear away the heaped-up earth at its base so she could read the inscription. Eliza Cartright, world traveler and would-be authoress, had lived to a ripe old age even by modern standards. She had been eighty-one when she died in 1912. She had never married; that, Karen realized, was why she was here, in her family plot. A married woman would have lost even that feeble and final independence, joining her husband in death as she had in life. A long poem praised Eliza's virtues and expressed her expectation of immortality. It was so bad Karen suspected Eliza had composed it herself.

As the day went on the sun rose over the trees and shone full upon them. Pollen, dust and bits of grass stuck to the sweat that covered exposed skin to form a conglomerate that looked terrible and itched like fury. Increasingly miserable though she was, Karen did not want to be the first to call for mercy. She was infinitely relieved to hear Simon announce, "We have visitors."

The other vehicle had pulled up behind Peggy's car. "Oh, Lord," Karen exclaimed, "it's a police car. Do you suppose we're breaking some law by being here?"

"Trespassing, probably." Bill didn't sound particularly worried. "Let's go talk to the gentleman. A bold front is the best defense."

One of the officers got out of the car and approached the gate. Apparently he decided not to get his nice neat uniform dirty by squeezing through, for he awaited them there.

"Good morning," Simon began.

"It's afternoon" was the unsmiling reply. "You folks enjoying yourself?"

"We are engaged in serious historical research," Peggy informed him.

The young man's official countenance cracked into a smile. "Right, lady. You look it. Mr. Hayes notified us you might be coming out here today and asked us to swing by and make sure everything was all right. No problems?"

"None at all," Karen said, relieved. "It was kind of you —"

"What kind of problems did you have in mind?" Bill interrupted.

"The usual. Vagrants, drunks, vandals, kids looking for some quiet place to do drugs and make out." He inspected Bill's tall frame and broad shoulders approvingly, and added, "Mr. Hayes only mentioned the two ladies. Some of these characters can get mean, especially if they're high on something. But there's nothing for you to worry about."

"Thanks anyhow," Bill said, squaring his shoulders and looking manly. Karen smothered a laugh, and he grinned at her.

The officer nodded. "We've had some complaints about a pack of dogs," he said casually. "Not rabid, so far's we know; just wild. They've savaged a couple of calves, but they won't attack people."

"How does he know they won't?" Karen asked, as the police car pulled away.

Simon, a city boy born and bred, looked apprehensive. "I should never have left the safe streets of Baltimore for this dangerous region. Vandals, drug addicts, wild dogs . . . We can't accomplish any more here without equipment heavier than those little trowels. Haven't you learned all you can, Peggy?"

Peggy shrugged. "If you guys are going to strike, I'll have to give in. Actually, you're right, Simon. The person who composed the genealogy must have gotten her information from the gravestones. I haven't found anything new."

"Then . . . then . . ." Simon choked. "This was a complete waste of time? All these hours of misery —"

"It was not a waste of time. I had to find out." Flexing her shoulders, she surveyed the sea of green, in which their hard work had made only a small island. In a low voice, as if talking to herself, she said, "I wonder if I've been on the wrong track all along."

Peggy refused to explain this enigmatic statement, and Karen did not press her. At that moment she was more interested in basic creature comforts, such as food and drink, cold showers and a flat surface on which to recline. Even Bill shook off his macho image long enough to mutter, "If this is what constitutes historical research I'm glad I took up literature instead."

"So you're not volunteering to join the archaeological dig?" Peggy inquired. Fatigue had not affected the panache with which she drove; Bill cringed as she made a wide, shrieking turn onto the highway, but replied, "The stone house, you mean? Wild horses couldn't keep me away. Or wild dogs."

Karen declined Simon's invitation to lunch, so they dropped her at the apartment.

"I'll call you later," Peggy said. "We'll worry about your car tomorrow, okay?"

Her recalcitrant vehicle was the farthest thing from Karen's mind just then. She was not so far gone that she forgot to retrieve the briefcase from Peggy's trunk, however.

After a shower and a late lunch she felt better. Her food supplies were low; Joan had made vast inroads on them. Damn the damn car; she'd have to ask Peggy to take her shopping. And how was she going to locate a mechanic who wouldn't take advantage of a woman and a stranger? Cameron was the obvious person to ask, but there was no way she could reach him if he was working at the house. Lisa would probably give her the name of the most rapacious mechanic in town, out of spite. After a moment of cogitation she reached for the limp, dog-eared telephone book and dialed.

Tanya sounded genuinely pleased to hear from her, and she was able to recommend a garage. "They've managed to keep me on the road, and believe me, that's no small feat. Sorry to hear you're having problems. If you need a lift —"

"I don't think so. But thanks for the offer."

A warm contralto laugh preceded Tanya's reply. "I owe you one, lady. You gave me one of the best hours of my life last week. The whole town's talking about it."

"So I hear," Karen said wryly.

"Mrs. F. giving you a hard time?"

"Trying to. She called me a trollop."

"Oh, God, really? How wonderful."

Under the gurgle of her laughter Karen heard a soft click, as if Tanya had let the telephone knock against some other object.

"Also a brazen hussy . . . a disgrace to the name of woman . . ." It was funny now. She could hear Tanya giggling uncontrollably. "Wanton, lewd, filthy-minded . . . And of course ill-bred, rude and crude."

"You've got to let me buy you a drink sometime."

"Aren't you afraid of guilt by association?"

"There is that." Tanya sobered. "She could get me fired."

"You're kidding."

"Unfortunately, I'm not. The old biddy wields a lot of power in this town. There's nothing she can do to you, though."

"I've been called worse things than trollop," Karen agreed, laughing. "I'll take a rain check on that drink — until it's safe. Maybe after I finish this part of the project."

"How's it going?"

"I've made progress in some areas; very little in others."

"You ought to talk to my mama sometime."

"Your mother? Why?"

"She's worked for the Cartrights off and on for fifty years. And her mama before her. Knows a lot of stories."

"I would like to talk to her," Karen said. "Does she live here?"

"Uh-huh. She takes care of old Miz Hayes. Cameron's mama."

"I didn't know that. When can I —"

"Gotta go," Tanya interrupted. "One of the trustees just walked in. I'll be in touch."

"Ditto. And thanks again."

Karen repeated the conversation to Peggy when she turned up later that afternoon. "I called the garage; they said if it is a rod, I shouldn't risk driving it. They'll send a tow truck around in the morning. Do you want to meet Tanya's mother?"

"Definitely." Peggy stubbed out one cigarette in the chipped saucer Karen had supplied as an ashtray and lit another. "We're running out of sources, Karen. Joan may have hit it on the head when she suggested pursuing oral tradition. The old lady could be a mine of information."

"She needn't be that old. Tanya can't be more than thirty."

"If she's a local girl her family has probably been working for the Cartrights for generations. Free and slave," Peggy added.

"I thought of that, but I didn't want to ask. What did you mean this afternoon when you said you'd been on the wrong track?"

"Just an amorphous idea." Peggy lit another cigarette. "I haven't got it quite clear in my head

406

yet. We're having dinner with Simon, by the way. If you're ready, we can have a drink in the bar before we meet him."

"All right." Karen gathered up the pages of manuscript and notes.

"That thing is getting to be a damned nuisance," Peggy said, watching her stuff the papers into the briefcase. "We really ought to figure out some safe place to leave it instead of hauling it everywhere we go."

"Anyplace safe is also inaccessible. I can't go running off to a bank every time I want to work on it."

Peggy drove slowly as they drove past the house. "No sign of Mrs. F. Doesn't she usually sit on the front porch this time of day?"

"She's probably afraid the mere sight of me will contaminate her."

"Not likely. I'll bet she watches you day and night from behind the curtains, hoping she'll catch you doing something . . . What's the matter?"

"My God," Karen exclaimed. "It never occurred to me till this minute. That funny click I heard when I was talking to Tanya — do you suppose my telephone is an extension of the one in the main house?"

"It never occurred to me either, but I guess it's possible." Peggy pondered. "She's the sort that would feel she was justified in keeping tabs on her tenants."

"But how would she know when I made or received a call?"

"Damned if I know. Maybe she just happened to pick up the phone. Or maybe she didn't. My telephone is always making strange noises. What difference does it make? We haven't discussed anything important over the phone."

"It could make a difference to Tanya," Karen said soberly.

"Surely not! The old bat can't have that much influence."

"God, I hope not. If Mrs. Fowler was listening she got an earful, to put it mildly." Karen groaned. "If Tanya loses her job it will be my fault."

"Let's not trouble trouble till trouble troubles us," Peggy advised.

"What?"

"It's a folk saying."

"So I imagined. Well, there's nothing we can do about it now."

"That's what I said." Peggy pulled into a parking space.

Simon joined them before long, but refused Peggy's offer of a drink. "I made a reservation at a restaurant in Williamsburg. The food here is an affront to the culinary art."

"Is anyone else coming?" Karen asked.

"Bill would have," Simon said. "I did not invite him. I wanted a quiet chat with you two."

"About anything in particular?" Peggy stood back and allowed him to open the door.

"About everything. I have an interest. I would appreciate being brought up-to-date."

He refused to discuss the subject, however, until

they had reached their destination and been shown to a table. Karen recognized the signs; Simon viewed dining out, as opposed to eating per se, as an art form, prolonged, leisurely and deliberate. It took him ten minutes to select the wine, after long consultation with a headwaiter who was obviously enraptured by his attitude toward food. They would be there until midnight, Karen thought resignedly.

After the most important matters had been settled, Simon looked at Peggy. "Begin at the beginning," he said. "And go on until you reach the end. "

Peggy was happy to oblige. Simon let her ramble on, with only an occasional question. The last question brought her up short. "What next?"

"Uh — well . . . We're planning to excavate the stone house . . ."

"Why?"

Peggy looked at Karen, who stared blankly back at her.

"What do you hope to find?" Simon asked. "Or, to put it another way, what can you possibly hope to find?"

"The fact that it was hers," Karen began.

"Not good enough," Simon said bluntly. "Let me summarize the situation as I see it. "

"I'm not going to like this," Peggy muttered, reaching for an ashtray.

Knowing Simon's views on smoking between courses, Karen took it as a meaningful sign when he gave Peggy an affectionate smile instead of a lecture. "I am not criticizing what you have done. All of it would have to be done at some time or other, and you seem to be enjoying yourselves hugely. But you remind me of Stephen Leacock's equestrian, who leapt onto his horse and rode off in all directions.

"The project you have undertaken has two major parts: one, the study of the manuscript itself; and two, the identification of the author. Yes, Karen, I know you have been working on the manuscript and I hope you will entertain me, later, with a summary of the plot. However, you have allowed yourself to be distracted. You ought to be in your apartment in Wilmington, safe and undisturbed."

"Safe," Peggy repeated, narrowing her eyes.

"Safe," Simon said. "Someone invaded her living quarters and attacked her physically. What on earth has come over you two, that you can coolly ignore that event? The intruder may not have intended to harm Karen, but she might have been injured, and the copy of the manuscript might have been taken. It would not be at risk — as it still is — if she had remained where she ought to be."

"You're right," Peggy murmured.

"But —" Karen began.

"Let me finish, please. The second part of the search is primarily Peggy's responsibility in any case, and it is also secondary to the main job. How can you possibly hope to identify this woman? You've already taken the obvious steps; you knew — at least I hope you knew — when you began that your chances of success were slim. What can you learn from that battered portrait? What can you find in the stone house? Even if it is the one she mentions in the manuscript, she left it a century and a half ago."

"There are other possible sources," Peggy said, frowning.

"Correct. And you were wise to purchase as many of the family possessions as you could. Some scrap of paper, some letter or diary may yet turn up. The chance is remote, however, and the search will be prolonged. I cannot understand why you are not concentrating on the manuscript. It has given you your most concrete evidence so far; you know you have found the right house, and that Ismene was most probably a member of the family. You've found absolutely nothing to connect her with a particular woman, and your best hope of finding that lies, it seems to me, in the text itself. Would you care for dessert?"

"You've taken away my appetite," Peggy said gloomily.

They settled for coffee and brandy. "Now tell me about the book," Simon said. "Start at the beginning and go on —"

"I don't know the ending yet," Karen said. "I've managed to resist the temptation to skip ahead; I want to get a feeling for the narrative, as an ordinary reader would do. And I'm horribly afraid we'll never know how it came out. Part of it is missing."

"Start at the beginning, then."

By the time she finished, the dining room was almost empty; except for one other party, they were the only ones there. "The pages I read this afternoon clear up the mystery of the old woman's identity. As Ismene cowers away from that groping hand, Edmund rushes into the room, accompanied by one of the servants. The old woman shrinks from him, mumbling incoherently, but she does not resist when the servant leads her from the room.

"Ismene is on the verge of collapse. Gently Edmund takes her into his arms and carries her to her bed. Rubbing her icy hands, he explains that the old woman is his poor, senile stepmother, his father's second wife. She is half-blind and so lacking in her wits that she must be confined and closely watched, for fear she might injure herself.

" 'She is completely harmless,' he insists, 'But the poor creature's appearance is so dreadful I do not wonder you were panic-struck. Even her daughter shrinks from visiting her. She has returned to infancy, physically as well as mentally, but rest assured that she receives the same tender care an infant would receive. Occasionally she takes these restless fits and escapes her guardian, wandering the house in search of heaven knows what fantasy of the mind. But you were in no danger, dear Ismene. Never will you be in danger while I am here.' "

She stopped speaking. "Then what?" Peggy asked.

"Edmund leaves, she falls asleep. That's as far as I got."

"She's in bed, vulnerable and quivering, he's leaning over her holding her hands — and he leaves?" Peggy exclaimed.

"This is at least a hundred years too soon for what you've got in mind," Karen said. "In its own way, though, it is distinctly sensuous. You'd have to read it to know what I mean."

"Oh, yeah? You could have a best-seller on your hands after all."

"I doubt it," Simon said, his lip curling. "The romantic sensibilities of modern readers have been blunted by anatomically detailed descriptions. Never mind your best-sellers. What concerns me — and should concern you — is to what extent you can interpret this story as autobiographical." He raised his hand and ticked the points off on his long thin fingers, folding them under as he touched them. "One: The setting appears to be based on reality — a specific house in a specific location. Two: The heroine, like her creator, aspires to literature and perhaps to the attainment of solitude in a 'room of her own.' "

Three fingers remained untouched. Raising his eyebrows, Simon looked from one of them to the other. "And that's it," he said. "That's all you have. Obviously the Gothic trimmings are pure fantasy. The grim labyrinthine old house, the vague hints of sinister secrets — and the characters themselves. Ismene's childish, helpless sister, her angelically handsome cousin, her dark, surly suitor the doctor, the elderly madwoman — don't you see, they are stock characters of Gothic fiction! What leads you to suppose that they have any basis in reality? If you ever learn Ismene's identity, you will probably discover that she was a smug, respectable Victorian matron who had a dozen children and a very lurid imagination!"

Silence fell like a damp, depressing fog. Karen could think of nothing to say. Simon was one hundred percent right. She ought to have known it. She had known it. And she knew why she had not been willing to admit the truth.

Peggy emitted a long sigh. "All right. So what do you suggest?"

"I suggest we take our departure," Simon said, beckoning the waiter. "It is getting late."

They were in the car heading back before he spoke again. "The only thing that puzzles me is why two intelligent, highly educated women should be so reluctant to face facts that must be even more obvious to them than they are to me. Have you any information you are keeping to yourselves? If you choose not to confide in me —"

"Don't be an idiot," Peggy growled.

"Then the answer is obvious, surely. Rid yourself of your preconceptions. Start again from the beginning, which is the manuscript itself. What you require is evidence that will enable you to fix the date of the manuscript more closely. You may find a specific reference to some historic or literary event. If not, you should be able to make an educated guess on the basis of the style of the writing itself. I fear you are letting your preconceptions influence your judgment on that question as well. The earlier the book, the more important the discovery; I quite understand that. But it sounds to me as if it is closer in time to the Brontës than to Mrs. Radcliffe."

"Karen is the best judge of that," Peggy said loyally.

Karen said nothing.

Simon didn't wait for her response. There was a new note of urgency in his voice when he spoke. "I must leave tomorrow. I have an important appointment on Wednesday. Please, Karen, won't you come with me? Have I not convinced you that remaining here is counterproductive?"

"He's right," Peggy said. "Much as I hate to admit it. Not that you're in any danger —"

"No, no," Simon said quickly. "I didn't mean to alarm you."

"Like hell you didn't." Karen reached out to pat his shoulder. "But I appreciate your concern, Simon dear. And your insightful analysis. You are right, of course, I should be concentrating on the manuscript. Anyway, I've accomplished most of what I hoped to do here. I can't leave until my car is fixed, but I promise, as soon as it's ready, I'll head for home. Are you satisfied?"

They were not as late as she had believed they would be; it was a few minutes before eleven when Peggy turned into the driveway. She and Simon followed Karen up the stairs and into the apartment.

"It's all right, you see," Karen said, switching on the lights. "You needn't look under the bed, Simon."

Simon gave her a cool stare and proceeded to do so. While he was looking into the bathroom and the closet, Karen whispered, "You aren't going to say anything to him about — about —"

"Of course not! I adore that man, even if he does treat me like a blithering idiot sometimes; I don't want him to think I'm a superstitious blithering idiot."

Simon emerged from the bedroom. "No one is there," he announced.

"Thank you," Karen said meekly.

"Not at all. Be sure you bolt the door securely. If you are ready, Peggy?"

Peggy gave Karen a wink and a grin, and she smiled back. Simon could lecture them all he liked about irrational romanticism, but he was not entirely immune; there was a certain swagger in his step as he strode to the door and held it for Peggy.

As soon as the car pulled away Karen turned out the light and prepared for bed. All that wine, and brandy on top of it, after a day of strenuous physical activity, had left her stumbling and groggy. She felt sure she would sleep soundly, in spite of Simon's deflating, depressing, devastatingly accurate analysis. She consoled herself by concluding that no real harm had been done. She hadn't wasted that much time. Viewing the house had not been just a romantic indulgence. Simon didn't understand; atmosphere was important, being actually on the spot had given her a new insight.

The dark figure came shambling down the corridors of sleep. Holding the candle high, she waited for it to approach. Knowing what it was, horror had been replaced by pity — or so she believed; but when the dreadful face lifted toward hers and the white eyeball shone yellow with reflected light — when the twisted hands groped blindly for her skirts — compassion faltered and she recoiled from the touch and from the hoarse mumbling voice.

"Is it she? Is she the one? She must be warned, it will soon be too late . . ."

And then, in the manner of a true nightmare, the film vanished from the creature's blinded eye. Both eyes opened to display dark dilated pupils rimmed with brilliant blue — the eyes of youth, clear and bright and wide with fear. The voice rose in a high woman's scream. "Wake! Wake, or it will be too late!"

The cry had come from her own throat. Gasping for breath, Karen rolled over. Her face had been buried in the pillow, but when she inhaled she found herself still struggling for air. The room was white with moonlight — strange, heavy light, like curdled milk. She sucked it into her lungs with the next breath, and burst into a fit of coughing.

Sheer instinct got her out of bed and to the window. A few deep breaths brought her closer to conscious waking. What had happened to the moon? The milky light was not white, it was reddish, uncertain, flickering.

Now wide awake and weak-kneed with terror, Karen ran to the closed bedroom door. One touch was all she needed; the wooden panel was so hot it stung her palm. Thank God some half-remembered lecture had kept her from opening that door. The living room must be engulfed in flames.

The air near the floor would be clearer. She remembered that too. A folder in some hotel room, telling guests what to do in case of fire . . . On hands and knees she crawled to the closet and dragged out the unwieldy bundle of rope and metal. Her head was swimming and she could hear the crackle of the flames through the closed door.

One hard shove sent the screen tumbling out. It seemed to take an eternity to locate the heavy metal strips that hooked over the windowsill, and push the ladder out. Filling her lungs with the relatively clearer air near the floor, she held her breath and ran to the bed. A tongue of flame bit through the smoldering wood of the door and licked toward her as she pitched the briefcase out the window and climbed over the sill, bare feet feeling for the topmost rung. She was halfway down when the fire broke through the wall of the garage next to the ladder. Without looking to see what lay below, she threw herself backward. Prickly branches broke her fall and tore her arms and legs. Rolling over, she saw the briefcase lying on the ground. The lurid light was as bright as the day of a planet circled by a red sun.

Clasping the briefcase to her breast, she retreated

to what seemed a safe distance and stood in a be-
numbed stupor watching the flames blow like
wildly tossing hair from her bedroom window. The
whole place was gone, it was too late to save it
. . . But what about the house? The miracle of
her own survival had overshadowed all other concerns till then, and she swore at herself in a shaky
undertone as she pushed through the hedge and
ran across the garden. The neighbors' house was
some distance away, it probably was in no danger,
but if blowing sparks caught the roof here, and
she couldn't wake Mrs. Fowler . . . The windows
were dark. Shouting, she banged on the back door.
There was no response. Mrs. Fowler's window remained unlighted.

Karen set her teeth, shielded her face with her
arm, and swung the briefcase. Glass shattered. She
cleared the jagged shards from the frame with another sweep of the briefcase and reached inside.
Bolts, chains — thank God, the key was in the
lock, Mrs. Fowler must also be aware of the danger
of fire — and of burglary, she had taken precautions for herself that she hadn't bothered to supply
for her tenants. The door finally gave way. Still
not a sound from upstairs. How could the woman
sleep through the racket?

She learned the answer after she had located the
telephone and called the fire department. Mrs.
Fowler was sound asleep in her bed, snoring like
a baritone.

Thank God, Karen thought. She had half expected to find the old woman stark and stiff, her

419

face set in a glare of Gothic horror. She leaned over Mrs. Fowler and shook her.

There was no response, not even a grunt. Karen stepped back, her nose wrinkling. The stench of stale whiskey permeated the bedclothes and Mrs. Fowler herself.

Chapter Fourteen

Western culture . . . was a grand ancestral
property that educated men had inherited
from their intellectual forefathers, while their
female relatives, like characters in a Jane Austen novel, were relegated to modest dower
houses on the edge of the estate.

SANDRA M. GILBERT,
"What Do Feminist Critics Want?", 1985

By the time Peggy arrived, the garage had collapsed into a blackened, steaming heap. The scene
had an insanely festive appearance; people in a
wild variety of informal costumes chatting and
drinking coffee and watching like spectators at a
performance, headlights crisscrossing the dark and
turning the sprays of water into sparkling illumined fountains. Peggy hadn't stopped to dress;
she had slipped her feet into sneakers and thrown
a coat over her nightgown. It flapped around her
calves as she ran toward Karen.

"Are you all right?"

"Fit as a fiddle. I told you I was."

"I saw the ambulance and I thought —"

"It's for Mrs. Fowler," Karen said without expression. "They don't believe she's in any danger.
Just a precaution."

"Shock, I expect." The little woman standing next to Karen shook her fluffy white head. "I near fainted myself when I saw that place on fire. Thought the young lady here was still inside. If I've told Miz Fowler once I've told her a hundred times she shouldn't keep paint cans and old newspapers in the garage."

"This is Mrs. Miller," Karen explained. "She's been wonderful. This is her raincoat I'm wearing, and her coffee I'm drinking. My friend Peggy Finneyfrock, Mrs. Miller."

"Ah, the owner of that handsome cat." Peggy offered her hand. "Thanks for coming to Karen's rescue."

"Well, my land, what else would a person do? I offered to put her up for the night, but she said she'd already telephoned you. Would you like some coffee, Peggy?"

"That would probably save my life," Peggy said gratefully. "If it's not too much trouble."

"Not a bit. Be right back."

As soon as she was out of earshot Karen said urgently, "Simon mustn't know about this. You didn't wake him, I hope."

"No, I didn't. But he's bound to find out sooner or —"

"Make it later. There's no need to worry him unnecessarily."

"Unnecessarily!" Peggy's voice cracked. "How can you be so cool about this?"

"I don't know," Karen admitted. "Maybe it hasn't hit me yet. But this doesn't change anything.

The garage was an accident waiting to happen. The fire may be — probably is — unrelated to anything else."

"Oh, Christ!" Peggy threw up her hands. "Let's get the hell out of here. It makes me sick at my stomach just to look at that charred mess."

"You have to drink Mrs. Miller's coffee first," Karen said calmly. "Besides, I expect the fire chief wants to talk to me."

The two arrived simultaneously. Mrs. Miller proffered a heavy mug, and the chief — a tall, stooped man with a face as long and melancholy as that of a bloodhound — took off his hat and blotted his wet face with his handkerchief. "All secure," he announced. "I'm afraid there's nothing left, miss. Any idea how it could have started?"

Mrs. Miller snorted. "The wiring in that place is fifty years old, Bill. And she had all that junk in the garage."

"I think it started in the garage," Karen agreed. "When I woke up, the living room was burning, but there was fire below, under the bedroom, too. It burned through the garage wall when I was half-way down the ladder. I had to jump."

Bill scratched his grizzled head and looked grave. "I told Miz Fowler time and time again she was in violation of the law; at least she went to the trouble of getting one of them ladders. Lucky for you she did, miss. If you'd had to jump from the upstairs window you could've broken something, or knocked yourself unconscious, and then . . ."

Coffee sloshed over the edge of the cup Peggy

was holding. Taking it from her, Mrs. Miller scolded, "That's enough, Bill. Why talk about terrible things that didn't happen? Oh, my land, look-they're carrying Miz Fowler out on a stretcher. I better go see . . ."

"There's nothing serious wrong with her, is there?" Karen asked, as Mrs. Miller trotted off.

"Don't guess so. But she's an old lady and she was whooping and carrying on and yelling about her heart, so we figured it was better to be on the safe side. Expect you're ready for some rest too, miss. Where'll you be?"

Karen supplied the information and led Peggy to the car. "I'll drive," she said. "No, don't argue; you're shaking like a leaf. Give me the keys."

"They're in the ignition. Mrs. Fowler didn't buy that ladder, did she?"

"No."

"I think I'm going to throw up."

"It's your car. Suit yourself."

A choked laugh from Peggy told her she had said the right thing.

A knock on the door woke Karen next morning. It took her several seconds to orient herself; the bed, the room, even the nightgown were unfamiliar. Then the events of the past night came flooding back and she sat up with a start, in time to see a man in a white jacket beating a hasty retreat. Peggy was pouring coffee. Carrying a cup to Karen she remarked, "Well, you gave one young waiter the thrill of a lifetime."

Karen pulled the nightgown back over her shoulders. It was Peggy's, and far too large for her.

"Sorry," she mumbled.

"He wasn't." Peggy sat down on the edge of the other bed. "I hated to wake you, but time's awastin'. Your car has been removed; I told the guy from the garage he'd have to figure out what to do about the keys, since you'd lost yours in the fire. Simon has gone, innocent and unwitting." Peggy made a wry face. "You may have ruined the romance of the century. When he finds out how I lied to him . . . Anyhow, he said to tell you if you weren't home by Friday, he'd come back and carry you off, bound and gagged if necessary. Tanya called. So did Lisa. So did Cameron. So did Bill."

"Wait a minute," Karen begged. "I'm still half asleep. Talk slower. When did all these things happen? I didn't hear the phone ring."

"I told the switchboard not to put calls through. I've been downstairs in the lobby for the past two hours; took the calls there. I had breakfast with Simon. Come and eat yours. And don't dawdle. We've got to buy you a whole new wardrobe, replace your credit cards, checks, keys —"

"Don't." Karen slumped into a chair and buried her face in her hands. "I don't want to think about it."

"Don't think. Eat."

Peggy waited until she had consumed a restorative amount of food before she spoke again. "The

425

most sensible thing, of course, would be for me to drive you back to Wilmington today. Even if your car were operable, you don't have a driver's license and you can't get a replacement until —"

"You needn't go on. It would be the most sensible course."

"Are we going to do it?"

Karen swung around to face her. "I wouldn't be here this morning if two things hadn't happened. First, an irrational premonition that prompted me to buy that rope ladder. Second, a dream that woke me in the nick of time. That's not a figure of speech, Peggy. The smoke in the bedroom was so thick I could hardly breathe. Another minute and I'd have been unconscious."

Peggy rolled her eyes, clutched her head with both hands, sputtered, and finally managed to speak. "I had a feeling you were going to say something like that. It's partly my fault. I should have slapped you down when you started talking about cold spots and premonitions and Screaming Ladies. Speculating about such things is entertaining; I've always had a halfhearted, shame-faced desire to believe in them. But wishing don't make it so, Karen. You're losing your objectivity in your sympathy for Ismene. You're seeing her as you want to see her. And if you're counting on her to warn you —"

"I'm not. I'm counting on your skepticism and good sense to keep me from going off the deep end. That's why I told you about the dream. I know I've allowed myself to become too emotionally involved in this business."

"Oh." Peggy sat back. "Then you're willing to do as Simon suggested?"

"Not yet." Peggy's lips parted; before she could speak Karen went on, "Simon made a good case, but he's allowing emotional considerations to affect his judgment too. So are you. You're both worried about me — with insufficient cause, in my opinion. Now just stop and think, Peggy. These last two incidents have been accidents, pure and simple. They can't have been anything else. Our original reasoning still holds. I don't present a threat to anyone and I possess nothing anyone else wants except the manuscript — and I don't even own it! It belongs to you. That fire would have destroyed the only accessible copy."

"Uh." Peggy looked horrified. "I hadn't thought of it that way.

"Had you thought of this?" Karen leaned forward, eyes intent. "Cameron said he had a potential buyer. Once the house is sold we may not have access to it. A new owner may demolish all or part of it, clear the woods for building sites, bulldoze that pile of stones. We can't count on Cameron's continued cooperation either. He doesn't owe us anything. Suppose he decides he doesn't want us hanging around? We've got to finish the job before we leave. We may not have another chance. At the very least we ought to take a few rolls of pictures. Well?"

Peggy sighed. "Your logic is irrefutable."

"Then you agree?"

"I have to agree. The only counterarguments I can produce are irrational. But I don't have to like it."

Having agreed, Peggy flew into action, as if she were determined to finish the business as quickly as possible. Shopping occupied the rest of the morning, in spite of Karen's determination to buy only the bare essentials. It was a relief to get into clothes that fit; Peggy's pants were six inches too short and several inches too large elsewhere, and her sandals left Karen's toes protruding painfully. When she could walk without limping she raced up and down the aisles tossing articles into the shopping cart and envying her primitive ancestors for the simplicity of their needs. On the other hand, as Peggy pointed out when she expressed this opinion, if your sole article of clothing was a bearskin, you had to catch, kill and skin the bear first. Time-consuming, to say the least.

"Now what?" Karen asked, after they had stowed two large bags of bare essentials away in Peggy's car and were recuperating with coffee and sandwiches.

"I made a list." Peggy extracted it from her purse. "We're going to go about this methodically for a change."

She handed the paper to Karen. "Family Bible," the latter read. "You still believe there is one?"

"I intend to find out for certain one way or the other. When I talked to Lisa this morning I told her it was time to put up or shut up — that we were leaving town in a few days and probably wouldn't be back."

"What did she say?"

"Just what I expected. She'd have another look around and see if she had overlooked anything."

"Okay. Number two: talk with Mrs. Madison.

"Who's Mrs. Madison?"

"Tanya's mother. I told you, she called this morning — Tanya, not her mother — to ask if you were all right and was there anything she could do."

"How did she know I was at the motel?" Karen asked, momentarily distracted.

"My dear girl, everyone in town knows you're at the motel. They probably know every grisly detail, including a few that never happened. The fire was undoubtedly the main topic of conversation this morning."

"Oh. What do you hope to get from Mrs. Madison?"

"One never knows."

"All right, be mysterious." Karen glanced at the paper. "Number three: take photographs. You brought your camera?"

"Yes. I had planned to take photographs of the house anyway. I bought some extra film this morning."

"Do you want to do it this afternoon?"

"Tomorrow. I told Cameron to have the workers there —"

She broke off, looking as if she wanted to clap her hand over her mouth.

"So," Karen said gently, "you told Cameron we'd be there tomorrow. I suppose we are calling on Mrs. Madison this afternoon? You made those appointments — you told Lisa we'd be around for a few days — and yet this morning you tried to talk me into leaving immediately."

"I made you an offer," Peggy corrected. "It had to be your decision. I wouldn't have blamed you for getting cold feet. Are you sure you want to go ahead with . . ."

Karen's eyes returned to the list. "Number four: investigate the stone house. Of course I want to go ahead with it. If I don't go back to that clearing I'll wonder all my life what it was we heard that day, and despise myself for being too cowardly to find out."

"It should be an interesting experiment," Peggy said dubiously.

"It's a lovely old house," Karen said, as Peggy brought the car to a stop in front of one of the sprawling Victorian mansions on West Main Street. "What a pity the Madisons have let it deteriorate. I suppose they don't have much money."

"It's Cameron's house," Peggy said.

"What?" Karen stared at her.

"Get with it, girl. Didn't Tanya tell you her mother babysits with Mrs. Hayes? According to Lisa, the old lady is a candidate for a nursing home; she must be bedridden, or, as Lisa nicely put it, senile."

"She's got a heart as big as all outdoors," Karen

muttered, remembering Lisa's cold dismissal of her aunt. "And Cameron's not exactly the dutiful son, is he? You'd think he could keep his mother's house in better repair instead of spending all his time and effort on something he expects to make money on."

The crumbling bricks of the walk and the overgrown lawn showed the same signs of neglect as the house. They approached the steps to the veranda cautiously; they were solid, though there was very little paint left on them.

Their knock was promptly answered. Mrs. Madison, a slim woman with a smooth, unlined face, had been watching for them. "It's nice to have company," she said ingenuously. "I get pretty bored with nothing to do all day except read and watch the soaps."

She must do more than read and watch the soaps. The living room was shabby but very neat and clean, and the silver tea set arranged on a table shone with polishing. "You shouldn't have gone to so much trouble," Peggy said, as Mrs. Madison offered a steaming cup.

"Oh, it's no trouble. Like I said, I'm pleased to have somebody to talk to."

"Mrs. Hayes doesn't . . . ." Peggy paused tactfully.

Mrs. Madison glanced at a closed door. "She sleeps a lot. This is usually one of her quiet times, so I hope we'll be able to have a nice chat. Tanya told me what you're doing. It sounds real interesting. I don't know if I can be any help, but go ahead and ask anything you want."

Peggy beamed approvingly at her. "Good. You don't mind if I take notes?"

Mrs. Madison looked dubious. Interpreting her reaction correctly, Peggy added, "This is off the record. If we want to publish any information you give us, we'll ask your permission first."

The other woman's face cleared. She nodded. "That's fair. It's just that I wouldn't want to embarrass Cameron, or make trouble for Tanya. Some of the folks in this town take old history too personally."

"I know what you mean," Karen said, feeling it was time for her to join in the conversation. "My landlady, for one."

The other woman's face rounded with laughter. "Tanya told me about your talk. She liked it a lot."

"I probably shouldn't have done it, though," Karen said ruefully. "I was rather rude. And now Mrs. Fowler won't have anything to do with me."

"She wouldn't be much use to you. She's a terrible malicious old gossip. You can't believe nothing she says."

"I'm sure you'll be a much more reliable source," Peggy said, folding back a page of her notebook. "You lived at Amberley when you were a child, didn't you?"

"Uh-huh. My mama and daddy worked for old Mr. Cartright back — oh, land, it must be forty years ago. Before he got so queer and mean." She settled back, hands folded on her lap. "We lived in the main house, in those rooms near the kitchen. The servants' houses had tumbled down long before and there was plenty of room, with just old Mr. Josiah living there. It was a quiet, peaceful place for children to grow up, but awful lonesome, no neighbors or nothing. We had chickens and dogs and cats, though, and all those acres to wander in."

"Do you remember a kind of hollow, a clearing in the woods, with an old ruined building of some kind?"

"We didn't go there much."

"Why not?"

"There were stories about it." She shrugged deprecatingly. "You don't want to hear them; they were just old tales, the kind kids tell to scare themselves with."

"That's exactly what I want to hear," Peggy said eagerly. "Please go on."

"Well." She settled back again, a reminiscent smile on her face. "You know how kids are. My brother Tyrone loved to tease the little ones. He was the one who told us about the slave house. That's what the stones were, he said. The place where the old devil — not Mr. Josiah; the old man that built the house all those years ago — where he put the slaves who'd stood up to him or tried to run away. He'd shut them up in the stone house, in the dark, without food or water, and leave them there."

"How horrible!" Karen exclaimed.

"It was just a story," Mrs. Madison said.

"Maybe not," Peggy said quietly. "I've heard of worse things."

"There couldn't be anything much worse," Karen muttered. "God, how awful."

"I'm sorry, I didn't mean to upset you," Mrs. Madison said. She and Peggy exchanged glances, and Karen realized she had sounded like a naive child. Of course there were worse things. And people had done them, all of them, to other people.

"Anyhow, it all happened a long time ago," Mrs. Madison said soothingly. "To us kids they were just scary stories. But we didn't go there much. The place had a funny feeling about it. Probably because Tyrone was such a good storyteller. He said he'd heard them screaming. Now you know that was just foolishness, because you couldn't have heard anything through those thick stone walls even if there had been people inside. There was no proof such a thing ever happened."

Peggy carefully avoided looking at Karen. "Was the stone house intact when you were a child?" she asked.

"I guess so. It was all covered with brush and vines, and we didn't look close at it."

"Do you know about Mrs. Fowler's book?" Peggy was scribbling furiously.

"The ghost book? Yes, sure. Lot of lies in it," Mrs. Madison said calmly.

"She mentions a Screaming Lady."

"Oh, yeah, that was another one of Tyrone's stories. I don't know where he heard 'em. He was the oldest."

"You never heard anything, or felt anything —
in the house or elsewhere?"

Mrs. Madison frowned thoughtfully. "Hard to
remember now what really happened and what's
imagination. I was real little . . . We didn't go
in the main part of the house much. We weren't
allowed to, you see. Tyrone said there was some
awful scary statue in the cellar, but I never saw
it; Mama wouldn't let us young ones go down
there, it was all mud and mess, she said. But Tyrone managed to have a look. He was a real curious
youngster, and not scared of anything."

"Tyrone sounds like quite a guy," Peggy said
with a smile. "What's he doing now?"

"He died in Vietnam."

"What a waste. I'm so sorry."

"Thank you." Mrs. Madison got to her feet.
"Excuse me just a minute. I think I hear —"

Karen hadn't heard anything, but when Mrs.
Madison opened the closed door, the sound came
clearer — a wordless whine, like the complaint
of a sleepy baby. A faint but unmistakable, unpleasant odor accompanied it.

"Excuse me," Mrs. Madison said again. She
closed the door, but Karen had already seen the
big bed and its occupant. The body under the
heaped up blankets was invisible, too wasted even
to lift them; the face might have been that of a
man or a woman or a waxen mask, vacant and
sightless. A stream of saliva trickled from the open
mouth.

Peggy had seen it too. Karen heard her breath

435

catch. Then she said softly, "For once Lisa seems to have understated the case."

"Good God," Karen breathed. "You sound so —"

"Don't lecture me about compassion, Karen. I've just seen my worst nightmare — the thing all aging people dread most. To be a prisoner in your own rotting body . . ."

"Let's go. I can't stand this."

"*You* can't stand it?"

"Surely she doesn't know —"

"We can hope she doesn't, can't we? Sit down. We'll take a gracious, well-bred leave when Mrs. Madison returns. I think I've got most of what I wanted from her."

Peggy studied her notes. Karen studied her. After a while Peggy said, without looking up, "Sorry I snapped at you. Your kind heart does you credit. You'll toughen up as you get older."

"Is that a threat or a promise?"

The walls of the old house were thick and solid. They had no warning of his approach; the door opened, and there he was.

The words of greeting froze on Karen's lips. She had once wondered what it would be like to see Cameron lose his temper. Apparently she was about to find out.

"What the hell are you doing here?" His voice was soft, but so distorted by anger it was barely recognizable.

"Why, Cameron," Peggy began.

He turned to face her, muscles squirming under

the stretched skin of his cheeks and jaw. "You, too. Of all the contemptible, filthy tricks! Forcing yourself in here, invading the privacy of a woman who's too sick to protect herself —"

The bedroom door opened, and Mrs. Madison said quietly, "Oh, hello, Cameron. I thought I heard your voice. You're early."

He stared at her, struggling for breath as if he were choking on the words he wanted to say. At last habitual good manners — or Mrs. Madison's air of conscious virtue? — prevailed. He muttered, "I — I had to make a few phone calls. Go home, Jenny, there's no need for you to stay."

"I have to wait for Tanya to pick me up," Mrs. Madison said.

"We'll be happy to drop you off, Mrs. Madison," Peggy said.

Cameron offered to call Tanya, and refused to let Mrs. Madison clear away the tea-things; he was obviously desperate to get rid of them, so Mrs. Madison agreed. "I changed her and got her settled down," she said in a matter-of-fact voice. "You should have a couple of hours to yourself."

Peggy cleared her throat. "Is it still on for to-morrow morning, Cameron?"

"Uh — yes. Right. Thanks, Jenny."

He stood in the open door watching them as they picked their way along the treacherous surface of the walk. They were in the car and on their way before Karen ventured to speak.

"I hope we didn't . . . He won't be angry with you, will he, for letting us come?"

"Oh, no," Mrs. Madison said placidly. "He doesn't like people seeing her like that, is all. But he'll get over it — two nice ladies like you. Some people in this town, not naming any names, aren't so understanding."

"It's very good of you to take on that job," Peggy said warmly. "Not everyone would."

"She's just like a poor little baby," Mrs. Madison murmured. "No harm in her at all. There but for the grace of God . . . Anyhow, poor Cameron's got enough to worry about. I'm only there eight, ten hours a day. He's got her the rest of the time. And it's harder, you know, when it's one of your own."

They dropped her off and headed for the motel. Neither spoke for some time. Finally Karen murmured, " 'Sometimes it is better not to see what lies hidden in the dark.' "

"Very philosophical. What brought that on?"

"Just thinking."

Peggy did not pursue the subject. To judge by her expression, her thoughts were running along the same uncomfortable lines as Karen's. But she's not the one who should feel guilty, Karen told herself. I interpreted his reserve, his refusal of my offer of friendship, as a personal affront. I despised him for being greedy and money-mad. In my consummate selfishness, it never occurred to me that he might have good reasons for behaving as he did, reasons that had nothing to do with me.

She twisted uncomfortably and raised one hand to shield her flushed face from Peggy's curious glance. "What's bugging you?" Peggy asked.

"I hate feeling like a jerk."

"So do I. You'll get used to it," Peggy said with a wry smile. "It's the inevitable consequence of being a human being."

They found a number of messages waiting for them. Peggy thumbed through them as they rode up in the elevator. "Aren't we popular? Here's one from Cameron; we needn't return his call, we've already heard what he thinks of us. At least he hasn't canceled our permit to excavate . . . Lisa! I'll call her first; she may have something for us . . . William Something or other — I can't read the writing. Is that the fire chief? Better call him, it's probably an official demand . . . Bill Meyer . . . Bobby Mansfield . . . The pimply brother-in-law. What do you suppose he wants?"

"He's probably wondering if I'm going to sue the old lady," Karen grumbled. "And hoping to charm me out of it. The hell with him, I don't want to talk to him."

"How about Bill?" Peggy unlocked the door.

"I don't want to talk to him either."

"He might buy us dinner."

"I don't want —"

"Oh, all right. I'll talk to him. You have no objection to his joining us tomorrow, I hope."

It wasn't a question, so Karen didn't answer it. She unpacked her purchases and employed her brand-new toothbrush while Peggy spoke on the telephone. When she came out of the bathroom

Peggy reported, "Bill is deeply hurt but resigned. He'll meet us tomorrow at Amberley. Lisa's on her way over here. I figured we might as well make her come to us if she's as eager as she sounds. She must have something good. You've got time to call Bill the Chief before we meet her in the bar."

She sat on the bed listening while Karen talked. "What was that all about?" she demanded, as Karen slammed the phone into the cradle. "I can see you're furious, but I didn't get enough out of your side of the conversation to make sense of it. Did I hear something about smoking? He didn't imply —"

"He didn't. Mrs. Fowler did." Karen bit off the words. "She claimed I must have been smoking in bed. There's no other way the fire could have started, she says."

"Well, she would say that, wouldn't she? A good offense is the best defense. How about the papers and paint cans in the garage?"

"She says Bobby Boy cleared the garage out that day. He supports her. It's my word against theirs, and I can't even swear the garage wasn't empty when we got there that night. I didn't look."

"Well, well. Now we know why Bobby Boy called, don't we? They can't prove negligence on your part since there was none, so he's hoping to scare you into a tidy little out-of-court settlement."

"It won't work."

"Of course not. Have the cops got any idea how the fire did start?"

Karen's furious scowl turned to a thoughtful frown. "I got the distinct impression that there is something suspicious about it. I mean, wouldn't the chief have told me if it was something like spontaneous combustion or faulty wiring?"

"Maybe not. Officials of all varieties are tight-lipped by nature." Peggy glanced at her watch. "We'd better go down and meet Lisa the Greek."

"The who?"

"You know about Greeks bearing gifts." Peggy picked up her purse and gestured toward the door.

Lisa was waiting for them. She had already ordered a drink — not a ladylike pastel concoction or a glass of white wine, but a stiff shot of Bourbon. Before getting down to business she wanted to know all about the fire. There was something almost ghoulish about her repeated questions and expressions of concern. Finally Peggy put an end to them.

"So how is Mrs. Fowler?"

"They sent her home this afternoon. She's still pretty upset, as you can imagine. Bobby is staying with her till she gets over the shock."

"Shock, hell." Peggy didn't bother being tactful. "She ought to be apologizing to Karen and thanking her. Her negligence was responsible for the fire, and if the house had caught she'd have been burned in her bed. She was dead drunk."

Lisa choked. "That's a terrible accusation to make."

"It's the truth," Peggy said. "I'm tired of gossip and innuendo and veiled threats. You tell the old bitch we know what she's trying to do, and she isn't going to get away with it. If she wants to start trouble she'll get more than she's bargained for."

"I don't —"

"Of course you don't. Let's drop the subject. What have you got?"

Wide-eyed and silent, Lisa produced her offering. It was a Bible — a huge folio four inches thick, with brass clasps and engravings from Durer. Lips set in a sneer, Peggy thumbed through the pages at the front. "No good," she said curtly.

"What? You said you wanted —"

"This edition was printed in 1890. We've already got this information, it's in the genealogy."

She laid the book on the table and held it open. The page was headed "Births" and framed by an elaborate border of vines and flowers and fat, doughy-faced cherubs. The first name was that of Frederick Cartright, born February 18, 1798. Karen recognized the name; it had been that generation, the third, that Peggy had investigated in such detail. Peggy closed the Bible and pushed it toward Lisa.

"You don't want it?" Lisa's face had fallen.

Peggy shrugged. "I'll give you twenty bucks for it. As a gesture of goodwill."

After Lisa had gone — with the twenty-dollar bill — Peggy paid the check and hoisted the Bible into her arms. "That was a bust. I guess I should have expected it."

Karen had remained silent, transfixed by min-

442

gled horror and admiration. Following Peggy into the elevator she exclaimed, "You were absolutely vicious. What happened to your policy of winning people over by tact and kindness?"

"I'm getting mad," Peggy said briefly.

"So I noticed. What are you going to do with that Bible? You're right, it's of no use to us."

Peggy tossed the book irreverently on the bed. "I'll give it back to Cameron. Lisa probably stole it from his mother's house, along with the other cartons. Now that you've seen the situation there, you can see how she got away with it. Mrs. Madison wouldn't dare interfere with her."

Karen sat down on the bed and opened the Bible. "It belonged to Eliza," she said in surprise. "I thought the handwriting looked familiar. She started with her parents' generation. Do you suppose there was an older Bible, with the earlier names?"

"Unlikely and irrelevant. If such a book existed it's long gone. Who's Eliza?"

"A Victorian bluestocking," Karen answered. "I ran across her diaries . . . Oh, Lord! They're gone too, in the fire. Mrs. F. will probably raise hell about that. She forced them on me the day I went to the Historical Society."

"Don't worry about Mrs. Fowler." Peggy brandished the hairbrush she had been using. "We're going to break that woman! Let's go have dinner."

The phone was ringing when they returned to their room. Peggy made a dash for it. From the way her face fell, Karen deduced she had hoped the caller would be someone other than Joan.

"We're fine, how are you?" she said. "Uh . . . No. Nothing new. What? Do you want to talk to Karen?" Karen had opened the briefcase and placed the manuscript on the table; she shook her head vehemently. "Good," Peggy said. "She doesn't want to talk to you either, she's working. Oh, yeah? Well, I'll tell her. We'll let you know."

She hung up. "Joan's bored."

"She hadn't heard about the fire?"

"It wouldn't make the wire services," Peggy said. "We can pray Simon hasn't heard about it either. He'd have a fit."

"Were you expecting him to call?"

"He said he would. Maybe I'll take the phone into the bathroom and call him instead. That way you won't be disturbed."

"You just don't want me to hear those erotic verses you quote at one another," Karen said with a smile.

"That too. Go ahead, I won't bother you again."

She vanished into the bathroom trailing the telephone cord behind her and shut the door with a decisive slam.

"We are fortunate indeed, Doctor, that you happened to be in the house when this occurred," Ismene said gratefully. "You have been a frequent visitor of late; I hope that means that you have acquired many new patients in this region."

A dark, unbecoming flush mantled his swarthy

cheeks. "My services, such as they are, were unnecessary; your sister suffered an ordinary swoon, from
which she would have recovered under your minis-
trations; but what was that wild talk of withered
faces and dark forms? Miss Clara's constitution is
delicate, I know; is her mind also given to morbid
fancies?"

Fairness to Clara as well as concern for another
moved Ismene to speak. "It was no fantasy, but an
actual living woman she saw — Isabella's poor mad
mother, whom Edmund, in the kindness of his noble
heart, maintains here in her home. From time to time
she escapes her guardian and wanders the house. The
sight of her is startling in the extreme, and Clara
did not know of her presence; to come upon her un-
awares would be a shock to the strongest system. It
was to mine the first time I saw her."

"Good heavens!" the doctor murmured. "I had no
idea such an individual existed. Is she not dangerous?
Should she not be confined more closely?"

"I do not believe she means the least harm," Ismene
said firmly. "She is too old and frail to constitute
a danger to any but herself. Indeed, she appeared
to be as terrified of Clara as my poor sister was of
her; I found her cowering against the wall, unable
or unwilling to move, when I rushed to the spot in
answer to Clara's cries. Her attendant had to carry
her away, and I fear she may have taken harm. It
would ease my mind if you would see her."

"Certainly." But the smile that altered his features
so attractively did not linger. In an uncharacteris-
tically hesitant manner he went on, "Are you certain

445

Mr. Merrivale will not object? He appears to have kept this woman's very existence concealed from the world —"

"Only out of compassion for her, I feel certain, and to spare the feelings of those who knew her in happier days. I would wait to ask him," she added, seeing that his countenance continued to mirror his doubt, "but he and Isabella will probably not return until later this afternoon, and I know you must be anxious to continue your journey."

He no longer demurred, but followed her toward the remote and lofty regions where Edmund had assured her his stepmother dwelt. The door was now secure; in response to Ismene's knock came a rattling of bolts and chains whose sound engendered awful suggestions of imprisonment. Yet when her arguments with the attendant, who appeared reluctant to let them in, had at last won them admission to the chamber, she saw Edmund had spoken no more than the truth when he assured her the unfortunate creature lacked no comfort he could provide. The windows were closely barred and a heavy screen covered the hearth, which was now dark and cold, for the mild summer weather required no other source of heat. Yet the chamber was clean and airy, and the low bed had been furnished with ample covering.

"Let her see and hear me first," Ismene urged, placing a hand on the doctor's arm. "She may take fright at the sight of a stranger."

The old woman was not sleeping, as the attendant had claimed, and as Ismene had believed. Hearing the soft low voice of her visitor, she opened her eyes.

Almost could Ismene have fancied she saw a gleam of intelligence in the single operative orb. It was short-lived; frenzy transformed the withered features and a gabble of agitated speech distorted the gaping mouth.

With an alarmed exclamation the doctor stepped quickly forward. "There is no cause for concern," Ismene hasted to assure him. "It is her old mania, the same vague, meaningless warnings she always utters. Who knows what dread phantoms her troubled brain sees around us? Dear madam" — taking the bony fingers in hers and leaning closer — "dear madam, here is a physician come to see you. He is my friend and would be yours. Will you allow him to examine you?"

She had not expected a response nor dared even hope for comprehension. Whether this occurred or not she could not be sure, but at least the old creature lay still, submitting without visible demonstrations of alarm to the doctor's cautious approach and gentle touch. One by one he lifted the bony limbs; delicately he ran his hands over the wrinkled scalp and frail body.

"There appears to be no injury," he murmured; and Ismene saw he had forgot all else in the exercise of his noble art. "She does not cry out in pain. What does she say?"

For his patient had begun to speak, if speech it could be called. Even Ismene could not distinguish words in the hoarse mumble.

"It is only nonsense, I fear," she began. "Her troubled mind —"

He broke in, with the same touch of irony she had

447

heard before. "If her mind were untroubled she would have difficulty expressing her thoughts with her organs of speech so impaired. It is difficult to articulate without dental apparatus. Speak more slowly, madam; I am listening. What would you tell me?"

There was no evidence of repugnance, only compassion and interest, on his face as he bent closer; when the clawlike fingers groped for his sleeve he folded them unhesitatingly in his. Ismene's heart swelled. To see him thus, to behold the tenderness he displayed toward the helpless and infirm was to comprehend the limitations of physiognomy as a designation of character. Who could suppose, having seen those forbidding features in their normal expression of sardonic silence, that they could soften so remarkably?

The chamber door opened. Edmund stood on the threshold.

His sudden appearance broke the spell. The old woman's mumble erupted in a ghastly shriek. Ismene started to speak, but was prevented by Edmund. His tones were soft, but they quivered with anger.

"How dare you come here?"

He addressed not Ismene but the doctor, whose expression had resumed its old harsh cast. Detaching the fingers that clutched at him he rose to his feet. "I must apologize —"

"No apology can compensate for this inexcusable intrusion," Edmund said in a low savage tone. "Begone, and never return to this house."

"Edmund, you are unjust," Ismene protested. "If anger is called for here, it should be directed at me. I proposed — nay, I insisted upon — this visit. You

448

do not know what transpired."

Quickly and tersely she told all. Edmund's furious color subsided as he listened. "I see. Well, sir, no doubt you meant well. If you have assured yourself there is no need of your services . . ."

"Yes" was the curt reply. With a final look at the old woman, who had slumped back against the pillows and closed her eyes, he walked quickly to the door and went out.

"Wait," Edmund said, as Ismene would have followed. "You are still angry with me. That condition must not endure."

"I am not so much angry as surprised — shocked — astonished," Ismene replied. "I had not supposed you capable of speaking and acting so rashly, without waiting to hear explanations."

"My dear." He drew her to the door and closed it behind him. The corridor was deserted. When he would have taken her in his arms Ismene stiffened and drew away.

"I was not angry with you," Edmund said softly. "How could I feel other than admiration for the benevolence that prompted your action? Seeing him with you, watching his false actions, I was overcome by jealousy."

At first she could not believe she had heard right. "What!" the cry burst from her. "You insult me, Edmund, if you believe —"

"My dearest girl." His arms enclosed her. Gently but inexorably he overcame her resistance and pressed her to his breast. "How can you be insensible to my overpowering affection? Is your modesty so great that

449

you have failed to observe that I love — worship — adore you? That same modesty and innocence veils his intentions from you, but they are no secret to me. Now that you have been warned you will avoid them. He is unable to offer you a heart worthy of your acceptance, Ismene. Your happiness shall be the sole study of my life. I cannot — will not — live without you."

Chapter Fifteen

There comes John, and I must put this away,
— he hates to have me write a word. . . .
She is all the time trying to crawl through.
But nobody could climb through that pattern
— it strangles so. . . .

CHARLOTTE P. GILMAN,
The Yellow Wallpaper, 1892

"So that's the way the land lies," Peggy said, returning the papers to Karen and signaling the waitress for more coffee. "I thought Edmund would declare himself before long. I'm betting on the doctor, though."

"Why?" Karen pushed the remains of her cereal away. Peggy had insisted she eat a hearty breakfast, in preparation for the hard day's work ahead. She hated cereal.

"Edmund's after her money. And," Peggy added, before Karen could object to this dogmatic statement, "the sister, Clara, has her eye on Edmund too. Ismene's too noble to find happiness at her sister's expense. Then there's The Horrible Secret to be exposed. The old lady knows what it is, and maybe she's not as crazy as she seems."

"You really are jumping to conclusions."

"I'm making educated guesses," Peggy corrected. "That's part of the fun of reading mysteries — trying to figure out the solution. Ismene has set up the plot, and unless she cheats by introducing a new character or a vital clue at the last minute, an intelligent reader ought to be able to predict what will happen. How much more of the manuscript have you got to read?"

"Forty or fifty pages. But I have a nasty feeling that 'Houses of Stone' is going to be another *Edwin Drood*. You know, the murder mystery by Charles Dickens that he never finished."

"Why didn't he?"

"He died."

"That's a good reason," Peggy admitted.

"Dickens set up the plot and the list of suspects," Karen went on. "And the victim. But nobody knows whether Edwin disappeared voluntarily, or was kidnapped or murdered, much less which of the suspects committed the crime — if there was a crime. Hundreds of books and articles have been written speculating on how Dickens meant to end the book."

"Is this going to be the same? I know you said some pages seem to be missing, but maybe it's only a few. Come on, don't tell me you haven't cheated and looked ahead."

"I peeked," Karen admitted. "The last page ends in mid-sentence; it seems to be a description of some damned rose garden. This isn't a typical murder mystery, where the explanation is left till the last chapter, so I'm hoping Ismene tied up most of the loose ends earlier and that the missing pages contained only unimportant moralizing. But I won't know till I've read the whole thing."

"Maybe you ought to stay with it, Karen. I can take pictures and supervise the workmen."

"The manuscript can wait. I'll have to go over it again and again anyhow. We may not have access to Amberley much longer."

"Especially after what we did yesterday." Peggy scribbled her name on the check and pushed her chair away from the table. "Not that we intended to misbehave; we were properly invited and had no reason to think Cameron would resent our being there."

"I suppose I might have suspected he would," Karen said slowly. "He never invited me to his home or gave me the address — only a phone number. He's made it clear from the beginning that our relationship was strictly business."

"Hmmm. Are you sure you didn't miss a cue here and there? I'm not criticizing, mind you, it's none of my business how you feel about him, but he's awfully thin-skinned; the slightest hint of rejection and he pulls back into his shell."

"I tried to be friendly," Karen protested. "He never —" She broke off in some confusion, remembering at least two occasions when Cameron *had*. "Anyhow," she went on, "he has nothing more to sell. From now on we're not potential buyers, we're damned nuisances. He'll be happy to see the last of us."

Cameron certainly did not appear happy to see

them that morning. The man who followed him out of the house was a stranger to Karen, but she knew who, or what, he must be.

Cameron was wearing a suit and tie and carrying a briefcase. He greeted them with a frown and a curt "I didn't expect you so early. Your crew won't be here for another hour."

"That's okay," Peggy said, deliberately misinterpreting this speech as an apology. "We wanted to take some pictures before we start work."

She turned her bright innocent smile on the other man. "Sleek" was the word that came to Karen's mind — slick, well-groomed gray hair, expensive tailoring, a smooth pink face. "Good morning," she cooed. "We won't be in your way, I promise. Just ignore us."

"Not at all, ladies" was the affable if meaningless reply. His eyes went over them with a curious absence of expression; Karen realized he was seeing them not as women or even human beings, but as potential business rivals.

Peggy said nothing to dispel this impression. Names were exchanged and hands were shaken, and then they excused themselves, leaving the men to talk.

"You were right," Peggy said sotto voce. "The guy's a developer if I ever saw one. I wonder what he's got in mind for the house. You could turn it into a conference center or bed and breakfast, I suppose, if you weren't sensitive to atmosphere. Me, I'd tear it down and start all over."

"Who gives a damn?" Karen demanded. "Honestly, Peggy, you can waste more time on —"

"Kitchen things," Peggy said, smiling. "Here, hold the light meter and the extra film. Where shall we start?"

They moved methodically from room to room. Karen was dreading the moment when they would reach the narrow stairs that led to the attic; she was determined not to shirk the job, but she wasn't anxious to repeat that experience. Luckily for her, Peggy was a finicky, fussy photographer; they were still on the first floor, in the library, when Cameron joined them.

"I'm driving Mr. Halston back to town," he announced. "The crew should be here anytime. Can you manage without me? I should be back in an hour or two."

"No problem," Karen said. She was dying to know whether Cameron had made his sale, but didn't like to ask.

Peggy was less inhibited. "Is he going to buy the place?"

Cameron's face mirrored his feelings — exasperation, reflection, and finally reluctant amusement. "There are a few details left to work out. Excuse me, I don't want to keep him waiting."

"I don't know how you get away with it," Karen said after he had marched out.

"It's my age. Old ladies are expected to be nosy, and in this part of the world at least, people don't hit grandmas. If we hurry we can finish the library before the men get here."

They were sitting on the front steps when a car

pulled up. Karen had forgotten Bill Meyer was to be part of the work crew but she discovered, somewhat to her surprise, that she was glad to see him — or at least not sorry to see him. His scraped face still looked awful, but it seemed to be healing.

"Not even a singed curl," he said, looking her over with an expression that contradicted his light tone.

"I told you she was fine," Peggy said.

He dropped down onto the step next to Karen. "I went by the place this morning," he said soberly. "How you ever managed . . . I guess you'd rather not talk about it."

"I don't see any point in talking about it. But it was nice of you to call yesterday."

"Nice, hell. You're making me very nervous, Karen. Try not to get mashed by falling rocks or bitten by a poisonous snake today, will you?"

"We'll let you boys do the dirty work," Peggy said. "This must be them. Or should I, in the presence of two English teachers, say 'they'?"

The noun fit the other "boys" better than it did Bill; they were all in their late teens and they introduced themselves by diminutives: Scotty, Jimmy Joe and Bucky. They might have been brothers or cousins, they looked so much alike, and Karen had a hard time remembering which was which.

At first they took Bill for the boss, but Peggy soon set them straight. Shouldering the tools they had brought, they followed in an obedient procession, with Karen and Bill bringing up the rear.

"You've been here before, Bill, I gather," she said, as they entered the woodland path.

"Once. I hope this experience won't be as unpleasant as the last."

"What do you mean?"

He glanced at her over his shoulder, holding back a branch that barred the way. "It was raining and foggy and very still. My five-year-old nephew would describe the ambience as 'creepy,' I suppose. I found a shed snake-skin while I was cutting away the vines, and that didn't cheer me up much. Copperhead."

"Oh." The sound of the brook grew louder. The hour was still early; sunlight slanted through the branches at an oblique angle. It had been midday or later when she and Peggy heard the cry. If it happened again, at a different time of day, in the presence of so many witnesses, she would know the phenomenon was not paranormal. Scotty, Bucky and Jimmy Joe didn't strike her as nervous or overly imaginative.

All the same she didn't offer to wield clippers or shears. Nothing had happened the last time until she got close to the ruin. If there was a danger zone around the structure, like an invisible fence, let one of the others set off the alarm.

She noticed that Peggy stayed some distance away too. Under her direction the others, including Bill, began cutting away the tangled vines. After a while Karen got nerve enough to edge closer and drag the mounting piles of brush out of the way of the workers. So far so good, she thought. The cheerful unconcern of the young men, their brisk movements and good-natured gibes at one another and at Bill — especially at Bill, the city slicker, the old guy — transformed the once un-canny spot into just another clearing in the woods. A woman who came here wailing for her demon lover would get short shrift.

Not only vines but coarse weeds and saplings had rooted themselves among the stones. Peggy moved in closer as the shape of the structure began to emerge from the greenery that had veiled it. "Be careful. Clip as close to the surface as you can, but don't try to pull any plant out by the roots. They're intertwined through the crevices like a net; you could dislodge one of the stones."

"Sure hate to have one of them suckers fall on me," Jimmy Joe — or possibly Bucky — agreed. "Wonder how come they cut 'em that big? Never seen anything like it around here."

By the time Peggy decreed a break for lunch they had cleared only two of the remaining parts of the four walls, but the shape of the structure was now plain. It had been approximately eight feet square; the height could only be estimated, since neither of the cleared walls had survived in-tact. No traces of window apertures were visible, but an opening on one side must have been a door; rusted spots on the stone indicated the presence of hinges, though these, and the door itself, were missing. Nothing of the interior could be seen. It was filled with rubble and with a luxuriant growth of plants, including two good-sized trees.

Back at the house, the boys piled into their truck, promising to return in an hour, and went in search of sustenance. "It had better be a drive-in," Peggy announced, gesturing the others toward her car. "We aren't dressed for anything fancier."

Karen had to agree. Bill was the most disheveled; he had worked as hard as any of the boys. Their jokes must have gotten to him. His wrinkled, sweat-soaked shirt stuck to his skin, his hair stood on end, and his face was flushed. If the M.L.A. could only see him now, Karen thought. He saw her looking at him, and read her mind; acknowledging her amusement with a wry smile, he got meekly into the back seat of Peggy's car.

Cameron had not yet returned when they got back. "Looks as if he's made the deal," Peggy said. "He'd be here working his little heart out if he hadn't found a buyer."

"Unless his mother . . ." Karen stopped herself. She was getting to be as bad as Peggy, gossiping and guessing about things that were none of her business. Poor Mrs. Hayes was none of Bill Meyer's business either.

"The boys are late," Peggy said critically. "Here they come. Shall I bring the cooler?"

He had suggested they buy it and stock it with ice and soft drinks, an idea Peggy had approved. The truck arrived and the boys emerged; one of them — Karen had given up hope of telling them apart by now — hastened to take it from him. If Bill's face hadn't been so flushed with heat it would have reddened with indignation, but he did not protest.

The temperature grew uncomfortably hot as the afternoon went on. Towering white clouds piled up and passed overhead, making the sunlight flicker like a faulty light bulb. "I hope to hell it's not going to rain," Peggy muttered. "One more day, God, just give me one more day."

Bill mopped his streaming brow with his sleeve and managed to laugh. "Sounds like a spiritual, Peggy. You can't do this job in two days."

"This isn't a proper dig, Bill. I just want to get a general idea of what's here." She had to raise her voice to be heard over the roar of the chain saw. "If we find anything that justifies excavation . . . well, we'll face that if we come to it."

One of the trees toppled, crashing to earth, and she let out a cry. "Dammit, boys, I told you to watch out. You could bring that wall down."

"No, ma'am, no chance," called Bucky or Jimmy Joe. "We made sure it would fall thataway. The back wall's solid rock, not cut stones."

"What? Let me see."

"He's right," said Bill, posing picturesquely atop a tree stump. "That's limestone, not earth — a good-sized outcropping. The builder of the house must have smoothed off a section and used it for one of the walls."

Curiosity, and the absence of anything unusual, had overcome Karen's fear of going too close to the house. Following Peggy, she looked over the top of the cleared wall.

The interior was still knee-deep in dirt, from which a few corners of fallen stone protruded, along with the stubs of the trees. The far wall was far from smooth, but it had unquestionably formed the fourth side of the structure. Just above the uneven surface of the earth Karen thought she saw a darker shadow, like a break in the stone. It might have been the top of a narrow opening.

Involuntarily she fell back a step. There had been no cry, no sudden wave of cold; only a sudden memory that carried a chill of quite a different kind. "Could that be the entrance to a cave or a tunnel?" she asked.

"There's no mention of such a thing in the book," Peggy answered.

Karen saw Bill's ears prick, but for once she didn't care what he overheard. "It might have been blocked up. But earlier . . ."

Peggy gave her a curious look. "Well, we can find out. Boys, I want the whole interior cleared, but there isn't time to do much more today; concentrate on that side and see if there is an opening in the rock."

The boys were losing their enthusiasm. Karen could hardly blame them; they had been hard at it for over six hours and the air was stifling, without the slightest hint of a breeze. They had all removed their shirts, against Peggy's advice; their movements increasingly slow, their bodies streaked with muddy sweat, they kept at it until the irregular top of a narrow opening could be seen by the watchers.

"Could be a tunnel," Jimmy Joe or Bucky reported, his voice hoarse with fatigue. "Or just a kind of hollow place. Can't tell. It's filled up with dirt. Want we should go on?"

"No, that's enough for today. It's after five, and you guys must be exhausted. You're really hard workers. I hope you're not too worn out to come back tomorrow."

Shoulders straightened and chests expanded. The spokesman, whoever he was, cleared his throat. "Hell, no, ma'am, we're not tired. We'll be partyin' tonight and back on the job first thing tomorrow."

Still showing off, they bounded up the path ahead of the others, who trailed wearily behind. "Rotten little bastards," Bill wheezed.

"Don't be so pompous. I'll bet you flexed your youthful muscles at the old folks when you were eighteen," Peggy retorted.

"Huh. Well, ladies, I'll be on the job tomorrow but I sure as hell ain't partyin' tonight."

"Me neither," Karen admitted. "I'm about to die, and I didn't work the way you did, Bill. If you don't feel like coming tomorrow I wouldn't blame you."

Bill was too far gone to straighten his shoulders or any other part of his body, but his face relaxed into a smile. "Wild horses . . . I said that before, didn't I? See you in the morning. Sleep well."

"So, you've decided to be nicer," Peggy said, as they followed his car along the drive. "Was that calculated, or are you willing to admit he's not such a bad guy?"

"He's not such a bad guy. I wonder what happened to Cameron. If he hasn't shown up by this time he probably isn't coming back today. Should we close the gate, do you think?"

Peggy considered the suggestion, and then shook her head decisively. "He's made it clear that he thinks we're a pair of nosy busybodies; in his present mood he'd probably interpret anything we did as unwarranted interference."

Bill's car was already out of sight when they reached the road. Peggy put her foot down. "We'll have a quiet evening," she said, with a glance at her companion. "You do look tired."

"Not really. It's mostly the heat — and the tension."

"I kept expecting it too," Peggy confessed. "Nothing happened, though. Or did it? Something was bothering you — something about that tunnel. I didn't want to press the point in front of the others; is it mentioned in the manuscript?"

"No." The air-conditioning was having its effect; Karen was beginning to feel chilly as perspiration evaporated. "It had nothing to do with Ismene. I was remembering what Mrs. Madison said, about the slaves being shut up in there, and then I happened to recall a grisly story Simon read to me once, called 'The Torture of Hope.' The Grand Inquisitor let the poor guy think he had escaped from the dungeon; after he had crawled through the dark on his hands and knees, he finally reached the garden — and they were waiting for him."

"My God," Peggy breathed, "I never realized you had such a morbid imagination! That's sick, Karen. And," she added firmly, "far too subtle for an eighteenth-century slave owner. Forget it."

"I wish I could. Oh, you're right, the tunnel is only a morbid fancy of mine — if it's there at all. But I can't get that story of Mrs. Madison's out of my mind. Burial alive; a long, slow, agonizing death from hunger and thirst, in the dark, all alone . . ."

She shivered. Peggy reached across and switched off the air-conditioning. "That's enough of that. We'll dig out the damned thing tomorrow and find it is only a natural hollow, as Bucky said. Or was it Jimmy Joe? Damned if I can tell those kids apart."

"Neither can I." Karen was glad to accept the change of subject. "We ought to be ashamed, though; we sound like those supercilious bigots who swear the 'natives' all look alike."

"Have you got energy enough to go out for dinner?" Peggy asked, after they had reached their room. "I'm getting awfully tired of the menu here."

"Just let me shower and change into my other pair of pants, and I'll be good as new. You can go first," she added generously.

"I will have a drink first. And see what that blinking red light on the phone portends."

When Karen came out of the bathroom toweling

her wet hair Peggy was still on the telephone. With a final "Fine, see you there," she hung up and started to undress. Karen noticed her glass was empty and that she looked unusually grave.

"That was Tanya," Peggy said. "I asked her to join us for dinner. Hope you don't mind."

"No, of course not. Is something wrong?"

"She said she had a few tidbits of news for us." Peggy headed for the bathroom, shedding garments right and left. "Gossip," she added. "The stuff of which great novels are made."

"The Hungry Hog?" Karen exclaimed. "Why here?"

"Any objection?" Peggy pulled into a parking space. "It was Tanya's idea."

"It's popular with the haut monde. We might see some familiar faces."

"If you're referring to Mrs. F., I hope we do. There are a few things I'd like to say to her."

However, the only familiar face was Tanya's. They joined her at the table. Peggy insisted they all have a drink, and Tanya did not demur.

"It was nice of you to ask me," she said politely. "We could have talked over the phone."

"We owe you one," Peggy said. "Anyhow, I like food and drink and talk, especially in combination. Kitchen things."

Tanya's eyes lit up. "You know 'A Jury of Her Peers'? It's a great story."

"Karen introduced me to it. She's been broadening my mind and trying to improve my manners

465

— though that's an uphill fight."

"And vice versa," Karen murmured.

"I hope we didn't get your mother in trouble with Cameron," Peggy went on. "She told you what happened, I suppose."

"Oh, that. Don't worry about it. He apologized to her later."

"He didn't apologize to us," Karen said.

An unexpected dimple made a brief appearance in Tanya's cheek. "In a way he did," she said cryptically.

The advent of the waiter and the business of ordering postponed further discussion; after he had gone Tanya said seriously, "It's Cameron I wanted to talk to you about. I guess you don't know what happened about the fire? Well, you knew it was his company that insured Mrs. Fowler's place? You didn't? You ladies sure don't get around."

"Tell," Peggy urged, leaning forward.

"She filed a claim the day after the fire," Tanya said. "And Cameron refused to pay it. The company's sent for an expert from Richmond to look for evidences of arson."

"Have they any reason to think it was?" Karen asked.

"I guess they must. There's some talk around town that it could have been Bobby set the fire, for the insurance. He's always after the old lady for money. I can't believe he'd take a chance on somebody being hurt, though."

"He might not have known anyone was there," Karen said, struck by a sudden revelation. "My car wasn't in the garage and I went to bed early."

"That's an interesting idea," Tanya said thoughtfully. "Bobby wouldn't deliberately set out to endanger you — he's too much of a cautious coward to risk a charge that serious — but he's so stupid he'd never think of checking to make absolutely sure the place was empty.

"Anyhow, he heard the talk and he blamed Cameron for it — and for turning down the claim. But I heard from somebody else, who was there, that it was what he said about you that started the fight."

"Fight?" Karen's jaw dropped unbecomingly.

"Wait a minute, you're leaving out all the interesting parts," Peggy exclaimed. "When did it happen? Where did it happen? Who said what to whom and who hit who first?"

Egged on by Peggy, Tanya let herself go. The encounter had taken place at high noon in front of Cameron's office on Main Street — as public a spot as anyone could hope to find. Accompanied by two of his "scruffy friends," Bobby had been lying in wait; he had prudently waited until after the prospective client had got in his car and driven away before accosting Cameron. He had begun by demanding that Cameron "stop effing around and hand over the insurance money," to quote Tanya. Cameron had tried at first to back off, but it had been he who struck the first blow.

"Bobby started calling you names and implying it was you who put Cameron up to denying the claim, out of spite against Mrs. Fowler," Tanya reported. "Then he said he'd found you two out there at the house — uh — making — um —"

"Never mind, we get the idea," Peggy said, lips twitching. Though what she found amusing Karen could not imagine. "Was that when Cameron hit him?"

"Uh-huh. Knocked him flat, too. Cameron started walking away, and then all three of them jumped him. A couple of people who'd been standing around watching intervened at that point; when somebody mentioned the police, Bobby and his pals took off."

"Was Cameron hurt?" Peggy asked.

"He left under his own steam, anyhow," Tanya replied. "Mama said he showed up at the house about two, and sent her home. He told her he'd fallen off a ladder, but he was okay. Nobody's seen him since."

"He must have known she'd learn the truth eventually," Peggy mused.

"Yes, well . . . He keeps things to himself. I wouldn't have told you," Tanya said apologetically, "except I thought you ought to know what that miserable kid and his aunt are saying about you. Mrs. Fowler's never forgiven you for that speech and she'll do you an injury if she can."

"She can't," Peggy said briskly. "And let us know if she tries anything on you." Her voice deepened into a growling drawl. "Ah won't leave this here town till I've cleaned out that nest of vermin and made it safe for honest folks."

This was too much for Karen, who had been

fuming with speechless embarrassment. "God damn it, Peggy, I don't see anything funny about this!"

"It is funny. It's also very romantic," Peggy said with an unrepentant grin. "What's wrong with you? I used to dream of having a handsome hero fight for my honor at high noon on Main Street."

Karen looked from her to Tanya, who had retreated behind her napkin. "Oh, hell," she said. "I guess it is funny. Sort of. But it certainly isn't romantic."

"That's the right attitude." Peggy sobered. "I'm sorry for Cameron, though. He's too thin-skinned for his own good. I'll bet he's a lot more embarrassed about this than you are."

"I'll bet he's not," Karen muttered.

They had finished their meal and were waiting for coffee when Peggy, who sat facing the tables at the front of the restaurant, said under her breath, "Brace yourself. Here comes one of those familiar faces, and she looks as if she's bursting with gossip."

Karen was glad she had been warned. Lisa did look pleased with herself, and that was usually a bad sign. She refused Peggy's invitation to join them for coffee. "I'm dining with a gentleman friend. I just wanted to make sure you were aware of what's being said around town. I expect Tanya's already given you her version."

"She told us what happened," Karen said, seeing Tanya's lips compress. "I hope that repulsive young man and his degenerate friends are in jail."

Lisa was momentarily taken aback, but she quickly rallied. "It wasn't Bobby's fault. Cam accused him —"

"That's not true, Lisa." Tanya was perfectly capable of defending herself. "All Cameron said was that there was some doubt as to how the fire started. Until the experts come to a definite conclusion, he's got no choice but to hold back on paying."

"If somebody set that fire, it wasn't Bobby," Lisa snapped. "He's got an alibi."

"From his buddies?" Peggy snorted.

"I didn't come over here to argue with you." Lisa was losing her temper; two bright, symmetrical patches of red showed on her cheeks. "I just thought you ought to know. And you can tell Cam he'd better stop playing the pious fool and hand over that money."

Karen was even closer to losing her temper. Lisa had looked directly at her. "Good gracious me, that sounds like a threat," she said, with a sneer as fine as any Peggy could have produced. "You can go back and tell Mrs. Fowler that she'd better stop playing the little dictator. I wouldn't advise Cameron to pay up on a claim as dubious as hers even if I had the slightest influence over him. Which I don't."

"That's not what I hear," Lisa snapped. She turned on her heel and stamped off before Karen could reply.

"Bitch," Tanya said clearly.

"One-hundred carat." Peggy didn't trouble to

lower her voice either. "We can assume she hasn't anything else to sell, can't we? She wouldn't be so rude to a prospective buyer. Well, this has been a fun evening. I told you there's nothing like gossip to liven things up."

They had to pass Lisa's table on the way out. She ostentatiously ignored them, breaking into bright chatter and leaning toward her companion. Karen remembered seeing him at the luncheon. He was a good thirty years older than Lisa, but he looked prosperous.

Not until they were on their way back to the hotel did she raise the question that had been troubling her. "It might not have been Bobby who set that fire after all."

"I don't think it was," Peggy said.

"Do you think we ought to tell the police about . . . about the manuscript?"

"About Dorothea Angelo, you mean."

"I suppose I did. It sounded so outrageous . . . I can't believe she'd do such a thing."

"I see no reason to say anything just now," Peggy said thoughtfully. "It is an inadequate motive, as you yourself pointed out. We'll see what the investigation turns up. Could be the fire was accidental after all."

After they reached their room Peggy retreated into the bathroom with the telephone and Karen went to work on the manuscript. She was still at it when Peggy went to bed, so absorbed that she only mumbled unintelligibly in response to the other woman's "Good night."

471

It was after one before she stood up and stretched creaking muscles. Unaccustomed exercise followed by long hours of sitting had awakened aches in areas that had never ached before, but she was too excited by what she had discovered to sleep.

Tiptoeing to the bed, she bent over the motionless form. "Peggy," she whispered. "Peggy, are you asleep?"

"I was," said a gruff voice. "What do you want?"

"I've found out what the Deadly Secret is!"

Peggy opened one eye. "And you woke me up to tell me that? Frankly, my dear, right now I don't give a damn."

She rolled onto her side and pulled the blanket up over her head.

Chapter Sixteen

I thought of how unpleasant it is to be locked
out; and I thought how it is worse perhaps
to be locked in. . . .

VIRGINIA WOOLF,
A Room of One's Own, 1929

"Sorry I was so unappreciative last night," Peggy
said, offering a cup of coffee as additional apology.

Karen sat up and yawned. "Sorry I woke you
up. Did you call room service? I didn't hear a
thing."

"You were dead to the world. I hated to wake
you, but I told the boys to be there at nine."

"I'm glad you did. Have you read it yet?"

Peggy glanced at the papers on the table. "Part
of it. I resisted temptation as long as I could —"

"Why the hell shouldn't you read it? Go ahead
and finish while I shower and dress."

When she emerged, fully clothed and in her right
senses, Peggy was ready for her.

"Did you suspect the truth?" she demanded.

"No. And don't claim you did."

"You're still grumpy. Have another cup of coffee," Peggy said, grinning. "I did suspect, believe
it or not. I told you I've read dozens of the modern
descendants of these books. It's only logical, if you

think about it. The old lady had to know The Secret, and The Secret had to have something to do with the quarrel between the two brothers, which happened in the distant past, while Ismene was still a small child. How could the old lady know if she didn't marry Edmund's father until later? He didn't even confide in his own son. He wouldn't gossip with a mere woman. The only way she could know was if she was herself involved, and one way she might be involved was if she was actually the first wife, and therefore Edmund's mother."

"And Ismene's. Don't tell me you anticipated that!"

"No, that was a shocker. It's a confusing story; let me see if I got it straight. Ismene and Clara are in fact older than Edmund. They were infants when their father discovered that he was being cuckolded by none other than his own brother. The guilty wife — already pregnant, one presumes — and the dastardly deceiver fled Papa's righteous wrath. He moved to another part of the country where the shameful story was not known and told everyone, including the girls, that their mother was dead.

"In the meantime dastardly deceiver and his paramour settle in Virginia, where they are accepted as man and wife, and proceed to have two children of their own — the half-brother and -sister of Ismene and Clara. The old lady gradually goes bonkers, shame and guilt preying on her soul, and is locked up in the attic. But she has enough wits left to know who the two girls are, and to realize that Edmund is about to commit the deadly sin of incest by proposing marriage to his own sister."

"But is Edmund aware of that?"

"The doctor says he is."

"He's prejudiced," Karen insisted. "And so are you. You never liked Edmund. The way the doctor discovers the truth leaves Edmund in the clear." She selected a few pages from the pile on the table and read aloud.

"It was some time before Ismene recovered from the swoon of horror that had bereft her of her senses to find a hand supporting her head and another holding a cup to her lips. A sip of the cordial restored her; dashing the cup away, she rose up in a frenzy of indignation and disbelief.

" 'It cannot be true! Reason, affection, simple decency recoil from such horror.'

" 'Good,' said Dr. Fitzgerald's quiet voice. 'You have recovered. I had not underestimated your courage and strength. You will not, should not judge until you have heard the facts. Listen now, while I tell you how I came to this discovery.

" 'I was struck when I first saw them together by the resemblance between Clara and Isabella — and to a lesser extent between them and Edmund. The trained eye of a physician observes characteristics of bone structure and of such seemingly trivial structures as the configuration of the ear, that others would pass over. Still, I thought little of it until I spoke with that miserable sinner who

475

has paid a terrible price for her crime. Her ravings might have been only senile wanderings; yet when she spoke of her "daughters" and of the sins of the parents' generation being repeated by the next, a dreadful suspicion dawned. It might be no more than that; but the horror of that possibility demanded investigation. I proceeded to carry this out, corresponding first with your father's legal representative in C——, where you had dwelt. He was able to inform me of the name of the northern city from which the gentleman and his infant daughters had removed; further correspondence with individuals in that place resulted in the information that there was no record of your mother's death and burial, and that certain elderly citizens of the city remembered the old scandal. You may say, and I would not blame you, that this does not constitute proof. To me it is proof enough to cast serious doubts upon the course you may be contemplating, and to require confirmation or refutation before you decide.' "

Karen looked up from the page. "See? Edmund wasn't even born when this happened — if it did happen. How could he know?"

"What do you mean, if it happened? Are you suggesting the doctor invented the story?"

"He's got a damned good motive for turning Ismene against Edmund. She's a wealthy heiress, and he loves her."

"Hmmm. That's true." Peggy lit a cigarette. "Quite a dilemma for the poor girl, isn't it? One of her suitors is a liar and a whole-hearted villain,

476

the other is lily-pure, and she has no idea which is which."

"And no way of finding out for herself," Karen said. "As a woman in that day and age she had no legal rights. If Edmund is a villain, she is completely in his power; she can't order his carriage or command his servants to drive it; she can't even mail a letter without his seeing it; and she has already prejudiced the neighbors against her. If she runs away with the doctor and he turns out to be a rat, she's equally powerless."

"I don't think the doctor is a rat."

"It's his word against Edmund's. I did read on a little more," Karen admitted. "I was too tired to write it out, but I wanted to see what she'd do."

"She confronts Edmund?" Peggy asked interestedly. "That's in character for her, isn't it?"

"Yes, I suppose so, though it's rather foolish of her. Actually he catches her off guard. In great horror and agitation she rushes off to her only refuge, her house of stone. Edmund finds her there and demands to know what has distressed her. Still shaken, she blurts out the story."

"And he says —"

"Denies it, of course. First he rages up and down, cursing the doctor and threatening to horsewhip him, set the dogs on him, and so on, if he ever dares show his face at Ferncliffe again. After he's calmed down he promises Ismene he will take all the necessary steps to prove the story is a fabrication."

"Such as?"

"He mentions locating the record of his parents' marriage, for one thing. He's a little vague about other steps. But," Karen insisted, "a marriage certificate would be enough. That's where I am at the moment; poor Ismene is in a distracted state, not knowing which man to believe, not wanting to believe either is capable of such villainy."

"Could you finish today if you stuck with it?"

"Possibly. I'm going with you, though. We may not have much time."

"I wish you wouldn't say things like that," Peggy complained. "It sounds so — so —"

"Gothic? I only meant that if the property has been sold, the new owner may not be as accommodating as Cameron has been. He'll have the bulldozers in as soon as the sale is completed." She hesitated for a moment, her frowning gaze fixed on the window. "Anyway . . . I've had it up to here with this damned town. I'm sick of Mrs. Fowler and Bobby and Lisa and their nasty gossip and their narrow little minds. I'm ready to leave."

"When?" Peggy rose and began getting her things together.

"As soon as my car is ready. I'd better call the garage. And don't tell me I can't drive without a license, I can and will. I've done it before."

"I wouldn't dream of telling you what to do," Peggy exclaimed, opening her eyes very wide. "Or not to do."

"That'll be the day. I'll be with you as soon as I make that call."

The garage assured her the car would be ready that evening. "Or first thing in the morning. Ten, at the latest."

"That probably means mid-afternoon, at the earliest," Karen grumbled.

"We'll see. We may not be able to work tomorrow anyhow," Peggy said, with a glance at the gray skies. "Looks like rain."

They had gone some distance before Karen spoke again. "Did anything strike you after you'd read that last section?"

"I'm not sure what you mean," Peggy said cautiously.

"I've insisted all along that the novel was semi-autobiographical. What we just read proves what we suspected — that the plot is pure fiction. The Horrible Secret, the long-lost mother, the metaphors of the cave, even the suspicion of incest occur in other Gothics. So do the women — the virtuous heroine and her rival, Eve and Lilith, the good girl and the female monster. Isabella and Clara are two aspects of the same character. But I still think we may be looking for sisters who were rivals. The fact that Ismene, the real Ismene, was an intellectual doesn't mean she wasn't interested in men — one man in particular. This book might have been a fairly inventive and rather vicious way of getting back at her sister."

"Who had married the man they both wanted?"

"It's a possibility, isn't it? You were the one who pointed out that marriage was a woman's only viable option in those days. And if it's true

. . ." She waited to see if Peggy would finish the sentence.

". . . then instead of two Cartright sisters we're looking for a Cartright wife and her sister of another name."

"Damn it!" Karen exclaimed. "You had thought of it. I thought I was being so clever."

"You are, you are. The thought had passed through my mind, yes, but your interpretation hadn't occurred to me. It's not only clever, it's damned good. I was afraid you were so besotted with Ismene you couldn't see any flaws in her character."

"I'd like to find flaws, they make her more human. As a fictional character she was too damned noble. And what she did — if our theory is correct — is a relatively harmless way of exorcising resentment."

"That's why mystery writers are, on the whole, such mild-mannered individuals," Peggy said, smiling. "They don't have to take an ax to the people they hate, they kill them with a pen. Or a word processor."

"So can you find the necessary information?"

"I can but try. It won't be easy. Genealogies are traced through the male ancestor; they don't pay much attention to women outside the direct line of descent."

Her face set in a frown, Karen did not respond. Glancing at her, Peggy said encouragingly, "Cheer up. There's a good chance this new line of inquiry will pay off. The genealogy mentions the maiden names of the Cartright wives, and only two or three of them fall within the likely time period. If I can trace their family trees —"

"There are too many questions we may never be able to answer," Karen interrupted. "Why did she choose Ismene as a pseudonym? What happened to the rest of the manuscript? How was it damaged? I didn't pay much attention to its physical condition, except to assure myself it was stable enough to be read; but I'm wondering now if some of the marks weren't made by fire. Where was it, and what happened to it, before someone hid it in the trunk in the attic?"

Peggy's forehead furrowed. "Good questions. You think it was in Ismene's stone house?"

"I don't know." Karen's hands clenched. "But there's something there. I feel it. Something . . . waiting."

Peggy looked at her uneasily, but did not speak.

Sunlight was breaking through the clouds when they reached the house. The gates had been open and their crew was waiting, but Cameron's battered pickup was not there, and neither was Bill Meyer's car.

"We don't need him, ma'am," said one of the boys, with a condescending smirk. "Likely he won't turn up; he was pretty bushed last night."

However, they had not been at it long before Bill did turn up, apologizing for his tardiness. "Damned desk forgot my wake-up call. How's everybody this morning?"

"In the pink, as you can see," Peggy replied briskly. "Here, Bill, have a shovel."

"Just what I wanted. They're predicting rain tonight," he added, glancing at the sky.

"I know." Peggy hoisted her own shovel. "That's why I want to get this place cleared out today."

She set to work with more enthusiasm than skill, pitching shovelfuls of dirt over the wall. The boys exchanged grins and glances and moved out of her way.

Bill leaned on his shovel and smiled at Karen. "I'm not going into that place until Peggy gets out of it. She's going to brain somebody if she isn't careful."

"Let her work off steam. She'll tire soon and then maybe I can persuade her to let someone take over." Karen spoke abstractedly, her eyes fixed on the narrow opening which Bucky (or Jimmy Joe) was digging out.

"How much longer are you planning to stay here?" Bill asked.

"If it rains tonight —"

"I didn't mean here in this wilderness. I meant here in town. Surely you've accomplished what you hoped to do by now."

The urgency in his voice drew her attention away from the excavation. Turning to look at him, she saw he was watching her with an intensity that made her oddly uncomfortable. "Why do you ask, Bill?"

"I can't stay much longer, Karen. I'm going to

England next week, and there are a number of odd jobs I ought to finish before I leave."

"Lucky you," Karen said lightly.

"Right. It would ease my mind considerably if I knew you were safe in Wilmington."

Once, only a few weeks earlier, she would have snapped back at him, denying both danger and the need of assistance — especially his. Now it was surprisingly easy to overcome her initial automatic resentment.

"Set your mind at ease, then. I'll probably leave tomorrow."

"So soon?" He laughed then, and shook his head. "Inconsistency is not, as my sex claims, limited to women. I'm glad, Karen. But I had hoped . . . Look, I'll only be gone three weeks. Can I call you when I get back?"

"Why not?"

"Great. I don't suppose you'll feel like going out for dinner tonight?"

"Let's see how we feel at the end of the day." She picked up her shovel. "Peggy is as red as a beet and she's about to decapitate one or all of the boys with that spade; come and help me persuade her to let us take over."

Peggy denied that she was (a), tired; or (b), in danger of committing manslaughter, but Karen finally convinced her that she would be better employed as a photographer. With her out of the way, the others were able to work more efficiently. Bill pitched in with a will, and by noon they had cleared almost half the interior, down to the floor.

Bucky (it was Bucky) had determined that the opening in the rock was a tunnel — three feet of one, at least.

"It looks more like a natural fissure than a man-made tunnel," Peggy said, aiming the camera. "The sides are rough and the roof is so low a person would have to crawl . . ." She stopped, with an uneasy glance at Karen, and repeated, "It couldn't be man-made."

"You want me to quit digging it out, then?" Bucky inquired hopefully.

"No," Karen said. "I have to see —"

"Not till after lunch," Peggy said firmly. "Make it quick, boys, the clouds are thickening."

They continued to thicken as the day went on, though the rain held off. Even without sun to warm it, the air was hot and oppressive. The boys shed their shirts, Peggy her light jacket. By mid-afternoon they had finished most of the soft drinks in the cooler and Bucky, backing out of the lengthening hole in the rock, showed signs of rebelling.

"There ain't nothing in there," he wheezed, mopping mud off his face with the back of his hand. "It's got so narrowed down I gotta lie flat. You want me to go any further?"

"I guess not," Peggy said. "The air is probably bad, we don't want you passing out while you're stuck in there. Have something to drink."

They were gathered around the cooler finishing the last of the drinks when they heard someone coming along the path. He stood in the opening for a moment, anonymous in the shadows, before proceeding. When he emerged into the light Karen saw he had a magnificent black eye, and he carried himself with a stiffness that suggested other bruises concealed by his clothing. One of the boys said something under his breath, and the others snickered.

"Sorry," Cameron said — as Karen had known he would. "I meant to be here this morning, but I was detained. How is it going?"

Peggy inspected him from head to foot but for once she refrained from tactless comments. "Very well," she said. "Come and have a look."

It was the first time Karen had paused for an overall view. The result might not have looked impressive to one who had not labored mightily to produce it. Most of the floor was relatively clear, but it was far from even; some of the stone blocks, too massive to be moved by a single man, had been heaved and tossed aside by the sullen, steady force of growing tree roots. Stumps and thicker roots, some as big around as her wrist, still protruded.

She picked her way carefully over the rough ground, following Peggy and Cameron to the far wall, where there was a small pile of objects. The excavation of those scraps had taken several hours; when the first of them showed up, Peggy had insisted they use trowels and their gloved hands instead of shovels.

"Rusty nails," she said, indicating them with the toe of her boot. "These scraps are wood, but not branches; they've been sawed and shaped."

485

"A table?" Cameron stooped awkwardly and lifted one of the longer pieces of wood. It crumbled in his hand, and he quickly lowered it to the ground again.

"Or a chair or a bed. There's not enough left to tell; most of it has rotted away."

"But . . ." Cameron turned to face Karen. "But that's evidence of habitation, isn't it? Furniture. That's what you hoped to find?"

"One of the things." At close range his eye looked terrible, half closed and surrounded by purpling flesh. Honesty compelled her to add, "I didn't expect anything like this. And there's no way of knowing how old it is."

"A laboratory might be able to tell you," Cameron said. "You aren't going to leave it here, are you? If it rains tonight . . ."

Peggy nodded. "We'll have to move the stuff, much as I hate to risk it; the wood's half rotted already. Do you have a tarp or some plastic bags we could borrow, Cameron?"

"Yes, of course. I'll get them."

"I'll go, if you can tell me where they are." Bill hadn't spoken till then. Karen didn't doubt he meant to be helpful, but Cameron's response was not particularly gracious.

"In the back of my truck."

"Right. I won't be long."

He went loping off and Peggy squatted in the corner, poking with a trowel at something that had aroused her curiosity. The boys had gathered around the cooler. Cameron said in a low voice,

"I haven't had a chance to apologize."

"What for?"

A wry smile further distorted his abused face. "The list is fairly extensive, isn't it? My rudeness to you the other day, the fire, Miz Fowler's insults and insinuations, Lisa's questionable business dealings, my brother-in-law's foul mouth —"

"None of them were your fault."

"You're lying in your teeth," Cameron said pleasantly. "They were all my fault, directly or indirectly. That damned apartment was a firetrap, and I let the old . . . lady. . . talk me into insuring it for more than it was worth. I let Bobby badger me into losing my temper and behaving like a jackass. And the things I said that afternoon, when you were a guest in my house —"

"Cameron, please." Karen put her hand on his arm, and saw him flinch at her touch. "Stop doing this to yourself. I don't blame you for any of those things — even for yelling at me that day. It was understandable. I don't know how you could do what you've done all these years; I'd have cracked up long ago with the misery of it."

"It hasn't been easy. She used to be so . . . The only way I can cope is to think of her as someone other than the bright, cheerful woman I used to know. In a sense, she is someone else. There used to be moments when she recognized me, but that hasn't happened for months."

Karen wondered how often he had allowed himself the indulgence of talking about his mother.

"Will you be able to get her the help she needs now?"

"I think so." He leaned back against the wall. "The place I have in mind won't take her without a sizable down payment. My share of the proceeds of the sale and the house should do it. If she —" He broke off with a sharp intake of breath and shoved Karen aside. "Peggy! Watch out!"

He reached Peggy in time to grab her around the waist as the stones at which she had been prodding sagged and shifted. Earth and twisted roots prevented a complete collapse; only one stone fell, and it would have done even greater damage if Cameron had not pulled Peggy out of the way. When Karen reached them she saw that Peggy was half-lying, half-sitting on the floor clutching her foot and cursing.

"Did it hit you? Is it broken? What happened?"

"Get back," Cameron ordered, taking Peggy into his arms. They both grunted as he lifted her.

"Cracked rib?" Peggy inquired.

"For God's sake," Cameron groaned, "stop prying into other people's business." He carried her outside the house and lowered her to the ground.

The boys converged, questioning and exclaiming. Bill ran up, dropping an armful of plastic bags. "What happened?"

"One of the stones fell," Karen said, kneeling by Peggy and reaching for her foot. "Is it broken, Peggy?"

"I don't think so." Peggy bit her lip. "It hurts too much to be broken. Oh, hell! What a stupid thing to do. I got so interested in . . . I've gotta go back, there's something buried under the —"

"You're not going anywhere, except to the emergency room," Karen said, taking a firm grip on Peggy. "Bill, will you drive her in your car? I'll bring hers."

"Does this mean you ladies are finished for the day?" Bucky asked hopefully.

Peggy was forced to admit that she, at least, was finished for the day. Two of the boys made a chair with their hands and carried her off, but she was still yelling orders at Karen as they vanished among the trees. "Don't you dare leave this place until you've collected the nails and the wood scraps! Look there by the wall where I was digging! But be careful! I think it — ow!"

"Don't you dare do anything of the kind," Bill said firmly. "Come on, Karen, I'm not leaving you here alone."

"I'm not alone." She indicated Cameron, who had backed away when Bill and the boys took over. He stood watching them, arms at his sides, his face unreadable.

"But —"

"Don't argue with me, Bill. Peggy needs you and I don't. Hurry up."

"Oh, all right. I'll see you later. I damn well better see you later," he added, with a sour look at Cameron.

Karen waited until the sounds of his retreat had died away before she picked up the plastic bags and turned. Cameron had not moved. "You'd better go," he said very quietly.

"I'm not leaving you here alone either. There have been too many . . . accidents."

"Accidents," Cameron repeated. "Yeah. All right, let's get it over with. Where are you going? I thought you wanted —"

"Did you see this?" Karen indicated the fissure in the rock, now gaping open. Beyond the entrance, narrow and low, darkness filled it.

"What is it?" Cameron came to her side.

"You have a flashlight up at the house, don't you?"

After a moment Cameron said, "I don't think I like what I think you're thinking. There can't be anything there; it's only a —"

"I've got to see for myself. This may be my only chance. You don't have to come with me."

"For God's sake, Karen! Never mind my damned claustrophobia, you could get stuck back there or mashed by falling rock, or . . . Look, let's collect Peggy's bits and pieces first, and have a look at that place where she was digging. If you're still set on this crazy stunt after we've finished, I'll get the flashlight. Okay?"

"All right."

She knew what he hoped: that it would start raining, and that that would put an end to her crazy stunt. They gathered the scraps of wood and nails and stowed them in the bags, not without damage to the objects. Leaving them to be soaked by water would have damaged them more, though.

Then Cameron climbed over the fallen stone and knelt by the wall.

"Hand me that trowel, will you please?"

"Be careful," Karen said anxiously.

"Mmmm." After a moment he sat back on his heels. "I can't see anything. But it's getting dark, and I'm not keen on digging out more dirt until I can see what I'm doing. Suppose we cover this with plastic and leave it till tomorrow?"

"I may not be here tomorrow."

He turned to look at her. "You're leaving?"

"Probably. If my car is ready."

"You should go anyway," Cameron said slowly. "You should go now. Back to the motel."

"I want to see what's in the tunnel."

"Karen, please. It's going to rain like hell pretty soon, and your friends will be worried about you." Slowly he rose to his feet. His face was under tight control, but she heard his breath catch.

"Are you all right?" she asked.

"If I tell you I feel like hell and I'm about to keel over, will you give up for today?"

"Do you? Are you?" She moved closer to him and put her hand on his arm.

"Yes. No, not really . . . I'll check out that filthy hole in the rock, and I'll investigate Peggy's questionable discovery, and I'll . . . do what needs to be done. If you can trust me to do it right."

He looked so tired. Not just tired — defeated.

"I don't know how to do it right either," Karen whispered. "We'll just have to do the best we can."

Her hand moved slowly, lightly, up his arm to

his shoulder. He stood rigid as a statue while her fingers curved over the back of his head. Even after it had bent under the gentle pressure of her hand, she had to stand on tiptoe to touch his lips with hers. His movements were as delicate and deliberate as hers had been until his arms held her; then they tightened with a sudden force that brought a stifled cry from her and a gasp from him.

"Was that pain or passion?" she asked breathlessly.

"Both." His lips moved to her closed eyes.

"You do have a cracked rib."

"I don't remember. Let's try that again. It was almost right, but I think we can do better."

"I don't want to hurt you —"

"I'm supposed to say that." His exhalation of laughter mingled with hers.

At first she took the distant sound for a rumble of thunder. Then it rose in pitch, like a scream, and she went rigid in his arms. "My God! What is it?"

Cameron said something under his breath. They stood listening for a moment, and then the sound came again. This time Karen heard the words. "Hey, brother! Where are you, boy? We know you're here. Come on out and play!"

"It's Bobby," Cameron said flatly. "He's been trailing me all day. I thought . . . Come on."

"Wait. What are you going to do? He's not alone." The chorus of high-pitched voices sounded like dogs, baying on a fresh scent.

"No. He likes to have company on these little jaunts." The air was dusky dark with the approaching storm; his face shone with sweaty pallor. "I'll go . . . talk to him. He doesn't know you're here."

"He knows someone else is here. Peggy's car —"

"Oh, God, yes. I'd forgotten." He turned in a desperate circle, scanning the clearing in search of a way out. The thorny barricade could have been forced, but only at the cost of painful scratches, and the signs of their passage would have been clearly visible. The voices were louder now, closer. One rose in a wild Rebel yell. "You'd better hide. They're probably drunk, and they might . . . That tunnel. Pull some brush over the entrance. I'll tell them there was an accident, that you all left together —"

"You won't have a chance to tell them anything!" She clung to him, fighting his effort to pull away. "They'll be four or five to one, and you've already got a cracked rib. We've both got to hide."

"Karen —"

"Cameron." She twisted both hands in his shirt and swung him around to face her. "Do you really think I'd cower in that hole listening while they beat the shit out of you?"

The taut muscles of his face sagged into a faint smile. "Well, if you put it that way . . . Let's go then. Is that your purse over there? Take it with you; if they see anything lying around they'll know you're still here."

Karen scooped up her purse and Peggy's forgotten jacket, and they ran for the tunnel. It was probably almost as hard for Cameron to enter that dark hole as it would have been for him to face four or five opponents. But he'd survive an attack of claustrophobia. He might not survive a meeting with Bobby and his buddies.

"Hurry up," Cameron gasped. "They've found the path."

A louder whoop from Bobby confirmed his statement. "Ready or not, here we come! Wheee-hoo!"

Ducking her head, Karen scuttled into the opening. Cameron didn't follow her immediately; she assumed he was hesitating, fighting his phobia, and was about to tug at his pant leg when a shower of dirt rained down across the opening. Shielding his face with his arm, Cameron came through it and dropped down onto the floor just inside. The shower trickled down and stopped, leaving a pile of debris, dirt mixed with cut vines and branches, half-blocking the entrance.

"Good thinking," she whispered.

He didn't answer. She could tell by the way he breathed how much he hated this, though he was still just inside the entrance, too close for safety.

"Can you move farther back?" she asked.

"No. You'd better, though."

Karen crawled back another foot or two. The air was warm but surprisingly dry, and she had no feeling of discomfort though the ceiling was too low to enable her to stand. The surface under her hands was rough enough to scratch them, even under the inch-thick layer of earth that remained. The womb, the enclosure, the primal cave; now she knew firsthand how the heroines of the romances had felt. Which was worse, to be shut in by impenetrable walls or to know that the walls were not impenetrable — that something threatening could get in? Right now I'll take the impenetrable walls, she thought, and prayed for rain as devoutly as any drought-afflicted farmer. A heavy downpour would cool the pursuers' enthusiasm.

The voices rose to a clamorous howl and then stopped. "Shit," said a voice loudly. "There's nobody here."

"Where'd he go?" demanded another voice. "I told you you shouldn't've yelled like that, he heard us and now he's run off like the yellow coward —"

"There's no place he could run to." That was Bobby. "You see any way out of here?"

"Well, damn it, he ain't here, is he? Maybe he's hiding in the house."

"Or someplace closer," Bobby said.

Turning, Karen saw Cameron's head and shoulders silhouetted against the opening. "Get back," she mouthed at him, but she dared not speak, and she knew he was probably incapable of going farther inside. She could hear the crackle of brush underfoot as someone approached the stone walls.

"Come on, Bobby," one of the others called.

"I tole you, he ain't here. Let's get out of this place. I don't like it."

"Is the little boy scared?" Bobby's voice was terrifyingly close. "Did his mammy tell him scary stories about bad things in the woods? Don't worry, little feller, Bobby'll protect you from the boogeyman."

The object of his derision muttered something obscene. Bobby laughed. "Here, have another drink. Nothing like it to chase the spooks away."

There was a brief silence while — Karen assumed — the bottle was being passed around. Then twigs snapped under approaching feet. He was so close she heard his breath go out in a soft, ugly sigh of satisfaction. The form silhouetted against the lacy fretwork of vines was not Cameron's. He had flattened himself against the wall.

Karen clawed at the rock beside her, trying to break off a fragment large and sharp enough to use as a weapon. The limestone crumbled under her nails. Lifting Peggy's jacket, she fumbled frantically in the pockets, hoping against hope there would be something there. Even a nail file would be better than nothing. Not much better, though . . .

Crumpled Kleenex, cigarettes, lighter. Nothing sharp, nothing heavy. Turning with difficulty in the cramped space, Karen snapped the lighter. The small flame wouldn't be visible from outside with her body shielding it. Anyhow, Bobby knew they were inside the tunnel. He had burst into raucous, off-key song — something about a fox in its hole.

Karen crawled forward, holding the lighter high. Through her mind ran a prayerful litany: a large rock, a forgotten trowel, a lost knife . . . Why don't you pray for a .45 Magnum while you're at it, she thought despairingly. The ceiling lowered till it brushed her bowed head. She saw it drop to meet the floor, marking the end of the tunnel, and at the same moment she heard the crackle and crunch of brush and a shout of triumph from Bobby. Cameron had gone out. Damn him and his gallantry! If he had stayed put, they would have had to come at him one at a time, and it wouldn't have been easy for them to drag him out into the open. But then they might have seen her.

The lighter was scorching her fingers. Her desperate gaze swept the rough surfaces. Nothing. Bucky had been too damned efficient: he had taken his tools with him and cleared out every rock larger than a pebble.

Then she saw it — a rounded shaft, brown, brittle and broken. Too fragile to serve as a weapon — but her fingers closed over it, and before the lighter died she saw other things in the dust.

The incredible message they conveyed would have meaning to her later; now she shunted it aside into a separate compartment of her mind. No time now, no time for anything except trying to stop what was happening. The sounds she heard, distorted though they were by echoes and distance, turned her stomach.

Her sudden appearance made the men start. They hadn't known she was there. Stupid of them, she thought with icy detachment; they ought to have noticed Peggy's car.

"Well, just look what we got here!" Bobby crowed. "Reckon this is your lucky day, honey. Take good care of my favorite brother-in-law, boys, while I give the little lady a hearty welcome."

Cameron raised his head. Two of them were holding him by the arms. He would have fallen if they had let go; his eyes had difficulty focusing and blood dripped from his mouth. "Don't be a damned fool, Bobby," he said thickly. "If you lay one finger on her she'll press charges, and so will I. Aren't you in enough trouble already?"

One of the men holding him relaxed his grip and said uneasily, "I don't need that kind of shit, Bob. Maybe we better —"

"It'll be their word against ours," Bobby said. Thumbs hooked in the belt of his jeans, he studied Karen from head to foot and back again. She knew, with the same cold detachment, why he hadn't moved in on her. He was waiting for her to run.

Somehow she doubted that the application of conscious virtue would have much effect on Bobby. Running or screaming would have been fatal, though. He'd love a show of fear. She stared back at him, unblinking, and said coolly, "My word carries more weight than yours, Bobby. I'll have your ass in jail if you don't let him go and get the hell out of here right now."

"You and who else?" He took a step toward her.

"The others will be back soon. Professor Meyer —"

"The big hero that saved you from being run over?" Bobby's grin stretched another couple of inches. "Who do you think it was set that up, honey? The cheap bastard only paid me fifty bucks, so I gave myself the pleasure of coming a little closer than he expected. He won't interfere with me. He wouldn't want the fuzz to find out about that stunt."

The low-hanging clouds parted momentarily, and the dying sun sent a last ray of lurid crimson light into the clearing, flushing the faces of the men and casting dark, distorted shadows across the uneven ground. When it died the darkness seemed even deeper. A distant rumble of thunder rolled and faded.

"I've had it," one of the spectators muttered. "Let's get the hell out of here."

"Five more minutes," Bobby said softly. He started toward Karen.

She stood her ground. It was not courage that kept her from retreating or screaming for help; it was a queer, cool sense of anticipation.

Cameron thought, as he later admitted, that she was too paralyzed with fear to move. With a sudden, violent movement he twisted away from the grasping hands, but one of the men stuck out a foot and he went sprawling.

It came then, as Karen had known it would,

rising instantly from a distant wail to a ghastly shriek that assaulted the ears and pierced the heart. It filled the clearing like dark water and shook the branches. When it died away, she and Cameron were alone.

Karen had dropped to the ground and covered her ears with her hands. It was that bad, even for someone who had heard it before and who had anticipated . . . something.

She rolled over and sat up. Cameron had raised himself to his knees. The fall must have knocked the wind out of him; he was whooping for breath, but he managed to gasp, "Christ Almighty! What in God's name was that?"

Karen crawled across the few feet of ground that separated them. Rising to her knees, she threw her arms around him. "Are you all right?"

"Yes, fine." The strain in his voice and the tremors that ran through his body made him a liar. She was trembling too, now that it was over. They clung to one another, shaking and panting.

"What was it?" Cameron repeated.

"A guardian angel, maybe."

"Didn't sound like an angel. We'd better get out of here."

He got shakily to his feet, raising her with him. "Just a minute." She moved out of his hold, toward the tunnel.

"For God's sake, Karen!"

"I'm coming." Carefully she wrapped the broken shaft of bone in Peggy's jacket. As they started down the path toward the house, the first drops of rain began to fall.

"So you were right," Peggy said. "It's another *Edwin Drood*. We'll never know how it ended."

Karen gathered up the last pages of the manuscript. They had finished breakfast; Peggy leaned back, her bandaged foot on a chair, a cigarette in her hand. The windows streamed with rain.

"We can make an educated guess, can't we?" Karen said. "Someone is following her as she steals through the night — darkened garden, her bundle over her arm. The reader knows that, if Ismene doesn't. The doctor is waiting for her at the gate, so the follower has to be Edmund. There will be a confrontation between the two men, a final admission of guilt by one of them, and Ismene will fly into the arms of the other."

"But which one? You don't know how many pages are missing. The confrontation could result in an entirely new plot twist. Even if the doctor is telling the truth, Ismene has to go back to the house with the proof he's promised her, to free her poor crazy mother and convince Clara that she'd better stop making eyes at Edmund. I must say," Peggy went on, reaching for her cup of coffee, "you were right about Ismene's feelings for her sister. That scene where she tries to warn Clara makes the latter look like a vindictive bitch."

"A lot of people will be speculating," Karen said. "There's another possibility, though. Ismene may not have finished the book."

Peggy had been trying not to look at the cotton-lined box and its grisly contents. They made an incongruous addition to the breakfast dishes. "It could be a woman's," she said. "Men were shorter back then, though. With only one bone —"

"It's hers," Karen said quietly. "I saw a few other bones before the light went out. Some are probably gone, smashed or carried off by animals. But there will be enough left to prove I'm right."

"I'm surprised you aren't heading back there, rain and all," Peggy said, shifting position with a grimace of pain.

"I've found what I had to find. The bones are just . . . left-over pieces. Anyhow, they shouldn't be moved by amateurs. There are people at Williamsburg or William and Mary who will know how to deal with them." Karen stood up and stretched. "We'd better start packing. I don't know how we're going to cram all that stuff you bought into your car."

"Oh, come on, it's not that bad." Peggy squirmed. "Damn this foot. Suppose we sort through the loot and see what can be discarded. We should be able to squeeze some more into the trunk."

Karen dragged the boxes and bundles nearer to the invalid. They made a discouragingly large pile. "What do you want with this petticoat?" she demanded, lifting a mass of white fabric and shaking it out. "It must have ten yards of material in it. It's way too long for you, and the waist . . ."

"Look at the tucks and the handmade lace,"

Peggy protested. "I have to keep that."

"Oh, all right." Karen raised the lid of the trunk and crammed the petticoat in. "How about this?"

After some heated debate Peggy consented to discard two pairs of knee-length split drawers and a bundle of long underwear. "See," she said with satisfaction, "the rest fits in the trunk."

Karen sat on the lid and managed to close it. "That finishes that box, except for these papers. You said they weren't —"

"Let me have another look." Peggy sorted through the bundle, accompanying the search with a muttered commentary. "I suppose I could dispense with the newspaper clippings, they're all about turn-of-the-century social activities. The recipe book . . . no, I can't part with that, it's too delicious. 'Take fourteen eggs and a pint of heavy cream . . .' "

"Hurry up," Karen said impatiently. "I want to get out of here before noon. It's a long . . . What's that?"

"Seems to be a diary," Peggy said, riffling through the pages. " 'I have been reading the new novel by Mr. Hardy. It does not seem to me to measure up to his earlier works.' "

"It must be one of Eliza's. Same binding, same metal clasp. I wonder why it didn't end up at the Historical Society with the others."

"My, my, she did think well of herself, didn't she? 'There are few individuals, particularly among the ladies, with whom I can converse without feelings of boredom. Their intellectual capacities . . .' " Chuckling, Peggy turned over a few pages.

"You can keep it if you insist," Karen said resignedly. "It's not that big, I can probably squeeze it in somewhere. Come on, we've got another box of clothes to . . . Peggy?"

She had stiffened, eyes wide, mouth ajar.

"Peggy! What is it?"

"It's the answer," Peggy said in a queer choked voice. "All the answers. My God, how could I have been so stupid? I should have known it was Eliza."

"Eliza was Ismene? That's impossible!"

"That's why she hid this volume of her diary," Peggy muttered. "She had enough intellectual integrity to refrain from destroying the truth, but that awful Victorian prudery kept her from publishing it."

"What are you talking about?" Karen demanded, leaning over her shoulder to peer at the close-written pages. " 'Houses of Stone' could not have been written by —"

"Listen." Peggy cleared her throat and began to read. " 'I watched the fire take hold and then I knew I could not do what I had contemplated. I took it out with the tongs and beat out the flames. Only a few pages were lost. They were the ones that mattered, for they contained the awful accusation that had moved me to destroy the papers. It is only a story, of course, pure fiction, without foundation in fact; but anyone who read it would recognize the individuals on whom she had based her characters, and those readers would believe the worst, as people always do. The malicious gossip, the whispers would ruin us and cast a stain on the character of my sainted mother. I cannot allow it to be published or even read by another. But neither can I destroy it. Would that I had never found that recess in the paneling of the room that must have been hers! Would that I had never read it, or the little sheaf of verses! Would that my antiquarian research, my pride in the antiquity of my family, had not led me to search out the evidence that has provoked such fearful doubts!

" 'My mother never spoke of her. She does not lie in the family plot. It was not until I began looking through old newspapers in the hope of finding information for the genealogy that I came upon the notice of her death. She had fallen or thrown herself from the cliff, it said; there had been a witness who tried in vain to hold her back, but the body had not been found. The river was high, it must have washed her far away.

" 'I know this is true. The story is only a story. But I will hide it away, with this journal. Fate will determine what becomes of it. I cannot.' "

For a while there was no sound except the patter of rain against the window. Then Peggy muttered, in obvious chagrin, "And I call myself a historian! The clothes in that trunk were Late Victorian in style, so the manuscript must have been hidden *after* that time. Well, there won't be any difficulty identifying Ismene now. Her sister was Eliza's mother. Hand me my briefcase, will you, please?"

Karen obliged. It didn't take Peggy long to find the genealogy. She was as methodical about her work as she was careless about her personal property. "Here she is. Helena Cabot, wife of Frederick."

"Her brothers and sisters aren't listed." Karen craned her neck to see over Peggy's shoulder.

"Well, you knew that. I understand how you feel," Peggy said with a wry smile. "We're so close now, closer than we ever hoped; and yet we still don't know Ismene's real name. But now we know her last name, and we can go on from there."

"Cabot's an awfully common name," Karen muttered.

"Not as bad as Smith. And it's commoner in New England than in the South."

"That's right," Karen exclaimed. "And according to the manuscript, Ismene's father came from 'a northern city.'"

"Interesting," Peggy muttered. "Am I stretching things, or is Helena's name significant?"

"You probably are stretching things. But . . . Peggy, look at the dates. Helena was two years older than her husband. Edmund was born after Ismene and Clara's mother left her husband, so he would have been . . . ."

"Younger than either of the girls," Peggy finished. "So — how much of the novel is autobiographical?"

"We'll never know. We don't even know how it ended."

"Ah, but we can make some educated guesses."

506

Peggy's eyes gleamed. Karen recognized the look; it was the pleasurable anticipation of scholarly speculation. Peggy went on, "If those bones are Ismene's —"

"There should be enough left to indicate sex, age and race. If they are those of a female Caucasian under thirty, she's the most logical candidate. Her body was never found, remember." Karen stared at her clenched hands. "Of course we can't be certain until the experts have examined them. I don't know anything about anthropology. I'm jumping to the wildest of all possible conclusions."

"But you're sure, aren't you?"

"Yes," Karen said quietly. "I'm sure."

Peggy nodded thoughtfully. "All right, let's accept that as a working hypothesis. Let's also accept the likelihood that the book had a happy ending; most of the novels of that type did. Even if Ismene the heroine met a tragic end, it would be too much of a coincidence to suppose the author died in exactly the same way as her heroine. However, Eliza did read the ending, and it horrified her so much she tried to burn the manuscript because it 'cast a stain' on her mother. Suppose it described a murderous attack on Ismene by her own sister? The novel would mirror reality to that extent at least — not the manner of Ismene's death but the motive for it."

"Motive," Karen repeated stupidly. She couldn't deal with the problem as dispassionately as Peggy.

"You can't get around it," Peggy insisted. "If

those are Ismene's remains, she was deliberately murdered. If she had been crawling around in the tunnel involved in some kind of antiquarian research and died of natural causes, they'd have gone looking for her and removed her body. She was trying to get out; that's the only logical reason for her to be there. Someone had shut her up in her own house of stone, and barred the door."

"And invented a story about her falling off the cliff in order to explain her disappearance." Karen shivered. "It fits, doesn't it?"

"Could Clara have managed that by herself?"

"It would have been easy." Karen's lips twisted. "Ismene must have had a key; she wouldn't leave the place unlocked, not with her private papers and books there. But when she was there, she'd have no reason to lock herself in, would she? She may have been in the habit of leaving the key in the lock — outside. So . . . just turn the key and walk away. No blood or mess, no unpleasant confrontation. The place had been long abandoned, none of the servants went near it. The walls were too thick for cries to be heard . . ." She broke off, biting her lip.

Her voice deliberately matter-of-fact, Peggy said, "But Edmund — Frederick — knew about the stone house. Even if he believed his wife's lie about Ismene falling into the river, wouldn't he have gone to the house to retrieve her books and papers? He knew how much they meant to her, and he was fond of her —"

"Are you talking about Edmund or Frederick?

We're back to the same question: how much of the novel is autobiographical?"

"Right." Peggy shook her head. "I can't keep them straight. But I still think Frederick must have been involved. Or guilty."

"I'm inclined to agree. But it was her mother, not her father, that Eliza mentioned. Maybe one of them did the actual dirty work and the other was an accessory after the fact. If there was a great deal of money involved, and Ismene was about to marry someone else, on the rebound, Clara would get the whole bundle if her sister died, and a woman's property belonged to her husband. That would give Frederick a strong motive. But we'll probably never know the truth."

"This answers all the other questions, though." Peggy shook her head. "To think this diary was lying there, in the box, while we were speculating and guessing! Eliza must have had the poems published as a kind of expiation. She wouldn't use her aunt's real name, so she chose that of the heroine of the book. Come to think of it, that's the one question we haven't answered. Why did she call herself Ismene?"

Karen got up and went to the window. The rain had slackened; it slid like tears down the wet pane. She followed the path of one drop with her finger till it melted into the puddle below. " 'There is no triumph in the grave, No victory in death.' She had no patience with the kind of martyrdom Antigone courted. She wouldn't walk meekly to her death. They had to kill her. And she was still fighting, still trying to get out when she died — at the farthest end of that pitiful tunnel, which had been begun and deepened by other prisoners with the same unconquerable will to live."

Peggy cleared her throat. " 'Dying for a cause is just one of those silly notions men come up with. It has always seemed to me more sensible to go on living and *keep on talking.*' "

After a moment Karen turned from the window. Smiling, she said, "Are you composing aphorisms now?"

"No, I read it someplace. It's not a bad motto, though. Keep on talking."

"Ismene would have agreed. That book is her triumph over death and silence. That's why I'm not concerned about her poor bones; she wouldn't have cared about them."

"You are going to get them out, though."

"Not me. Cameron said he'd take care of it."

"Are you going to marry him?"

Karen stared at her friend in openmouthed astonishment. "Good God, no. I hardly know the man. What put that idea into your head?"

"The way he looked at you last night. And you weren't exactly scowling at him."

"I like him a lot," Karen said primly. "And I feel very sorry for him. He's had a hard time and —"

"Good Lord, you sound like Jane Eyre. No, Jane Austen! Jane Eyre had at least the guts to admit she was sexually attracted to Rochester."

"So I'm sexually attracted. A long-term relationship requires a lot more than that. Something may develop," Karen admitted. "But as Joan might say, why should I deprive all those other guys of a chance to win my heart?"

"Huh." Peggy lit another cigarette. "Then I guess it's up to me to provide a romantic ending. Though it's going to look more like Abbott and Costello than Bacall and Bogart."

"You and Simon are going to be married?"

"I guess so." Peggy shrugged. "He's such a stick-in-the-mud he won't consider any other arrangement. Wanna be maid of honor?"

"I'd rather be best mensch."

"Fine with me," Peggy said, laughing. "What are you going to do about Bill Meyer?"

"I'll think of something."

"Something with boiling oil in it?"

"Oh, no," Karen said gently. "Nothing as nice as boiling oil."

"He was also the burglar, I suppose."

"I've always believed that. He pushed Dorothea's guilt too hard. I don't think she could have climbed in that window, she's not exactly built like Jane Fonda. And it's easy to spray yourself with perfume. I imagine he lured Dorothea down here so she could be a suspect. The fire scared the hell out of him, though; he thought she set it and he started feeling like Dr. Frankenstein. That's why he's been so incredibly civil and helpful lately."

"Dorothea didn't set the fire."

"Go ahead, astonish me," Karen said. "I suppose

511

it wasn't Bobby either."

"I shall now proceed to force a confession from the culprit," Peggy announced, reaching for the phone. "And finish another little matter I promised myself I'd tend to before I left town."

After she had finished the conversation she turned a self-satisfied smile on Karen. "I thought she'd crumple under pressure. The woman's got no guts."

"You flat-out lied!" Karen exclaimed. "There was no witness. There couldn't have been!"

"She doesn't know that. She was blind drunk. To do the damned woman justice, she thought you weren't there. She was tucked up in bed boozing when I dropped you off, and your car wasn't in the garage." Peggy leaned back, smiling smugly. "I don't think she'll give Cameron any more trouble. Poor guy, he's had more than he deserves. You're sure you don't —"

"I'm sure," Karen said firmly.

Epilogue

The crimson rambler climbing the porch pillar was past its first exuberance of bloom, but a few flowers still shone satin-red among the emerald leaves. Peggy broke off in the middle of a sentence and dashed toward the plant. "Goddamn Japanese beetles!" she shouted, swatting wildly.

Karen pressed a sandaled foot against the porch floor and set the swing swaying. "Relax while you can," she said lazily. "Tomorrow is going to be hectic. How does the guest list stand at the last count?"

"I've lost track." Peggy returned to her chair. "Simon has more friends than anyone I've ever met, and he keeps inviting people without telling me. When I complain he says it doesn't matter, we've ordered enough food and champagne for a regiment anyhow."

"He's right about that. I just hope it doesn't rain so we have to move the ceremony inside."

"So do I. A few tears are appropriate for a wedding, but a maid of honor who is sneezing her head off and weeping copiously may not strike the proper note."

Karen laughed. "Only for you and Simon would I have made the supreme sacrifice of starting those allergy shots. They won't be fully effective for a while longer, though."

"You're a noble woman," Peggy said gravely. "But if you hadn't made the sacrifice, we'd have had to continue entertaining you on the front porch. It gets a little chilly in January."

Karen gave the swing another push. "So you're going to live here?"

"We're still arguing about that," Peggy said cheerfully. "I imagine that in the end we'll be here part of the time and at Simon's place part of the time, and part of the time he'll be there and I'll be here. We're both used to living alone and we both need periods of solitude."

The screen door opened. Simon came out and settled himself in the chair next to Peggy's. He didn't kiss her or take her hand, but the glances they exchanged brought an odd but pleasant lump to Karen's throat. "Where's Cameron?" she asked, not so inconsequentially.

"He insisted on bringing the tray," Simon replied. "The man is unnaturally well-mannered, Karen. Can't you do something about that?"

"I'm working on it."

Peggy lowered her voice and glanced over her shoulder. "So how's it going? Are you two —"

Simon's exclamation of protest blended with Karen's laughter. "Stop pushing, Peggy. I'm in no hurry, and neither is he. We've both got a lot of emotional baggage to get rid of before we make any decisions."

"How very cool and mature," Peggy said, wrinkling her nose. "All I was going to say was: Are you two having fun?"

514

"Oh, that." Karen smiled reminiscently. "I am, and I believe I am safe in stating that he —"

She broke off as Cameron backed through the door carrying a tray. Depositing it on the table, he reached for the bottle. "Shall I open it?"

"I'll do it," Simon said irritably. "Sit down and behave like a guest."

Cameron joined Karen on the swing and took one of her hands in his. Most of the cuts and scrapes had healed; Karen ran a caressing finger along one white scar.

"Champagne?" she asked, as the cork flew into the shrubbery. "Celebrating early, are we?"

"This is a celebration of quite another kind," Simon said, pouring. Cameron jumped up to take two of the glasses from him. Simon handed one to Peggy and then, still on his feet, raised his own glass. "To Ismene," he said solemnly. "May she rest in peace."

Cameron had brought the pathologist's report with him when he arrived that morning. It had taken a while to get it; antique bones did not have a high priority.

Peggy was the first to break the thoughtful silence. "Where are you going to put them — her?"

"In the old cemetery," Cameron said. "We can't be one hundred percent certain of the identification, of course, but it's good enough for me. I thought I'd put up a stone of some kind."

"Absolutely," Peggy said. "Can I suggest an epitaph? It won't be 'rest in peace.' That wasn't her style."

"What did you have in mind?" Simon asked apprehensively.

Peggy grinned at Karen, who grinned back. "Keep on talking," they said in chorus.

"She'll do that, certainly," Cameron said, after Simon's scandalized protests had died away. "How much of her story are you going to include in the introduction, Karen?"

She turned her head to look at him. He was frowning a little. "I wish I could say that's up to you, Cameron," she said gently. "But I can't. I have to tell the truth as I see it."

Cameron's frown deepened. "Of course. Did you think I was suggesting you falsify the facts to spare some sort of meaningless family pride? What kind of a pompous ass do you take me for?"

"I'm sorry," Karen began.

"I thought I'd never see the day!" Peggy exclaimed. "She's apologizing and he's talking back. Are you guys going to have a fight? Can I join in?"

"Depends on whose side you're on," Cameron said.

"Yours."

"Oh, well, in that case . . ." He put an arm around Karen's shoulders and pulled her closer.

"It isn't that simple." Simon was obviously trying to keep the conversation on a sensible plane. "How much of the truth do we know? Legally one cannot slander the dead, but morally one would not wish to make accusations when the accused cannot defend himself."

"Or herself." Karen raised her head from Cameron's shoulder. "I have to present all the evidence, though. Some of the true history of these people is paralleled by the plot of the novel. Ismene's name was Cassandra Cabot — another name from Greek literature, you notice. Her father was born in Boston, but at some point he moved to Charleston, South Carolina, because that was where he died. We know he was a widower, and that he left two daughters. There was no record of a will, so he may have died intestate. We know nothing of what happened to the girls after that, until 1820, when Helena married Frederick Cartright."

"None of that has anything to do with Ismene's — Cassandra's — death," Simon objected. "You can't offer a motive for murder; you don't know the size of Mr. Cabot's estate, and you've absolutely no reason to suppose that Mrs. Cabot didn't die a natural death in Boston or Charleston."

"I'm not a prosecutor in a court of law," Karen retorted. "Just a poor hard-working scholar. I don't have to produce evidence."

There was one kind of evidence she would not, could not mention, without destroying her reputation. In her own mind however, it was irrefutable. There had been something in the attic of that terrible old house — some thing, or someone, who had suffered and despaired and died without forgiveness or reconciliation. She could never prove it; she did not want to prove it. She could only pray the remnant of that suffering was impersonal, an echo of past pain and not the bodiless survivor of it.

A slight, almost imperceptible shiver ran through her, and Cameron's arm tightened its grasp. He knew about the cold in the attic; it had been a step forward in their relationship when he had been able to admit he had felt it too and had found it so unbearable he had hired workmen to carry the contents of the attic to a lower floor.

"Stop hassling Karen, Simon; she'll do a proper job," Peggy ordered. "Let's talk about something more cheerful. Such as how many more people have you invited since yesterday?"

"Only one but he's not coming," Simon said. "He got back from England three days ago, and he was too —"

"Not Bill Meyer!" Peggy exclaimed. "Simon, how could you?"

"He's not coming, I said. Why shouldn't I have asked him?"

"After he bribed that moronic Bobby to pretend to run Karen down so he could heroically save her life, and broke into the apartment trying to steal the manuscript —"

"You have absolutely no proof of that," Simon declared. "Professor Meyer's manner was completely open and forthright. He asked me to convey his best wishes and regrets . . ." He stopped, his mouth ajar.

"That's about as close to a confession as we'll ever get from Bill Meyer," Peggy declared.

"Good heavens," Simon muttered. "It never occurred to me that . . . I thought he was making a tactful and manly reference to his — er — broken heart. He certainly gave me the impression —"

"Oh, I think he was beginning to harbor the delusion that he was in love with me," Karen said calmly. "At least I hope he was. It would add a particularly sweet tang to my revenge."

A smile curved her lips as she told the others of her meeting with Dorothea Angelo.

Angelo had been deeply suspicious but too curious to decline Karen's invitation. They had met at a restaurant in D.C. — neutral ground — and the expedition had taken an entire day of Karen's time. It had been worth it, though.

"I don't suppose you're going to offer me a chance to help you edit the manuscript." Dorothea had opened the conversation with that remark; meaningless courtesies weren't her style.

"No. Would you like a glass of wine? Lunch is on me."

Dorothea's blackened brows lowered. "What are you up to, Holloway?"

"I wish to see justice done," Karen said solemnly.

It had been glorious to watch Dorothea's face as she heard, in the most lurid terms Karen could invent, how Bill Meyer had set her up, and worth every penny of the very expensive lunch Dorothea consumed as she listened. They had shared a carafe of wine. Karen had one glass. At the end of the conversation she raised it. "Shall we drink confusion to a certain person?" she asked.

"Damned right." Dorothea had chewed most of her lipstick off, and her expression would have sent small children howling for their mothers. She refilled her glass. "You're not such a bad sort, Holloway," she said awkwardly. "Thanks."

"What for?"

"For believing me when I said I didn't do those things. And for telling me how that bastard Meyer tried to use me. Don't worry, I'll take care of him."

"And I'm sure she will." Karen finished her story, while the others stared at her in horrified fascination. "She's the worst gossip in the M.L.A. and by the time she gets through embroidering the story it will make Bill look like an even greater horse's behind than he actually is."

Cameron drew a long breath and pretended to flinch away from her. "Remind me never to do anything to irritate you."

"That was brilliant," Peggy declared respectfully. "Absolutely inspired. You deserve a medal."

"I learned from you," Karen said with a fond smile. Then her face sobered. "It was a perfect case of making the punishment fit the crime. Bill didn't try to kill me. Nobody tried to kill me. I kept telling you that. In real life people do commit murder for extraordinary reasons — but cautious, careful, sane academicians don't endanger their reputations and safety for a step up in their careers.

"And yet all the threatening incidents stemmed

from a single event: my acquisition of the manuscript. It got Bill and Dorothea on my trail; it took me to Virginia, and my presence there activated animosities that might never have erupted if I hadn't unwittingly acted as a catalyst. Mrs. Fowler wouldn't have dared set the fire if there had not been someone living in the apartment. Destroying the property of someone she detested was an additional incentive, and she believed that, like Peggy, I was a smoker. Cameron's refusal to pay the insurance brought Bobby's resentment to the boiling point . . . The whole intertwined plot had the inevitability if not the dire consequences of a Greek tragedy."

Simon had dissolved into silent laughter. Wiping his eyes he sputtered, "Machiavelli couldn't have done better, my dear. With one stroke you avenged yourself on Meyer and won Dorothea over to your side. You do deserve a prize. We were going to wait until tomorrow to present it, but this seems a more appropriate occasion."

He rose and went into the house. When he came out he was carrying a flat parcel wrapped in brown paper and tied with string.

"You aren't giving me Eliza, are you?" Karen asked, deducing the nature of the gift from the shape of the parcel. "Not that I wouldn't appreciate it, but —"

"You hate it," Peggy said calmly. "I want Eliza for myself. She'll look great in the living room. Go ahead, open it."

Karen's hands were shaking with excitement as

she untied the string and stripped off the paper. It had to be a picture. If it wasn't Eliza, it could only be . . .

The painting had been beautifully restored and set in a simple frame of softly polished walnut. The faces looked out at her, unmarred by filth or flaked paint. They wore matching blue bows and there was a strong family resemblance between them, particularly in the soft brown eyes. They were the most charming pair of King Charles spaniels Karen had ever seen.